THE ENE~~MY OF FREE~~DOM

"Forward!" Waterman commanded as he and his men moved into the ravine. Sporadic gunfire erupted. His men opened fire, running at top speed.

"Follow me!" He charged ahead, pausing to fire his pistol at a resistance fighter. In the distance, between explosions of the mortar rounds, he could hear the roar of gunships coming from the north. The machinegun fire from his own positions whistled over his shoulder.

He advanced and saw the resistance camp scatter, men and women running in panic before the onslaught of Waterman's Special Operations forces. One woman stood her ground, firing a pistol in each hand now. Waterman recognized her.

She was the daughter of resistance commander Martin Deacon. She would pay the price for her father's folly. Waterman approached her and shouted, "For your crimes!" He burst-fired the assault rifle, killing her where she stood.

The brutality of his action left a sweet taste in Waterman's mouth. Now he wanted Michael Hope— and the war against these subversive guerrillas would be won.

MIES OF FREEDOM

THE
FREEMAN

Jerry Ahern
and Sharon Ahern

BANTAM BOOKS
TORONTO · NEW YORK · LONDON · SYDNEY · AUCKLAND

THE FREEMAN

A Bantam Book / November 1986

ISBN 0-553-21674-6

Published simultaneously in the United States and Canada

Bantam Books are published by Bantam Books, Inc. Its trade-mark, consisting of the words ''Bantam Books'' and the por-trayal of a rooster, is Registered in U.S. Patent and Trademark Office and in other countries. Marca Registrada. Bantam Books, Inc., 666 Fifth Avenue, New York, New York 10103.

PRINTED IN THE UNITED STATES OF AMERICA

O   0 9 8 7 6 5 4 3 2 1

ACKNOWLEDGMENT

We would like to thank our friend and medical adviser,
Joe L. Griffeth, M.D.,
of Commerce, Georgia.

BOOK ONE
AT ANY PRICE

Chapter One

He depressed the play and record buttons simultaneously as he ducked, the texture of the granite rough-feeling and cold to his skin. "This is Jean-Pierre Petrovitch reporting for Independent News of France." His voice was a whisper and his eyes watched the audio level of the machine—it was picking up. Marc Lumierre, beside him, nudged him. Petrovitch looked up over the rocks. Lumierre's black eyes lit—Petrovitch nodded. Lumierre shouldered the video camera slightly higher, aiming it across the yellow-streaked, khaki-colored rocks, beyond the scrub brush and the rapier-thin pines that clung to the side of the gorge, toward the men moving along the gorge below them. Petrovitch watched, then looked away—the hum of the video camera would record on his cassette tape machine, with the pause button actuated, the recording level indicator would waver slightly upward. Lumierre was too close, but there was nothing for it.

Petrovitch stared down into the gorge as his finger found the pause button and hit it. He began to speak again, the machine six inches or so from his lips. "With my cameraman and friend, Marc Lumierre, we have been traveling the back roads and animal trails of the Tennessee Mountains near the Ocoee River, searching for the almost mythical James Hope, former United States senator, former Federal Bureau of Investigation agent, outspoken critic of the Peace Party, and perhaps the most wanted man in what once was this bastion of freedom known as the United States. But we do not search alone, Marc and I. For three days now, units of the United States National Police Force with fatigue-clad men whom some earlier reports have indicated are Soviet Special Forces advisers move through these glorious mountains as well. Here, in a setting that could well be some Garden of Eden,

3

there is violence and death. In their search for James Hope
and his band of Resistance fighters, National Police Force
units routinely interrogate and sometimes torture the disarmed
and all but defenseless residents of the small towns and
hamlets that dot this magnificent landscape. James Hope is
their goal—and he is our goal as well. In—"

"Hey—Jean-Pierre!"

Petrovitch pushed the pause button, following the vector
of Marc Lumierre's camera: There was movement on the far
side of the gorge. At first Petrovitch thought it was an animal.
There were many wild deer here, and supposedly there were
bears. The idea of bears frightened him, for he had no gun.
They had barely been able to smuggle themselves out of
Chattanooga. And to have obtained a weapon of any sort
would have meant stealing one from an armory or a member
of the National Police Force or the National Defense Force.
Neither he nor Lumierre were commandos. Now, as he
watched along the far side of the gorge, he could tell: These
were not animals. These were men.

Petrovitch hit the pause button, speaking again into his
machine. "Below us, as the National Police unit—heavily
armed—traverses the course of the gorge, on the height
opposite us other men move. The Resistance, perhaps—a
battle may be imminent." Petrovitch hit the pause button
again.

"Shit, my friend," Lumierre said with a hiss. "There is
going to be a little war here, I think."

"Yes." Petrovitch nodded—he realized he was breathless
and sweating. His eyes riveted to the far side of the gorge.

He moved along the rim of the gorge, the M-16A2
clenched tightly in both fists, dropping down to his knees for
an instant beside Lobo, the red-haired kid grinning at him.
He slapped the boy soundlessly on the shoulder, then was
up, moving again. When the Soviet Special Forces personnel
were with them, the National Police units were harder to kill.
Harder but not impossible. He kept running, slinging the
M-16A2 behind his back, the rifle banging tactilely but not
audibly against his left combat boot; the right one (the two
were knotted together over his left shoulder) was at his left
breast.

He stopped, glancing back—she was barefoot, Jennifer Hope. He couldn't understand how she could run the rocks and the brush that way. He wore tennis shoes. Panting, she dropped into a crouch beside him. Her blue eyes bored into his eyes, and he nodded. Jennifer Hope set down her boots, then slipped the sling for her submachine gun higher, cinching the sling tightly so the weapon would be locked diagonally across her chest, the inwardly telescoped butt stock beneath her right breast, the suppressor-fitted muzzle over her left breast. Her hands moved to her blond hair. Her hair was shorter now, settling only just past her shoulders—he remembered when his wife had helped Jennifer cut it. She knotted a camouflage bandanna over it now, tying it under her hair at the nape of the neck.

She nodded, drawing the short-sword-sized BuckMaster knife from the sheath at the left side of her pistol belt.

He turned away from her, starting forward and down—the Soviet Special Forces people always sent one of their "advisers" and one of the National Policemen ahead, to scout. He reached to his belt for the big Life Support System I. He stopped where the trail dropped. Against superior odds—as always—there was no other tactic than surprise. There were hundreds of folks in the mountains here who would have swollen the ranks of the Resistance, but new weapons were obtained only by killing the enemy, the weapons then filtered out to arm more of the populace. When he himself had been arrested by the National Police, they had taken the handgun he had carried almost all his adult life, his Smith & Wesson stainless steel four-inch .44 Magnum. He had never seen the gun again. According to the Civilian Disarmament Act, individual weapons were forbidden. All weapons. The Life Support he held clenched in his fist now as he slipped off the M-16 and his tied-together boots was identical to the knife confiscated along with the revolver, his shotguns, his rifles, his other handguns, and other knives—all but the ones he had buried in the survival canister. He held the knife. His lips were dry as he licked them with his tongue.

He was frightened of battle—and he always had been. He had reasoned once that fear was what made him survive battle, giving him a perceptual edge.

He glanced back once to Jennifer. She nodded, flicking

her lids closed once, the lashes like the wings of a butterfly. The only prettier eyes he had seen in his life were his own wife's.

He started down along the trail they had cleared earlier of interfering brush and broken twigs that might betray movement with sound. The trail was steep as it descended into the gorge.

He stopped at the edge of the low ground, feeling Jennifer Hope stop behind him.

A flash of movement—the green was unnatural. The camouflage-patterned battle-dress utilities of the Soviet Special Forces were the wrong shade for the Tennessee mountains in winter. Once before, the incongruity had saved his life. He counted that it had saved his life now—and Jennifer's. The wrong color of green took form—it wasn't bright enough. A man, his beret cocked low and his hat brass gleaming. In the Soviet soldier's hands was an AKS-74, the best of the Soviet assault rifles. Some farmer would be happy tonight, he thought.

The cammie-clad man walked past, gray eyes scanning the high ground. The black-uniformed National Policeman, his M-16A2 at a sloppy high port, followed after.

The National Policeman's back was to him now—it was a broad back, but the shoulders were stooped; too many shoulders stooped to the Russians since the Peace Resolution. At the corner of his peripheral vision, he could see Jennifer Hope—the massive Bowie patterned knife with its hacksaw teeth on the spine, its rope-cutting teeth on the clip. She held the knife in both hands, again giving the image that somehow it was a sword.

The trick—he had learned that long ago—was to concentrate on your weapon, on your movement, on anything but your victim. Because the concentration was what somehow imparted that sixth-sense impression to the person whose life you were about to take. He focused his attention on the massive knife in his right fist, on his left open palm. He started forward in a low crouch, running from the cleared path, then hurtling his body into space toward the Soviet soldier, his left knee impacting the Russian square in the back, the knife in his right hand arcing downward as they both fell to the rocky ground. His left palm found the man's mouth to stifle the cry. His right knee crushed the right kidney. His right hand swiped one of the knife's edges deep across the throat. His right arm came out of the backswing, then hammered downward, his fist molded to the weapon, the blade gouging into the larynx.

He rolled to his knees as the dead man's body went limp beneath him.

The National Policeman's throat spurted blood from a wide gash, arms flailing as he attempted to raise his assault rifle. But then Jennifer's arms drew back, the knife in her tiny hands arcing outward from shoulder height, the knife's tip biting flesh, catching flesh for an instant, ripping, the policeman's head partially severing, Jennifer wheeling away as the artery burst and blood was everywhere in a cloud of pinkish spray.

He rolled the dead Soviet soldier over, stripping away the AKS-74, the magazines in the shoulder-slung case, the equipment belt at the waist, the fighting knife lashed along the thigh.

He searched the pockets quickly—no documents. There never were.

The National Policeman's body—the M-16A2 was gone. Jennifer would have it. He looked up into the trees and rocks—she had disappeared there, would return in an instant, her boots on, his rifle and boots in her hands, just as she did each time they did this thing together.

There was casual talk among the National Policemen who moved along the gorge; some of it was intelligible. Women. Liquor. They always spoke of the same things. The second Soviet Special Forces adviser moved along near the head of the column. An officer, but very young.

Jennifer skidded down from the higher rocks, whispering, "Martin—"

He nodded, handing her the AKS-74, taking his M-16 from her.

"Martin—there's somebody in the rocks on the other side of the gorge. I saw something move."

Martin looked to the far side of the gorge and let his vision follow the striated granite outcroppings upward toward their height. He saw nothing, not even a hint of movement. But if Jennifer saw something, then there was something, without doubt. Her eyes were not only pansy blue, they were also animal-keen eyes, young eyes.

"There's nothing we can do. If it's a trap, we run for it. If it isn't, and we blow this, we can't get away any easier," Martin said, hissing.

She nodded, blinking her eyelids.

Jennifer hunched closer to him. "You start when you want. I'll keep my eyes on the far side of the gorge—and this," and she gestured with the AKS-74 he had handed her.

Martin nodded.

The National Police unit was starting up along the dry course of the streambed. He had lived in these mountains as a child, lived in these mountains on and off as an adult, lived in these mountains steadily again since he had escaped from the National Police and joined the Resistance. Never once had he seen the streambed with water coursing through it, not even in the heaviest rain.

His right thumb worked the M-16's fire selector to "auto" and he waited.

Martin considered his wife: frail, gentle, a hairdresser when he had met her. After they had married, she had given up her job and helped him to manage the school. He had tried teaching her many times, but violence was not part of her nature, no matter how far removed the violence was from reality, no matter how stylized. Linda Elizabeth Kelsoe Deacon and the martial arts had never gotten along. When he had fled into the mountains, she had fled with him, the life harsh for her at first until they had linked with a large Resistance group that utilized semipermanent camps, but not as harsh as the enforced poverty when the martial arts school had been closed by government edict. She had never been a warrior, but she fought in her own way. Warm meals for the men and the women when they returned from the field, caring for the children, some of whom had been born in the wild country, some of whom had no surviving parents. Linda had become a good nurse. Dr. Huntley, who worked with them, treated them, had several times commended her for her natural gifts, as he had called them.

Martin concentrated on his wife now. The National Police were largely stupid, brutal, insensitive. But the ruddy-cheeked Soviet Special Forces officer—the young man would feel Martin's thoughts.

The National Police unit was almost into the killing ground.

Martin Deacon glanced once at Jennifer Hope—she smiled at him for an instant, her eyes flickering back toward the height of the gorge on the side opposite from where they hid. She looked like Melissa Hope—blond, blue-eyed, tall, lean of build, athletic, fair skin deeply tanned. But she fought like James Hope. And that was the finest compliment he could pay anyone, man or woman.

There were some in the Resistance who thought of James Hope as some sort of Messiah. Martin Deacon imagined that part of that was because of James's last name. But James had been Messiah-like to them. He was a natural military leader, at once prudent yet audacious.

The National Police were too close for real aimed fire—Martin Deacon barely looked across the M-16's sights as he opened fire. His target was the young Soviet officer. He ripped the first three-round burst across the man's chest, then a second burst and a third, sawing diagonally from abdomen to throat, the Soviet soldier falling back, dead, the pale gray eyes wide. . . .

"Marc—get it!"

Lumierre raised to his full height, swinging the lens of the video camera toward the bottom of the gorge, Jean-Pierre Petrovitch recording the unfolding battle as he watched it, the gunfire making the monitor pop. "This is Jean-Pierre Petrovitch reporting for Independent News of France. Forces of the American Resistance are attacking an apparent superior force of the National Police. What you hear in the background is the sound of gunfire: assault rifle, machine guns, pistols—" The gunfire was punctuated by a scream, but the unnatural-sounding scream of a man. A woman—the bandanna that had covered her hair ripped away in her left hand, blond hair cascading to her shoulders—held a weapon in her right hand. The bandanna in her other hand blew in the breeze before her. Petrovitch was cold. The weapon in her right hand was spitting fire in bursts, cutting into the black-uniformed National Police.

Petrovitch started speaking again. "A woman—graceful, by any standard beautiful, her blond hair caught in the wind—she is one of the Resistance, perhaps one of its leaders. Her description matches that of Jennifer Hope, daughter of James Hope, leader of the Resistance. There she goes. My God, she has just killed three of the National Police. Wait a moment: They are counterattacking. As men and women of the Resistance seem to pour down from the opposite side of the gorge here, the National Police apparently are consolidating their position. The woman who may be Jennifer Hope—her weapon has stopped firing, for some reason! She has a knife—she is hacking with it like some sort of sword. My God! She just severed a man's head from his body. I have never seen such as this! Another of the Resistance—a man, tall, lean, dark-haired—is coming to her aid. My God! The man is leaping up. He has kicked one of the National Policemen in the head. He is whirling around, like the funnel of a hurricane! His foot has kicked one man in the jaw, another in the chest! In his right hand is a knife now. This man is incredible!"

Lumierre shifted position, clambering onto the rocks, the power pack for the video camera swaying precariously at his side now, gunfire from beneath them in the gorge more sporadic now. Petrovitch cleared his throat, speaking into his cassette recorder. "The National Police unit is falling back; guns are being raised by the Resistance toward our positions in the rocks here—"

Lumierre started to shout, his English less accented than Petrovitch knew his own to be. "We are journalists—we are not armed. Do not shoot us!"

Petrovitch stood, too, his left hand raised high in the air over his head, the cassette recorder in his right hand near his lips. "They are aiming their guns toward us. My friend and photographer, Marc Lumierre, has just called to them in English, telling them that we are journalists and not to shoot us. We wait now, not knowing whether they will try to kill us."

Petrovitch had the sudden urge to urinate. He had been in combat before, seen it—but never had the guns pointed at him.

The girl—she had to be Jennifer Hope—shouted up to them in perfect French, "Identify yourselves!"

Petrovitch suddenly wanted to let it go, not hold it anymore. He began to breathe again. He called down to her, "We are with the Independent News of France. We were sent here to interview"—he guessed, dared himself to say it—"we are here to inteview your father, Senator Hope!"

Petrovitch waited. Lumierre was cursing softly under his breath, "She will kill us, my friend. We are in deep shit, my friend."

The blond-haired girl in the depth of the gorge shouted again, "Keep your hands raised and don't get out of sight!"

Petrovitch found himself nodding, trying to talk into his recorder now without moving his lips, to avoid provoking any response from the Resistance. "The woman speaks perfect French. She has all but admitted to being Jennifer Hope, daughter of the leader of the Resistance."

Chapter Two

The rock was cold beneath him, but he sat there. He had been told to by the woman. She was incredibly beautiful. And she was the daughter of James Hope. Marc Lumierre sat beside him, their equipment taken away some distance. It seemed to Petrovitch that Jennifer Hope and the dark-haired man who had fought so much like a demon were coleaders of this Resistance unit. The man, Petrovitch had learned, was named Martin.

Jennifer Hope, a small machine gun of some sort slung beneath her right arm, a pistol on her right hip, the massive knife she had used in battle on the other hip—and such hips, he thought—approached them now.

Petrovitch would have risen but didn't, less he provoke a response. Lumierre said with a hiss, "We are here for a story, and to get out alive—not a woman, hey, my friend?"

Petrovitch licked his lips, looking at Lumierre for a moment, then back to the woman. He knew he was staring at her.

And when she stopped walking, her weight resting on her left leg, her right hip slung slightly forward, she smiled. She spoke in French again. "How did you find us?"

"Miss Hope, we asked for this assignment—Marc and I. We wanted to get the true story of your father from his own mouth. The stories that come out of the United States are all controlled by the Russians; we do not know what is true and what is not true. Your father—he is called a bandit, a butcher, a murderer of small children. But it is whispered he is a hero. Marc and I have come for the truth."

Jennifer Hope laughed. "I failed to see your lantern. But that's for seeking an honest man, isn't it? I'm afraid I was terrible at ancient Greece. I was going to be an interior decorator. I have an M.B.A. from—well, what does it matter? So you want truth," she almost whispered. Her voice was a rich, warm, alto. Sensuous, Jean-Pierre Petrovitch thought.

"And what will you do with truth once you get it?"

"We will tell it to the free world."

"Free world?" Jennifer Hope laughed—and her laughter was music. "A French reporter with a Russian last name talking about a free world?" She doubled forward, laughing, dropping to her knees, her right fist tightening on the grip of the little machine gun but not in any menacing way, as though instead she were holding it to keep her sides from splitting with laughter. And then she stopped laughing, very suddenly. Her blue eyes were tear-rimmed and he didn't know if the tears were there from the laughter or from the thought that had evidently so suddenly sobered her. "You honestly believe there is a free world out there—still?"

"Yes—I believe this," he whispered. "A place where beautiful women do not carry"—and he used the English words, gesturing with his hands—"machine guns like that."

She broke from French into English. "This isn't a machine gun. Years ago, before Daddy—well, when Daddy was still a senator, I would have called this a machine gun, too. But it's a 9mm Parabellum-caliber Uzi submachine gun. When you're a real pro, like I am, you call it a sub gun, or a

squirt gun, maybe. I remember once my younger brother—"
And her eyes suddenly became sad.

"Stephen Hope," Petrovitch said slowly, in English, too.
"And he works with your father's former partner in the FBI,
Arnold Borden, the director of the National Police Force."

She laughed, tossing her head, her hair dancing in the
gray sunlight, a wisp of the hair caught up in the breeze that
intermittently raked the defile in the high rocks where Jennifer
Hope and the dark-haired man named Martin had brought
them. "I should—ahh—say something very dramatic," and
she repeated herself in French, then lapsed back into English. "Something like 'My brother is dead' or 'I have no
brother'—shouldn't I?"

Petrovitch said nothing. To be a good reporter, he had
once told a journalism class, one had to be a good listener
first.

Jennifer Hope smiled, laughed again, then began again
to speak. "This one time, I helped Stephen fix his ten-speed,
you know. He conned me into it. Big sister help little
brother—that kind of shit. So I did—and I broke a nail on the
derailer gears or whatever." She raised both hands now,
letting her submachine gun fall to her side on its olive-drab
sling. On both hands the nails were as short as a man's nails,
dirt under them, unvarnished. "I can take this submachine
gun apart with my eyes closed, and I haven't had a nail to
break in two years. I used to bitch at my mother when I had
to wear the same dress to two different Washington parties—
right?" And her fingertips tugged at the T-shirt beneath her
open fatigue jacket. She was not large-breasted, but even so,
he could tell she wore no bra. "I've been wearing this
'ensemble' for the past three days. I used to smell of perfume—
the expensive kind, the kind that cost some poor working
guy's monthly mortgage payment just to buy by the ounce.
Now—well, I just smell," she concluded dismissively. She
stood up. "So—now you've got a story. Jennifer Hope, former
socialite, bitter about her life in the wilderness as a freedom
fighter. But I'm not—bitter. I don't have time to be bitter.
Because there's too much to do. Too many battles to fight."
And she laughed—a girl's laugh, full of confidence in her
beauty, full of confidence in her charm and her wit.

And in the setting, Petrovitch suddenly felt a sadness for

her he did not want to feel. Because if the first rule of journalism was to be a good listener, certainly the second rule was to be dispassionate. And as he looked at her, the great blue eyes that belied the smile that dimpled the corners of her thin, pale-lipped mouth—he realized the moment he had first seen her, he had lost the ability to be dispassionate at all. . . .

Martin Deacon had been against it, but somehow she had felt she could trust Jean-Pierre Petrovitch and Marc Lumierre. Martin Deacon had snapped, "Women!" "Damn right," Jennifer had snapped back. She had ordered that Lumierre stand by while the camera equipment was checked for weapons, stand by so that the camera equipment and tapes not be damaged, that Petrovitch stand by while his own things and the things of his cameraman—backpacks and the like—were searched as well. There had been an attempt five months earlier to assassinate her father, men pretending to be Resistance from Pennsylvania. Her father had been wounded in the right arm but with his left hand he had taken down two of the assassins with a pistol, Martin Deacon getting the other two.

But as much as it was now a war of weapons, it had always been a war of words, and the strength of her father's words was the reason he had been branded an outlaw. And the strength of her father's words could—and she almost verbalized it—maybe make a difference.

They had been moving northwest for some time now, taking a more intricate route toward the mountain stronghold in the National Forest than necessary, but necessary now to confuse the two Frenchmen. When their equipment had been checked for weapons, it had also been checked for homing devices and hidden microphones and, as an added precaution, Jennifer had confiscated Petrovitch's two tape recorders. One had not even held a cassette, the other had. She had felt as though she were peeping through a window, but she had listened to bits and snatches of the tape. She remembered something as she walked along: "A woman— graceful, by any standard beautiful, her blond hair caught in the wind—" She had shut off the tape machine, feeling dirty inside somehow for having listened to it. But the words had not left her.

Her father called her that: beautiful. But sometimes she thought that her beauty was gone, because she no longer felt beautiful. She didn't quite know what feeling had replaced that.

She kept walking, Martin Deacon just ahead of her, a few more of the Resistance band behind her, then the two Frenchmen, then more of the band. Single file to minimize the effect of ambush. There was always the unexpected National Police unit to contend with—they, too, roamed these mountains. And increasingly more, the Soviet Special Forces personnel led the National Police units in their patrols. And the Soviet Special Forces personnel were better trained, better equipped, and vastly more cautious.

Jennifer Hope felt a shiver along her spine—the cool breeze that rustled the trees around her was not the cause of the chill. It was the inevitability of the Soviet advisers sooner or later assuming full responsibility for killing or capturing her father. And entire patrols of Soviet Special Forces personnel, airborne reconnaissance or attack—all of this might prove to be an irresistible force.

Martin Deacon raised his right hand. Jennifer signaled the halt to the Resistance personnel behind her.

Martin turned and glanced back toward her. There was worry on his lean face, around his eyes. His lips pursed for a moment to signal silence. His fists held his rifle. He turned away.

Jennifer Hope strained her ears. She could hear it now, too. Movement of the trees that was not caused by wind—it was too irregular. She dropped to a crouch along the deer trail, signaling the others behind her to do the same. Martin moved his left hand in a side-to-side motion. Jennifer repeated the signal, glancing back once as the company of the Resistance vanished to right and left paralleling the trail, the two Frenchmen being pulled almost bodily along, out of sight.

She tightened the sling of her Uzi, reaching across to her left side with her right hand and drawing the BuckMaster from its sheath.

But then Martin stood up, turned to her, and called out so loudly that all of the Resistance could hear it: "It's all right—McDowell and Habersham."

She stood up, resheathed her knife, loosened the sling of her submachine gun. Habersham stood very tall and very black and very young and very good at killing the enemy. McDowell—in his midthirties, red-haired and fair-skinned, short, overweight—was one of the strongest men she had ever seen. McDowell was also good at killing. She walked forward, Habersham smiling good-naturedly as he always did, McDowell ignoring her as he always did. Habersham spoke, Martin nodding as he listened. "The shit has hit the fan, Martin, Jennifer."

"What shit has hit what fan?" Martin asked, his voice low. She studied his eyes and the hard set of the muscles around them. He didn't like surprises, and bumping into Habersham and McDowell ranked as a surprise. Her father had sent them on long-range reconnaissance ten days earlier and they weren't due back in the area so close to camp for another four days.

"A Russian patrol—real big one—three dozen men and two officers. Workin' their way this direction—killin' everybody they think is lyin' to them. And they're lookin' for James and the rest of us. And they're gonna find us—people aren't gonna hold up under 'em, ya know?" Habersham's voice calmed. What he had said had made tangible Jennifer's greatest fear.

Martin spat.

"Jees—"

Jennifer Hope realized her hands were trembling. And she realized she was speaking though her voice belied her feelings, because it was perfectly calm. "Those French reporters. They wanted a story—"

"What French reporters?" McDowell asked with a drawl. Jennifer Hope was a Northerner by birth and education and still, despite her years in the South, sometimes was aware of what she termed an accent that men such as McDowell and Habersham and Martin Deacon considered just normal speech if they considered it at all.

"Back there," she said with a sigh. "You'll meet them. But they wanted a story. And if the Russians are finally coming out of the damn closet and coming after us, this is the first time Soviet troops have gone into operation on American soil outside the capacity of advisers to the National Police.

Petrovitch and Lumierre can document it to the world. They'll get more story than they bargained for. Have you warned my father yet?"

"No. We were just—"

She cut Habersham off. "That's what I thought. Stay with us—we'll cut back onto the main trails, and we can be in camp in two hours or so. Need any water, any food?"

"No. Could use some .223, if anybody's got it. Bumped into a National Police unit—McDowell and me. Burned their asses good and blew out most of our ammo doin' it."

Jennifer Hope licked her lips, nodded. Where was lipstick when you really needed it? she thought absently. "All right." She looked at Martin. "Let's go?"

He spat again. "Let's go," and called back in a loud stage whisper along the bunching column of Resistance fighters behind them. "Russians—looking for the base camp. We gotta warn James, maybe evacuate the camp, figure out a nice warm welcome for those fuckers. We're going back to the main trail 'cause it's quicker—but it's more dangerous, 'cause if they do force people into telling 'em anything, they'll find the main trail. Be extra careful and extra fast. Hardesty, Gruber—take drag."

"Right!"

Hardesty—lean, muscular, short—brandished his riot shotgun in the air and tapped the older Gruber on the shoulder. The two men disappeared back along the secondary trail.

Martin continued talking. "Jess, you take point—about two hundred yards ahead. And keep your safety off," he added. The woman nodded, brushing past Jennifer, running past Martin Deacon, and disappearing into the trees. "Let's go," he commanded in a louder voice, his M-16 at high port.

Jennifer Hope tried to swallow, but something was very hard in her throat and she was very much afraid.

Jennifer Hope had returned his tape recorder—the look in her eyes told him she had listened to his words. He was happy she had. She had said nothing except, "Stick with us and do exactly as you're told. Russians."

It would be the story of his career, he had told himself. But Marc Lumierre had put it well: "We could die here."

Petrovitch used his machine sparingly, talking into it

when he had the breath. Toward the camp, the main trail's cutoff—which was what he understood the rocky, goat-pathlike trail to be—was steep and hard to navigate. The Resistance moved along it so quickly that he was half out of breath almost constantly. Lumierre fared better. Petrovitch reasoned that was because Lumierre's body was more hardened from the perennial burdens of his equipment. And Lumierre played tennis and swam a great deal.

They had climbed along a narrow ledge, then branched upward from the ledge, following the outline of what Petrovitch judged to be reclaimed land. It bore the signs of the devastation of hydraulic mining or some similar earth-scarring technique. The pine trees that grew here on the reddish soil were smaller, spaced more evenly, the high grass thinner somehow, and there were more weeds.

The ledge suddenly turned into a broad path, but none of the Resistance personnel behind him or ahead of him paired up, the men and women still walking single file. There was no sound, no idle conversation, only background noises: insects, the rustling of the high tops of the skinny-trunked pines, the occasional crackle and snap of a twig being crushed or broken under foot.

Ahead of him now, he watched as Martin (he had learned Martin's last name was Deacon) raised his right hand, signaling a halt. Petrovitch hoped it was for rest. Despite his own fatigue, he had taken on the burden of some of Lumierre's equipment and was exhausted.

The men and women of the Resistance started spreading out into the scrub brush and the pine trunks and the high grass and weeds. For a moment, Jean-Pierre Petrovitch thought they were preparing for battle rather than rest. But then he saw men sitting beside tree trunks, and women dropping to their knees in the high grass, freeing their hair of bandannas or crusher hats.

Petrovitch edged off, Lumierre already seated a few yards from him. Petrovitch whispered into his machine, his eyes fixed on the level indicator. "We have traveled for an hour or better since the change of course when the two men intercepted us on the trail. I have been told that we were shifting cross country from one of the secondary trails to the main trail leading toward the base camp, where presumably

James Hope presides over his Resistance army. I have been told that Russians are coming—but as yet I have seen no sign of Russian presence beyond the dead Soviet advisers in the battle earlier. Lumierre and I are very tired—"

"So am I."

He looked up, automatically hitting the pause button. Jennifer Hope stood over him, her small submachine gun held limply in her left hand, her hair free of the camouflage bandanna, her eyes weary but beautiful. The wind was cool here in the mountains, he thought. And he pushed the stop button on his tape recorder. It would be more than a pause now with her here.

"You are beautiful—but you know I think that," he said with a smile. "My English—it is not so good, I am afraid."

"I like it," Jennifer Hope told him.

"Please—sit beside me?"

She nodded slowly. Then in one fluid motion she dropped into a cross-legged sitting position on the ground beside him. "I'm sorry about listening to your tape player. Ahh, I needed to know for certain that—"

"We are newsmen?"

"Yes." She nodded, smiling briefly; then the smile faded. The sun was stronger here and gave a warmth to the color of her skin. "Anyway, I felt like a Peeping Tom."

"A Peeping Tom," he repeated.

"Yes. Don't you know what a Peeping Tom is?"

"No."

"Well, legend has it that when Lady Godiva—"

"The English noblewoman who rode naked through the streets of Coventry—"

"Yes," she said with a smile. And he could have sworn she blushed a little. "But that when she made her ride only one man looked at her: Peeping Tom. I felt like that—like the one who looked, listening to what you said about me."

"A voyeur," he supplied. "But you are not. You are doing your job, as I, indeed, do mine."

"You and your photographer friend—"

"Marc Lumierre," Petrovitch supplied.

"Yes—Marc Lumierre. You and your friend could get killed here with us. If you like, we can try to get you out—before we get involved with the Russians."

"And miss the story of a lifetime?" He tried to laugh. He couldn't. "No. If we can get Soviet regulars on camera, what your father has said these years since the Peace Party has come into power here will be vindicated to all the world."

He watched her—she was studying her hands. He reached out his hands instinctively, touching her hands, holding them. They did not draw away. Her eyes raised toward his. "You really think that will do any good?"

"Yes. At the least, the rest of the world—it will know the truth of Soviet intentions."

"I'm very tired, Jean-Pierre."

"You are very beautiful. Very desirable. You should not be tired."

"Do you want to—ahh?" and she lowered her eyes.

"Yes—very much I want this, " he almost whispered.

She smiled. "If we live until tonight." And she drew her hands from his, raised to a standing position, and ran off, her bandanna trailing in her right hand, her submachine gun in her left hand. And Jean-Pierre Petrovitch closed his eyes to keep the sight of her with him for an instant longer.

Chapter Three

James Hope. Jean-Pierre Petrovitch assessed the myth. Tall—what the Americans called a six-footer, and then some. Petrovitch had read the biography, read and reread it, practically memorizing it. Hope was fifty-four but looked barely forty. His forehead was high and etched slightly with wrinkles, but the wrinkles of thought rather than age or dissipation. His hair was full, and long to the point where it touched over the collar of his gray-green epauleted shirt. The photographs in the biography had shown Hope at varying ages—in his twenties in the Federal Bureau of Investigation, in his thirties as the chief of the FBI counterterrorist team, in his forties as a fledgling United States senator, in his fifties in the last photograph taken of him on the day Hope was to have been arrested. Instead he had escaped with his family.

In the first photo, even in the second and third, Hope's hair had been a dark brown, almost black. But in the last photo, taken after he had publicly denounced the Peace Party as pawns of the Soviet Union and pledged to fight the party's assault on the United States Constitution, the hair had already begun to turn gray.

It seemed grayer now—and now as an outlaw, he had the appearance every politician so zealously craved, that of the elder statesman, still fit, hardy, strong, keen of eye. The eyes, unlike his daughter's eyes, were brown. They studied men, analyzed their hearts and souls, Petrovitch realized as he watched Hope's eyes studying him.

Hope appeared unarmed except for a gunbelt at his waist, a holster on each hip, but the flaps of the holsters concealed what was inside them.

Hope was arguing with his daughter. His wife, Melissa, stood beside him. If Jennifer Hope would mature into such a woman, she would be a goddess forever, Petrovitch thought. Melissa Hope was very pregnant, her long fingers gracefully stroking her abdomen as she listened with interest to her husband's words, her daughter's words. That James Hope and Jennifer Hope argued was obvious, but they were too far away from him to be overheard except for the occasional syllable, and Petrovitch's English was not that good that such occasional pieces of words were intelligible to him.

The argument ceased—or perhaps was only suspended. Petrovitch had no way to tell. But James Hope was striding toward him now.

Lumierre whispered, "My friend, should I film him?"

"No—not until he gives permission. It might lose the tape for us."

"Very well. It might lose our lives, too, eh?"

Petrovitch grinned at Marc Lumierre, then refocused his gaze on James Hope.

The man's voice, like his eyes, was magnetic. Hope asked nothing; he stated only. "You want to interview me. Your friend wants to film a battle between us and the Soviets."

"Yes."

Hope thrust his right hand forward. Petrovitch took it—there was strength, firmness, but the grip wasn't the handshake of a man who had to prove anything, either. It was simply there.

Lumierre murmured something Petrovitch didn't catch, but he caught its motivation. "Senator Hope, may I have the honor of presenting my friend and associate, Marc Lumierre."

Hope turned to face Lumierre, extending his hand. "It's not Senator anymore. Glad to meet you, sir. I'm afraid our daughter's the only one who's terribly gifted with languages."

"It is a true honor, sir. You are a legend everywhere."

Hope seemed almost to ignore the remark, Petrovitch thought. But he smiled graciously. The voice was like iron. The teeth revealed in the smile were white and even. "You and Mr. Petrovitch are either very intrepid journalists or you have a death wish."

"They are one and the same, sir," Lumierre said with a laugh.

"Very similar to being a Resistance fighter," Hope remarked offhandedly. He seemed to clear his throat, to draw himself to attention, but in reality Hope did neither. Hope merely closed away the smile, saying, "Jennifer tells me we have a Soviet force heading our way and suggests that we evacuate the camp." Jennifer Hope drifted over to stand beside him, Hope encircling his daughter's shoulders with his right arm, her head resting against his shoulder. "Militarily, she's perfectly correct, of course—but the Soviets will expect that. And we have several women among us who are pregnant, several infants, and many small children. So we'll meet them instead. You gentlemen are welcome to accompany us. We leave tomorrow at dawn. But I doubt that you'll be treated as neutral journalists if captured."

Petrovitch remembered Jacques Martel. Lumierre spoke of him. "A friend of ours was killed during the terrorist bombing of the National Rifle Association headquarters. But he was shot with a rifle, and his photos showed no one armed in the crowd that formed there—except the National Police."

Hope thrust his hands into the pockets of his blue jeans, his holsters looking strange as they were pushed away slightly from his hips. Hope looked down at his combat boots for a moment, then at Lumierre, Jennifer Hope holding his right arm at the crook of the elbow now. "That wasn't a terrorist bombing. The Soviets with the help of the National Police entered the NRA headquarters illegally, seized all membership records to use as an arrest list, then bombed the building themselves. They wanted the old membership files that dated from before the Gun Control Act of 1968 and the yellow Form 4473's. They used the Form 4473's to go after gun owners for confiscation of their weapons, sometimes for arrests and sometimes for murder. But before GCA '68, the closest thing to a list of gun owners would have been NRA files. Of course, that was illegal—taking the lists. And in those days..." Hope's voice sounded suddenly old and far away, and Petrovitch felt filled with sadness for the man.

"In those days, the Peace Party tried to maintain the appearance of legality, and the Soviets were only our 'friends' and not our 'advisers.'"

"You have always been anti-Communist, Senator Hope?"

Hope shifted his gaze from wherever it had gone, to Petrovitch's eyes. "Yes—but not so anti-Communist as to provoke armed conflict over mere ideological differences. I was a strong supporter of expansion of U.S. ties with mainland China, for example. No—communism is the Soviet excuse, not the Soviet religion, as it's sometimes branded. I'm against communism. It is morally wrong, and I'd like to see it obliterated from the face of the earth. But the inevitability of logic, the peaceful evolution of nations once gripped by Communist dictatorship—those will destroy communism, if not in name, then in practice. The Soviet leadership has recognized that for decades. As much as I dislike communism, perhaps the greatest crime of the Soviet leadership is that they fail to practice it. They use the word 'communism' as a synonym for martial law, police powers the like of which have been seen only in Nazi Germany, for a false war-footing economy. They are criminals, not ideologues."

Petrovitch asked another question. "You focused your fight on what you called the individual right to keep and bear arms. Why?"

James Hope smiled. "Our Founding Fathers viewed the militia as every able-bodied man. In those days, of course, women were not considered full citizens."

"Hmm—only in those days." Jennifer Hope smiled.

Her father folded his arm about her again. "In the modern era, that would mean every able-bodied man and woman. It's well to remember that there was great distrust of standing armies and centralized government. I sometimes feel they had a crystal ball. With every man and woman a potential citizen-soldier and armed for the defense of the nation, the rights delineated in the first ten amendments thus were guaranteed. And remember, the right to keep and bear arms follows only in order of precedence freedom of speech, press, and assembly. It seemed clear to me that if the Peace Party leadership was so dedicated to disarming the American people, there had to be a reason. And subsequent events have proven that the reason for disarming the American people was to render them defenseless. At first, when friends would disappear into the mountains, into the deserts, I deemed their actions stupid, perhaps even cowardly. Stay and fight through the legal system. Then the Subversion Acts were passed and the NRA, the Citizens Committee, the other pro-firearms rights organizations were listed as subverting the peace effort and ordered disbanded. Those who kept firearms or fled from the law were not only felons, they were also classed as subversives, and under optional penalty of death. It was a license for Arnold Borden and the National Police Force to murder anyone who was a potential undesirable, a potential spokesperson against government oppression, against our growing domination by the Soviets."

"About Arnold Borden, sir?" Petrovitch began.

There was fire in James Hope's eyes. "He was my friend. The best man at my wedding. Jennifer's godfather. My partner when I was in the FBI. They dangled power in front of him, and he sold out. He was a decent man once. Now he's a butcher, a traitor. And Gentlemen"—Hope cleared his throat—"if I continue talking about Arnold Borden now, well . . ." He forced a smile, the muscles around his eyes very tight. "Well—it's not good for my sinuses." The smile died away. "You look hungry. I know I am. We can talk later. Come on!" Hope clapped Petrovitch on the shoulder. Petrovitch fell in at Hope's left side, Hope's arm across his shoulders. "What part of France are you from?"

"Now, of course, I am from Paris, but . . ."

And he saw Jennifer Hope's eyes as she walked at her father's right—the eyes were so beautiful....

It was like an old movie he had seen once: the American actor Errol Flynn as Robin Hood leading Maid Marian through his camp, showing her the poor, the downtrodden, the physically abused—the people he had rescued from the oppressors. He was not Maid Marian, Petrovitch thought with a smile, but the tour was very much the same. No green-clad archers—only green-clad people with rifles and pistols and shotguns and submachine guns. No legs of mutton; instead, bowls of stew largely vegetarian, chunks of bread without butter. And no chests of gold overflowed from a usurper prince's ill-gotten coffers, but rather crates of arms and vastly fewer crates of ammunition.

The stew had been good. It had been warm. The woman who had ladled it into his borrowed bowl, he had learned from Jennifer Hope, was Martin Deacon's wife. Like James Hope's wife, who shared their rough-hewn table beneath a camouflaged tent, Deacon's wife was pregnant, but not as far along.

James Hope ate heartily but almost thoughtfully, as though considering his food as he consumed it. Petrovitch watched as Lumierre wolfed his own food away, was offered more but declined. Lumierre would eat until he could barely walk and show no sign of weight. Perhaps it had been all the children about the camp and the small size of their food bowls.

James Hope took a cigarette, and Petrovitch began to laugh. It was a Virginia Slim. Hope looked at him from across the table. "I know...." From his shirt pocket Hope took a small knife shaped like a pen, opened it, then cut away the filter tip. "I used to smoke quite a lot. Pall Malls. Up here, well—you can't get cigarettes. And even the Russians we kill smoke the ones made in this country. I took these off a National Police commander. And I checked—it was really a guy." He lit the cigarette with a battered brush-finished wind-lighter.

Petrovitch eyed his tape recorder. It was as if Hope had read his mind. "Turn on your machine and ask away. We have some time, I suppose. But if we're leaving at dawn, we need a good night's rest."

Petrovitch felt himself smile. "But, yes—thank you." He felt Jennifer Hope sitting beside him, but their bodies did not touch. "I would like to ask you to give me a chronology of the events that brought you here. I realize this is a question that is very broad, but if you please—try, sir."

Hope inhaled his cigarette, nodded as he exhaled, smoke coming from his mouth as he talked. "The obvious, immediate cause was the *Northstar* incident."

"Did you consider it an accident, or were the remarks attributed to you in the Soviet press true?"

Hope laughed, shaking his head. "For once, the Soviets told the truth. I should say *almost*. I didn't accuse them, I merely said it was a deliberate act of sabotage. I didn't say who did it. You see, of course the national elections were coming and it was the off year and all the various antinuclear, antiwar, anti-everything parties had formed a coalition, were running candidates against every Republican and Democrat who held office, except for some who were certified by the Peace Party as being politically acceptable. At the time they did it, most political observers felt they were being terribly naïve, that running a few candidates and being able to concentrate media efforts and financial support in a few key races would have been vastly more sensible. But at the same time, no one really wanted to advise them on this. I mean, no one wanted them to win. They advocated total unilateral nuclear disarmament. I mean, nobody in their right mind wanted nuclear war—I don't think the Russians any more or less than ourselves. But if we had scrapped our nuclear arsenals... Well, we did. And here we are." James Hope stubbed out his cigarette, stood up, and announced, "Gentlemen, why don't we continue this on the trail tomorrow. I'd like to spend some time with my wife."

Petrovitch didn't have time to answer. He merely hit the stop button.

Jean-Pierre Petrovitch's hand closed over Jennifer Hope's. He wasn't looking at her, but instead at the sky, at the stars that were so clear here, so beautiful. "I will say this," he said only half aloud. "If someone must hide from the authorities and live in the wilderness, there could not be a more beautiful place."

Jennifer didn't answer him, but she spoke. "What did you think of my father?"

Petrovitch laughed. "He sounds like a senator. He is very intelligent, I think. An easy man to respect, to trust—but—"

"But not an easy man to live with."

Petrovitch looked at her; her hand moved away from his. "Yes, I think this, too. He is too right—always correct—I cannot think of a better word, darling...." He stopped.

She was looking at him. "Why did you call me that?"

He licked his lips. "Why did you, earlier today—why did you ask me if..." He didn't finish it.

"When you look at me, you see a woman. Everybody else sees James Hope's virginal daughter who fights for freedom."

"Are you?"

"Virginal?" She laughed.

"I didn't mean that. I mean, I know that you are James Hope's daughter. I mean—"

And she turned to him, and she was in his arms. "I'm not virginal—and I know what you mean. Make love to me—please."

He licked his lips again. His palms were sweating. "I want to make love to you very much. But for different reasons."

"What reasons?" she whispered.

He looked away from her. He looked at the stars instead. "I don't want you to want me because I am here and you are here."

"You talk like a woman," she told him.

He laughed. "I don't think so, darling. If I didn't care, if I didn't want you so much—then I would take you on your terms. But I do care."

She whispered to him. He could hear the scraping of her pistol belt's buckle, felt it fall, heard it fall. "Then on your terms—love me."

Petrovitch folded his arms closer around her, her head cocking back, her eyes closed. He whispered to her. "Eyes opened, Jennifer—eyes opened." And she opened her eyes and he bent his mouth over hers and touched at her lips.

There was a sweetness he had never experienced. And he tasted at it harder still.

Her hands moved along his chest—he felt her fingers working the buttons of his shirt open. He let her do it. But then his hands moved from her waist to her hands and stopped their progress. "No. You do not want me." He released her hands and reached down to the ground and picked up her pistol belt. It was heavier than he had thought. The pistol in its holster, her knife, other gear. He held it out to her, but she had turned her back. "Here," he whispered.

"The Frenchmen I knew were different."

"The American girls I knew—they were different, too."

She turned around, quickly, looking at him. She took the pistol belt, holding it in her hand, clutched to her abdomen like a woman might ordinarily clutch a handerchief. "What the fuck do you want?"

"The woman, not the daughter of the legend. If you are bored, I am sorry. If you are horny—"

"Hell, it's a cinch you aren't."

He didn't say anything. She did.

"What did you expect? I look into your eyes and cry. I don't touch you but you touch me? I don't want—just let myself be wanted?"

He didn't reply. She went on.

"You asked me if I was bitter."

"I didn't ask you—you told me you weren't."

"Damn it!"

"I will go back to camp."

She buckled on her pistol belt. "Go—go on."

He turned around, starting toward the camp, trying not to think about her. And he heard her voice from behind him then, and he turned around to face her. "What do you want?" she asked.

"I will know when I see it," he told her. He waited, not knowing really for what.

"Yeah—I guess I will, too." And she smiled.

"You will be all right? I can see you back to camp."

"Have you ever killed a man, Jean-Pierre? Or a woman, for that matter?" But she didn't wait for him to answer. "If you haven't, you'll say 'no.' But if you have, you won't want to talk about it."

Now he answered. "I haven't. I was in a fistfight once, when I was a little boy. And once when I was covering a riot someone broke a bottle over my left arm—my arm broke. I broke my tape recorder over the man's face and ran away to the police lines."

"I never wanted to grow up—like this."

It started to rain, and he looked skyward—one patch of dark cloud, no lightning illuminating it from within, and surrounding the patch of darkness the pinpoints of light that were stars and planets. He looked back at Jennifer Hope. She was laughing. "Used to be, I'd come in out of the rain." And she stood there, her head rising, her face tilting upward into the rain. He could barely see her now, because the clouds obscured the bright crescent of the moon that had lit the ground with a dull glow.

"Come over here, to me," he told her.

"Why?" She didn't look at him, her face still upturned to the rain.

"I want you."

"You forgot to snap your fingers."

And now her face turned toward him. He raised his right hand almost to the level of his chest, slowly bringing his thumb and second finger together. He snapped them, then let the hand fall to his side.

Jennifer walked toward him. He asked her as she stopped a few feet from him, "Is there a place in the camp?"

"Aren't you going to kiss me in the rain? I saw a movie once where the man did that to the woman."

He walked toward her. He touched his hands to her face and raised her chin, bending his face to hers, touching his lips to hers again. Her face was wet with the rain. But he tasted a saltiness as he moved his lips across her face to touch at her eyelids. "You are crying."

"Yes."

"Why?"

"Because I think you care."

"You should cry, then—very much." He folded his arms about her. The rain became more intense, but he made no effort to move her from the spot. He simply held her.

Chapter Four

He had showered after leaving the tent where he had eaten and spoken with the French newsman. He had come to bed in the tent he shared with Melissa, his wife, and she had been waiting for him, both of them wanting to be lovers again. With her swollen abdomen, it had been impossible for weeks to use any position that was not some form of rear entry. Afterward, she had fallen asleep in his arms.

James Hope sat up in the cot. His crotch was sticky from what had dribbled out of her in the night as he had slept against her. In books he had read, they used to call it sleeping like spoons. There was no time for another shower, so he took his old underpants from the foot of the bed and rubbed at himself and it seemed less sticky.

Barefoot, naked, shivering slightly in the damp chill of predawn, he picked up the bedside oil lamp and stood, starting across the tent to where his things were.

"Jim?"

"Go back to sleep, sweetheart," he told her, his voice low.

"Is it time already?"

He looked at the Rolex on his left wrist, the white of the luminous markings seeming yellow in the lamplight glow. "Yeah—it's time already."

"How long will you be gone, Jim?"

"I don't know," he told her honestly, putting down the lamp on the old dresser one of the Resistance members had given him. One of the drawers was missing. He opened the top drawer and took out a clean pair of underpants, stepping into them. He found socks, balancing on one foot to put them on.

"Is Jennifer going with you?"

"Yeah—I'm leaving Martin in charge of the camp here. If you have any problem—"

"No, I'll be fine. How many Russians? I heard a lot of different numbers last night."

Her voice was a soft alto, a little throatier than it had been a quarter century ago, when they had married. But it was still something that he could get lost in, just listening to. "Thirty-six—at least that's what Habersham and Bob McDowell say. Plus a couple of officers."

"They finally did it."

"Yeah," he agreed. *They finally did it.* He pulled on his Levi's, zipping the crotch halfway up, looking for a shirt. She always kept his few things clean. She had never washed anything by hand except her underwear, and that only when they stayed in a motel overnight. She had been rich before marriage—before birth, really, her father a third-generation millionaire. She had risen to every occasion in their marriage— even this, he thought, pulling the gray-green Army shirt on. A truck they had stopped had contained hundreds of them. He had found his sleeve length, but not his neck size—but he never buttoned them at the neck, anyway. He buttoned the rest of the buttons now. "They finally did it. But this news crew being here—it's a real break, kid."

"Kid—I'm almost as old as you are."

"Close counts only in horseshoes. Anyway, any woman with a cake in the oven's automatically a kid."

"Pregnant at my age—can you imagine? And I'm happy about it, that's the crazy thing."

"It isn't crazy," he told her, making the sign of the cross as he put the sterling silver crucifix around his neck. From the top of the dresser, he took the little pen-shaped Grande knife, slipping it in his left breast shirt pocket. The crucifix was all that had been left of his father's rosary, nearly all that had been left of his father. D-Day. June 6, 1944. For a lot of people of his generation, the "D" stood for death. He had never known his father, but this mother had told him he— James—was like the man who had died leading his platoon against a machine-gun nest. The posthumous Congressional Medal of Honor. Stephen had thrown it away in the Potomac, and he had struck Stephen. Not like a father might slap a son, but punched him in the face, knocked him down, drawn blood.

He exhaled, very tired of it all. He pulled his pants up and cinched the belt. A thirty-five-inch waist—he still had the stamina. But he no longer had the patience. He picked up his combat boots and walked the lamp back toward the edge of the cot, sitting down. "You still awake?"

"Sure I'm still awake. What's bothering you, Jim?"

"I was thinking about Stephen. Shit, I shouldn't have hit him that time."

"It was your father's Medal of Honor and he threw it in the river. What the hell were you supposed to do?"

"But you don't punch out your own son." He had both feet in his boots and began lacing the upper eyelets so he could tie them.

"He wasn't your son anymore."

"Now the truth comes out—the milkman. I thought he had that guy's eyes."

"Ohh—"

He turned toward her, barely able to see her in the lamplight. She was beautiful, more beautiful than when he had married her, and she was beautiful then. "You're a neat-lookin' woman, you know that?"

"Yeah—better believe I know it." And she laughed and leaned her head toward him, their foreheads touching first, then his lips touching her skin "You get back from this Russian thing quick—it's cold in bed without you."

"Great—I'm reduced to a walking hot-water bottle."

"Hot-water bottle, back scratcher—you're very versatile."

James Hope put his arms around his wife, holding her tightly. "I'm sorry," he whispered.

"For what?"

"Well, hell—I mean—"

"For this? Why? You're doing something you believe in. Doing something I believe in. You got me pregnant, and that was fun. And you promised me after Jennifer was born and then—after Stephen—you promised me you'd do all the diaper-changing on the next one and I'm gonna hold you to it."

"Got a deal—when I'm here."

"Just because you're fighting for truth, justice, and the American way isn't an excuse, Jim."

"I'll go put a big letter 'S' on my chest."

"Yeah—and I'll be the only woman in camp who knows what it really stands for."

He kissed her lips. They had always tasted good to him, better than anything.

He tied his last boot, sticking the loops and ends of the bow knot into the tops of the boot, then stood up. "So—you sleep as late as you want."

"It's because of me, right? And Martin's wife? And the other women who are pregnant? And the little kids?"

"What's because of you?" he said, finding his gunbelt on the chair alongside his side of the bed. The gunbelt was slung from the back, the two Detonics Scoremasters on the seat of the chair. He strapped on the belt.

"The reason you aren't moving the camp, the reason you're going out to brace these Russian whatever-they-are—"

"The name means Special Forces—like we used to call our guys."

"They're tough, aren't they?"

'Well, hell, I sure hope so. Don't want the world press saying I'm taking advantage of the bastards when I kill 'em."

He could hear her laugh. "Uh-huh. We could go to England—you could run it from there. They already offered."

"That was a very private offer. They're just as afraid of the Russians as everybody else. Anyway, I can't do that."

"I know you can't. I just thought I'd mention it," she added with a sigh.

He would check the pistols later, in the light. He holstered them for now, closing the flaps over them, the weight familiar to him. Arnold Borden had publicly demanded them. He had laughed at Borden on national television and told Borden, "I don't give away things with my name engraved on them—it's tacky." "Hope"—it was engraved on the right-slide flat of each pistol.

He walked back to the bed, sitting on the edge of it. "Gimme a kiss, kid," he told his wife.

"Okay," she told him.

*   *   *

She never trusted to loaded chamber indicators—so she worked the Beretta's magazine-release button and let the fifteen-round magazine bounce off the cot once and then come to rest in a fold of blanket. She worked the slide back, popping the sixteenth 9mm already chambered. She held the pistol toward the lamp so she could inspect the bore for any obstructions; there were none. She replaced the chambered round, letting the slide run forward, replaced the magazine, then put the gun into the holster and picked up the belt.

Jean-Pierre Petrovitch asked her, "Is that a phallic symbol?"

"No—you are. And you'd better get up if you and your buddy, Marc Lumierre, are coming with us."

"Ah—the campaign against the Russians. It is all coming back to me."

She laughed as she buckled her pistol belt, walking across the tent holding the lamp, setting the lamp on the upended fruit crate she used as a nightstand. A two-year-old copy of *Vogue*, a book on the British Special Air Service commandos, a crocheting needle and a ball of dazzle yarn hijacked from a truck, and the first two rows of a shawl she was trying to make. Her mother was teaching her. She set the lantern down on *Vogue* rather than the SAS. In the lantern's light she could see Jean-Pierre. She thought he was good-looking. "Well?"

"You are into critiquing?"

"No. I mean—hell was I?"

"Yes—very."

"I think I'm in love with you, Jean-Pierre. So just think of me as stupid."

"I don't think you are stupid. I will not call you stupid. Because you could call me stupid." She leaned her head against his bare chest, felt his hands push up her clean camouflage T-shirt and find her breasts. She moaned. "You should stay here—at the camp."

"Daddy needs me—and you'll need me to keep you alive. You're great between the sheets. . . ." That wasn't true. He was great, she thought, but she hadn't slept between sheets in more than a year—they were too good as bandages. "But you aren't exactly G.I. Joe."

"Who is he?"

"He was a doll for little boys. Instead of dresses, he wore fatigues. Then they made a cartoon show about him."

"I remind you of him?"

"Not a bit," she said, hugging her arms around his neck. "Except I wouldn't mind dressing you."

He held her—so tightly she could barely breathe, but she didn't say anything because it felt good.

She heard movement outside the tent; it would be Martin. Regardless of who left on what operation, he was always there to see them off, and there to welcome them back. Unless he was leading the operation himself.

The hard-to-breathe part finally got too tough and she said with a gasp, "I'm gonna faint on you, and I'm not the fainting type. But I need to breathe."

He let go of her.

"Not that much."

He took her in his arms again and she cocked her head back so he would kiss her, and he did.

He had never been a rifleman. He had qualified as an expert with the M-16 but never liked long-distance shooting at all. So as he always did, he took up his riot shotgun and left the M-16 behind. He had kissed her many times. All he said was, "I'll be back, kid."

"Better be," he heard her whisper.

He snatched up the shell bandolier and went through the tent flap—the landscape was already gray except for where the deep shadows still hung, places blocked from the low-hanging sun by the higher rocks that etched the skyline about the valley. The air was cool, and he liked that. Field operations in hot weather always were twice as difficult and three times as tiring. He left his coat open despite the cold. It was good for his image. He laughed at that—but not outwardly. The only persons he was honest with were his wife and his daughter, and sometimes he wasn't sure if his daughter saw it that way at all. "Honest" was the wrong word, as he considered it—"relaxed" probably was a better word. Outside the tent, he was the heroic commander simply because the Resistance needed a heroic commander, whether he felt heroic that day or not.

And James Hope wasn't quite sure how he felt today. He knew one thing: He felt every day of the fifty-four years he carried. It wasn't stiffness, nothing physical. It was something else.

He hailed Martin Deacon, but not too loudly—no sense awakening the entire camp. "Marty!"

"Right, James." Deacon ran to him. Hope waited, working the Remington 870 pump's slide just slightly back, not far enough to catch a shell and raise it and chamber it, just enough to verify the empty chamber.

"So—what the hell are you up for?"

Deacon laughed. "I'm always up, James." He had told the man to call him "Jim" for almost two years. It had taken six months to get past "Senator Hope" and another three months for Martin Deacon to use any name at all. Marty finally had settled on "James." "From the gear, you plannin' ten days?"

"I'm planning on five," Hope told his friend.

"I know what you're planning. Let 'em know it's you—because it's you they want, then lead 'em away from the camp and into an ambush."

Hope laughed. "Now, how the hell would I let 'em know it was me?"

"You get close enough to let their scouts see you, then knock off all but one of 'em. So they know it's you, and even if their orders say get the camp and not get you, they'll be pissed enough to come after you."

"Hold my shotgun for a sec."

Martin Deacon was a shrewd man, James Hope reflected. Too shrewd for comfort sometimes, but the ablest man he had.

James Hope began to check the condition of readiness of each of the two .45s in turn, walking slowly toward the far side of the camp as he did it, talking with Deacon. "When I die—and this isn't some kind of premonition thing, Marty— well, if Stephen were one of the good guys—well. Anyway. Melissa feels like she's gonna have a boy. I guess she should know, since she's already had one of each."

"Makes sense," Deacon agreed.

"Well, give these to him, huh?"

"What makes you think I'll outlive you?"

"I'm almost thirty years older than you are. You sure as hell better, Marty. Promise me?"

"Yeah, sure. But don't talk like that. You're gonna be around a long time."

"I know that. Like I say, this isn't any of that premonition crap. Just a simple favor any man might ask his best friend—"

Deacon stopped walking.

"Well, I know you mean it if you say it, but—ahh—"

Hope looked Deacon in the eye. "Suddenly you've discovered politicians aren't all bad, I know."

"You mean, I'm your best friend?"

"Yeah."

"I mean, I always felt you were my best friend and like that—but I'm your best friend?"

"No shit," Hope agreed.

"Okay—you got a deal, James."

"Thank you."

"Thank you," Deacon said solemnly. "Very much."

Hope nodded, holstering the last of the two pistols, closing the protective flap. He could see his daughter coming out of her tent and see the French reporter Petrovitch with her.

"That bother you, James? I mean, I can..."

"No. Does it bother you?"

"What the hell do you mean by that?"

"I mean, you think the guy's okay—on the level?"

"Yeah, I guess—for a foreigner. Yeah."

"Yeah," Hope nodded. "So do I." And he waved to his daughter. "Hey, glad you could make it, Jennifer."

The smile on her face told him what he had suspected: Anatomy always stated the obvious. James Hope shrugged it off. She was twenty-four years old, and that meant she was a grown woman—more or less. He'd talk with her about it, Hope promised himself.

He didn't know how many miles they had covered, the rain starting only an hour after leaving the base camp. Lumierre shot some videotape of the march only after James Hope had given permission. The ferocity of the rains had increased, and they had been forced to retreat to the cover of a rocky overhang overlooking one of the most beautiful vistas Petrovitch had ever seen. A niche—wide and only partially obscured by trees—was cut in the valley wall, the valley spreading before them for miles, farmhouses dotting the far edge, checkerboarded fields nearer, virgin wilderness at the near edge of the panorama of a thousand subtle shades of green. In the distance, at the far edge of the valley, it was not raining; bands of sunshine and intermittent bands of localized rain were visible, haze rising like smoke from the far rim. He wondered if their elevation was a mile high, because it seemed as if it was. The rain clouds that blanketed the summits and the near portion of the valley seemed so close from the trail they had walked that although he knew it were impossible, he had almost felt as though he could in fact reach up and touch the clouds.

Rain cascaded through rocky rills in the rock overhang, at first flowing like tiny streams as they had gone beneath the overhang, but the tiny streams were swollen now, he thought—they had become small waterfalls. It was dry in the cave, although the dampness was chilling as the wind heightened from the intermittent breeze of yesterday and the early morning of today.

The hardwood of the small fire—he warmed his hands toward it—smelled like something delicious cooking, but in fact nothing cooked at all. It was only the scent of the wood.

Petrovitch had changed batteries and put a fresh audiotape in his cassette recorder. Jennifer squatted down beside him, her right hand brushing at his left thigh. From the far side of the fire, his face appearing phoenixlike over the licking flames, James Hope began to speak.

"So anyway, the Peace Party had its candidates for a significant number of the off-year Senate and House seats. The President—and I think the political motivation wasn't as great as the Peace Party people made it sound—announced that within two months, which would put it almost on the eve of the general election, the *Northstar* would be activated. *Northstar* had been a focal issue to the Peace Party people, in large part responsible for the coalition among the peace splinter groups forming in the first place. At least we thought that at the time." He stopped speaking for a moment, taking out his little knife and whittling the filter from a cigarette. "Are you sure you want all this background, Mr. Petrovitch?"

"Please—your perspective on the events is what I seek." Petrovitch could hear Lumierre running the video camera.

Hope fired his cigarette from a glowing log. "The Peace Party people were doing miserably in the polls, just as everyone had anticipated. NASA gave the word that all was in readiness. I was on the committee that dealt with NASA, and it was a foregone conclusion that even if the slightest glitch seemed possible, activating *Northstar* would be put off. We weren't about to play games with people's lives. But NASA said everything was go for the event. The Space Shuttle was launched carrying the nuclear core. The Peace Party people were demonstrating in the streets—it was almost like the sixties—but you're probably too young to remember much of that—you and Jennifer both, and Mr. Lumierre. Some of the demonstrations turned into riots. It was the perfect issue for them, really. The *Northstar* itself had been controversial: Why build a space station when there were people starving? The dopes never wanted to believe that the information the space station would allow us to gather would be the first step toward accurate long-range weather predictions and would do more to alleviate world hunger than billions of dollars spent elsewhere could ever do. And then the nuclear engine for the *Terra*. 'Nuclear weapons in space!' they cried. Bullshit. It wasn't a weapon, it was a nuclear engine that would allow sufficient fuel supplies for the practical exploration of the solar system." His face suddenly looked old as he said it. "And then, of course, on the night before the election, the test-firing of the *Terra*'s engine—ah, God help us."

"How many were killed? I have seen conflicting reports," Petrovitch interrupted.

"The *Terra*'s crew, of course; they were all on board for the systems checks. The NASA team that had been working on the installation of the engine. The Space Shuttle crew. The space station work crew. Everybody aboard the *Northstar*. The *Northstar* itself was vaporized. The Space Shuttle. The *Terra*. Everything. Two hundred and seventy-nine people were killed. There was no way in a free system to suppress news of such magnitude. The Peace Party people got equal time with the government from some of the networks. The election was all of a sudden up for grabs. The Russians were shouting that we had tested a nuclear weapon in space and that the *Northstar* was to be a weapons platform. If they were trying to help the Peace Party—and they may have been—

they couldn't have done a better job of it. When the votes were counted, seventeen House seats and three Senate seats were held by the Peace Party."

"What has always amazed me," Petrovitch said, unconsciously finding himself stirring the fire now, "is that in two years' time they were able to take control of the White House."

"Well, you have to remember something: Who's going to say they are against world peace, huh? A lot of the senators and members of the House were scared—I mean really scared. The ones who were up for election two years later were petrified. The Soviets were building up, we were building up. To the general public at least, it looked like World War Three was in the offing. And then Lester Saile went to Moscow just before the campaign for the presidency got under way. He was already the Peace Party candidate for the presidency. The networks covered their convention the same as those of the two major parties. They were doing moderately well in the polls—especially among eighteen- to twenty-five-year-olds. Both major parties conceded they were going to lose some seats."

The rain was getting heavier, if that were possible, huge drops of it pelting against the floor of the overhang, ricocheting into the fire occasionally, the fire hissing in commentary to Hope's words, it seemed. "Lester Saile went to Moscow when the United States had been holding at DefCon Two for two weeks, the longest we had ever held at that condition of response. All that was needed was one wrong radar blip and it would be DefCon One—we'd send our planes in, open the silos, be ready for launch. And Lester Saile stood in Kremlin Square with the leader of the Soviet Communist Party and they made a joint announcement: The Soviet Union was stepping down from Alert status, they would trust to the good intentions of men like Lester Saile, work with those Americans who hated war to achieve a lasting peace. Sort of a 'peace in our time' speech. The election followed, and Lester Saile was the new President of the United States. And all of this began."

The cigarette with the excised filter had burned out in James Hope's right hand. He seemed to study it for a moment, then threw it into the hissing and crackling logs of the fire.

Chapter Five

Spetznas.

He inhaled the fresh mountain air, feeling it fill his lungs, swell his chest. There was rain in the distance and he could smell it now, faintly. It was good to be free of the simperingly stupid National Police—almost free. There was a certain almost admirable ruthlessness in Arnold Borden, their director. He had respected Borden's decision to turn prisoner interrogation over to Spetznas personnel—and the Intelligence data had begun to flow.

He exhaled the air, feeling a freshness that was undeniably good.

His right combat-booted foot was perched on a flat, angular rock, and he shifted his weight to his left foot. A caterpillar—yellow and furry—crawled across the surface of the rock. He studied it for a moment. Blotsky had the outdoorsman's distaste for things that crawled into sleeping bags, and he realized full well he lacked the classic out-doorsman's respect for harmless life forms. He raised his right foot—

"Comrade Colonel!"

He turned around. "Here, Martinevitch!"

He gestured toward the man, then looked back to the rock. The caterpillar was gone. Blotsky shrugged his shoulders and continued instead to stare down into the valley, toward where it rained.

"All is in readiness, comrade Colonel!"

"Good," he answered dismissively. "They are there—in the rain. I can feel it. If I were James Hope, I would know about our search by now. My scouts would have told me, or perhaps my Intelligence network. And I would realize that to move an entire encampment was an exercise in futility. I would take a substantial but easily maneuverable force and tantalize our force away from the camp. It is the only logical choice. But he will not suspect I appreciate his guile."

"Comrade Colonel?"

"Lieutenant, this is most elemental. Hope has no formal military training, yet he served as the American Secret Police terrorist hostage rescue commander. He is familiar with small-unit tactics only. So he thinks like a field commander rather than a general. It is why the United States Defense Force and the National Police have never been able to engage him. He will not engage. He hits; he runs. That is the way of it. Whether James Hope is brilliant or not is academic. He is skillful in utilizing what he knows. Unfortunately for Hope, I am more skillful. Brilliance is for pedagogues and theoreticians and scientists. It is not always practical."

He turned away from the valley. "You will take thirty of the men, as we have discussed. Hope will know the composition of our force. Sergeant Voss will wear my rank, and you will bend every effort that Sergeant Voss be thought, to the observer, to be me. He is my height and coloring and approximate size—it will be good enough. You will continue toward the coordinates of Hope's encampment. You will be open, but not obviously so. The six men and myself will be there."

He watched Martinevitch's face.

"Move out, Lieutenant—and the best of luck." Blotsky didn't offer his hand. He merely turned away, to stare back toward the side of the valley where it rained. In a few moments, his six men would be waiting for the word to move out. He rested his right hand on the flap of his belt holster. In a few moments, he would begin to close the trap.

Arnold Borden studied the photograph from his wallet, then raised his eyes to study the face that looked at him from across the olive-drab camp table. "You look like your dad, Stephen."

Stephen Hope said nothing, his eyes showing no emotion.

Borden reconsidered his remark. He had no idea what James Hope had looked like at Stephen's age, just twenty-one. He tried to think back. James would have been twenty-nine or so when they had met. He was the one who had been twenty-one. Hope's case record in the Federal Bureau of Investigation was already being talked about then—and he, Borden, was just a rookie cop on a small-town Maryland force. But together, they had broken up one of the most publicized kidnapings since the Lindbergh case. And they had been friends ever since, the notoriety pushing James Hope's career in federal service, getting Borden pushed along the ladder toward detective, now with the Baltimore Police Department. At age twenty-eight, Borden had entered the FBI Academy at the insistence of James Hope. Upon graduation, Hope had pulled the right strings to make them partners. There had been the Matuszak case—civilian employees at an Army computer installation using their equipment to raid the Defense Department computers for access to classified information, then selling it to the Russians. Borden and James Hope had netted the entire spy ring, including two KGB officers.

Arnold Borden found himself smiling. He had lunched with one of those KGB men less than a week ago. The KGB man was no longer a case officer but one of the ever-growing number of consultants and advisers and planning aides supplied by the Soviet Union since the Peace Resolution and the Civilian Disarmament Act had taken effect.

He looked at Stephen Hope again. "What's 'a matter—don't you think you look like your dad? Even my wife thinks you look like him."

"Yeah—I guess I look like him. But the important thing is I don't think like him."

Arnold Borden shrugged. He could hear the choppers warming up outside. "There's nothin' wrong with thinkin' like your dad—he's an honorable man. Always has been."

"He's a fascist, a warmonger, a killer—"

"Bullshit. Look, boy, I'm goin' after your dad because it's my job. I love the man like a brother, but I'm gonna kill him. He knows that. I know that. Either I kill him or he'll kill me."

He was tired of talking to Stephen Hope. He replaced the picture in his wallet—it was a black-and-white glossy taken right after the Matuszak case, and the photographer had told them to shake hands, sort of like "this case is closed" or something. They had shaken hands. Many times before that, many times after that. But they never would again.

Arnold Borden stood up. He slipped into his shoulder holster, which had been on the back of the camp chair. He pulled the Colt from the leather and looked at it a moment. "You actually like those things," Stephen Hope said suddenly.

Borden held the Gold Cup in both hands. "Yeah—and so does your father. You ever see him use those two Detonics Scoremasters of his with his name engraved on the sides? Huh? Maybe the best .45's ever made—before we closed all the arms factories here. On the Matuszak case, right—"

"To hell with the Matuszak case."

"Just your old man and me against fifteen Americans and three Russians, and we didn't know how many of them were armed. Your dad had those Scoremasters and I had this Gold Cup and the H-K MP5 SD A3 sub gun we had in the trunk. Trouble was, one of the KGB guys had the same brand of sub gun, and he wanted to use it real bad. That's where I got this." Borden held up his left hand. Stephen Hope had seen the spot where the little finger had been before, and he didn't look at it now. "That KGB guy opened up and a 9mm slug tore my finger right off. He was dodgin' to his right, and I was dodgin' to mine. I one-handed the H-K as I went down, but I missed the guy who shot me. Your dad didn't miss. Both those Scoremasters opened up—boom-boom, boom-boom—double taps from each hand. Blew the son-of-a-bitch away. The second KGB guy was scared shitless and dropped his pistol. Everybody else raised their hands. Your dad had Mrs. Matuszak bandage my hand, and I was back on my feet by the time our backup and the news guys got there."

"What the hell does that prove—except my father is a killer?"

Arnold Borden looked at Stephen Hope. "I'm gonna kill your dad—but I wouldn't say anything bad about him. And you ever do it again, I just might kill you." He holstered the .45, found his coat and started for the tent flap, went through and into the daylight. It was overcast, misting. He glanced skyward and judged they were on the boundary line between rain and light. . . .

The rain was not slackening, and Jean-Pierre Petrovitch turned his cassette machine on again, with a fresh tape inserted, pressing the play and record buttons simultaneously. Jennifer was stoking the fire, which had burned down considerably.

"How did the Peace Resolution get started?"

Jennifer Hope sat down beside him, saying, "It was just a logical outgrowth of Lester Saile's election and the Kremlin Declaration, wasn't it, Daddy?"

"I don't know if 'logical' is the correct word for it, sweetheart, but it was an outgrowth, all right. Saile was swept into office on the basis of what he had achieved in Moscow: peace. At least that's what the majority of the electorate thought. And on his coattails he gave the Peace Party a substantial number of House and Senate seats. And now the majority of the Senate and House members who were Rupublicans or Democrats realized the handwriting was on the wall. A large number of them stuck to their convictions and were promptly voted out of office in the next off-year campaign. Some managed to stay in office by voting with the Peace Party. There were only a few of us whose constituents were loyal enough—and my last race was a squeaker. But I kept saying what I thought rather than what was popular. And don't mistake me, here: I'm not trying to paint myself as an outspoken hero. I just had some things that I believed in and considered inviolate. There were a lot of men and women like myself, and there still are. A lot of them are in federal prisons, and some of them—God bless them—some of them are in the so-called mental institutions. Another innovation we can thank the Soviets for, I'm afraid. Obviously, someone who disagrees with the government can't be right in the head. Therefore he belongs in a mental institution. It makes sense to them, or at least to their leaders.

"But I'm not answering your question," Hope said. "The Peace Resolution wasn't that big a thing, and I don't think everyone who voted for it realized what they were

voting for. It authorized and encouraged the president to
work with the Soviet Union to bring about a lasting peace and
nuclear disarmament and a reduction of forces. It was supposed to be bilateral. I didn't vote for it. A lot of my
colleagues didn't vote for it, but enough of them joined the
Peace Party, and it passed both houses. So we had it. Saile
invited the Soviet Communist Party chairman to Washington.
A few months later, Saile went to Moscow again. A few
months after that—and there was a lot of enthusiasm for it,
momentum for it—there were talks in Geneva. All of a
sudden Saile had an arms agreement. He signed it, but it
needed congressional approval to have the force of law. I was
one of the senators Saile called into his office. He told me
that if I voted for it, supported it, the Peace Party wouldn't
put a candidate against me when I ran for reelection. I told
him the treaty had no safeguards, no way of checking on
Soviet compliance. I told him, very respectfully, of course"
—Hope smiled—"to go to hell. I left his office. The treaty
was ratified by the Senate. Not much happened, really. The
Soviets supposedly made the grand gesture and began cutting
back on arms production—but as it turned out, they didn't.
We did. Then Lester Saile began the 'Peace Is in the Heart'
campaign. We were sharing medical and scientific technology
with the Russians, there were massive exchanges of students,
all that. And Lester Saile's number two in the Peace Party
was assassinated—"

"You were quoted," Petrovitch began. "I am sorry to
interrupt, but at the time you were quoted as saying that you
doubted the validity of the investigation into Harlan Cox's
assassination."

Hope nodded. "Cox was jockeying for power. He was the
actual founder of the Peace Party coalition, and Saile stole all
his thunder. He wanted the presidency after Saile ran for and
served out his second term. That was common knowledge
around Washington. And it was also common knowledge that
Saile wanted Wilmer Bogen, his vice president, to run next,
because Bogen never had an original thought in his head and
Saile could still run the White House even if Bogen were
living there. I always felt that there were too many unanswered
questions about the Cox assassination. For one thing, the
assassin was carrying an NRA membership card, yet friends

of mine at the NRA had no record of the assassin ever even applying for membership. The gun used to shoot Cox was stolen from a private collection, and the owner claimed that the gun was registered, had registration documents to prove it, but the official records of the registration were missing. And the man who had originally owned the gun was an outspoken proponent of the Second Amendment. All of a sudden it looked like a conspiracy was hatched by the progun people to knock off Cox because Saile had just appointed Cox to head a study group aimed at achieving the prohibition of the private ownership of handguns. A setup."

Hope raised both palms upward, then closed his hands into fists. "When the gun registration turned up missing, when the NRA claimed there were no records of the assassin's membership, the truth was turned against the NRA and everyone else involved. Because they told the truth, it was obviously a lie and a cover-up, more proof of a conspiracy against Cox. There were always a few antigun members, of course, in both houses, and they jumped on the bandwagon with the Peace Party. And the media got on the bandwagon with 'Peace Is in the Heart.' You saw the damn slogan everywhere. I mean, fine—peace is any rational man's goal, but not peace at any price.

The Civilian Disarmament Act got rolling. Some of my colleagues came to me—because of my former career in the FBI, I suppose. I started an investigation. We came up with positive evidence that Cox's assassin had not spent the past two years in West Germany, as his records indicated, but that he had spent three months in East Germany. There was no record at all of the other twenty-one months. None. There was no evidence to link the Russians to Cox's death, but there was enough evidence to prove conclusively that it was a frame-up concerning the NRA and enough evidence to warrant an inquiry into what if any involvement there was on the part of the Soviets. And, of course, the assassin, Phillip Chester Nicholson, was killed during the attempt. So he wasn't around to ask. Nicholson's wife insisted that her husband had been paid to do something—she didn't know what—by some mysterious group. And she'd overheard part of a conversation once where one of these men who had hired him called Cox 'an antigun pussywhip.' Well, he was antigun—

but a lot of people were until they realized what a gunless society would be like. And he was a pussywhip. But neither one of those reasons is sufficient for killing a man. And there was evidence that supported the theory that Mrs. Nicholson was paid off—not by some progun group, but by the Peace Party to help build the case that Nicholson was a progun fanatic and not a KGB-trained assassin. Nicholson had been in and out of lunatic asylums. And nothing in his background suggested he had ever owned or used a gun. But when he shot Cox, he did it in a very professional manner, right where Cox's bulletproof vest wouldn't protect him. I watched the videotape of the assassination over and over." Hope laughed bitterly. "In those days I still trusted Arnold Borden. Arnold said it before I did: 'That guy had professional training—he's an assassin. Being a whacko is secondary.' And Arnold was right.

"The Civilian Disarmament Act went forward. Handgun ownership was banned. The National Police Force was formed to go after handgun owners. When handguns weren't turned in. When the law wasn't complied with. Hell—I didn't comply with it myself. And then they amended the Civilian Disarmament Act to full measure: All private ownership of firearms was abolished. And every law-abiding gun owner was automatically a criminal unless he turned in all his weapons and opened his home to a police search. I wouldn't have done it. A lot of Americans felt the same way. The next election came. Saile was sent back to the White House, but it was one of the smallest voter turnouts ever, because so many people were either convicted in the C.D. courts and couldn't vote, or ran off to evade the law and couldn't vote. By now, Saile had a Peace Party majority in both houses of Congress. That's when he pushed the Subversion Acts, since there was massive civil disobedience to the Civilian Disarmament Act, and the Russians were claiming that this was hindering the disarmament procedure. What right-thinking Americans had once called a nation of armed citizens the Russians and the Peace Party called a nation of armed warmongers. Neighbors were turning in hardworking, otherwise law-abiding people for the gun bounties. And the gun bounties were so high, people were being turned in who never even owned a gun. And unless you could somehow prove you hadn't owned a gun, well—you were up the creek. After more than two centuries of a system where innocence was presumed until guilt was proven, the situation had reversed. How could someone who had never owned a gun prove they had never owned a gun? By informing on everybody else they could think of. And that didn't always get them off the hook. In a period of eight years, the entire fabric of the nation had changed."

Hope lit a cigarette—he merely broke the filter off first, not bothering to cut it. "And Saile found himself more powerful than he had ever imagined. And he had his Peace Party majorities abolish the Twenty-second Amendment, which limited the number of presidential terms. Saile made himself dictator—and he was voted back into office. And now he has the power of the KGB and the Soviet Army to back him up."

"And Daddy tried to stop him," Jennifer Hope added.

"Daddy didn't succeed," James Hope stated—perhaps with a note of bitterness, Petrovitch thought. "But Daddy still is trying."

"After your reelection," Petrovitch began, changing tapes and checking his battery levels, "what transpired that brought you here?"

Hope laughed again—a genuine laugh this time, no bitterness in it at all. "That's sort of asking me to explain Einstein's Theory of Relativity in twenty-five words or less, young man. But I'll give you the fast version." The rain was beginning to slack. "After my reelection, I got together a few senators who weren't Peace Party and who had the guts to buck Saile. We began hearings on the constitutionality of the Civilian Disarmament Act and the Subversion Acts. The Civilian Disarmament Act was in the courts already and we were certain that if the Supreme Court reviewed it, it would be declared unconstitutional. The Subversion Acts were the things to hit. So we did. The Civilian Disarmament Act was ruled unconstitutional. But Saile refused to accept that, and he instructed the National Police to continue enforcement while the government appealed the Supreme Court decision. Donald Smithwicke was the director of the National Police. Smithwicke was an old FBI man like myself. A bastard, but a bastard who could be pushed only so far. He refused to

enforce the Civilian Disarmament Act further until Supreme
Court clarification. Saile removed him from office and appointed
Arnold Borden. I never thought Arnold would take the job.
But he did. Maybe Arnold saw himself getting older—I don't
know, really. We never talked after that—except that last day.
But Arnold took over. He brought new vigor to enforcement
of the Civilian Disarmament Act and the Subversion Acts. I
started calling for Saile's impeachment. I knew it wouldn't
come off—he controlled both houses. But it was worth a try.
That's when Saile ordered Arnold to arrest me for holding
firearms in contravention of the Civilian Disarmament Act
and for direct violation of the Subversion Acts."

James Hope cleared his throat. "Arnold brought three
men to my house in Virginia. My wife, my son, my daughter—
we were all there. Arnold placed me under arrest. I agreed to
go—a trial would be a public forum, and I could afford the
best lawyers. After I had turned over my guns—these"—and
he patted the holsters on his hips—"I told Arnold where to
find the rest of them. Hell, Arnold knew already. He practically lived at our house on weekends, with his wife, Margaret.
They took me outside, cuffed, and I noticed one of the
National Policemen—a uniformed guy—laughing. I asked
him why he was laughing. Arnold answered for him. He told
me he was sorry, but I would never get to trial. It had to be
that way. And I realized Arnold was going to kill me. In a
situation like that, you can't hope for things to get better, and
anyway, Arnold's guys were kicking the crap out of me. And
one of 'em put a gun to my head. That next second I heard an
assault rifle go off. I'd hidden a stainless Mini-14 and some
loaded magazines in a place where the National Police would
never find them, so Melissa and Jennifer and Stephen would
have some means to defend themselves against prowlers—
crime against individuals was at an all-time high, and home
invasions were so common the papers didn't even report most
of them. Any home that was still occupied by its owners and
known to be gunless was easy pickings. Jennifer had grabbed
the gun. Stephen tried to stop her; Melissa grabbed it.
Melissa killed two of Arnold's National Police. I killed the
third one with the chain from the handcuffs. Jennifer took up
my two pistols—Arnold dropped them onto the grass when I
kicked him in the crotch and started the fight. Stephen ran

into the house. I ran after him. Stephen was trying to use the phone to call the National Police. I didn't let him. I used my old handcuff key and took the cuffs off, and we took what we could from the house and fled. We stopped near Mount Vernon—I wanted one last look at it . . . ." Hope closed his eyes, lowered his head.

"That's when Stephen took our grandfather's Congressional Medal of Honor and threw it into the Potomac. That's when Daddy—"

"I hit him," Hope said, raising his head, opening his eyes wide. "I haven't seen Stephen since then. He works with Arnold Borden now. And I understand he's helping Arnold to track us down."

Jean-Pierre Petrovitch drew in his breath, glancing down automatically to see how much remained of his tape. It would likely be a short answer, anyway. "Why did you not kill Arnold Borden? He had announced his plans to kill you."

"How do you murder your best friend, Mr. Petrovitch? You answer me."

Petrovitch could not answer; he shut off the machine. The rain had stopped.

Chapter Six

It had started him thinking about Stephen—and thinking about Stephen had always deadened him. He had, if anything, treated his son preferentially over his daughter, because Stephen was a son. And a son was something special. He had stopped along the river near Mount Vernon to take a few moments to plan their flight, to compose his thoughts. They would expect him to go to Virginia, not to the state from which he had been elected. It was too far. And getting to Tennessee was just what he had planned. He had gone walking with Stephen along the river, telling the boy his feelings. "I know you were confused back there, son. You thought Arnold was somehow acting independently of the National Police—but he wanted to kill me, son."

"What the hell is wrong with peace? Not enough profits in it?"

"There's nothing wrong with peace. Here, I brought this to give you. In case something should happen to me." The sun had been very bright. He had taken the velvet box from his hip pocket and opened it, the left-profiled face inside the five-sided star surrounded in a green circle shining in the light. "Your grandfather fought for liberty against tyranny; he fought for peace. Like I said, in case something should happen to me, I want you to have this." He gave the box to Stephen.

They had stopped walking. Stephen took the medal from the box. "He got this for killing people. You oughta give it to my mother for killing those two National Policemen. Or give it to yourself for killing the third one. My God, what kind of animals kill each other? You can take your fucked-over medal—" And he threw it into the water, so far out that there would be no hope of finding it in the sediment. He turned around and stared into James Hope's eyes. And James Hope punched his son in the face and hammered the boy to the ground, picked up the empty box, dropped to his knees, and wept.

Stephen didn't return to the overloaded station wagon. Stephen didn't ever come back, and after a time he realized Stephen would be calling the police from the nearest telephone. So Hope had packed his weeping wife and his stunned daughter into the front seat of the station wagon and they had driven the Ford along every back road possible to avoid the major arteries where the National Police would be searching for them. They had ditched the car and all the belongings they couldn't carry. Then they had hitched rides and walked, on their long, never-ending trek to freedom.

They had reached the Ocoee River area, and Hope had found himself once again stunned by its beauty. Few people these days utilized the river beneath the dam for whitewater rafting and kayaking, but of necessity the water still was released periodically. When they had first taken sight of the river, the release had been at full surge, the rapids stunningly beautiful. He had run them in a kayak several times, and again he had thought of Stephen—they had run the rapids together. James Hope had wondered then as he wondered now, walking once again toward the Ocoee River, where he had failed Stephen as a father.

He signaled a halt. The trees still were dripping water, though the rain had long since moved toward the far side of the valley beyond.

The report of his scouts Habersham and McDowell had only confirmed additional Intelligence data—not only that the Spetznas force was coming, searching for him, but also their approximate route.

"We'll rest here before going down to the river and crossing over," he announced, moving ahead along the trail, not looking back to see if Jennifer was coming, or anyone else. He pushed away a low-hanging branch, and the rainwater that had been cupped in its bright green leaves drenched the shoulders of his coat.

But he was at the lip of rock that overlooked the river—and the river was low, the dam still holding back the water. He could make the crossing farther up then, not having to move along the river for several miles to a shallower ford. It was all still now, and except for sunlit puddles in the gaps between the smaller of the yellow and gray rocks strewn along the riverbed, it was dry.

He found a flat rock and perched against it, the Remington 870 pump shotgun across his lap. He looked at the twelve-gauge, then back to the rocky bed of the river. The Spetznas.

They were as well trained as their American Special Forces counterparts had been, warriors in heart and mind like the Navy SEAL teams, the Delta Force personnel. But they were trained in other ways as well. The specialized use of torture in interrogation was one of the ways. James Hope had appreciated the inevitability of the encounter in which he was about to engage when he had first learned through his Intelligence network that Arnold Borden had turned over prisoner interrogation functions of the National Police to his Soviet advisers—the Spetznas.

Their weapons were state-of-the-art. The Spetznas and subsequently the most elite units of Soviet paratroops were issued the minor-caliber AKS-74 assault rifle, a new, light, maneuverable weapon. Although the Spetznas in advisory capacities with the National Police carried handguns rarely, they all would have the AKS-74. Also, the Spetznas habitually carried the excellent Czechoslovakian-made CZ-75 9mm X19, or Parabellum, rather than the standard Soviet military handgun, which was not noted for high capacity or ease of ammunition resupply in the field.

Some units were allowed individual weapons: a favored fighting knife, a secondary or backup handgun. Some elements of the typical Spetznas unit would be carrying the Soviet PPSh submachine guns, these converted to the more standard 9mm Parabellum, the same caliber as their pistols. Some would be equipped with the Samozaridnyia Vintovka Dragunova (SVD) sniping weapon, with its special PSO-1 telescope with a range-finder scale, battery-powered element to illuminate the reticle, and ability to detect infrared nightvision devices. Some would be equipped with more exotic weapons—the spring-powered knives that could be fired from a yarawa-stick-type device and were lethal to distances of fifteen feet or beyond. These were used primarily for assassination, occasionally for defense or for sentry removal.

Their training enforced physical perfection in them—running everywhere, body-building with logs, rappelling, free-rope climbing, each man an expert marksman with shoulder-fired and hand weapons, each trained in a special blending of the martial arts that formed their basic hand-to-hand combat techniques, each skilled in knife fighting.

They were not supermen he was about to brace, but they were very close: expert trackers, mountaineers, climbers, hunters of men.

He considered his own force. He had left the base camp outnumbered approximately two to one. His force—men and women—were trained in grocery clerking, gasoline pumping, accounting, kindergarten teaching, farming, house painting, chiropractic medicine, plumbing, heating and air conditioning, and the like. Some had advanced training—running coon dogs, deer hunting, trout fishing, and skeet shooting. One had been a police officer, but the female kindergarten teacher handled a gun better.

James Hope reviewed his plan—to cross the river, intercept the Spetznas and let himself be seen from the far side of the river, then lead them into a killing ground he had already chosen. Where he planned to intercept them was where the water still would be deep and they would either have to waste time with inflatable rafts or waste time going upriver to where it would be dry enough to ford without them.

He had left Martin Deacon in charge at the base camp. Should this operation fail, Martin would have no choice but to evacuate, leading the women who were noncombatants, the children, the elderly, and the infirm higher into the mountains, leaving behind the best of his fighters—men and women—to fight holding actions against the Spetznas until another trap could be set. But each of the Soviet Special Forces personnel killed was one less to worry about.

James Hope consoled himself with that.

He looked back from his perch overlooking the dry and rock-strewn Ocoee's bed and saw Jennifer. His exquisitely beautiful daughter was now more of a son to him than Stephen had ever been. And he wondered at the child his wife, Melissa, carried in her womb. Boy or girl? He smiled; that hardly mattered anymore. He had learned—albeit the hard way—that the person counted and not the shell of body the person wore.

James Hope stood. He saw that Jennifer and the others were looking at him. He said nothing, but instead raised the shotgun high in the air over his head in his right hand. And he signaled his force—heroes, all of them—forward.

Feyodor Mikhail Blotsky signaled a halt, his six warriors still exuding the energy that the clean mountain air imparted to him as well. It was a place of true beauty—a strategic blessing for an adversary, and a tactical nightmare for him. If his operation were to fail, he would personally oversee the use of napalm in these mountains, turning the millions of trees here into an inferno in which nothing could live— not even James Hope. The National Police units served only to supply Hope with weapons—they penetrated this wilderness in search of him and never returned. In the small village of Ducktown, he had personally overseen the interrogation of a man found with an AKS-74 taken from one of his own Spetznas. The Spetznas personnel who had died would never have died had it not been for the incompetency of the

National Police, whom they served as advisers. After the
interrogation, he had shot the man possessing the AKS-
74—in the head, once, but not in such a manner as to achieve
instantaneous death, but rather excruciating pain. And he
had staked the dying man in the village main street, to let
him die where all could watch and hear. It had taken over
three hours. The man had been very strong physically.

"Check your weapons," he announced as he leaned
against a bare-trunked white pine. Silently his men began the
methodical procedures he had rehearsed with them so often,
then had practiced so often before the moments of combat
that brought them glory. The thirty-six enlisted men and the
lieutenant—Martinevitch—were the cream of his country's
Special Forces. Their selection and his own had made him
realize fully the dire necessity for the death of James Hope.
And it should best be provable death—revolutionary figures
tended to live on so long in memory they sometimes tended
to live on as ghosts—yes, James Hope made that raid; James
Hope attacked that National Police armory. He would like to
present Hope's head to the American puppet administrator,
Lester Saile. But someone who advocated peace might well
be put off being given a human head on a platter. Bad for the
public image that seemed so important in the West, a cult in
which his own leaders were beginning to indulge—charisma.

He had been checking the AKS-74. Satisfied, he set it
against the tree trunk. He dumped the magazine from his
CZ-75 pistol, inspecting the chamber—empty as he carried it
except during battle. From a pouch at his belt, he extracted a
solitary 9mm X19 round, dropping it into the barrel chamber,
then depressing the slide stop to let the slide run forward.
He reinserted the magazine and holstered the pistol, closing
the flap securely over it. He glanced to his six men—their
assault rifles were checked, their pistols checked. The three
who carried them inspected their PPSh submachine guns.
The other three set to inspecting their special-purpose weapons: the SVD, the RPG-7V antitank rocket launcher, the
7.62mm RPD light machine gun.

Sheathed on his right leg was the spear-pointed killing
knife. Sheathed at his left hip was the sawtooth-edged Bowie-
bladed survival knife. The other weapons secreted about his

body he did not check. They would be there if he needed them; they always were.

Blotsky turned to address his six men. They were a silent lot, and he preferred that.

"We are approaching the Ocoee River. So are the men under the command of Martinevitch. If they have been observed, they will have been observed to be the full complement of Spetznas, which we have so painstakingly established to be present here over the past four days. They will parallel the route of the Ocoee River along the highway, leaving themselves readily observed but exercising all due caution less the mere fact of their being observed should alert the Resistance fighters that something is wrong. I have estimated that James Hope will bait our main force from the opposite side of the river along which our comrades travel. On that assumption, we are on that opposite side. Nevitsky— you will break off from the main body."

"Yes, comrade Colonel," the shaven-headed corporal responded, all six and one half feet of him springing to full attention.

"You will make contact with the dam workers. When I fire the red-star flare, you will order the floodgates opened. Brasnevitch..." The shorter man, stocky, brought his Dragunov to his right thigh and snapped to. "You will accompany Nevitsky, finding a suitable position for yourself near the dam site and overlooking the dry riverbed with full fields of fire."

"Yes, comrade Colonel."

"The red-star flare will be fired when I see Hope and his force crossing the river—as they will do near the dam site. But there will be no action. Nevitsky, Brasnevitch..."

"Yes, comrade Colonel," both men answered as one.

"No action until the red-star flare is fired. This will also serve as a signal to Lieutenant Martinevitch, who with his men will close up against Hope's rear. I and the remaining members of this team will move down into the dry riverbed area and engage Hope and his fighters. But we shall not enter the riverbed. As the floodgates are opened, Hope and his force will be made to flee for their lives, and their only avenue of escape will be along the riverbed itself. When Lieutenant Martinevitch sees the red-star flare, he will break radio silence, alerting Director Borden of the National Police that the helicopter gunship unit should proceed along the course of the river from downstream. Theoretically, our fire, the force of the water itself, and panic should eliminate our quarry before the National Police gunships need fire a shot. There are questions?"

There were none. He was always clear in his instructions to his men, each man knowing his assigned task. It was one of the reasons he was always successful.

Blotsky closed with, "Good luck, comrades," and turned back to the tree trunk and snatched up his rifle. Silently he gave the order to move out.

She didn't need his offered hand—she could navigate the rocks and escarpments and defiles better than he could. Women generally had a better sense of balance, anyway. She wondered if it were inborn or inbred, from wearing high-heeled shoes and taking shorter steps and carrying coffee cups and soup bowls without spilling their contents. They spoke in English. She said, "Thanks—it's nice to be in the company of a gentleman again."

"And for me—to be in the company of a lady, of course," he smiled.

There was an actual trail here, the riverbed clearly in sight, stretching its rocky course from the dam farther than she could see. "It is beautiful here, I think," Petrovitch told her. "And sinful that men and women, too, should come here to fight and die."

"Maybe it's because the land is so beautiful—maybe that's part of it," she whispered.

"Perhaps that is so," he answered. But she wondered where his thoughts really were. In the next moment he told her, "I am in love with you, darling. That is so crazy to say, I know. We have only just met."

"Yes, it is crazy."

"Insanely stupid. Soon I must leave these mountains. If we can somehow reach New Orleans, there is a contact there who helped us to enter the country. She can help Marc and I—help us to leave. But I have to leave you."

"What is she like—your contact, I mean?"

"This woman is very resourceful."

"Is she very pretty, too?"

She watched his eyes, and his eyes—they were a pretty shade of brown—laughed. "Oh, yes—she is pretty. Marc could tell you better. They slept together for two nights."

"Can we sleep together tonight?"

"I wish that we could sleep together always, Jennifer."

She liked the very soft sound that his speech imparted to her name. "I love you, too. Even if it is crazy, I really don't give a damn."

He stopped walking. She was afraid some of the others of the Resistance would bump into them, but they were strung out over a considerable distance to reduce the losses if there were an ambush. He took her in his arms—she had to push the submachine gun out of the way of his body and hers. He bent his face over hers and she didn't wait for him to kiss her, her arms encircling his neck, her lips finding his.

She kept her eyes open—and she could see as Jess Bloch the kindergarten teacher and Elwood Jensen the chiropractor passed them by into battle. . . .

James Hope raised his right hand, signaling a halt. He turned, waiting for his people to bunch up, seeing Jennifer and the French reporter at the rear of the column now. Lumierre was filming again, and Hope heard the whirring of the camera. "All right, listen up. Jennifer, you and Elwood fan out. You go upstream, sweetheart, and Elwood—"

"I know," the gray-haired, bespectacled man said with a laugh, "downstream."

Hope let himself smile, then nodded.

"The two of you will be our security in case something goes wrong crossing the river. Once you see the last of us to the other side, wait three minutes or so, then come on quickly. Watch those rocks out there." Jennifer had broken an ankle playing tennis once, and he always considered that with her. "We'll be in position then to cover you." And he let himself smile again. "Mr. Petrovitch, I hate to separate you and Jennifer," he said, ignoring the stifled laughter from the men and women of his company, "but you and Mr. Lumierre should stay with the main body of the force."

Lumierre volunteered, "I would film better from here, Senator Hope."

Hope shrugged. "Fine—then you stay with Jennifer and

keep down and do exactly what she tells you. When she gives the signal to move, don't waste time filming it, just move."

"But, yes—of course."

"Jennifer, Elwood—we'll give you a couple of minutes to find good positions."

"And just remember—if anybody does pull any muscles or anything, develop any inflammations of neck or sciatic nerves crossing the river, my services are available," Elwood Jensen said with a grin.

"We'll remember," Hope agreed. He had never tried Jensen's brand of medicine, never needed it, but Jensen was one of the bravest and most dependable men he had. Jensen held his deer rifle at high port and took off along the side of the road on the far side from the riverbed and near the high rocks.

Hope watched his daughter—and Jean-Pierre Petrovitch. They were holding hands. Petrovitch kissed her cheek, and she kissed him full on the mouth and smiled—first at Petrovitch and then at her father. Hope watched her, her submachine gun in her left hand, her hair loose of the God-awful-looking camouflage bandanna she usually wore. It bounced, almost danced as she ran. It reminded him of his wife, who was eight years his junior and as beautiful as the day he had married her twenty-five years before. "Be careful!" he shouted after her. It would have been just as good to shout after her, "Be reckless!" because she always seemed to combine both qualities skillfully. For a son like Jennifer, he thought.

She disappeared around a curving section of road where there were high trees. Lumierre the cameraman followed after her.

Hope looked at the rest of his people. "All right, we'll spread ourselves out upstream and down. Have your weapons ready. If the Spetznas have a trap set for us, this is the place to spring it. But we have no choice: If we engage them on this side of the river, they'll be too close to our camp. Let's move out."

He clutched the 870 pump in his left fist, his right fist closed on the pistol grip. James Hope started down, toward the dry, rocky riverbed. It had been a good decision to leave Jennifer behind—she was smart enough to make her own decisions. Elwood was a dead-eye marksman when he had a rest for the old Winchester bolt action; he could trim pine cones from a tree at a hundred yards with the well-worn .30-06, given time to settle in for each shot. So Hope was not worried about those two.

Hope looked to the dam house on the far side; nothing seemed odd or strange about it. He glanced across the river; there were no signs of anyone waiting in hiding, no subtle glint of steel in the fading sunlight.

His clothes still felt damp from the rainstorm that had delayed them throughout the morning and the early afternoon. He made a mental note to treat his leather gear this night; the gear had taken a soaking. He reached the cement of the kayak and raft ramp, glancing again across the river, again to the dam house, this time scanning the narrow suspension bridge that ran over the spillway itself. Nothing. The spillway was a mossy green and brown, seeming to exude a smell even though no smell would have been noticeable at the distance.

He descended the boat ramp. To his left near the guardrail, which ran upward to the level of the spillway, there were permanent dark stains from the water, which overflowed in billows of spray when the waters flowed. But the dark spots seemed dry now. It had not rained here, he surmised.

He did something he never did: He tromboned the pump of the shotgun, chambering a round. He always waited until the round was needed before working the action—a safety precaution ever since his earliest days in FBI, something taught him by his shotgun instructor, something proven valid to him a hundred times in the field. But he walked now among the rocks with the chamber loaded.

Jennifer loosed the sling of the Uzi to keep it comfortably ready for use. Marc Lumierre, beside her, whispered, "It is not my business, of course, but Jean-Pierre loves you, I think."

"Uh-huh. I think he does, too."

"He is a fine fellow."

"I know."

She could hear his camera going now—filming as she watched—her father's force crossing the dry riverbed, scrambling over the rocks.

"You must hate that camera equipment after a while," she told Lumierre, making idle conversation.

"Because this is heavy?"

"Yes."

"It is my job to carry it, to use it—as it is with you and the Uzi, I think."

"You know guns?" she asked.

"Yes—my father was a policeman. He taught me to shoot his gun. Sometimes he would take me along when he and his fellows would use some of the other weapons stored at their police station. I served in the Army. For a time I was a regular soldier, and then they taught me how to use this camera. I made training films of weapons being used, of men jumping from airplanes. I think it is why I am good with my camera—it is like shooting. You pick a target, do not lay down a barrage. You understand?"

"Yes." Her eyes scanned the dam house on the far side of the riverbed. There was nothing to see.

Her father and the others, fanned out upstream and down, were at what she eyeballed to be the midpoint of the riverbed, equidistant from either bank.

She heard something—the sound of a skeet load or something like it—and she swung the Uzi up to the level of the rock behind which she crouched, her eyes scanning for some puff of smoke, some sign. Then she saw it. A red starburst flare.

It was useless at the range, but she fired the Uzi across the riverbed, toward the origin of the flare. She stood to her full height, hearing the whizzing sound of Marc Lumierre's camera. "Daddy! Daddy!"

The rockface in front of her exploded and she fell back, Lumierre on his knees beside her. "A sniper! He uses a silencer, I think."

She was on her feet, Lumierre trying to hold her back. "Daddy!" She started to run, then dropped to her knees, swinging the Uzi toward the suspension catwalk over the spillway. She sprayed the Uzi toward it, hosing the bridge, the Uzi bucking in her hands.

Another shot—a tree branch crashing down on her. She pushed herself to her feet, the Uzi empty now, running. The sniper was on the bridge—and Elwood would have seen him.

Gunfire came from the riverbed, toward the sniper, and more gunfire erupted from the far side of the river.

The boom of her father's shotgun—he would be near enough to the opposite bank to risk it.

She looked to her right. There was Elwood standing perfectly erect, his deer rifle to his shoulder. She looked to the bridge—an impression only of the silhouette of a man. She looked behind her. Lumierre was running, his camera to his shoulder, filming.

Elwood's rifle—she heard the ripping sound of it on the air.

She looked to the bridge—the silhouette had become a man, falling back, catching his balance, extending an ungainly-looking rifle from his right shoulder, his left arm limp at his side. The weapon seemed to rock—a faint puff of gray-white smoke? She wasn't sure. The Soviet sniper's body fell backward over the bridge railing. She glanced toward Elwood. His body swayed like an axed tree, his bolt-action rifle discharging into the rocks near his feet, rock chips spraying upward. He fell, vanishing from sight through the trees—to the rocks below.

Tears flooded her eyes, and she wiped at them. Then she heard a roar—not the roar of a rocket, or of any sort of explosion. But a duller, pulsing roar.

Ramming a fresh thirty-two-round magazine up the well of the Uzi, the empty magazine already stuffed into her belt against her abdomen, her eyes scanned the river again.

The spillway was opening, the green of the water above giving way to roaring white water, the water in a massive, tongue-shaped wave, crashing down the narrows at the base of the spillway, surging at full power over the guardrail, rolling across the concrete ramp, powering into the main course of the riverbed.

She screamed, "Daddy! Run!"

She started to run, Lumierre beside her now, shouting in French, "My God!"

They had opened the spillway—it had to be the Russians. The water would inundate her father, her friends—people who would risk their lives for her, for her mother, for her father. And these Soviet Spetznas had opened the spillway to use the killing force of tons of white water to dash her father

and her friends against the rocks. There was mortar fire now
from the near side of the riverbank. The Spetznas would have
split into two groups for their trap. Machine-gun fire. She
looked to the dam house—a machine gun had opened up
there.

She saw her father. The riot shotgun he carried was
inverted in his hands, and he was using it to club one of the
Spetznas near the opposite riverbank, the wall of white water
closing inexorably toward them. She screamed again, "Daddy!" And she stopped her headlong lunge, Lumierre crashing
against her.

"You get to some cover—fast. You aren't even armed,"
she said. "And if I get myself killed—tell Jean-Pierre—" She
broke into a run, but at a right angle to her course toward the
river, toward the suspension bridge that spanned the river
just above the spillway—to get the machine gunner, to turn
his machine gun against his own people. If her father or any
of the others survived to come out of the water, they would
be shot, helpless to defend themselves.

She glanced back once. Lumierre was rushing downstream. If he took her advice and took cover, he might live.
But she knew he wouldn't take her advice—because the
camera still was mounted to his shoulder as he ran.

James Hope swung the Remington 870 hard, the pistol
grip catching the Spetznas at the temple, the man's face
already battered, bloodied. The Spetznas went down, Hope
wheeling, two more Spetznas advancing from the trees that
came along to the edge of the riverbank. The 870 was empty,
and he hurled it toward the two Soviet soldiers to get their
attention—they were opening fire into the rocks in the
riverbed now.

One of the soldiers turned. Hope had both .45s in his
fists now, the hammers jacked back to full stand. He fired
both pistols simultaneously from the hip. The Soviet soldier
went down.

Hope looked behind him—the wall of water was closer
to him now. It would be only seconds until it hammered the
Resistance fighters to death against the rocks.

Mortar fire from the opposite bank rained down on the
rocks at the center of the riverbed, rock chips spraying in fine

clouds of khaki-colored dust, white puffs of smoke as the mortar rounds impacted, balls of red and orange flame. Machine-gun fire came from the catwalk suspension bridge, chewing into the rocks near him. He broke into a run—back toward the middle of the riverbed, toward his people pinned there, awaiting death. The Detonics Scoremasters in his fists spit fire as he ran. Automatic-weapons fire was coming from the trees, then a whooshing sound and a loud, angry hiss.

"Rocket!" he shouted, throwing himself down into the rocks. The impact made his body shudder, a hail of rock chips and dust pelting him as he pushed himself up to his knees— the water. "Jesus," he said with a hiss.

Hope leaped to his feet, thrusting his pistols into their holsters, closing the flaps. "To the far bank—hurry!"

He heard a scream over the roar of the rushing wall of white water. It was Jess, her assault rifle in her right fist, the butt of it wedged in the rocks. "I'm coming!" Hope shouted. Her right ankle was wedged in the rocks, and she was trying to pry herself free with the butt of the M-16.

The others were running for the far bank where the gunfire had begun, where the red flare had originated.

He ran for the center of the riverbed and the crackshot kindergarten teacher who was about to be crushed to death under the tons of water hammering toward them. He wouldn't leave her to die alone.

James Hope jumped a high boulder, skirting another, clambering over a third, skidding downward. He wouldn't reach her in time. "Jess—get your M-16—pull the bolt. Use the barrel like a snorkel and stay down behind the rocks. Do it—Jess!"

The woman only stared at him for an instant—he was in motion toward her. Then she started to move, the magazine flying from her hands, the M-16 breaking open, the bolt flying skyward. Hope glanced hard right—the water was almost on him. He scanned the rocks around him, finding the largest one. He threw himself behind it, both hands gouging into it for a purchase he already knew was futile. The chances of Jess surviving the rush of water were less than futile where she was—but a chance was better than meeting death and surrendering to it.

Hope looked back to Jess. She was a smart girl. The

muzzle end of the rifle barrel was to her mouth, the boltless chamber end wedged above her, the buttstock of the rifle flopping against a niche of sand-colored rock.

He sucked in his breath as the water came.

It slammed against him, pummeling his body, trying to crush the breath inside him. The water itself was like a living enemy. His body slammed back, his hands clawing outward again, the pressure of the water too great for him to open his eyes against it. His left hand found a purchase, holding to it, his right hand now, his left boot wedging against a rock, the water tearing at him, beating his head, his chest, his back, his neck, then tearing at his flesh.

The air inside his lungs was starting to go bad. Hope forced his head upward, his left hand slipping, losing its purchase. His body dashed back, his arms splaying outward, his body spread-eagled against the unyielding surface of a rock. The water crushed him against it now, the pressure against his chest tightening. The water beat at his face, his eyes squinted tight against it, his ears feeling the pressure. He wanted to open his mouth and shout the pain away.

Hope arched his back, his head breaking the surface, his mouth gaping open, his lungs seeking air. Water filled his mouth. He spit it out, turning his head away from the surging waters, gulping the air, his lungs aching with it, his ears ringing dully from the thunderous howl of the rapids where an instant earlier there had been only the rocks.

A high, flat, gray rock lay ten yards from him, perhaps only eight.

Hope launched himself outward, reaching for it, the current sweeping him downstream. As his left hand slid over the slick granite surface, his right hand locked onto a sharp edge, the rock gouging into his flesh. But he held on.

He looked toward where he thought Jess had been. There was no sign of the rifle, no sign of the woman at all.

Hope thrust himself against the gray rock, sagging his weight across it, arms and legs wide for friction against the slick surface. He raised his head again, scanning the foaming surface of the river for the woman.

He gasped for breath again, a wave crashing over the rock, over him, his head pushing up.

Some of his Resistance people had reached the far side of

the river; others he could see foundering downstream among the rocks. As his people exited the water, they were being cut down. The Spetznas closing toward the riverbank were murdering the unarmed men and women as they dragged themselves from the waters. Hope raised his voice, shouting over the roar around him, "Mother-fuckers! God-damned Communist mother-fuckers!"

He looked toward the spillway. The water still was coming, even now that it had done its work.

But on the catwalk bridge James Hope saw a flash of blond hair against the red-tinged sky—his daughter. . . .

Jennifer Hope had climbed to the catwalk, the narrow, precarious expansion bridge stretching before her. Spray washed over her, a high wind rising from the riverbed now, cold and wet. The Uzi was clutched in both hands. She could see the Spetznas at the bipod for his machine gun on the far side by the dam house.

He must have killed the man who controlled the spillway; they would never have opened it for him to do this.

Her father was dead, she told herself. This man she had fallen in love with so suddenly was dead as well. *Jean-Pierre* . . . she rolled the name on her tongue. What had tasted so beautiful to her before, now tasted only of bitterness. She had told him almost when they had first met that she was not bitter—there was no time. It was that way still. If she lived to be old, she would be cold and alone and bitter then.

The thing was to charge across the suspension bridge, firing as soon as the man tried to turn toward her and kill her. He would be armed with a pistol—likely his only other firearm besides the machine gun. It was an LMG by the look of it—light enough for a quick and deadly return fire.

To her feet, running, slipping, catching herself against the mesh-covered guardrail of the suspension bridge. She ran on, the white water of the spillway roaring beneath her, the Soviet machine gunner starting to look toward her. The Uzi in her hands opened up in three-round bursts, just as her father had taught her from the first.

The planking of the suspension bridge splintered and ripped. The Soviet machine gunner was on his knees now, reaching to the flap holster at his right side.

It would be a CZ-75, she told herself. She fired, again and again and again. She remembered as a young woman seeing movies where there were commandos and their submachine guns seemed to fire endlessly. Hers didn't. She worked the bolt; the Uzi was empty.

No time to reload. As her hands dropped the Uzi to her side, her left hand moved to the holster on her right hip, her right hand to the flap. The Beretta 92-F was there, her right thumb working up the safety as she freed the weapon.

The Soviet Spetznas had his CZ-75 in his right hand, aiming it like a target shooter. A chunk of the guardrail blew away near her.

Jennifer Hope locked her left fist forward of her right, her left thumb hooking into the front of the Beretta's trigger guard. The Beretta glinted wet with spray. Her right first finger worked the trigger back. The double-action pistol bucked gently in her hands. The Spetznas slumped back, still holding his pistol. He fired again, Jennifer feeling the searing heat, then the cold near her left breast. She staggered, fired, then fired again, screaming, "Die, you Commie son-of-a-bitch!"

The machine-gunner's body fell against the guardrail and didn't move, the pistol falling from his right hand into the white water of the spillway.

She ran forward, the Beretta in both fists, dropping to her knees behind the light machine gun. She set the Beretta on the bridge floor beside her, then swung the muzzle of the machine gun away from the center of the riverbed, toward the riverbank she had just left. Soviet troops were there, potshotting into the riverbed, standing perched on the rocks, calmly shooting fish in a barrel.

Her wound burned and bled, but she ignored the pain. There was something more important to do.

She kept swinging the machine gun's muzzle—then she stopped. Her father was fighting his way from rock to rock, the current tearing at him, sweeping him downstream. He reached out, grabbing hold of another of the larger rocks. Assault rifle fire hammered into the rocks near him.

She swept the muzzle to the greatest concentration of the Soviet Spetznas, opening fire. She estimated the range at a hundred and fifty yards, holding high, firing in three-round bursts, just as she would have with her submachine gun.

Some of the Spetznas went down under her fire, some returned fire to the bridge. Jennifer Hope looked away from the sights. Her father was moving closer to the riverbank now but was well downstream of the greatest concentration of the Spetznas.

She started to open fire again when she heard the bridge rattle, felt it shudder. She looked left: A Spetznas, his clothes soaked from the spray, was clambering onto the bridge from just below the dam house.

She reached to her holster—the Beretta wasn't there. There was no time for anything else. She drew the BuckMaster from its sheath at her left side, throwing herself toward the Spetznas as he crossed the bridge railing. The knife gouged into his left shoulder, his right hand backhanding her.

She fell, spread-eagled on the bridge surface.

The Spetznas stood to his full height now, saying something in Russian she didn't understand. His left shoulder dripped blood. In his right hand he held a double-edged fighting knife, and his face was lit with an insane smile.

She struggled to her feet now—and edged slightly back, holding the massive handle of her knife in her right hand, point up, her left arm extended toward her opponent, palm outward. Martin Deacon had taught her the use of kendo in knife fighting. She had no idea who had taught the Spetznas, but something in his eyes said that he had learned well. He started toward her, holding the knife as if it were a rapier, like a swordsman would hold it.

She turned full-face toward him, raising her left hand, bringing both hands together, the left hand at the base of the knife hilt. A man's hands would have been too large to hold the BuckMaster with two hands comfortably; hers were not. She positioned the tip of the blade on a level with the Russian's throat. He was coming closer. She drew her right leg back, flexing the knee. The knife was like a short sword in her hands, completely inverted, the flat of the blade almost touching her left bicep. Without moving her left foot, she drew her right foot forward, flexing the knee again, arcing the blade in the air. The blade edge turned outward, the hilt and the right hand forming an inverted V.

The Spetznas lunged for her abdomen. She drew her right leg back, arcing the blade left and downward, with full

momentum parrying his blade. She pivoted three hundred
sixty degrees on her right foot, addressing him now with the
blade held in a guard position at the level of his bobbing
Adam's apple. Again she drew the blade back, point up, her
left palm toward him. She made herself smile. "Speak English, asshole? Well—you're a dead mother."

The Spetznas lunged again. She moved to the presenta-
tion of the knife with the blade flat against her left bicep but
didn't hold that, going immediately into another three-hundred-
sixty-degree turn but not presenting the blade for his throat,
instead hacking with it, downward, across his forearm as he
threw himself toward her. She sidestepped right. The knife
fell from his fingers. The Spetznas stumbled to his knees. Her
left palm extended toward him, the right arm arcing high
over her head, then arcing downward, cleaving the beret,
into the skull of the Spetznas, and as his body fell away, she
wheeled. With the full force of her body she hacked the knife
across his throat. The artery ruptured, blood spurting in a
fine reddish spray across her hands and clothes. The man's
head was half severed from the torso, and the lifeless Spetznas
fell to the bridge floor.

Gunfire came from the two riverbanks now, and Jennifer
Hope threw herself down, cleaning the blade of the Buck
Master against her trouser leg, then sheathing the knife. She
picked up the Beretta, working the safety to lower the
hammer, holstering the pistol. She crawled now, gunfire
ripping into the planking of the bridge floor, dragging herself
prone along its surface. She reached the Soviet light machine
gun. She set her hands to it, swinging the machine gun on
line with the near bank. She fired, spraying into the trees
where the assault rifle fire originated, then swung the muzzle
across the width of the river, firing into the massed riflemen
there. Her father would have made it by now, and if she
could keep them busy he would have a chance to escape
them. She kept firing.

Her left breast burned now from the gunshot wound; she
fought against thinking about it.

She would never see Jean-Pierre again. He could not
have made it out of the water, even if he were a good
swimmer. He was an innocent. And if he had made it out, he
would have been killed.

A gust of wind wafted a wash of cool spray from the spillway across her—and it refreshed her. The machine gun would be out soon, and she had seen no extra ammo for it.

She would never see her father again, either—no matter what he tried, he couldn't draw enemy fire from the bridge long enough for her to escape.

And there was her mother, too—and the baby she carried. James Hope would have to get to them, warn Martin Deacon that the Spetznas had trapped them. The base camp must be evacuated.

Jennifer wondered—would it be a son her mother carried? Not a son like Stephen. She could not bring herself to hate her own brother, but she hoped there would not be another son like him. She realized she was smiling. She had played with dolls, loved dresses with outlandish frills as a little girl, been the spoiled socialite—and finally been the son to her father that he had never had.

And now she would be his dead son. Already she felt a sickness in her stomach, a light feeling in her head. She glanced to the bridge surface at her left side—a growing puddle of her own blood, her left breast, her abdomen, her left leg covered with blood.

She fired the machine gun until it was empty.

She scanned the bridge right and left. If the machine gunner had carried extra ammo, it had gone with him over the spillway. She crawled now, her left arm numb, almost useless to her, toward the man she had fought with her knife. Strapped across his back had been an AKS-74. She dragged herself toward him now, rifle fire rattling from both riverbanks, chewing into the fabric of the bridge, chunks of the flooring ripping up.

She closed her eyes—only for an instant, Jennifer told herself—letting her head fall forward. . . .

James Hope edged along the tree line, trying to catch sight of his daughter on the bridge. Brutal rifle fire tore through it, and there was no return fire. From his position among the rocks above the river, he could see clearly now: Two fatigue-clad Spetznas charged the bridge from the near side of the river.

A last ray of sunlight glinted on the blade of one of the men's bayonets.

Hope broke cover, starting to run toward the bridge, the Detonics Scoremasters raised.

He stopped. He dropped to his knees. The Spetznas. His daughter. From where he knelt, he could see clearly now. Her body lay on the bridge near the dam house, and the Spetznas were bayoneting her. She wasn't moving. Hope began to cry—more than he had when he had lost Stephen. Much more.

Chapter Seven

The helicopters that had swept along the course of the river, hovered over the spillway. One of them landed in the boat ramp parking lot, another in the parking lot beyond the cement-block building that held the chemical toilet facilities the rafters and kayakers had used. The helicopters were black, with the American eagle symbol inset within a white star. The star should have been red, it was whispered in the cities and towns and everywhere free men and free women gathered in the night. And the eagle, rather than the mighty guardian of freedom, had become nothing more than a bird of prey.

He had watched the helicopters, watched as Arnold Borden had walked along the bridge, watched as Borden had removed his jacket and covered Jennifer with it. James Hope had seen Stephen. His son had walked with Borden, then simply walked away, not even looking at Jennifer's body.

James Hope could not wait any longer. If Borden and Stephen were there, and more Spetznas arriving by stabilizer-winged Hind A helicopters, there would be a full-scale assault on the base camp. Hope capped and cased his binoculars, fed an eighth-round into each of his .45's, and started to run.

There was a far less demanding trail from the spillway to

the base camp, and far more open. He had rejected its use earlier because a large number of men and women, even moving in twos or single file, were easily spotted from the air. But a man alone had a chance.

Hope ran.

As an FBI agent, he had worked to keep his body fit; as a senator he had worked harder at it because the physical demands were different on him and more potentially deleterious. Running, pumping iron, swimming—he silently thanked his Maker for the swimming and the body-building—they were all that had kept him alive in the rapids. He saw the images of death as he ran: Jean-Pierre Petrovitch cut down with multiple bursts from assault rifles as the young French journalist, visibly unarmed, had emerged from the raging waters. Jess, the crackshot kindergarten teacher—drowned, helpless to free herself, himself helpless to free her. And his daughter—who had saved his life at the cost of her own. He vowed that if he lived she would be remembered—a beautiful golden warrior, heroic beyond reason or devotion.

Hope ran on. There was no sound of helicopters now—and he knew why. Borden knew him well, and would give him just the right amount of time to reach the camp, then attack. If the attack came first and Hope were not there, then Borden would be forced to continue to search the mountains. But Borden and his Spetznas allies could now hope to end it all at once.

Hope ran on. . . .

His first martial-arts master had spoken of expanding the mind, enlarging the horizons of the mind beyond the mere five senses of ordinary men. He had never felt the strength of these words more than now. Because of this, Martin Deacon had ordered the posting of extra sentries, had all the aged and infirm and the young children and those few women who tended them, including his wife, moved to the cave a quarter mile above the camp. The cave was used for supply storage and also was held as a last-ditch redoubt.

He sat on the corner of his bunk. He checked his weapons. The full-sized Randall .45 had been customized for him by Peter Dunn, one of the country's top pistolsmiths. The stainless steel pistol was modified to function with a

Detonics Competition Recoil System and fitted with Peter's own Bridgeman feed ramp modification. Deacon found himself smiling, wondering if somewhere the tall, good-natured man were fighting for freedom, too.

Deacon hefted his principle knife high. Handmade for him by Jack Crain, it was the ultimate in survival/fighting knives, a Life Support/System I. He inspected the second, smaller knife Crain had made him and that, like the first, he had buried along with the .45, buried in a survival canister. The hollow-handle, Tanto-like Commando. He sheathed the Life Support at his left side, the Commando in the sewn-in sheath of his well-worn brown leather vest, holstering the Randall as well. He had loaded it with an eighth round and carried it cocked and locked now—ready.

It had begun to rain as the sun slid behind the western horizon, and as Martin Deacon made to exit his tent he picked up the G.I. surplus rain poncho and pulled it over his head, pushing his dark hair back from his eyes. His wife had always cut his hair for him. He told himself to remember to ask her to cut it again, the first chance available. But then he felt himself smile. She would tell him, "Marty, if you don't let me cut your hair soon, then some morning when you wake up you're going to find it all full of curls. And I'll bet that'll be the last time you let it get that long."

He loved her very much, Deacon thought.

He snapped together the sides of the poncho, then grabbed up his M-16 and the small bag in which he carried spare loaded thirty-round magazines. He shouldered the bag at his right side, letting the poncho fall over it to protect the thirties carried inside it.

He stepped off the board and through the tent flap and into the rain. "Shit," he said with a snarl. He used his right hand to haul up the poncho's hood, his left hand holding the assault rifle.

It was almost fully dark now, and if something went wrong—as he felt inside himself—then darkness could be both an enemy and an ally. He thought of the old toast— "Confusion to our enemies"—but sometimes confusion was contagious.

Almost no one moved about the encampment. Each man, each woman had a task, and there was no time for idle movement. Deacon made the rounds of the interior guard, then crossed the camp on its axis, toward the far perimeter of interior guards and toward the outer boundaries of the camp. As a boy, he had read Elliot Arnold's book *Blood Brother*. Stories of the mythic Apache war chief Cochise had intrigued him. He had read everything he could on the subject, vacationed in the Southwest, studied the tactics, the life, the spirit of the Indians. He had liked the way Cochise had structured his stronghold. This camp was such a stronghold, as well as terrain would allow. He had discussed its layout, its protection—and James Hope had placed him in charge of the security of the camp. The rain had increased to a downpour, and his combat boots squished and slipped in the mud as he moved ahead. He carried his rifle inverted, to prevent accumulation of water in the bore.

He exchanged knowing nods with the men who held the nearest post as he left the interior perimeter; then he moved ahead, but more cautiously. The rain would make people angry, jumpy, nervous. That his far-perimeter guards would be more jumpy was a mixed curse and blessing. There was a greater chance of one of them potshotting another, or firing a betraying shot that might draw the enemy near. But there also was more chance that an enemy would be detected, because it was a lousy night to fall asleep on guard duty. Few of the men had ponchos; many wore nothing over their ordinary clothes except plastic trash bags with head- and armholes.

What was needed—and Deacon told himself to talk with James Hope about this—was a raid on a National Police supply depot for ponchos, combat boots (some of the men were lining their boots with cured deerskin patches), medical supplies, and field rations. And if that raid worked, then make the long-awaited raid on one of the National Police armories.

The armory in Chattanooga was said to be brimming with M-16 A-1's, Beretta 92-F's, LAWS rockets, grenades, plastique, and ammo galore—all just waiting to be taken. If they could standardize even a single unit of men and women, then that unit could be molded into a disciplined fighting force. As it was now, the Resistance simply had to make do with what they had.

Martin Deacon walked on, nearing the closest perimeter
guard.

"Hey!"

"I read it in a book, even saw it in war movies," Deacon
said with a grin, the rain blowing in sheets now on the wind,
lashing his face at the face opening of the poncho's hood.
"You're supposed to say, 'Halt. Who goes there?' Got that,
Rodriguez?"

"Yeah, Marty. But it sounds kinda dumb, huh?"

"Fine—you go ahead and say what you wanna say."
Deacon nodded, then cut up among the rocks. He found one
to perch on that wasn't so flat that water would stand on its
surface and make him wetter than he already was. He could
just make out Rodriguez's short, stocky frame. "You hangin' in
there, Rodriguez?"

"It doesn't rain like this where I come from in Mexico."

"How does it rain—up?"

"No, man—shit—I mean it rains down, but not down
this hard. And it isn't this cold."

Deacon let himself laugh. "Tell you what: After we beat
these suckers and get the U.S.A. runnin' again, I'll go down
to Mexico with you and help in the war down there. And
after we win that one, you show me this paradise on earth
where you used to live."

"Man, you got yourself a damn deal. You better bring
your wife, man, 'cause you never gonna want to come back."

Deacon thought for a moment. The rain was hitting his
right side now, and when he turned his head slightly left, he
could see Rodriguez a little better. "Tell me somethin', huh?"

"Sure, Marty. What you wanna know?"

"You're not even a citizen, right?"

"So what the fuck does that prove?"

"No—don't mean nothin' by it. But how come, Rodriguez,
you're risking your life for the United States and you aren't
even a citizen?"

"See, it's like this, Marty—man, you're fuckin' dumb. I
wanna be a citizen. I started bein' a citizen. My brother was a
citizen. He's still in some jail 'cause they caught him with a
gun in the house. Anyway, just 'cause I ain't no citizen don't
mean I don't know right from wrong, man. The Commies and
the Natpos are bastards, man. I wouldn't wanna be no citizen

under those mother-fuckers. So I gotta get rid of 'em all so I can wanna be a citizen again. Hey—you think I gotta take the Constitution test again when this is all over?"

"When this is all over, I hope we can elect James Hope president. And if we do, I'll lay you even money he'll make you a citizen by executive decree or whatever the hell they call it."

"Ya think so?"

"Sure." Deacon nodded to the darkness. His hood guttered when he did, and a stream of the icy rain poured across his face. "I think so."

"That's all right. But we still go to Mexico—gotta put them bastards away down there, too."

Deacon agreed. "Listen: Don't shoot me with that old beat-up lever-action when I come back, okay?"

"Sure—I think about it." Rodriguez laughed.

"See you." Deacon pushed himself up off the rock, the flash hider of the M-16 scraping against the rock as he moved away.

Mexico, he thought, clambering down out of the rocks, moving farther ahead into the blackness of night and rain. When the food riots had started there and the government had started shooting rioters, the Commies had walked in as though the government of Mexico had given them a gilt-edged invitation. The Communists hadn't brought the Mexican people food—just more firepower to kill rioters with, and the KGB and the Spetznas to kill anyone who wanted a democracy.

He reached level ground and kept walking.

If James and Jennifer and the others had carried out the bait job on the Spetznas, they would be pursued now, deeper and deeper into the mountains, farther and farther from here. But something told him that wasn't it.

He kept walking, taking a deer trail he had found. He felt somehow that he should, if there were any sense at all in getting drenched (the poncho had long since lost much of its water repellency), go to the farthest-perimeter guard posts.

The deer trail dropped down into a narrow ravine. He could hear water rushing through it now; it was too dark to see. The water had never been so high that it couldn't be waded, and as he half skidded, half climbed along the mud of the ravine's embankment, he hoped this rain hadn't somehow caused the water to rise higher. As he slid the last few feet, his rifle held high in his left hand over his head, he was suddenly in water to his knees. "Shit," he said with a hiss. It rose higher.

Deacon moved cautiously now, feeling the muddy water as it sloshed about his legs, tore at him. He almost stumbled once, which wouldn't have meant disaster, just dumb bad luck. His clothes were already as wet as they could be, except for the few dry spots where the waterproofing still really worked, and his weapons would all need to be cleaned and oiled.

He started up the opposite embankment, slipping in the mud, his rifle slung across his back diagonally. It would mean the longer way, but he could accept that—the mud was just too slick. Now there was no choice.

Halfway up, he slipped, skidding, getting a faceful of the gritty-tasting mud. He spat, reaching under his poncho for the bigger of the two Crain knives. He unsheathed it, clutching the sword-sized hilt in his right fist, then hammering the knife into the mud. If it encountered a rock, there would be no real damage.

The knife held, and he pulled himself up with it, getting his left hand on a large tree root at the lip of the ravine, wrenching his knife free, hammering it down again beside the tree. Again the knife held and he pulled himself up the lip, then from his knees to his feet.

"Damn it," Deacon muttered.

He wiped the knife clean of mud on the exterior of his poncho, then tried to wipe the knife dry against the interior of the poncho. He sheathed the knife. The rain—almost impossibly, it seemed—was driven harder as the wind whipped up again.

He kept walking.

He could see where the ground broke and rose and he aimed himself toward it, calling softly, "Angela—it's me—Marty!"

"Advance and be recognized," the soft, lilting soprano came back.

"I saw the same movie," he said, laughing.

"I see you, Marty. Come on."

That was why Angela McTavish was here, on the most remote guard post, "manning" it. She had the best night vision of anyone he had ever known. There were better shots, more stealthy infiltrators, more hard-nosed killers—but no one could see better at night than Angela.

"How ya doin', kid?" he asked her.

"Better than you—you're covered with mud."

He climbed up toward her, slipping on one of the rocks, catching himself, then continuing on. As he reached the niche where she stood, he asked her, "Quiet?"

"Till you came along, Marty."

"Gee, I'm sorry. I'll leave."

"No, I can use the company. Heck of a night for guard duty."

"Yeah," he agreed. "Heck of a night to be checkin' guard posts," he added, feeling slightly defensive. He always felt on the defensive around her. She was so level-headed, so calm—it was unnerving. "Count how many rabbits are slinking around within a hundred yards of us—that'll give you somethin' to do."

"Cut the jokes. How's your wife put up with you?"

"She's nuts about me."

"Much as I like your wife—well, the nuts part I'll agree with. How's she doing?"

Deacon shrugged. "Baby's kickin', she told me—that was a couple of hours ago, though. Kid probably wore out by now. Gonna be a football player."

Angela laughed—it was a nice laugh. "How's Melissa?"

"Missin' James and Jennifer. Worried about 'em like she usually is. But she's fine. James told me the baby shouldn't be due for another week or so. Melissa seemed great. How you doin'?"

"Heck, I miss my husband. But I'd never go back to him."

It was a can of worms as Deacon saw it—and he didn't want any part of it. Her husband was on the National Police—a Natpo, as Rodriguez and some of the others called them. She had left him, joined the Resistance, and brought her two children with her.

The silence was too long, and he finally said to her, "Hey—you'll find somebody. Not all the good guys like me are scarfed up. There're a lot of nice guys out there."

"What I want's a guy like Roger—but not without guts!"

"Hey..." He felt crazy saying it. "Maybe he figured bein' on the National Police was the right thing. Then I'd say he was crazy—but not gutless."

"Look, Marty, you're sweet. A pain in the rear, but sweet. He joined the National Police because if you get asked and you don't join, they pull your Social Security number and you can't get any other kind of job. So you join the Resistance and starve in company or you don't join and you starve alone. He was a coward—wouldn't stand up for his rights, for my rights, for the country. And one of these days when the children are older, I'm gonna tell 'em. So help me God, I'm gonna."

Deacon shook his head. More water guttered down off his hood and into his face. He was past caring about being dry. "You won't tell 'em. You'll wind up lyin' to 'em and tellin' yourself it's better that way."

"No." She hissed emphatically.

"Hey—I'll catch ya in ten years or so, even twenty. You see if I wasn't right, kid."

"Go peddle your papers, huh?"

"How'd a girl from Murfreesboro wind up talkin' like you?"

"New York—I moved to Murfreesboro after I met Roger."

Deacon knew that—she had told him before. But he had wanted to change the subject, and that she hadn't called him on it meant that she had wanted to change the subject, too.

"Look—want me to send somebody out to spell ya?"

"Shh—"

He held his breath, releasing it slowly, hearing the movement as she shouldered her M-16. He could see her in profile, see where she pointed the weapon, and he unslung his own as silently as he could.

From the darkness he saw nothing but heard a voice. "Gag me with a rubber banana."

It was the code phrase—he had picked it up from one of the young girls around the camp, something like Valley Girl talk. It was a cinch the Russians or the Natpos wouldn't fall to a code phrase like that.

And the voice called out a second time now from the darkness. It was very strange hearing a man of such stature using such words. It was James Hope.

Chapter Eight

There was no time. When James Hope had returned alone, his shotgun gone, all his equipment gone except his matched pair of .45's and his binoculars, Martin Deacon had realized things had gone badly.

Between the post Angela still guarded—now doubly diligent because of the news of the Spetznas' ambush and the National Police helicopters—and the base camp, Hope had stopped Deacon as they had walked. It was a brisk, long-strided commando walk, best for covering significant distance. But Hope had stopped them, and Martin Deacon had not been able to see Hope's face, and had he been he would not have seen the tears he knew were there, because of the volume of the rain.

Hope's voice broke. "They killed Jennifer, Marty—Jesus—they killed her."

Martin Deacon had folded his arms about his friend's shoulders. Hope had let his head sag against Deacon's shoulder, and Martin Deacon had embraced him as James Hope wept.

According to the luminous face of his wristwatch, Deacon judged they had spent five minutes sitting there in the rain, talking. James Hope told him things Deacon had never known before about his friend. Hope had stood, rubbing his hands across his face, his voice still sounding strained but more under control. "If anything—hell—you would, anyway." And James Hope had started back toward the camp, Deacon walking behind his friend. He knew the words Hope had not said—take care of Hope's wife, Hope's unborn child. Martin Deacon swore silently that he would. . . .

Martin Deacon had told James Hope for the first time since they had first met, "No." But as he had known he would, he had relented. He had cleaned his personal things out of the tent he had shared with his wife, packed them in pockets and his knapsack, then quickly field-stripped his M-16, swabbed the bore, lubed the assault rifle, and reassembled it. The rain still was falling heavily, but he would feel better knowing the weapon was clean, even if only for a moment.

As he crossed the compound, his poncho dripping water inside and out, he could see James Hope. Hope had been soaked to the skin but still wore no poncho. His fists were balled and rested on the flaps of his holsters now as he stood at the head of a group of some eighteen men and women, addressing them.

Deacon slowed his pace to avoid distracting them from Hope's words. Deacon already knew them.

These eighteen, under Deacon's own leadership, would take the aged, the infirm, the children, the infants, the pregnant women—take them up into the mountains and away while Hope himself would lead their remaining forces in a divergent direction, leaving a trail an idiot could follow, drawing off the Spetznas.

Deacon drew near now, Hope still speaking. "They are most important—those children. They are our future. Now, I know I'm splitting up families. I don't want to—you know that. But we need fighters here to draw off the Spetznas and the Natpos. And we need fighters to take the noncombatants to safety. We're buying time. I'd be lying if I said I felt we had a chance of defeating a force this large after splitting our own force. This may be the end for us—but only for us." Deacon watched the faces of the men and the women as they listened. Deacon felt tears welling in his eyes. "But it won't be the end for freedom. Maybe I'm sounding too much like a politician. But I do know that there are others fighting the Russians and Lester Saile and Arnold Borden and all of them. And someday, the Civilian Disarmament Act, the Subversion Acts—all of it—will be a bad dream this country went through. It's people like you who will make that day a reality. I've never known finer Americans, finer people. God bless all of you—and your families. And God bless your unborn children—that they'll live in a free America again." Hope rubbed his balled fists against his eyes, then looked at the people individually, it seemed. "All of you have your assignments. We've got to move."

Martin Deacon started to walk toward James Hope, but one of the older children was slogging toward him through the mud, shouting, "Senator Hope—it's your wife! She's havin' her baby, sir!" The boy just stood there. James Hope turned around.

Martin Deacon muttered, "Shit!"

Chapter Nine

The contractions were irregular, sometimes as little as five minutes apart. Martin Deacon alternated looking at his wife as she attended Melissa Hope and at Melissa herself. Linda looked concerned. Her own labor was not that many weeks away, Deacon knew. Melissa was trying to look confident, to smile for her husband, who knelt there in the lamplit cave beside her. It was horribly damp—and the sound of the rain was a constant, absorbing all other noise, making the whispers of encouragement, concern, and love between James Hope and his wife embarrassingly audible.

Reverend Bleeker knelt on the opposite side of the pallet on which Melissa writhed.

He raised his eyes. He spoke to Hope, but Martin Deacon could not help but hear. "I'm no doctor— but I was a volunteer fireman in this one community where I was called. I saw EMTs deliver babies a couple of times. I was with my wife—God rest her soul—when she delivered two of our kids." His wife and children had been killed by the National Police when his house had been raided for his deer rifle. He had been away with a member of the congregation who had been recovering from surgery. The rifle was never found by the Natpos. He had returned to find his family dead, taken the rifle, and come into the mountains. He had not become a killer, as Deacon knew he himself would have. But instead he had ministered to the spiritual needs of the Resistance in the mountains, helped with their medical needs. He was a man respected by all.

"Make your point, Harry," James Hope whispered.

"All right: You move her, and you'll lose the baby, maybe lose her. Gut feeling. Take it or leave it, James."

"Listen," Melissa began, forcing her face into a smile. There was pain in her pretty eyes. "I've had two children before. I know my body. I can handle being moved. I've got to."

Deacon began to speak before realizing it. "I know what we can do."

Hope turned and stared up at him from where he knelt beside his wife. "What, Marty?"

"All right. She can't be moved. We've got a couple of others who would be better off not being moved. Fine— instead of two forces, we can have three. I can bleed off a few of the guards from the escape party. You can bleed off a few of the fighters from the diversionary group. A smaller diversionary group will have a better chance of staying out of an engagement, anyway. We can cover the entrance to the cave. You stay here with your wife and take charge of the fighters here. I'll take charge of the diversionary force. And we don't pull out until the Natpos attack. They'll be too busy following us to look for this cave. Probably leave a few Spetznas behind to search for documents and stuff. You can lead some of our people against them. It's the only way, James."

It was one of the things he admired about James Hope: the man had an open mind.

"All right—you pick your own man to take the kids and the rest of the sick and injured out. I'll stay."

"No!"

Hope looked at his wife. "Jennifer died today. I didn't want to tell you. But she's gone. I don't consider Stephen our son anymore. You're all I have. You and the baby you're carrying. I can't sentence you both to death."

"Then leave me—for them. Arnold Borden wouldn't kill me."

Deacon spoke again. "The Spetznas would torture you, torture the baby, maybe—until James came back. You stay behind for them, you're sentencing James to death."

She began to cry.

Harry Bleeker said, "I'll stay—might need me."

Martin Deacon left. To lead the sick and injured to safety

he could think of no one better than Angela, the woman with the phenomenal night vision and a cool head.

James Hope crouched beside the concealed mouth of the cave. There could be no fire for warmth—the smoke would have become unbearable. Through a niche in the brush covering, he could watch the main camp area several hundred yards below. The women of Martin's diversionary force tended cook fires. Several of the men busied themselves with cleaning weapons, sitting in small groups under improvised shelters not too near the fires. This was to create the impression of normal activity—to make it appear that Hope had never reached the camp, had not warned them.

He looked at the Rolex on his wrist. The choppers would be coming any instant, perhaps holding back to coordinate with a ground attack by the Spetznas. But each moment they delayed the attack was a moment longer for Angela McTavish to lead the children, the infirm, the pregnant women to safety.

He looked back into the cave. At its far end, he could see his wife—her body torn with agony. It would be a big child, everyone said. Probably a boy. And her age worked against her.

Hope looked away, back through the niche. He had six men, well armed. Harry Bleeker made a seventh, but the good Reverend had only his Remington bolt-action. All the arms and equipment normally stored in the cave had been removed, buried, hidden. Hope had intentionally disallowed himself the knowledge in the event of his capture.

He waited. . . .

The Plexiglas of the helicopter's main bubble opened and the Spetznas commander, Colonel Feyodor Mikhail Blotsky, forced his bulk through, tugging the door closed behind him as he sat down opposite the pilot. Blotsky was at once massive yet lean. His height was over six and a half feet, and his shoulders wider than most doors, Borden thought. "So, Comrade Director Borden—all is in readiness with you?"

"Yes, Colonel—all is in readiness."

He watched Blotsky's gray eyes as they drifted from him

to Stephen Hope, who sat behind the pilot. "And you, young comrade—are you ready for the hour of vengeance?"

"I don't give a shit about your war. I just want to get on with my life. And I can't do that while my father's killing people and pretending he's some kind of goddamned commando."

Blotsky laughed, tossing his head back, snatching his beret from his head. His hair was almost nonexistent, it was so short. But it seemed thick, healthy, though graying. "What do you believe in, young man?"

"I want world peace—and as long as the United States fought against the inevitability of you and your people, there wouldn't be peace. So now we've stopped, except for outlaws like my father. Once you kill him, you won't have to worry about him anymore and I can live in peace."

"You don't make any sense, young man. Agreed, your father must be killed. But likely your mother will die, too. You did not even weep at the death of your sister. When I offered you her knife, or her pistol—you rejected both."

"I have no interest in weapons. I have no right to own weapons. I wouldn't own them if I did. And Jennifer was a killer, just like my father. As long as people have these archaic ideas of good and evil, there's going to be fighting and killing. Good was causing evil. Once people realize that, once evil triumphs, then there will be the inevitable transition of universal evil into universal good and there will be peace."

"I am evil, young man?"

"Yes—you kill. But the Soviet Union was ready to take over the world. The United States merely wanted to perpetuate the struggle. The Soviet Union wanted to end it. That's why I'm siding with you until this war is over. Then all I want is to be left alone."

Blotsky no longer smiled. "You are right that I am probably evil. But I am better than you because I believe in something. I fight for something. You believe in nothing, fight for nothing. I kill to serve the ends of my people, not wantonly. But you have nothing in your heart, I think." And Blotsky's eyes flickered back to Arnold Borden, who felt uncomfortable under them. "This man—Comrade Director Borden—is motivated by power, I think. Before, he was just a secret-policeman. Now he is a leader. And when James Hope is dead, great rewards will await him, even if it is my Spetznas who do the killing. He has purpose." His eyes traveled back to Stephen Hope. "But you are sick. There is nothing in you. You are the animal, young man."

Borden cleared his throat. "I think it's about time to get airborne, isn't it?"

Blotsky laughed. "Yes. I will join my men and put aside this most uncomfortable conversation. And Comrade Director Borden"—Blotsky's eyes smiled, and then the face only smiled and the eyes became hard—"if you make a mistake that costs me James Hope, you will be a casualty in this battle. Because you or Hope will die tonight. I have decided that."

"What the hell do you mean, Colonel?"

"Had you not insisted to our government and your own that you alone could outthink James Hope, my men would have been called in long ago. We could have found Hope and killed him more easily. Some of my men died today. That would not have been were it not for your blind stupidity, comrade Director. And so, I swear, James Hope dies or you die." The cold eyes shifted to Stephen. "And you, young man—I feel great sorrow for your father, my enemy. To have such a son must be the ultimate shame."

Blotsky wrenched open the door of the helicopter and in a single stride was gone, into the darkness and the rain.

"Pilot, shut off the dome light," Borden said softly. He had to reach out into the rain to jerk the door closed again so they could take off, and Borden's left arm became soaked in the process. It was too cool to remove the jacket, and even had it not been, there was really no place to put it in the cramped quarters. So he rested his left arm on his left thigh and felt the dampness pervade his trousers. "Stephen, when this is over, I never want to see you again. Do you understand?"

He looked at Stephen Hope. His father's height, but nothing near his father's build. And the eyes, neither those of his father nor his mother. There was a deadness in those eyes. "Is it that you believe in peace so much, or just that you're afraid of the alternative if you stood up for something?"

Stephen Hope only stared ahead.

Borden heard himself sigh. Then, "Take her up, huh?" And he felt the vibration increase as the rotor speed overhead increased. Tonight he would see James Hope dead. The best friend he had ever had. He felt a tightness in his throat and a heaviness in his chest and he knew the feelings would never go away.

Feyodor Mikhail Blotsky charged the chamber of his CZ-75 in his usual manner—with a loose round from his belt—then holstered the pistol.

He glanced to right and left. Blotsky could no longer see his men without great difficulty, which meant they were in position. He had kept the key survivors of his original force under his personal command, reinforced his unit with additional Spetznas brought from Chattanooga and placed at his disposal. He had kept the National Police units back, held airborne five miles from the battle area. But he would use them this time—to spring his trap.

With great difficulty, he had infiltrated to within seventy-five yards of the camp, observing movement and activity there for some time. The numbers seemed smaller than he had anticipated. But only fools would have stayed behind if Hope had reached the camp and warned them. Men who fought against vastly superior forces for something as intangible as "liberty" were fools.

He considered Stephen Hope an idiot, not even an idealistic one. Just mindless. If there were more like Stephen, it would be a depressing world, but a world easier to conquer. He raised his radio receiver-transmitter to his lips. "This is Blotsky—now!"

The helicopters would move. He rolled onto his back, staring up into the rain, letting it wash his face. Satellite reconnaissance of the base-camp area showed a large cave several hundred yards above the main encampment. He would lead his force through the center of the encampment like a wedge driven into a log that was to be split, then up into the rocks toward the cave. He had already matched the high-altitude photos and the infrared image of the cave with night-vision instant photos taken during his infiltration. He had matched these two duplicate sets of coordinates to the physical terrain—slightly to the north of the camp, at approximately a forty-five-degree angle to the central campfire.

Bushes and hedges showed there through his starlight

glasses; the entrance to the cave being camouflaged meant that it either held important supplies, perhaps a communications center, or even the elusive James Hope. That, by attacking, he was playing into the hands of the Resistance had not escaped him.

He checked his wristwatch—it was a Rolex that he had purchased in Switzerland. No Soviet watch was truly satisfactory for the rigors of the field. In two minutes, he should hear the rotors of the National Police helicopters, and so would the Resistance. They would move; he would move. Battle would be joined.

His watch showed him that helicopters should be within earshot.

He got into a crouch, the AKS-74 clutched in his right fist, the flare pistol in his left, his ears straining over the falling of the rain.

Blotsky heard them, triggered the H-K flare pistol in his left hand, the yellow skyrocket streaming upward on a tail of almost pure white, then bursting into uncountable numbers of stars, hissing, dying almost instantly in the rain.

He was to his feet, running forward, the assault rifle in both fists now, gunfire already coming from his men, directed at the camp, gunfire from the camp, gunfire from the rocks surrounding the camp. It had been a trap but he smiled. Hope was here.

Blotsky fired his assault rifle, a three-round burst into the nearest of the enemy, a shotgun discharging, something tearing at his left cheek as he wheeled left, sidestepped, and fired.

He knew the faces of the Resistance leaders. At the far end of the camp, lit orange and red by firelight a tall, dark-haired young man. Martin Deacon was marshaling his forces about him.

Blotsky turned toward Deacon, shouting to his Spetznas, "I want that man—alive!"

A woman in a rain jacket leaped from beyond one of the fires, an M-16 in her hands, firing. Blotsky threw himself to the mud, rolled, firing his own assault rifle. The woman staggered, then fell backward, her skirt catching fire, a scream issuing from her lips. Blotsky fired again, blowing her face away and putting her out of her misery.

To his feet.

A flamethrower. A tall black man held the device. It was
Soviet. Beside him was a white woman in camouflage clothing, some sort of riot shotgun in her hands, the shotgun
firing. The flamethrower opened up; two of his men were
down. Blotsky fired toward the black man, one of his two
men hit by the flamethrower charging forward like a living
torch, the second rolling on the ground screaming. Blotsky
fired his AKS into the man on the ground, dropping the
weapon on its sling.

The Spetznas who was a living torch now grappled with
the woman who held the shotgun, her clothes afire.

The black swung the flamethrower. Blotsky threw himself into the mud, grasping for the 9mm pistol in his holster.
He had it.

Rifle fire chewed into the mud beside him, plowing
furrows in it. To his left Blotsky fired crossbody, killing a
short, reddish-haired man. The flamethrower licked into the
mud inches from Blotsky's face.

He rolled, his beret gone somewhere, water streaming
into his eyes. He squinted against it, leveling the CZ-75,
firing once, then again and again, aiming for the head of the
black man.

The flamethrower suddenly went wild, the gasoline rolling in waves about the man who held it, consuming the
woman who grappled still with the Spetznas who refused to
die despite the flames engulfing both their bodies.

He was up, firing the pistol as he closed the gap toward
the black man, whose body was now aflame. The black man
ran into the bonfire that hissed and crackled at the center of
the encampment.

The body fell. Blotsky threw himself away from the
bonfire as the jellied gasoline exploded. His eyes burned,
etched for an instant with the light of the orange-and-black
fireball.

He looked to the far side of the camp: Martin Deacon
was gone, trailing behind him some two dozen of the camp
defenders.

Blotsky knew now; it had to be.

"Spetznas! Spetznas! Lieutenant. You! And you four. And
you two! With me—hurry!"

He rammed the pistol into his belt, not bothering with the holster, dumping the spent magazine for his assault rifle, running into the rocks at a forty-five-degree angle from the bonfire at the center of the camp.

He could hear the helicopters' guns firing now, toward the escaping camp defenders.

Blotsky didn't look back; his men would be with him. The National Police could pursue Martin Deacon. And without James Hope, Deacon and his kind would be worthless killers, annoyances sniping at convoys and attacking small patrols. But dead soon enough.

He reached the rocks now, letting his rifle fall away on its sling, starting to climb.

"James!"

It was a loud, hissed, stage whisper. The battle in the camp was over. Marty Deacon had gotten away, and it seemed that the bulk of the attacking force had followed him.

"James!"

He pushed himself up from the niche in the shrubbery and ran back along the central passage of the cave.

Harry Bleeker and one of the women defenders flanked Melissa. Her knees were up, her body half-tented.

James Hope dropped to his knees. "Your baby—it's coming—it's crowning," Bleeker said, panting.

Hope reached out to his wife. She grabbed both of his hands, her nails biting into the flesh of his fingers. "Jim—oh, sweet Jesus—Jim!"

"It's all right—Marty got away. I think the battle's over," he said.

His eyes and Bleekers's met. The minister only smiled, but the eyes told him that Bleeker knew.

"Hold on, sweetheart," Hope whispered. "It's gonna be a beautiful kid—just like you."

"Jim—Jim!"

"Hold on. . . ."

The woman was starting to manipulate the baby's skull as it broke through, the flesh ripping a little, Melissa screaming.

He started to put a hand over her mouth, but he heard a shout from the main entrance. "James! They're coming this way!"

"Hold her legs down," Bleeker ordered.

Hope loosed his wife's hands, holding her pelvis. The baby's face was mottled and blood-stained. A little bluish; but he told himself that was normal.

Blood mingled with soap from around her crotch—a yellow-and-red mass that nauseated him. But he saw the face clearly now: It was at once his face and his wife's face.

Bleeker's voice: "For the child's eyes—and for them."

Hope looked up. Bleeker held a bottle in one hand—Hope couldn't read the lettering. Bleeker had a rifle in the other hand.

One shoulder came, Melissa panting loudly, hissing, saying his name. "Jim—alive?"

"Beautiful—like you."

The second shoulder and suddenly the baby was in Bleeker's hands. Bleeker raised the child by its ankles—and the child urinated across Melissa Hope's abdomen and Bleeker's hands.

The baby screamed.

"A boy—it's a boy!"

Melissa laughed hysterically.

Gunfire—the smell of burning brush.

"Spetznas!"

It was not one of his men who shouted the word. Hope wheeled, drawing his pistols.

Bleeker said to the woman who had delivered the child, "Stay here—use that solution on the eyes like I told you!" Bleeker ran past Hope, the deer rifle at high port.

Submachine gun fire. An assault rifle. The roar of a shotgun fired again and again

The baby screamed.

Melissa cried, "I want to hold my baby!"

Hope heard the other woman. "He's beautiful. Like some kind of angel. Here—hold him."

Hope was to his feet, edging back, blocking his wife from the entrance of the cave. His wife and his son.

Smoke—they were using a flamethrower.

Bleeker's rifle discharged. It was the heaviest-caliber rifle in the cave and unmistakable in its report.

Hope dropped to his knees, cradling his wife's head in his lap.

He had never seen her more beautiful.

"I love you—always," he told her. He looked at his son.

"Take him—get out," Melissa pleaded.

"No," he told her. There was nowhere to go, anyway. He would not leave her.

He set down the pistol in his right hand, reached out to his child. He held his son's face, the body still smeared with blood. The child cried out.

Melissa hugged the child to her breast. The baby groped for the nipple.

Assault-rifle fire—a woman's scream.

"Spetznas!" A Russian voice.

Another voice, this one familiar. "He's mine, Colonel!" It was Arnold Borden.

They came. Hope gripped both pistols, his wife and son wedged against him.

"You bastards—leave us alone!" Melissa said, sobbing.

Hope said nothing.

"Holy shit," Arnold Borden whispered. "Jim—I didn't know."

The Spetznas colonel beside him held a pistol in his right hand. Hope also saw the pistol in Arnold Borden's hand.

Borden smiled. "Same one, Jim—the one I used when we nailed—"

"I remember," Hope whispered. "Take her out of here. Melissa and the boy. Please, Arnie."

"Jim—Jesus—I—"

"Please!"

Stephen entered, an assault rifle in his hands. "Go to hell!" The rifle fired.

Melissa screamed. Hope felt the heat of it in his chest, both pistols in his hands. But he pulled them back. He couldn't kill Stephen.

James Hope slumped forward, his fists locked on his pistols, Melissa's face tight against his abdomen, the baby screaming.

He stared into her eyes. The eyes stared back only death.

James Hope reached to his wife's breast, the pistol gone from his left hand, clutching his baby son to his chest. The child was covered with blood now—Melissa's blood.

He had the second pistol, edging back on his knees. He braced the Scoremaster in his left hand against his son's left shoulder, the child strangely quiet now.

The Russian colonel and Arnold Borden turned to Stephen Hope.

"I shot the fucker for you!" Stephen threw down the assault rifle.

The colonel and Borden fired their pistols simultaneously into Stephen's body as Hope was trying to raise the Scoremaster in his right fist. His vision was blurring.

Hope aimed the pistol at Arnie Borden. "Arnie! Christ—why?"

James Hope started to squeeze the trigger as the wave of coldness swept over him. He had only enough left in him to roll his body left to cushion his infant son in his arms as he fell to the floor of the cave into the darkness.

BOOK TWO
FORGE OF HONOR

Chapter Ten

Svetlana Drusznina touched her fingertips to her dress as she spun on her toes before the full-length mirror. The sunlight streamed through the open windows warm, orange, making soft, warm pastels of the flowers on the fabric of the draperies.

It was important to look perfect for Michael.

Hair. Eyes. Jewelry—not too much because he didn't like very much jewelry on a woman. And not too much makeup either, for the same reason.

She tugged at her hair ribbon now, shaking free of it completely. The sun of the weeks spent at Miami Beach with her father had lightened her hair almost an entire shade—it was now more golden brown than auburn. Last summer, Michael had told her he liked what the sun did to her hair. It was why she had spent so much of this summer in the sun.

He had told her he liked her hair long, and she had not cut it—it was to the middle of her back now, a length she hadn't worn it at since she was a little girl. But she liked it that way, too. She had taught herself to like what he liked.

Svetlana, her fingers toying with the ribbon, glanced back through the open window to the lawn outside, where her father and Michael's father waited.

With a final glance in the mirror she saw herself once more, her dress, her hair flowing in rhythm with her body. She was beautiful—and it was all for Michael.

Svetlana ran through the doorway and down the three low steps, looking right and left. Her hands bunched her dress up as she hurdled the low, squared-off hedgerow and slowed her pace. She reached the corner of the house and stopped, sucking in a quick breath, smoothing her clothes, touching at her hair, fixing her official smile.

The special smile was saved only for Michael when he

made love to her, when he touched her with his hands, or his eyes, or his voice.

She had nearly twisted an ankle making the hurdle over the hedge, and if she had, her father would have told her, "Svetlana—you are a lady. You are twenty-four years old. You do not jump over the hedges anymore."

Michael liked to jump with her. He did it better, of course. Three consecutive gold medals in the Olympic decathlon, the first won at age sixteen.

Michael did everything better.

She could hear the laughter, the tinkling of glasses, the small talk. It was fashionable for the Americans to do their party chatter in Russian these days, and it was fashionable for the Russians to make theirs in English. It made for interesting parties.

She always spoke English with Michael, except when they were in bed and he told her dirty things in Russian that drove her crazy with lust. They had both been bilingual since childhood, but English suited him better, and so she let it suit her better, too.

"Svetlana! Little one—come to me!"

It was her father's voice and she smiled and walked toward him—very ladylike.

He smiled and the lines of his face seamed into deeper creases and she nuzzled her cheek against his as he folded his arms around her. Her hands touched at his sides—his girth was too massive to encompass. She could smell aftershave on his skin. It smelled like vodka, and because of the smell people had always made jokes about him that he drank too much, though he rarely drank at all.

He had a perpetual five-o'clock shadow. Svetlana had marveled, as a little girl, watching him shave within the cleft chin of his lanterned jaw, within the lines at the sides of his full lips.

"Let me look at you," he whispered. As she leaned back so he could, he whispered into her ear in Russian, "You have hurdled the hedge again—you are"—and he used the English word—"glistening."

Svetlana turned around for him once, letting him see how pretty she was, letting him see that the money he gave her for clothes was well spent. "It's only the warmth of the sun, Father."

"James Hope will get you if you lie to me," he said with a laugh, shaking his massive belly under his black suit, shaking his long and spatulate finger at her, smiling on the edge of his frown.

He had told her that ever since she was a little girl—that the American gunman and killer and terrorist would know if she lied and claim her from hell. It was a story told to frighten children, and she had always wondered how it seemed to frighten Arnold Borden, director of national security. Because the real James Hope—if there ever had been one—would have been only a few years older than Comrade Director Borden.

"And James Hope will get you for threatening your only child so terribly, Papa."

She laughed and she kissed him. "Now I am not glistening—not much, anyway."

He grinned at her. "I see the cars coming."

"Michael!" She turned and ran, threading her way past the black waiters and maids, past the guests in their colorful dresses and conservative suits, across the lawn, onto the driveway's gravel.

She waited there. The lead Mercedes, with the American flag on the left fender and the flag of the Union of Soviet Socialist Republics on the right fender, was coming.

She looked back once. Her father and the other dignitaries were coming toward the driveway. The chauffeur of the Mercedes would time his speed so the receiving line would be formed up just as the gray sedan stopped.

Because of the tinting of the glass, she couldn't see inside. But she knew how it would be arranged. Peace Party Chairman Lester Saile—in his late seventies by now—would be seated in the rear seat. Arnold Borden would be seated facing rearward in the folding jumpseat, and Michael would be seated facing rearward, behind the security man.

She imagined Michael talking with Lester Saile. Did Saile ask Michael for his opinion? Did Saile congratulate her Michael on the fine job he had done as head of the Sports Council for Youth? Did he discuss Michael's upcoming marriage? She moved her hands from her hips and folded her arms across her breasts—*their* upcoming marriage.

She liked the way it sounded in English. *Dr. and Mrs. Michael H. Borden*. She smiled—the "H" was a big joke because it stood for absolutely nothing. Michael had no middle name, and when he had filled out his first official documents a middle initial had been needed and his mother had supplied it.

The Politburo's committee for space exploration had wanted them both in the coveralls of the crew of the *Beacon of Peace*. But she had done something she rarely did—and because she rarely did it, it had worked perfectly. She had cried, pouted, carried on as though her world were ending, and her father had pulled the right strings. Michael would wear his uniform, but she would wear a wedding dress that dripped with yards of handmade Polish lace. She giggled thinking of what the Politburo had wanted. She in the uniform and Michael—

"What are you giggling about, little one?" Her father stood beside her now.

"Nothing, Papa—nothing. Young girls are supposed to giggle. Didn't you know that?"

"Especially young girls who will be in bed with their young man in a little while, hmmm?"

"Papa!"

"You never lie to me. Do not now."

She licked her lips, thinking it was better to say nothing.

"Just be sure and I am happy for you," he said in his reassuring monotone.

She looked at her father and spoke honestly. "I love him, Papa."

He folded his arm about her bare shoulders. Despite the warmth of the sun, the warmth of his hands against her skin felt good to her. "Then I promise not to ask any embarrassing questions when the two of you disappear tonight. But do not disappear until after the main course." He laughed as he slapped at his abdomen, his suitcoat buttoned tightly over it. "That way I can have two more desserts. Chocolate chiffon pie—no wonder the Americans were so easily conquered. They ate so much they could not move."

"Shh, Papa—they're our allies."

He laughed. "They think that. The Soviet people think that, too—but you and I and Lester Saile, and perhaps even your handsome young lover, know better, do we not?"

The cars were well past the interior gate of the circular driveway now, the guard car easing over left, the second Mercedes passing it. She was standing on her tiptoes to see, she realized.

"You embarrass me—you are like an overeager puppy, little one," her father said.

"I am not. Well—maybe I am," she said with a smile. She knew she was.

"Remember one thing," he told her, holding her still. "He is not Russian."

"We're all one people, Papa."

"If you really believe that, I envy and pity you, little one." She felt his hand tighten against her skin for an instant, then leave her.

She glanced at him—he had pulled himself up to his full height and thrown his shoulders back and was tugging down his jacket. Automatically, she reached across to him and straightened the four-in-hand knot of his tie.

The gray Mercedes stopped. The black Mercedes behind it stopped, as did the other vehicles. The doors of the black van opened, the black-uniformed personnel of the National Police exiting, their rifles clutched against their chests.

The front doors of the gray Mercedes opened, then slammed shut under the hands of the driver and the sunglassed security man.

Both men looked about them as though expecting some kind of attack. Men took themselves so seriously, Svetlana thought, laughing. Michael took himself seriously—but he was still a lot of fun.

The rear doors were opened. Arnold Borden stepped out, his gray beard closely trimmed, his gray hair combed back slick.

Michael stood to his full height—six feet, four and a half inches in his bare feet (Svetlana had measured him, in not only his bare feet)—his shoulders back, his brown hair longer than officially preferred, but neatly combed. His face was tanned from survival-school training in Dasht-i-Kavir, or Salt Desert, in Soviet-occupied Iran. She had cooked when she had been there and gone through half a jar of moisturizer a night for weeks afterward. His face was lean, long, his head with its high, wide brow in perfect symmetry with his body. The muscles rippled under his blue blazer with the patch of the United States Olympic team. She watched as he stepped back from the Mercedes, his left hand touching at the black silk crocheted tie he wore, pressing it against his blue shirt as he buttoned the blazer's center button.

He half disappeared into the vehicle, then reemerged, his left hand at the elbow of Peace Party Chairman and President of the United States Lester Saile.

Comrade Saile seemed so frail beside Michael, Svetlana thought.

Michael's gray eyes flickered toward her, and the fingers of his left hand pushed back a comma of brown hair from his forehead. Lester Saile raised his arms to the dignitaries from the U.S. Senate and House of Representatives, from the Politburo, from the various government agencies. A cheer went up, Michael beginning to clap his hands in applause, others joining him, Svetlana clapping her hands. She didn't like Lester Saile at all, but Michael was her lover and—

But then Lester Saile bowed slightly, turned, extended his right hand to Michael, and Michael took it and their locked hands raised high over their heads, Lester Saile seeming almost child-sized beside Michael.

And the applause grew and she realized she was whistling and clapping like someone at an American football game rather than a girl at a garden party. She was laughing. Michael was home.

Svetlana extended her foot as far as she could without slipping out of her chair, her right foot out of her shoe. As Michael leaned back in his chair, smiling, his eyes alight, she could feel his stocking-clad foot touching at hers. She felt her cheeks dimpling when he touched her. And her face felt hot. She picked up her wineglass, quickly downing the contents so that if anyone noticed her face they would also notice her empty wineglass.

Michael was talking, and she listened. "I hardly think the Canadians have much of a chance, Mr. President. After their attacks on our borders—"

"Ah, but Michael—if you were only a little older." Lester Saile had been drinking a little too much, and his tongue always loosened when he did that. Her father had told her that once years ago, as if it were some sort of revelation from the Christian God, but it was obvious. The newspeople covered it well because he never looked that way on television. "If you only remembered what it was like three decades ago. This border fracus with Canada—it brings me back, Michael, it really does. Sit down sometime and talk with your father."

Arnold Borden stroked his white beard. "Mr. President—"

"Arnie, if an old man has any rights, it's the right to talk when he's drunk a little wine."

"But Mr. President—"

"Those Canadians..." Saile smiled, sipping at his port again—everyone else drank a California Chablis Blanc—"they are as stubborn as the damned Brits. The fuckers think they can take on the might of the United States and the Soviet Union. Goddamned crazies, that's what they are. Michael, you should see the pictures I've seen—bolt-action rifles against our modern weapons."

"Now, there you go, sir," Michael said with a smile. "A bolt-action rifle? I thought all rifles had bolts." He gestured expansively as he smiled. "I'm afraid I'd make a terrible soldier."

Marshal Blotsky spoke for the first time since he had joined them at the end of the soup course. "If I may, Mr. President, young Dr. Borden—well, some sixth sense tells me that you would make a fine soldier." Marshal Blotsky spoke in his faultless if heavily accented English. Svetlana thought she caught Arnold Borden's eyes looking daggers at old Blotsky, who had to be seventy at least. Blotsky laughed. "You are such a superb athlete—and you already possess some of the vital skills of the soldier."

"Running?" Svetlana suggested, laughing.

Blotsky looked at her and smiled. "A more useful skill than you might imagine, my lovely comrade." Marshal Feyodor Mikhail Blotsky smiled, and she liked his smile because it was so sad, like her father's smile. "But you are a leader, Michael, and you are supremely fit. And you fly as well as one of my own pilots in the Army. The hand-and-eye coordi-

nation you apply with such excellence on the athletic field—
you would be a fine marksman."

Michael laughed. "I'm afraid I wouldn't know which end
of a gun shoots, Marshal Blotsky."

"You would make a fine marksman. Someday I will show
you, Michael."

Michael smiled at him good-naturedly. "I can't say that
I'd enjoy using a gun—killing has never fascinated me. But
out of respect for you, Marshal, I would be honored."

"Excellent—tomorrow morning, hey?"

"Tomorrow morning—ah—"

"Best not to put things off—especially when it concerns a
fellow my age," Blotsky said.

"All right," Michael agreed.

"Eight in the morning, still a respectable hour for a
soldier and not too horrible an hour for a civilian."

Michael laughed good-naturedly. "When I was in training, I'd already swum two miles, run six miles, and showered
by then."

Blotsky clapped Michael on the right shoulder with his
massive left hand, and he looked at Svetlana. "I see you have
broken training just a bit." He laughed again.

This time she knew she was blushing.

Her father broke the chain of conversation. "The Canadian problem—I fear that it grows, Mr. President. Mercenaries
from England and Australia, dissidents from the United
States, and of course the arms smugglers."

"Where do they get the damned things? That's what I'd
like to know," Michael interjected.

Arnold Borden spoke, clearing his throat as he began.
"Michael, you'll have to appreciate that during the Times of
Trouble, there was a small percentage of Americans who tried
to make this country an armed camp. Whether you believe it
or not—and the history books will bear me out—the time was
when anybody could walk into a store that sold guns and
plunk his money down and fill out a yellow piece of paper—
Form 4473, it was called—and walk out with a handgun."

"That's disgusting," Michael said soberly.

"Well, disgusting or not, there were so many people who
ascribed to this cult of the gun that the large arms factories
flourished. Thousands of people were employed in them—

just making more and more guns and ammunition to crank down the throats of the American public."

Svetlana watched Arnold Borden's eyes. She had never liked Michael's father, even though soon he would be her father-in-law. He seemed to be seeking approval from Lester Saile.

"There were even magazines devoted to guns and teaching people the techniques of killing and maiming," Borden went on. "It was disgusting, as you said. But there still are enough of these old gun fanatics out there that they've set up illegal factories and they manufacture the ammunition to keep these old guns going. It could be centuries before these old guns are no longer operable. And, of course, in the capitalist countries of Europe such as Germany, Austria, Italy—they build every gun they can crank out. Some of these weapons get into the hands of smugglers who get into the United States, into Canada, into Mexico. Dealers in death—that's what they are."

"They ought to be stopped," Michael said rather lamely. Svetlana could feel his foot. He was more horny than philosophical tonight, she guessed.

"Yes—and you are sitting next to the man who's doing the best job of guarding our borders against these pirates." Arnold Borden clapped Comrade Marshal Blotsky on the shoulder.

Blotsky grinned devilishly. "And your father, Michael— without his devotion to duty, well, I just shudder to think what your beautiful nation would be like. The search for malefactors is endless, I know."

Michael nodded gravely.

Svetlana screwed her toes harder against his toes, and he looked at her from across the table and smiled. Lester Saile raised his head, as if from drowsing, saying a little too loudly, she thought, "We must knock off the Canadian problem before winter."

Marshal Blotsky raised his glass of wine. "Yes—and here is to ending the problems with Canada before winter."

Michael sipped at his wine, then looked at Blotsky. "I don't think I quite understand, Marshal."

Borden cleared his throat as if to speak, but Marshal Blotsky spoke first. "It is very simple. The people whom we fight are not particularly well armed. Canadian Army forces are decently equipped, of course, though their weapons are outmoded. But the Resistance in Canada is very much a group of diehards. Not just Canadians, of course, but people from your own country, from all over. And the Canadian wilderness is perfect for them—like it was in the old days of James Hope."

Arnold Borden's eyes became pinpoints of light. Svetlana laughed. "You mean there really was a James Hope?"

Blotsky looked at her, looked at Michael, then looked at Arnold Borden. There was a decided twinkle in his eyes. "He is more than a story told to frighten little girls, my pretty comrade."

"There is no mention of him in the history books," Michael began. "I'd always thought he was some myth of the gun crazies."

"Ohh, he has achieved mythic stature, to be sure—among those who support his ideas. But you should ask your father. Because your father and I were there when James Hope died."

Michael looked at his father. "You were there? The two of you? You never—"

Arnold Borden looked at Michael hard. "Some things you don't want to remember, Michael. That's one of them." Borden downed the contents of his wineglass and refilled it.

Marshal Blotsky said, "Hope was killed by his son—his one surviving child, Stephen. And Stephen was cut down by gunfire before either your father or I could act, Michael. It was a bloody scene. Hope's wife had been ill. She was a beautiful woman."

"Yes," Borden murmured.

"Hope was trapped, his Resistance fighters all but wiped out. I'll give the man credit for decency—more than his son Stephen had. Hope stayed behind to care for his wife."

"What was wrong with her?" Svetlana asked. Arnold Borden looked at her severely.

"Yes," Michael added. "Professional interest, let's say."

Lester Saile just sipped at his wine. Marshal Blotsky smiled, staring at his glass, swirling the clear, greenish liquid within it as though studying wave motion. "She had just delivered a baby."

"The poor woman," Svetlana whispered.

Her father, in his sonorous voice, intoned, "I think we are upsetting my daughter, gentlemen."

"No—what . . ."

Blotsky looked at her. "All right. She had delivered the baby. Stephen Hope had aided the National Police from the very first days of his father's outlawry. But Stephen was insane. Sometimes hatred can develop between parent and child—but with Stephen Hope it was more than that. He actually wanted to see his parents dead. I don't know why— I'll never know, I suppose. The three of us—Michael's father, myself, and Stephen—ran to the rear of the cave. All the opposition had been cleared away. Stephen picked up an assault rifle from the floor of the cave. It was the first and only time I'd ever seen him touch any weapon. He positively hated them. His mother's head was cradled in his father's lap. His father held those forty-fives of his—"

"Those are handguns, aren't they?" Michael interrupted.

"Yes—they are handguns." Blotsky nodded.

The corners of Michael's mouth turned down with evident distaste.

"Hope's wife, Melissa, held the baby in her arms, suckling at her breast," Blotsky went on softly. "Stephen took the rifle and fired toward the three of them. Apparently Mrs. Hope died instantly. James Hope clutched the baby to his chest, trying to protect it. The baby was in no danger, as you can understand. Men do not kill helpless infants, regardless of whom their parents may be. We were about to place Hope under arrest, but he was wounded by the burst from Stephen's assault rifle. Hope raised one of his pistols, as if to kill one of us, or perhaps Stephen—who can say? Who can say what goes through the mind of a dying man? Although I'd venture that a few of us at this table will soon find out." Blotsky smiled.

"What about the little baby?" Svetlana asked.

Arnold Borden spoke. "Like Marshal Blotsky said, apparently there were some Resistance fighters in the cave. They shot Stephen Hope to death. Either their gunfire or Stephen Hope's original burst of assault rifle fire killed the baby."

Michael didn't look up from his wineglass as he spoke.

"There are different sizes of bullets. Wasn't it possible to tell from an autopsy?"

"No. In battles like that—the bodies are all put in a mass grave. The child's body was put between his parents'."

Svetlana felt as though she were going to cry. She drew her foot back from Michael's, found her shoe under the table, stuffed her foot inside it, and pushed her chair back. "If you will all excuse me, comrades, Father, Michael—Comrade President Saile. I . . ." She turned and walked from the table, holding her abdomen.

As she reached the doors leading to the garden, pushing them open, the heat of the night like a humid wall of darkness, she felt hands touching her bare shoulders.

"Hi. Thought you might use a little company?"

They stepped between the doors, Michael moving his hands from her for an instant, closing out the noise and most of the light of the dinner party. And then his hands were on her again. She rested her head against his chest. "Hold me—please?" And she closed her eyes as his arms cocooned her.

She stood with her arms limp at her sides, the bedroom door closed, the windows wide open. A night breeze filled the curtains like sails in a wind. He reached his arms to her shoulders, drawing her close. He could smell her hair.

"Undress me," she whispered to him.

"All right," he told her softly.

His hands moved to her waist. He found the knot of the sash and undid it, then his hands traveled around her waist, up her back. He found the tab of the zipper, the little hook-and-eye closure just above it. He undid the hook and eye and drew the zipper down.

He pushed the opened dress down over her hips, hooking his thumbs into the waistband of first her slip, then her panties beneath it. She stepped back a small step—out of her clothes bunched on the floor.

"You didn't take my stockings off," she whispered to him.

"You can take off your own stockings. How do you keep those up?"

"Antigravity—I learned all about it in astronaut training."

"Hmm." He kissed her neck, her head lolling back, her

eyelids flickering as he raised her face, looked at her, held her body tight against him, and pushed his mouth down hard against hers.

Michael Borden had left her in bed at six forty-five, according to his wristwatch. He had pulled on underpants, shorts, a T-shirt, and his track shoes and gone as quietly as he could downstairs.

Thirty-eight minutes later, the run was over and he retraced his path up the stairs and into Svetlana's rooms. She still slept. He let her sleep, grabbing up his blazer and slacks from the chair, his underpants and socks from the floor, using the open adjoining door to enter his own suite of rooms.

He stripped, except for the wristwatch. It was the same stainless steel Rolex given him by his father when he had reached twenty-one.

He entered the shower. It was nearly a quarter to eight. He kept the water steaming hot as he washed his hair, conditioned it, washed his body, and then rinsed. When the last of the soap had spiraled down the drain, he turned the hot water fully down and the cold water fully up, the adjustable shower head set for the most stinging spray.

Michael smudged water from the crystal of the Rolex— eight minutes before eight.

Half dressed and shaved—only two minutes remained.

He grabbed up a blue knit shirt with short sleeves and pulled it on over his head, running his hands through his wet hair. He stuffed his pockets with the necessities and crossed back into Svetlana's room. She still slept. He walked to the bed and touched his lips to her cheek. She smiled but didn't waken, her body seeming to tighten up into the sheets.

He liked the smell of her in the morning best of all.

Michael left through her doorway, breaking into a jog trot along the upstairs corridor, reaching the half-circular staircase leading to the main hall of Svetlana's father's official summer residence, taking the stairs two at a time. He had taken sunglasses and he put them on now as he reached the front door, letting himself out as he nodded to the security team stationed just outside. He had read studies that indicated that shooting could result in the discharge of gases and particulate matter that could be harmful to the eyes.

Coming along the driveway, he saw Marshal Blotsky's staff car. Michael stepped out into the driveway, raising his left hand in a wave. The Mercedes slowed, stopped, the gravel crunching under its tires. The right passenger door swung open, Blotsky leaning out. "Michael—I thought you might forget."

"No, Marshal—I'm honored. But I'll warn you again: You'll probably find me a terrible marksman." And Michael slipped inside, pulling the door closed before the chauffeur reached it.

Michael leaned back beside Blotsky as the Mercedes started ahead, around the driveway's horseshoe and toward the main gates. "I brought a number of different pistols, Michael—so that you might find which best suits you. You probably know, members of the Party and scientific, military, and certain sports stars are allowed certain privileges. Your father could easily get you the papers that would allow you to own a weapon."

Michael laughed. "No—I don't think I'd really have any use for it. And if someone were ever to break in and steal it, who knows what might happen? But thank you."

After a twenty-minute drive, the Mercedes stopped and Marshal Blotsky handed one of the pistol cases to Michael. "Carry this, Michael. I'll have the other case. Ivan, my driver, will bring the ammunition and control the targets."

Michael stepped from the Mercedes. It was cooler here, near to the sea, the sound of breakers crashing in the distance. It was partially the psychological effect, Michael thought. Neatly painted wooden tables and benches were lined for at least a hundred yards on either side of them, a vast mound of dirt and stone raised what seemed three hundred yards away. "What is this place, Marshal?"

"Thirty years ago, I understand it was a range used by the people of Seattle for recreational shooting."

"Barbaric," Michael noted.

Blotsky smiled. "And now my Spetznas use it for polishing their marksmanship skills in their spare time."

The chauffeur had outdistanced them, Michael walking slowly not to get ahead of Marshal Blotsky. But he had to say, for his age, Blotsky seemed remarkably fit. They were nearly of equal height and stature, but Blotsky carried more bulk.

Michael's professional eye judged the body-fat level as acceptable for a man Blotsky's age.

The chauffeur set down two large cases, extracting two objects that looked like the sound-muffling devices worn on the ears of aircraft ground crew and maintenance personnel. There were two sets of these, both bright orange.

As Michael and Blotsky drew nearer, Michael could see the contents of the second case—small boxes, he imagined of ammunition for the various handguns.

The chauffeur withdrew at a jog trot toward a high structure roughly equidistant from the Mercedes and the benches and tables. "The targets here in recent years have been made electronic for the use of my Spetznas. Ivan will run them. But it will take him a few moments to activate the systems."

They had stopped now, Michael setting down the case he carried, Blotsky doing the same.

"These things," Michael asked, gesturing to the orange earmuffs, "to protect our hearing?"

"Yes—mine was starting to go a bit. I recently started using hearing protection when practicing."

Michael fell silent.

Blotsky opened one of the pistol cases, then the other. "I selected only the most interesting handguns from my collection."

"You collect these?"

"The spoils of war, Michael. I brought you out here for another purpose as well." Blotsky picked up a gleaming, flat-sided handgun Michael guessed to be made of stainless steel. "This is a Detonics Scoremaster .45—identical to those used by the infamous James Hope. But not one of his own, unfortunately. Those guns disappeared. Here." Michael didn't reach for it. "It's empty, I assure you, Michael."

Michael took the pistol in his right hand, his fingers closing slowly on the butt. "Heavy," he observed. "It seems well balanced, like a surgical instrument should be."

"And this is a Beretta 92SB-F, what the National Security Forces and the National Police are issued. Your father has one of these." The gun was almost black in color, more streamlined, more modern-looking than the first gun. "And I imagine your father still has one of these." This gun looked like the first, only a dark bluish-black in color, and the grips were

brown wood rather than black rubber, as with the first gun.
"A Colt Gold Cup National Match, a .45 like the Detonics
pistol."

"So my father and this James Hope—they both carried
these .45s?"

"Yes."

"Is that what you carry there?" Michael nodded toward
Blotsky's holster.

Blotsky shook his head, then drew the pistol from the
holster. It was bluish-black and smelled faintly of oil. It
looked like a cross between the second .45 and the Beretta
service pistol. "This one is loaded, Michael. I carry it constantly,
unless I'm wearing my dress uniform. But I am always
armed—if anyone should ever ask you."

"Why would someone want to know?"

"One makes enemies—simply at times by doing one's
job." Blotsky looked away. "This is a CZ-75, made in
Czechslovakia. A 9mm Parabellum, like the Beretta—this
one."

"Yes." Michael nodded.

"You can shoot all or any of these."

"I'll try the gun like my father's first," Michael decided.

Blotsky picked up both the gleaming stainless steel gun
and the other .45. "Yes—I had imagined you would." He set
down the stainless steel gun, still holding the other one. "I
have been instructed by the Politburo to ask you a question. I
need one of three answers. And I must ask it in a specific
way, Michael."

"What is it?" Michael asked, staring at the guns in the
cases. His eyes were drawn to the one like James Hope had
used. What kind of man killed with a gun? he wondered.

"I am to ask you this: When Lester Saile dies, would
you have any interest in being the next chairman of the Peace
Party, the next president of the United States?"

Michael leaned against the bench. "What?"

"Would you like to be your country's leader, Michael?"

"But that's crazy. I'm no politician. I'm not even a
member of the Peace Party, or the Communist Party, either. I
always felt that athletes should avoid politics."

"It is known what you have thought." Blotsky began to
load some of the pistols from the small boxes of ammunition.

"And that is precisely why I'm asking you, on behalf of the Politburo. Not only do you have youth and vigor, you also have the respect of men and women of every nation, even our countries' enemies. You could be a great instrument, Michael—for whatever you wished. Svetlana would be an excitingly beautiful First Lady at your side. It would be the ultimate union of our two nations, begun on the *Beacon of Peace* with your wedding."

"But—I'm not even thirty yet. You have to be thirty-five—"

"That can be waived."

"But—I don't—"

"Know how to be president?" Blotsky smiled.

"Well—yeah." Michael nodded. "I mean—what do you—"

"Very little. But your mere occupancy of the office would be important. I need one of three possible answers from you. *Yes*—which would be a foolish answer. *No*—which would be even more foolish. Or, *Ask me again when Lester Saile dies*—which is the most sensible answer."

A buzzer sounded and Michael jumped involuntarily. He pegged the origin of the buzzer as a loudspeaker mounted near them. "The targets are ready. Put on your hearing protectors. Keep your thumb down and out of the way of this—it is the slide, and each time the pistol is discharged, the slide moves back and then forward again." He handed Michael the gun. "This is the safety. When you wish to shoot, lower the safety before you pull the trigger. Hold the pistol tightly so the grip safety will be fully depressed. Here—keep the web of your hand lower. Don't choke the pistol."

Michael adjusted his hand on the grip of the gun—the bluish-black .45 like his father used to carry. He thought he remembered vaguely from his childhood seeing his father carrying a gun.

"Point the pistol at the target—there." Blotsky gestured toward a silhouette in the shape of a man's torso and head. "The front sight should be just beneath what you hope to hit, the rear sight lined up with the front sight so there is even light on either side of the front sight and so that the front sight is on the same level as the top of the rear sight. Do you have that?"

"Yes."

"Now, take the safety off and shoot, Michael."

Michael used his thumb to move the safety catch down.

He lined up the front sight and the rear sight on the target. He aimed for the head, since it was the most obvious feature of the silhouette. He felt a sickness creeping into his stomach. He knew he could never shoot a man. He looked away from the gun. "Tell the Politburo to ask me again when Lester Saile dies," he said to Blotsky. He looked back to the gun and pulled the trigger, almost losing the gun as it discharged, never imagining that it had felt that way to shoot a firearm. There was a pinging sound, and the silhouette snapped back and downward.

Marshal Blotsky, laughing, said, "Put the safety catch up. You have made a good shot."

Michael just stared at the gun in his hand.

Marshal Feyodor Mikhail Blotsky just kept laughing.

Chapter Eleven

They sat in the gazebo some two hundred yards from the house. All day long, since the shooting session with Marshal Blotsky, he had found himself judging distances. Svetlana held his hand. The sunlight streamed through the lattice-work; it was nearly dusk. Michael looked at her face, at the checkerboard pattern the sun made on her skin, on the white blouse she wore. She edged close to him, drawing his hand up, resting his hand and her hand against the fabric of her blue skirt. He could feel the heat of her body through it.

"What's wrong?"

"You can't tell anyone this," he told her. Blotsky had said it would be all right to tell her but that she must not tell her father. "And you can't tell your dad."

"All right." She nodded. "I'm going to be your wife— we'll have lots of secrets we can share together, Michael."

Michael nodded. "The Politburo wants me to be president after Lester Saile dies."

Her hand tightened on his. "What?"

"They want me—"

"I hear you. Oh, Michael, that's wonderful news. I mean, isn't it?"

He shrugged his shoulders. "Yeah, but what did I go to medical school for? I studied hard. I specialized in space medicine. Learned how to fly everything they'd let me near. If I take the presidency—I mean—"

"What good is it?"

"Yeah—what good is it?" He nodded. "Maybe I could do some good, you know. But—"

"What did you tell them?" she asked, her voice soft, breathless.

"I told them to ask me again when Lester Saile dies. Blotsky seemed to think it was the best answer."

"You should do what you want to do, Michael. Whatever you choose, I'll be happy. I really will."

He put his arms around her. "I know you will. It's just that this is something I never imagined."

"I mean—well, are you supposed to do anything—or not?"

"No. Sometimes I wish we could just run off and get married instead of have all the fanfare. Yeah, it's terrific being the first couple ever married on the *Beacon of Peace*—but they keep wanting to turn it into a circus. All I want is to be married to you and for both of us to get on with our work up there. I'm pushing thirty. All the time off from school to practice for the Olympics and everything. The years add up."

"How's your mother doing?"

Svetlana was changing the subject and not too deftly, but he let her, answering, "Dad says she's doing better. I want a look at her. Her doctor's a good man—you've met him; I've read some papers he's written. I guess he's the best available." He let out a long sigh.

"I'll miss you."

"We still have tonight. You just keep your promise to meet me in Moscow."

"I like New York better—the GUM doesn't stack up against Saks, even Macy's."

He laughed. She rested her head against his right shoulder. The light in the gazebo was getting fainter, and he could

see her features only in outline now. He felt the fingers of her
right hand as they touched at the inside of his thigh beneath
the leg of his shorts. He turned around to face her.

"I love you, Michael Borden," she whispered, leaning
her face against his, his lips touching her forehead.

"I know that already," he whispered.

"You going to do something about it?"

"Yeah—I am," he answered. His left hand moved downward along her thighs, finding the hem of her skirt, then
pushing it up. Her hand found his as he tugged down her
panties. He explored her with his fingertips, his fingers
entering her, her forehead against his chest. His lips touched
her hair, her body beginning to tremble. "Do you like that?"
he asked her.

"If you stop it I'll die, Michael. I really will."

He didn't stop. Her body shuddered against him again
and again. But then he did stop, his fingers wet from her. She
kissed his fingertips, then dropped to her knees beside the
bench where they sat. He felt her hands at his zipper,
opening it, her hands kneading against him; his hands held
her shoulders. She pulled his underpants down in the front
and he felt her tongue touch him—like something that had a
life of its own. . . .

Chapter Twelve

They had lived in Washington until he was ten, and then
Michael's father had been appointed director of national
security, which gave his father not only the control of the
National Police—some of the street punks and the antigovernment radicals called them Natpos—but also the National
Defense Forces. These were the elite troops that had been
trained by the Spetznas to replace what had been the United
States Armed Forces. Their dual function was to guard the
borders with Canada and with Mexico and to maintain do-

mestic order when something more drastic was called for than the National Police were trained or equipped to handle.

He had gone with his father on several occasions to observe some of the training sessions for the National Defense Forces. The first jet he had flown had been one of their comparatively low-speed trainers.

But it was when his father had been named director of national security that they had moved to Denver. He had instantly fallen in love with the mountains, hiking in the "safe" areas, sometimes with friends, sometimes alone, often without his father's or mother's permission. Eventually he had realized that crossing from a safe zone into a zone where some of the few pockets of armed Resistance still held out was simply crossing an imaginary line. He had crossed it many times, reasoning that if he wore a sign saying "Arnold Borden's son," he might have been in some danger from the armed lunatics that roamed the mountains killing the National Police sent to apprehend them for reeducation. But he wore no such sign, and his photo never was published until he was fourteen and had won a regional decathlon. For four years he roamed the mountains in anonymity with his schoolbag packed with sandwiches and cookies snitched when the cook wasn't looking—he wondered sometimes when he thought of those days if the old black woman who had cooked for them had known all along and just never told.

His father's voice interrupted his reverie, the mountains beneath them endless as they made the approach to the military field west of Denver. "What are you thinking, Mike?"

His father had called him Mike about five times in their lives. "Nothing, really. How about you?"

"What'd you and Blotsky talk about when you went shooting?"

He felt uncomfortable with it—so he told the truth. "Marshal Blotsky told me something in confidence, made me promise I wouldn't tell anybody except Svetlana. If it works out—kind of an opportunity for me—it'd be good for you and Mom, too."

His father nodded, stroking his beard. "All right. Anything else about this James Hope business?"

Michael thought for a moment. "One of the guns he

brought for us to shoot—he said it was like James Hope's guns. I can't remember the name."

"Detonics Scoremaster—two of 'em were what Jim carried."

"Jim?"

"Hope used to be an FBI agent—until he went bad. We worked together. We were good friends."

"God—that must have been tough, Dad. I mean, going out to arrest your friend."

Arnold Borden nodded. "Yeah, more than you know, Mike. More than you know."

The subject needed changing. "Marshal Blotsky showed me a gun like he said you carried—a Gold something?"

"A Gold Cup. That's a Colt .45 with whitewalls and factory air, son."

"What?" Michael laughed.

"Old joke. What'd you shoot? How'd you do?"

"The first gun I shot was the one like yours—and my first shot hit a silhouette at ten yards and knocked it down."

"How'd you shoot—I mean, with one hand or two?"

"One—that's the way Marshal Blotsky showed me." Michael shrugged.

"Yeah, well, Feyodor always shot that way—stand on your hind legs like a man—that shit. Sometime, maybe before you go up there"—he gestured skyward—"to the *Beacon of Peace,* I'll take you out and show you how to *really* do it." Arnold Borden cleared his throat. "So, ah— how'd you do after that first shot?"

"Kinda downhill." Michael laughed. "When the thing went off it scared the crap out of me."

"Time was," his father said, after taking a swallow of his drink, "when a man'd take his son out and teach him how to shoot soon as the boy could hold the muzzle higher than the ground. That's the way my dad taught me. Always meant to teach you."

"Yeah, but why would a man want to teach his son how to kill people? I mean, that's what guns are for, right?"

"Only some of the time. You listen to too much of the guff my propaganda people put out. Guns aren't just for killing people. And remember, sometimes people need killing. Guns aren't any better or worse than the men who use them. Like anything else."

Michael looked at his father. "I never heard you talk like this."

"Your mother never approved of such talk, so I guess I never had the opportunity."

Michael didn't know what to say. But then he did. "I love you, Dad."

Arnold Borden closed his eyes, barely whispering. "I love you too, Michael—a whole hell of a lot. Sometimes—well—maybe you'll hear things about me you won't like."

"What do you mean? You're just a law-enforcement officer doing his job. I mean, I know those whackos out in the mountains don't like you, but they're criminals. They're not supposed to like you."

"Yeah, well." The elder Borden shrugged. He pinched his nostrils with his right thumb and first finger, sniffed. "Anyway—"

The pilot's voice came over the intercom. "Comrade Director, Dr. Borden, we'll be touching down in five minutes. Would you both please fasten your seat belts and extinguish any smoking materials and place your lap tables in the upright position."

"The son-of-a-bitch knew I was gonna light up," Arnold Borden said with a laugh.

She heard the knock at the door and made the sign of the cross. "Just a minute, Helen." Each day it was harder for her to get down to her knees beside the bed, and each day it was harder still to get up. She had made it her penance. And she would not let Helen see her praying, because then Helen would have helped her to her feet, and the hardship would have been taken from her.

She needed it.

Her hands knotted on the bed post and she pulled as hard as she could, making the joints unbend, straighten. Her hands hurt from the strain of lifting her own body weight and from having held them clasped tightly together, the fingers intertwined. More penance.

But Margaret Borden finally stood erect, and she forced herself to calm her breathing, her dress feeling slightly damp against her chest and under her armpits from the exertion.

"You may come in, Helen."

She turned her face to the door and put on the smile Helen would expect. "Did I keep you waiting long, darling?" Margaret Borden cooed. "I was just lost in thought, about Michael coming home. To me."

"Yes, ma'am." Helen nodded, standing beside the doorway, the door half open under her chocolate brown hand. "Dr. Borozoi is here to see you, ma'am."

"Dr. Borozoi?"

"Yes, ma'am—like he comes every Thursday this time, Mrs. Borden."

"Yes," she answered. "I guess I was just hoping that Dr. Borozoi would forget today."

Helen crossed the room on her tiny feet, her maid's uniform rustling as she walked, her little white apron and the little white cap stiffly starched. Margaret Borden had always liked the girl—but never completely trusted her. There was no one to trust.

Helen stopped, settling her hands over her apron against her thighs. "Would you like Dr. Borozoi to come up here to your room, Mrs. Borden? He don't have to see you in the library."

"Oh—yes, he does. I'm not so sick that I can't leave my room."

Margaret Borden pushed herself away from the bedpost and started across the room. Her balance was slipping a little and Helen reached out for her, but she tugged her arm away. "I'm healthy enough to walk, thank you, Helen."

"Yes, ma'am, Mrs. Borden. I just figured—well, I was just fixin' to—"

"I know what you were 'fixin' to,'" Margaret Borden mimicked. She paused opposite the full-length mirror. The damp feeling under her arms and on her chest had left her, and the light gray dress showed none of it. She walked on, primping at a stray strand of hair she had caught sight of in the mirror.

"You sure do have pretty hair, Mrs. Borden—so white and full and everything."

Margaret Borden stopped by the partially open door, looking at Helen. "I started to turn gray at thirty. By thirty-five, the gray started turning white. When you are my age, if you are smart you'll dye your hair. I just never liked it." The lecture over, she continued on her way from the room. She had early on decided that Helen needed an education, then set about giving it to her. In the past twenty years, the schools had become specialized, and Helen had taken tests that had clearly shown her best suited to household or institutional service. So Helen's formal education had ended at the sixth grade. But there was a quickness in Helen that Margaret Borden had always liked, and so each day for the past two years she would sit in the library with Helen, who would read to her from the Bible. Helen had at first balked at this, because in the schools children were taught now that the Bible was merely the colorfully embellished, pseudodocumentary story of the Jews and the Roman Catholics. And the Jews, of course, were no different from their Zionist brothers and sisters in Israel who had resisted so far—and successfully—two attempts at Soviet invasion. They were now allies of Egypt, according to the Bible once their mortal enemy. She had tried explaining this to Helen—that what they taught her in the schools was wrong and what Helen's parents had taught her (until at age six she had gone to live at her education center) had been true. And the Catholics—the New Testament was scorned as Roman Catholic propaganda because the pope had spoken out against communism since his ascent to the Throne of St. Peter, as had his predecessors.

Helen had at first read from the King James Version merely to humor her, Margaret Borden knew. But in recent months, she had felt something in Helen, a growing depth, a longing to know, a feeling for the Word.

Margaret Borden reached the head of the stairs—it was not so bad going down. Helen hovered near her. She smiled at the girl. "You worry so much about me falling down these stairs, well—my Lord, girl—you're going to make me do it. You just stand back and if I fall and I don't die instantly, well, you can say, 'I told you so.' Is that all right?"

Helen forced a smile. "Yes, ma'am."

She attacked the stairs slowly, holding to the railing but only with her left hand.

Margaret Borden knew what people thought of her— early senility complicated by her circulatory problems, by her arthritis, by her heart condition. But she let them think that.

She had no desire to see her husband's friends, to hear their talk of power and greed, no desire but to live long enough to see Michael well settled with little Svetlana. The concept of private wills had been legally abolished, but she had set aside a packet of things for Helen: Krugerrands, diamonds, and instructions telling her what to do with them. And a Bible, of course.

She was halfway to the base of the stairs, and in the library doors she could see Dr. Borozoi. She disliked him—for no other reason than that Borozoi was Russian and there was a shortage of doctors and this one came to her house when he should have been working at one of the state-run clinics. Helen had confided to her the horror story of a woman who had died in childbirth while forced to sit on a straight-back chair in the clinic waiting room for six hours. No doctor, not even a nurse, had been free to see her.

Dr. Borozoi smiled at her. He always smiled at her, and she didn't like that, because a man who always smiled was always covering up something, and she didn't like liars. It was why she had stopped liking herself thirty years ago, stopped liking Arnie.

He was walking from the library doors. He would extend his hand to help her down the last few stairs, and she would take it because it was only politeness to take it, though inside herself she would scream at him.

He extended his hand to her. "And how are we today, Comrade Borden?"

She looked at him and didn't smile. "I don't know how we are, Dr. Borozoi—but I feel better than horse manure and worse than I did when I was a girl." She didn't like saying things like that because they weren't planned, and people always thought it was proof that her mind was gone. She knew that—even though nobody ever said it to her. "And I'm not a comrade," she added hastily.

"Very well, Mrs. Borden. I will rephrase the question: Do you feel any better? Has the medication given you any relief?"

"I don't take your damn medication because it makes me want to sleep all the time." She didn't tell him that one time it made her wet the bed because she had been so drowsy. But Helen had cleaned it up and sworn to tell no one.

"But you must. Otherwise, there is nothing I can do for you except put you into the hospital, Mrs. Borden." He was still smiling at her.

"You will never put me in a hospital. Nobody ever leaves the hospital."

"The hospital is only a place to make people well."

She looked at him. "You have to examine me today?"

"Yes. I must."

"My son is coming home today."

"All the more reason to feel your best, Mrs. Borden," he told her, helping her across the main hall and toward the library. Helen would wait outside, just as she always did.

"No more of your medication—it's no good for me."

He nodded, still smiling. "All right. We will try something else. Is that all right?"

She wouldn't answer him.

Michael wanted very much to tell his mother that he was home, but instead he stood beside the six-car garage that flanked the massive white house that looked like something one of the capitalist exploiters of the African slaves would have lived in in the days prior to the Civil War. On the parking apron was a very black, very polished Cadillac, customized to be a convertible. Comrade Dr. Elias Borozoi leaned casually beside it.

Michael Borden waited. Borozoi spoke. "Should I speak to you as the concerned son of my most dear patient, or as a medical colleague, Michael?"

"Try both—give it to me straight, Doctor." It sounded to him like it should have been a line from some of the old black-and-white movies, which were of course proscribed now because they promoted the wrong ideals. But he had seen some of them at an underground cinema run by one of his friends in medical school. He had never been invited back after that first night because, as his friend had put it, it made the others uncomfortable to have the son of the head of the secret police sitting there with them. He had insisted there was nothing secret about his father's police work. But he had never returned to see any more of the movies.

Dr. Borozoi spoke. "Your mother's condition—she has what might be called a not too often observed form of

Alzheimer's disease. This is complicated by her arthritis and her generally sensitive constitution, which precludes my use of some of the more common drugs that seem to have some efficacy in these matters."

Borozoi finished. The diagnosis matched exactly Michael's own based on his more intimate knowledge of her condition. And the prognosis was exactly what his own mind had told him but his heart had refused to accept.

"There is nothing that can be done?"

"I will speak to you now as a colleague, Michael. There is nothing that can be done, except to ease her pain, make her last months as pleasant as possible. The circulatory condition has resulted in what appears to be an insufficient supply of blood to the brain at times. You should notice that in the months since you have seen her, her mental condition seems to have deteriorated markedly. If I may say so, for her own sake, I hope the disease claims her before much longer."

Michael reached out his right hand, clapping Borozoi on the left shoulder. Michael lowered his eyes.

Borozoi, his voice strained, spoke. "Michael, I know she distrusts me. But I feel very much for your mother. I shall miss her."

Michael studied the concrete beneath their feet in intimate detail. "I'm sorry for that, Dr. Borozoi."

"In her mind, Michael, I am her persecutor. The examinations sometimes are uncomfortable and for such a woman, always distasteful. The shots—she despises them. The medication—even though it helps her overall condition, she sees it as restricting her still further." And Borozoi took Michael's hand in both of his. Michael looked up. "But we all do what we can. The love you show her is better medicine than I could provide."

Michael couldn't speak. He nodded, clasped Borozoi's hands tightly, then turned and walked away toward the house.

Helen opened the door. He gathered she had been watching for him ever since the car had pulled into the driveway. She smiled, saying, "Mr. Michael, it's good to—"

"Just gimme a hug, Helen," Michael told her, folding her into his arms.

"Mr. Michael, Mrs. Borden's real bad—I love her so—"

Michael just held her tightly. "I know," he whispered. "Without you I don't know what she'd do, Helen. And if I've told you once, I've told you a thousand times: Knock it off with this 'Mr. Michael' routine," he said with mock severity, raising her chin, looking into her eyes. They were tear-rimmed. "Now, you go dry your eyes and tell Mr. Halsey I said you're taking a little while off just to walk around in the garden, get yourself together, maybe lie down. Doctor's orders, okay?"

She forced a smile. "Okay—Michael."

He kissed her forehead—she was a foot shorter than he and small as a doll.

"Okay." He smiled. "The library?"

"The library—uh-huh." And this time the smile wasn't forced.

"You go on—do as I said. And tell Mr. Halsey that if he tries carrying my luggage upstairs at his age, all he's gonna do is get me pissed."

She laughed. "I can't tell Mr. Halsey that, Michael—he'd fire me!"

"Well, you rephrase it, then." He stopped, turning around. "When I was in Africa. I got you something called a dashiki—I asked for extra short."

"Michael!"

"Give it to you later. And tell Mr. Halsey I found him a new pipe. That'll calm him down."

He could hear Helen's shoes clicking on the slick marble floor, his own shoes slapping against it as he crossed the main hall.

Without really thinking to do it, he straightened the knit tie at his collar, smoothed the ends across his shirt front, buttoned his blue suit jacket. He stopped at the double doors, drawing himself up almost to attention, then knocked lightly. He didn't wait for a response but opened both door handles simultaneously, drawing the doors outward as he stepped through.

He tugged at his shirt cuffs as he drew the doors closed behind him.

He couldn't see his mother, but from the smell of her perfume he knew she was sitting where she always sat in the library, in the high wing chair that faced the hearth. The chair needed reupholstering, but she refused to let it be done, so it matched none of the other overstuffed furniture dotted about the room.

He didn't speak but instead played the game, walking up behind the chair slowly, leaning over the chair—her white hair, her frail shoulders. He reached out his hands and gently covered her eyes.

"Who is it?" Her voice sounded somehow older, but at once young, soft, beautiful to him.

"Who do you think?" he whispered.

"A handsome prince?"

"I would have thought you would have gotten better at this over the years," he said with a laugh, coming around the chair, dropping to one knee beside her, looking on level into her eyes.

"You are a handsome prince." She smiled.

"You just want a kiss, that's all," he told her, leaning toward her, folding her into his arms, kissing her lightly on the mouth, then hugging her to him.

"You were right." She sighed. There was an unnatural sweetness to her breath.

"Well, I'd be a fool if I didn't—the sexiest lady in Denver and she's all mine."

"Hmm. And how's the sexiest lady in Russia doing?"

He drew back and looked at her. Her eyes were smiling. "Svetlana is just fine—sent her love."

"She had some to spare, huh?"

It was the moments such as these that made it all the harder. Her mind seemed as sharp as ever, her tongue as quick. But in an instant, it could be gone. "You got some to spare? How about another hug?"

Margaret leaned forward, and he put his arms around her again, her head against his chest. "I missed you, Michael. Even Mr. Halsey must have missed you, and you know what a grouch he is. But he's the best butler in Denver, and he figures he can be a grouch and get away with it."

"He's right—on both counts." Michael laughed. "I got you a present, sweetheart."

He drew back. She clapped her hands together, pressing them tightly against one another over her lap, her face lit with a smile. "What did you get me? Come on! I'm an old lady. I could croak right here just waiting for it." And she laughed—he made himself laugh. He reached into his right pocket for the tiny box, took it out, and handed it to her.

Like women everywhere, Margaret seemed to enjoy frustrating the giver by dawdling over the gift. She tugged gingerly at the ribbon that sealed the box, gradually undoing the bow, even more slowly undoing the ribbon. She set the box on her lap, carefully folding the ribbon as though it were the gift. "That was a beautiful bow—it was a sin to open it."

"Uh-huh." He nodded.

She began at one end of the box, carefully tugging the Scotch tape away so as to avoid tearing the dark blue paper that covered the box. One end free, then the other end. Carefully, the sculptured nail of her right first finger explored the joint between the two ends of the paper—apparently she found the tape, sawing at it with her fingernail.

He could feel the gray hairs growing on his head.

She pulled the paper clear of the box, setting the box into her lap again, neatly folding the paper, placing it along with the ribbon just rescued from her lap on the small reading stand at her left.

"Ah—more tape." Margaret smiled. She sawed at it with her nail again, saying, "There," just looking at him, not opening the box. "You know, Michael, you don't have to bring me presents. I love it when you do. But you really—"

"Open the damn box," he told her softly.

"Michael!"

"Please?"

She laughed, then raised the hinged cardboard lid of the white box. He had forgotten about the cotton—he wondered what she could do with it. She removed it from the box and set it neatly on the small table beside the folded paper and folded ribbon. She returned her gaze to the box, looked at its contents, then closed the lid. "Oh—earrings. You know how I love them. Thank you, Michael!"

He closed his eyes. "So—hold 'em up—try 'em on—something." Margaret laughed and took the earrings from the box and held them up to her ears. He knew that her fingers were no longer capable of putting them on, but Helen would help her.

"You like?" She smiled.

"Yeah," he told her, smiling.

Chapter Thirteen

"Do you mind if I ride along with you? Your father told me I could ride the horses. That they needed exercise when you were away."

Michael Borden looked around from the wall where some of the tack was hung. A tall, thin man, clean-shaven, short-haired, his clothes immaculate—spotlessly new blue jeans and a blue and white checked shirt beneath a black leather jacket. The jacket he recognized: It was uniform wear for the National Police.

The man's face seemed all at once to crack—into a smile, Michael supposed it should be called. "I'm Captain William Waterman." He walked from the stable doors with a broad, easy stride, extending his hand as he stopped and said, "It's a true pleasure to meet you, Comrade Dr. Borden. I have followed your athletic accomplishments for years. I, too, am something of an athlete."

Michael made himself smile as he took Waterman's hand. The grip was firm and almost as cold as ice. "Well, what do you do—I mean, besides being a captain in the National Police?" It was always good to set someone at ease, and the origin of the compliment was obvious enough. Waterman did seem marvelously fit.

"I pump a little iron."

"Yes—so do I." Michael nodded.

"I run."

"Yes—well, I do, too."

"I am training officer and commander for the National Police Special Operations Group."

"Well, then—you rappel, you climb mountains, you jump out of airplanes—"

"But only with a parachute," Waterman said with a laugh.

"Yes, you do look the sensible type." Michael Borden released Waterman's hand. "I'd welcome the company on a ride. Sometimes it's good to ride alone—as I'm sure you'll agree. But sometimes company is the thing."

"You and your parents have some fine animals here." Waterman walked toward the big black gelding with the three white stockings and the white blaze, slapping the animal on the neck like someone would heartily pat a friend on the back. The animal edged back from him slightly. "But I'll confess," Waterman continued, "that this is my favorite—a fine beast."

"I'd somehow thought he would be," Michael said good-naturedly. The color of the animal matched the color of Waterman's hair, eyes, and jacket. He had been planning to ride the black himself simply because almost no one else could ride the black. The horse was hard to handle and sometimes bad-tempered. But if Waterman wanted him, Waterman could have him. Michael took the bridle he wanted off the wall—a different one than the one he used with the black, a different bit. And he grabbed up the hand-tooled, high-cantled stock saddle. He started across the stable. "Now, this one—Scheherazade, I call her. She's my favorite."

She was more than part Arabian and had the coloring of an Appaloosa but not the conformation. She was incredibly large for a mare, but lean from the long runs he gave her every chance he got. "Come here," he whispered to her, and Scheherazade ambled from the rear of her stall, tossing her black mane. If an animal could have eyes that held human expression, she did.

"Don't like mares, myself," he heard Waterman remark from behind him. He didn't look away from Scheherazade.

"Well, if you ever ride Scheherazade, you'll change your mind."

"I did once—" Michael Borden turned around. Waterman was taking down a bridle from the wall. "She just didn't do a thing for me."

Michael turned away, to look again at Scheherazade—he

stroked her wide forehead between her big soft eyes. "You just have to treat her like a lady, that's all."

They had ridden in the same area, but it was in no way riding together. Michael had not given the mare her head, holding her back—letting her build to it gradually over the first twenty minutes or so. Captain Waterman stayed several hundred yards distant, reining the black gelding with the white stockings back as well.

The house bordered the mountains, the estate encroaching upon them, long grassy plains, long enough to land one of the MiG-Boeing SW-9 Shuttle craft, angling gently upward toward lower slopes. The green here was brilliant, seeming even more so to him after his most recent sojourn in North Africa, speaking before the troops there who fought against the Zionists and the Egyptians. He was a hero to them—and it was a thought that sobered him greatly. He had visited a field hospital, a dying boy trying to raise his head from his pillow, his eyes alight. "Comrade Michael Borden!"

Michael had gone to the boy, sat with him, overstayed his schedule. The boy—no more than eighteen—had memorized every detail of every event in which he, Michael, had competed. Heights, distances, times, world and Olympic records—and the boy had died of his wounds before Michael left him.

Michael stopped Scheherazade in a glen of sparkling icy pools of blue silver and pine trees of subtly different greens, holding the animal back for a while before letting her approach one of the pools from the stream nearby. He let her drink as he dismounted, but only a little, drawing her head back, walking her, watching the clouds of steam from her breath mingle with the steam of his own.

He buried his left hand in the muff pocket of the Soviet paratrooper winter jacket he wore. They had been fashionable in his college days, and it was so warm and durable that he had never gotten rid of it.

Michael heard the snorting of the black gelding. It was Waterman, dismounting, walking just a few feet away from him now. Michael asked, "Why am I so favored with your company, Captain?"

Waterman said, "I have heard rumors, Comrade Dr. Borden—very interesting rumors."

"One always hears rumors. The wise man ignores them."

"Yes," Waterman said too quickly. "But the wise man remembers them nonetheless for the rare instance when one of these worthless rumors becomes valuable fact."

"And what rumors have you heard?"

"That an important post—supremely important—may await you in the near future."

Michael stopped walking, holding Scheherazade's reins more tightly, her head nuzzling against his right shoulder. He looked at Waterman. "Some rumors are truly best forgotten, Captain."

"And I will take your advice, Comrade Dr. Borden. But before I totally wipe it from my mind, I feel compelled to speak."

"Compulsion can be a disease," Michael almost whispered. The air was very cool—and so was Waterman. Michael wondered how cool.

"But there are always risks—so I will take mine. If these rumors are true, and come to pass as fact—then I would like to put myself at your service."

Michael licked his lips. "The National Police already has a director—a fine one—if that's what you mean."

"Certainly—a finer director could not be found. It would require someone of almost infinite wisdom to select the proper man to be Arnold Borden's successor—when, of course, Comrade Borden might choose to retire or for some other reason leave his post."

Michael smiled. "You're asking me to promise you my father's job—I mean, if your rumors come to pass?"

"Yes."

"I should base this choice on your consummate discretion, perhaps?"

"No—but on my loyalty. If the opportunity ever presents itself and you should care to peruse my record, you would doubtlessly agree with me." Waterman smiled again. "Have you considered why I was placed in charge of the newly formed Special Operations Group?"

Michael continued walking, urging Scheherazade ahead.

"Just a random guess, of course. Ruthlessness? Physical abilities?"

"Yes, I suppose. Many men possess such qualities. But when coupled with absolute loyalty, well—the possibilities should seem obvious."

"A hatchet man—I believe that was the term?"

"Hatchet man?"

"Yes," Michael told him, drawing Scheherazade's reins back to the horn, gripping the horn in both fists and swinging up into the saddle. She reared back a little and he held her. "A hatchet man, if I understand the term properly, is someone who does the dirty jobs without question and without complaint. And is usually splendidly rewarded."

"Then I am a hatchet man."

"Yes—but they were originally Chinese, I believe. And considering Sino-Soviet relations these days, calling oneself a hatchet man might smack of counterrevolutionary tendencies. Race you to the rocks—there!" And Michael pointed to the far side of the plain, beyond the stream, letting Scheherazade rear back. Waterman vaulted into the saddle. "And you won't make points with me by letting me win, Captain."

Michael dug in his heels. Scheherazade leaped forward, as though jumping a hurdle, Michael molding his torso against her neck, knotting his hands in her mane as well as the reins but letting her go. "Come on, lady—move it!"

He glanced back. The black gelding was coming down, leaping ahead now, Waterman low in the saddle, lashing the tails of his reins back and forth across the animal, shouting to it, "Damn you—run!"

Michael Borden fell into Scheherazade's rhythm, the soft, steady thrumming of her hoofbeats against the grassy ground. Her mane lashed at his face; his eyes squinted against it, against the slipstream that ripped and clawed around them, his elbows down, flanking her powerful neck muscles. Gray clouds had intermittently obscured the sun since they had left the stables, but the clouds broke now, and as Michael's eyes scanned the ground ahead, he could see their silhouettes—his and that of Scheherazade, man and animal one, it seemed.

A different rhythm—heavier-sounding but no stronger, on his left.

He broke the silhouette—Waterman on the gelding. And Michael Borden cooed to the lady under him, "Scheherazade, come on, sweetheart—come on—faster, baby—come on."

Scheherazade reached the stream first, bounding into the water, the icy spray from her hooves surrounding them like a cloud shimmering in the new sunlight. The black gelding stepped into the stream now, too.

Michael urged Scheherazade ahead. "Through the water, lady—come on." The opposite bank—Michael wedging himself against her again, holding her back a little as she scrambled up, slipping once, catching herself, the black passing her. Waterman was reckless, but the gelding wasn't as fast. Like any wise man, Michael Borden wouldn't have proposed the race if the gelding had been.

But Waterman seemingly didn't care for the animal, hammering his heels into its sides, lashing it with his reins, shouting at the gelding as though he were some demon.

Michael Borden eased into the ride again, letting Scheherazade out slowly. The rocks that made their finish line were some five hundred yards ahead.

"Come on, girl—show them up." Scheherazade seemed to him as though she flew now, again his eyes focusing on their silhouette against the ground, the movement of her legs a shadowy blur, her mane whipping across his cheeks, froth from her lips spraying him, sweat glistening along her body.

Waterman and the gelding—Scheherazade was closing the gap.

"Everything, baby," Michael whispered to her over the wind that surrounded them. "Everything now." He held his elbows down, his fists curled back, barely holding the reins but locked to her mane, his knees drawing up, his feet tucking the stirrups up.

Four hundred yards . . . three hundred yards . . . Scheherazade was even with the gelding now.

Michael looked to his left. His eyes were even with Waterman's black eyes—and the eyes were strangely lit through the squinted lids. Waterman's right hand moved, a flash of steel, the steel arcing downward. Michael tried to pull Scheharazade away. He felt the saddle slipping beneath him,

Scheherazade's stride broken. Michael's hands locked tighter into her mane, the saddle going, Michael starting to lose his balance, pulling back on Scheherazade now, the mare reeling hard right. Michael's balance was all but gone, then letting himself go as she reared up, he rolled away from her, falling, his left shoulder hitting the ground. His body automatically went into a roll—like coming down from a less than graceful try over the high bar.

On his knees—he looked up. Scheherazade bounded away in a lazy circle, rearing again, then starting back for him.

Michael looked away from Scheherazade to William Waterman. The black was no longer black but veined with white lines of sweat and froth, Waterman's jeans stained with it as he vaulted down from the saddle. In his teeth the knife he had used to cut the cinch strap of Michael's saddle. "You called me a hatchet man. Well, I thought I'd impress you more by winning than losing—whatever it took."

Michael was to his feet, walking past Waterman, whistling up Scheherazade, the mare coming to him, whinnying, lowering her head to be stroked. He patted her, looking to her side where the cinch had been cut. There was no wound.

Michael turned to face Waterman. The National Police captain was folding his knife closed. "I wanted you to remember me, comrade Doctor. I think you will."

Michael started to swing to his left, then hammered his right forward, the middle knuckle catching Waterman on the left cheekbone. Waterman's head snapped back, and he sprawled backward.

Michael stood there—waiting. He had never been in a fight in his life—not even in grammar school.

Waterman stared up at him. "You know I could kill you with my bare hands."

"Yeah—I know."

"Because I cheated you in our race?"

"No—because you cheated her." And Michael jerked his thumb back over his shoulder toward Scheherazade.

Chapter Fourteen

He had told his father that he would not go to Moscow but instead spend the last few months his mother had to live, with her. But in the end he had seen his father's reasoning and spent a last few hours with his mother, promised to call her, to write, kissed her, held her in his arms, and left her. She had been sitting in the library in her wing chair. She had been wearing the earrings he had given her.

His father's line of reasoning had been simple and direct: Margaret Borden's obsession was and always had been Michael. That his life get under way, that his marriage to Svetlana go as planned was the greatest way to ensure her peace, her happiness.

It was the same plane in which he and his father had flown from Seattle to Denver—the newest, most comfortable, and fastest of the twin-engine jet passenger planes in the service of the National Security Directorate—and now he flew that plane.

He had tried reading the curriculum notes for the training session he would undergo to serve aboard the *Beacon of Peace*. He perused the *Beacon*'s history and purpose, though he knew it as well as he knew his own name.

"The Earth's first permanent manned artificial satellite was conceived early in the Era of Understanding between the United States and the Union of Soviet Socialist Republics, discussed in fact in the earliest talks between President Lester Saile and the Politburo of the Soviet Union. In the years separating conception and reality, an image of the *Beacon* emerged as a symbol for peace, harmony, and brotherhood throughout the world."

One hundred eighteen men and women could live,

work, exercise, recreate—thrive for the first time in the otherwise hostile environment of space, aboard the *Beacon*. There had been the wholly automated, periodically human-serviced factories, the heroic efforts of Soviet cosmonauts in long-duration space flight, and the abortive attempt by the warmongering United States military to construct and man a nuclear weapons platform in space. This last effort—culminating in the *Northstar* incident—had brought the world to the very brink of thermonuclear annihilation. Only due to the courage of Lester Saile and the wisdom and foresight of the Soviet leadership had global annihilation been forever averted.

He stopped to reflect upon the broadening scope of deterioration in Sino-Soviet relations; the Canadian situation; the volatile Middle East, where to prevent the slaughter of non-Jews by the Zionist militarists, the Soviet Union had twice tried to intercede, only to face still another threat, the treachery of Egypt. And of course there were still rebel bands of armed lunatics who haunted the high reaches of the mountains of the West, and some in the Appalachian chain as well. They lived like animals. It was reported that they at times resorted to cannibalism, that they reveled in rape and pedophilia.

Considering the state of the world was a sobering thought and at times a disheartening thought.

To the north there were thunderheads, rolling in quickly as he stared through the cabin window. It might well be a bumpy ride. He pressed the intercom button on the arm of his seat, speaking toward the grilled microphone within it. "Captain Letjak—what is our position?"

The voice came back through the speaker. "Comrade Doctor—we are ninety miles south of Chicago. I'm afraid we have been advised that due to severe weather conditions, we must divert our flight still farther southward until crossing the Appalachians, then proceed northeast along the coast to Brezhnev International."

He pushed the button again. "I thought we were landing at LaGuardia."

"LaGuardia has had an accident on the ground, comrade Doctor. All traffic is being rerouted to Newark or Brezhnev—but a helicopter will be standing by to take you to LaGuardia. It is only the main runway closed."

"Very well. Thank you." He nodded to the unseen pilot.

Michael stared again out the cabin window. The storms were fast-moving and looked heavy.

It was the curse of being a pilot relegated to the status of passenger—you flew the plane without being able to touch the controls. He would have climbed—but he told himself he did not know the full weather picture, and Captain Letjak, aside from being quite personable, also was quite competent. They had flown together once, Letjak piloting, Michael copiloting. That was perhaps the best way to judge the skills of the man at the controls.

For some reason, as he returned to his course notes, he thought of Captain Waterman. If Michael Borden someday became president and at some future date his father chose to retire as head of the National Security Forces, a man such as Waterman would be the last choice. A ruthless man who wielded such power would be a tyrant, not a guardian of the people.

Michael shook his head. He would have discussed Waterman with his father but had always avoided discussing his father's professional affairs. The National Defense Forces and the National Police were none of his concern—at least not yet.

Michael decided on the best course of action: to think of Svetlana and to sleep. It was far easier to sleep in her absence.

The explosion awakened him and he started to slump forward, then slammed backward, bracing himself with his hands against the arms of his seat. The cabin lights were out, the sky greenish and glowing as he looked through the cabin window. Chain lightning crackled across the sky.

"Shit!"

He punched the button on the console arm of his seat—nothing; the red diode did not even come on.

He looked up. The emergency power would have gotten the seat-belt sign illuminated if they had been struck by lightning, unless the emergency power was out. The seat-belt sign was not on.

Michael Borden hit the release button for his seat belt, lurching to his feet, steadying himself with his hands against the cabin bulkhead to his left and the overhead, moving forward, fighting the downward slope of the cabin. He slammed himself against the cockpit door. The aircraft pitched violently under him, his body sprawling back against the portside bulkhead. But he caught himself with his hands against the wet bar, the wine bottles in the racks behind the glass bursting, the glass shattering. Pressure. He could feel the changing pressure in his ears now, in his shortness of breath.

He launched himself toward the cockpit door again, wrenching at the handle with his right hand, nearly tearing the handle clear of the door. The door swung outward. Michael pushed himself through the opening, rain battering at his face and his hands, wind tearing at him.

The copilot—John Farmer—was dead, a shard of glass the size of a butcher knife through his throat. The pilot—Milton Letjak—fought the controls, hands, face streaked with blood, the windshield smashed on the copilot's side.

It was as if Letjak sensed him there, because Letjak's face never turned from staring straight ahead and down. "Lightning—struck the avionics package in the nose! Must've been a short! The windshield blew in and the instruments are gone!"

"So's the cabin pressure!" Michael shouted back, wrenching the dead John Farmer from his seat, the head half severed. He shouted to Letjak, "I'm going to clear the rest of the big shards from the windshield—protect your eyes!" He lurched forward, grabbing at the bulkhead-mounted fire extinguisher, tearing it clear of its mounting. He used the butt of it to hammer out the glass fragments, the fragments flying inward as he turned away. Again he used the extinguisher, a large fragment just missing him as it was blown inward.

Satisfied it was at least halfway safe to take the copilot's chair, he threw himself down, strapping in. "What can I do?" He grabbed the copilot's yoke and tried pulling back. Nothing responded.

"We're goin' down, comrade Doctor!"

"No shit!" Michael shouted back, his eyes squinting against the rain. "Damn Russian wiring!" None of the gauges showed anything but malfunction. He peered to starboard—the starboard engine was running. "How's the port engine?"

"Dead, sir!"

"Radio, is that gone?"

"Yes, sir—dead, too."

"You got anything at all?"

"Negative—but I'm tryin'."

"Right!" Michael thought of Svetlana, of his mother—of his father, too. "Damn," he said with a rasp, tugging at the yoke. Nothing.

"Any flaps, Captain?"

"I don't—wait—"

"Here..." Michael reached up, working the controls for the flaps, slowly, so slowly that if they were reacting it was almost impossible to tell. But if he moved the flaps too fast— "Landing gear was up, right?"

"Right."

"Gonna make this sucker a glider as soon as we break through the clouds. Lock her into a flight path with the flaps and just ride her down—only chance."

"Like they landed the early Space Shuttles. That's suicide."

"We can't kill ourselves if we're dead already—and so far that's what it looks like. Can you cut the starboard engine?"

"Yeah—just cut off her fuel—"

"Do it—when I say."

He turned his face at a forty-five-degree angle to the wind and the rain that assaulted him through the open windshield, peering into the cloud layer, lightning crackling about them, hail now adding to the rain. "We're comin' down fast, Letjak." And for an instant the cloud covering broke— mountain peaks, a valley beyond, incredibly green, the rain coming at him more heavily now. "Do it—cut the fuel!"

He worked the flaps, the nose coming up, up, the drone of the jet engine gone, only the dull roar of the wind drowning out all other sound.

He had no way of knowing if the flaps were really responding—but he used them now to turn the aircraft to starboard, slowly. He aimed it into the valley floor, giving both flaps less angle now, trying to bring the nose up—it was rising.

"We're gonna die, comrade Doctor!"

Michael played the flaps now, holding the yoke under his right fist. Slowly now, very slowly, he was lowering them. It was futile—because they were coming in too fast. As soon as the fuselage undercarriage made ground contact they would start to roll, to break up. But at least if you told yourself defeat wasn't inevitable, it gave you something to do, he told himself.

If he had tried the landing gear, the first touch would

pitch them forward, he knew—and manually braking the aircraft would be impossible even now. And if when the electrical system had gone, the landing gear had inadvertently, undetected, dropped... He didn't consider it any longer—if it had, he wouldn't be alive to consider it, anyway.

The ground—it was foolish to think of the ground coming up, because it was just the opposite: You and the plane went down. He gave the craft full flaps, bracing himself as he locked both fists against the yoke—not for control, but to wedge himself. The sound of impact—thudding, scraping, tearing, the fuselage vibrating insanely. The plane twisted to starboard, the starboard wing ripping half away, dragging now—rocks. He thought of the name his mother sometimes called in the throes of her pain: Jesus. He whispered it. The portside wing was gone, the fuselage rocking to right and left, bouncing. He braced his neck with his hands, his left shoulder against the instrument panel—nothing else he could do....

Chapter Fifteen

Michael opened his eyes. His left shoulder began to shudder with pain as he moved it. But he was used to assessing his own injuries. He moved his fingers before moving his body any further, feeling first at the shoulder, then at the collarbone, for dislocation or a break. Then along the upper arm, then the elbow, then the forearm. It was trauma only, and slowly, as he raised his head and inched back from the instrument panel, he mentally cataloged each muscle group, each joint. All worked, seemed free to move.

He smelled jet fuel—but the smell of it was somehow more unnatural than it should be.

He sat fully upright, banging his head—part of the overhead had buckled inward.

He looked to his side. Milton Letjak was unconscious or

dead. He reached out and touched Letjak. Unconscious only; certainly not dead, the pulse strong.

Michael on one level began to assay their surroundings; on still another level of consciousness he examined Letjak as best as could be done without either of them moving. The cockpit was partially crushed—rocks jutted out some three feet away from the windshield opening. The fingers of Letjak's left hand had what felt like multiple fractures. "Wonderful," he murmured. Letjak's right temple was bleeding. Apparently they were on solid ground. If the jet fuel hadn't caught fire yet there was no reason to suppose it would, but the smell meant something very serious in the offing. To move Letjak might be murder. He began exploring the vital areas that movement might exacerbate, and he released his own seat belt and Letjak's to do that.

No obvious major fractures of the limbs. He felt at the ribs. "Shit." The third and fourth right ribs felt broken. "Shit," Michael muttered again. He looked behind them—at the door leading from the cockpit to the main cabin. The doorway was blocked, and the first-aid kit was in the main cabin. His medical bag was in the luggage compartment. He made a mental note never to do something that dumb ever again.

He completed examining Letjak—no broken back or broken neck. The right leg—the tibia seemed broken. "Fucking wonderful, Captain Letjak. Thanks a whole lot."

The funny smell of the jet fuel was getting stronger. It was time to leave the cabin.

He reached to his waist, undoing his trouser belt. It was lucky for Letjak that the man wasn't broad-chested—Michael thought it just might fit. It did, around the rib cage over the breaks. He secured it on the last hole. The leg was a different problem. The bone didn't protrude through the skin, but dragging Letjak through the cockpit door or a window might make it do so unless the bone had some support.

But there was nothing in the cabin he could use as a splint. "Oh, boy," he said with a groan, removing Letjak's trouser belt. But as he did, he noticed a clipboard with flight information logged into it.

The clipboard would serve as a splint, at least for the moment.

He stripped the data from the clip, then braced the leg with the clipboard and tightened the belt.

Michael began looking for a way out. There was no cockpit door. It would have to be the already-broken window. He searched the floor for the fire extinguisher. Finding it, he logged this as another possible splint, but now used it to knock away the remaining pieces of glass in the windshield frame in front of him. He could hear the drumming of rain, even hail on the remnants of the fuselage; he could hear the sounds of high winds whistling through the aft section.

He set the fire extinguisher on the copilot's chair as he stood in a crouch. Flashlight—another splint if needed, but more important as a light source. It would be dark soon. And in the mountains there could be wild animals, sudden drops into an abyss. He set the flashlight beside the fire extinguisher.

Between the seats was Letjak's flight bag—a large, accordion-style briefcase. He grabbed it up, placing it on the seat.

Letjak was beginning to stir. Michael began to talk to the man. "How you doin' there, huh? Man, I tell you—I'm gonna fly with you every time. You gotta be the luckiest damn pilot born, Milton. They call you Milton? Or how about Milt?"

"I hurt, comrade—"

"Cut the 'comrade,' huh? I mean, the name's Michael—leave it at that. And sure you hurt—got a couple of ribs that got banged up and got a little fracture in your right leg and a bump on the head; but don't worry about the blood. Head wounds do a lot of superficial bleeding but they're no big thing, Milt. We're gonna get outa here—and unfortunately it's going to be through the window. Always hate leaving by the back door, I tell you."

He started to move Letjak, who passed out, which Michael considered under the circumstances as being just as well. But he kept talking to the pilot anyway, in case Letjak was just on the edge. It wasn't bedside manner, just common sense. Distract the patient from his injuries, bring him out of his pain with something else to think about. Sometimes this kept the patient alive because you kept him too busy to die.

"So—where you think we're at, Milt, huh?" He judged they had been blown considerably off course to be in mountains such as he had seen when the clouds had parted. The smell was getting worse. "I figure Tennessee or North Carolina—maybe Georgia—but somewhere in that knot of mountains. Don't have to talk—I like to talk. They give doctors a special course in talking to patients—helps out the people who make pain pills. The patients need more of 'em that way. Hey, Milt . . ." Michael had the man already out of the seat. "You ever do this before—I mean, climb through the window of an airplane? Boy, I tell ya, it's the first time for me. Quite a thrill . . ." Almost as much as being on the receiving end of a proctoscopy, Michael mused.

Michael rested Letjak half in one seat, half in the other, moving the leg as gently as he could. He searched his sport-coat pockets—his identity papers, his travel permits, his wallet with the pictures of his parents and the picture of Svetlana—he stuffed all of these into his trousers. He cursed himself for not smoking—he didn't have matches or a lighter with which to start a fire. He stripped his coat away, making the tweed jacket into a drag, tying the sleeves across Letjak's chest but safely under the armpits and clear of the rib cage. It was easier to haul him this way, tugging at handfuls of his coat rather than handfuls of Letjak. He pulled, watching it with the leg, dragging Letjak up, then catching him under the armpits.

He began easing the pilot through the window. "You know, just between you and me, Milt, I don't think windows are ever going to replace doors—no shit." He held Letjak half in the cockpit, half on the burn-scarred nose of the craft. There was enough room, so Michael climbed up, pushing himself through, across, and over Letjak, then out onto the nose. The surface was wet and a little slippery. He could see now: The fuselage was crammed between two outcroppings of rock, but solid ground seemed to be beneath them. It was coming onto darkness, or perhaps it was only the rain. He looked at his Rolex for an instant; it had survived the impact. And it wasn't coming onto dark, just the rain and the cloud cover.

Michael pulled Letjak the rest of the way through, rain washing over him as it was driven on the wind against the rocks.

The jet fuel smell was stronger out here.

He looked to both sides of the fuselage. The side on his

right—the aircraft's port side—seeming more even. Then he jumped down.

Rain washed across him. The smell was even stronger here. Michael reached up, taking Letjak into his arms, easing the stricken pilot from the nose of the plane. The skid marks of the aircraft were visible across the green of the clearing, long furrows of black-and-copper-colored mud. His feet sank in it under the combined weight of his body and the pilot's. Getting the man clear of the aircraft was his primary concern. Twenty yards. Another twenty—he wanted at least two hundred for safety. Half the length of one of the wings, from the stem outward, lay perhaps a hundred seventy-five yards to the right. Michael started for it—shelter, however meager, for Letjak.

The mud squished beneath his feet, the rain slashed at him, driven on the wind, hailstones of varying sizes—some impossibly large—still falling, chain lightning crackling through the sky, and the dull booming of thunder.

He reached the wing section, balancing on one foot, kicking against it to verify the sturdiness of its position wedged into the mud. The wing section barely moved. Satisfied, he set Letjak down, removing the sodden sport coat he had tied about Letjak's body, folding the dry side up into a pillow so he could rest Letjak's head against it. "Milt, be right back—hang in there. I'll be able to see you and you'll be able to see me all the time if you open your eyes."

Letjak groaned something in reply. Michael had no time to worry what. He threw himself into a sprint, slogging across the mud and back toward the aircraft. Getting his medical bag from the fuselage luggage compartment would take longer. He went for the briefcase, flashlight, and fire extinguisher instead, clambering back onto the aircraft's nose, half crawling back into the cockpit. He grabbed all three objects, opening the briefcase—it was unlocked. No time to look inside. He stuffed the flashlight into it, closed the briefcase, then stood to his full height atop the nose, hurtling the briefcase in the direction of Letjak and the wing section as far from the aircraft as he could. There was no need to keep the integrity of the fire extinguisher canister—he wanted it only for possible splinting use. Michael hurtled this away as well, jumping down to the ground now.

A piece of granite of irregular shape but similar in size to a house brick would help. He picked it up, crawling beneath a sheared section of the fuselage—the smell was stronger now and acrid, as though burning. But he must reach the medical bag and warm clothing. Here in the mountains it could mean the difference between life and death for Letjak, perhaps himself.

He tried the compartment latch—jammed.

He smashed the chunk of granite against the locking mechanism again and again, the lock shattering just as the granite chunk split. Michael threw it down, tearing open the luggage compartment. His medical bag. He set it on the ground beside him. He grabbed his flight bag with his Russian paratrooper jacket lashed to the outside. He stood, hurtling the bag as far from the aircraft as he could. His suitbag—he left it, clean shirts his last concern. Another bag—presumably the pilot's. He grabbed it up, his medical bag now in his other hand, pushing up to his full height, telling himself the starting pistol had been fired, running.

There was a crackling sound now. He didn't look back. A roar—something slapped against his shoulders and back. He hurtled Letjak's bag away, throwing himself forward, tucking his medical bag against his body to protect it, his left hand and arm covering up to protect his head. The roaring sound was impossibly loud, his ears ringing with it as his body slid across the mud ruts in the field. He could feel things—hot— impacting his back, his legs, his face buried against the mud.

The rain of debris stopped, hailstones still pelting the ground, rain coming in torrents. He rolled onto his back in the mud and stared back toward the origin of the explosion. The fuselage was gone.

"Did you see that?"

"What?"

"Well, you didn't see it then or you'd know what—at least what you thought it was."

"What the hell are you talking about?"

"Remember—a half hour ago—that funny sound you said was thunder and I said was an explosion?"

"Yeah. I remember the thunder—you remember the explosion."

"All right. But did you hear that?"

"I thought I was supposed to see something."

"That loud thunderclap?"

"You can't see thunder—I've told you that ever since you were a little girl. You hear thunder, you see lightning."

"Okay. Well, I heard something that was louder than thunder and saw a fireball."

"Where?" Martin Deacon stood up and walked to the mouth of the cave, where Alice stood.

She stretched her right hand out into the rain. "There— that way, Daddy." She was still pointing. Martin watched her fingers—her hands were delicate, like her mother's had been. But she was strong, could outrun most men, was tough. But like her mother, she was also gentle, pretty. It was the strength that mattered. Alice was alive because of it, and her mother was not—because of it.

"I think it was a plane, Daddy—I think a plane crashed and blew up."

"You see how it's raining out there—we got six people plus ourselves who just started to dry out." The smell of the pecan wood burning was strong, the crackling and hissing of the wood was its sound.

"Okay, I'll go. Just the other side of the ridge. Can't be more than a mile or so."

"Women and distance—Jesus! Try three miles, maybe four."

"Okay, so three or four miles."

"I'm not lettin' you go over there alone. What about the Natpos?"

"Fuck the Natpos. You should pardon the expression—"

"I don't like you talkin' like that, Alice."

"What if—well, what if?"

"What if what? It had to be a Russian plane, or a Natpo plane."

"What if it was a civilian plane, a passenger plane? There could be people hurt, Daddy."

Martin Deacon looked back to the fire. He could sense its warmth. Showalter, Hotchkiss, Chen, Mary Stankowski, Rainwater, and O'Brien were all there.

"Alice and I'll be over the ridge just north of here. If we're not back in six hours, come looking for us, huh?"

Harriet Rainwater volunteered, "Hey, I'll go with Alice—couldn't help overhearing." Her chubby face lit with a smile.

Martin Deacon shook his head. "Good excuse for a walk alone with my girl."

All of them laughed except Hotchkiss, who hadn't laughed in a very long time—but Hotchkiss had reason not to laugh, Deacon reflected. They had been walking for two days, evading Natpo and Spetznas patrols searching for them, not even trying to reach their base camp but instead to link up with the Cherokees. Isolated members of the Cherokee Nation had been involved in Resistance work since the beginning, since the days of James Hope. But it had been only a little over a decade since the Eastern Cherokee Tribal Council had elected a war chief and declared a policy of total resistance to the current puppet government and the Soviet Union. It had come too late to turn things around, but the declaration had infused much-needed new blood and finances into the Resistance, and more and better places to hide. The reservation lands were virtually unknown to the Natpos at the time of the Declaration, and under the inspired military leadership of Horace "Jake" Brown, the deepest parts of reservation land were impervious to everything but aerial reconnaissance and air strikes. Brown had simply outsmarted the Natpos and the Spetznas.

And it was to the stronghold of Jake Brown that they were headed—to rest, to bum fresh supplies of ammunition and medical stores, to have a safe place to hide until the Natpos cooled down and cut their strength in the mountains again. With the help of the Western Cherokee and other Indian tribal councils throughout the United States, Brown had formed a decent Intelligence network and almost more importantly, a supply network. The most ready source of ammunition supply was through Canada, most of it from Canada. After the Civilian Disarmament Act and the Subervision Acts many of the designers and engineers from the larger American ammunition manufacturers had fled across the border to avoid persecution and to continue their livelihood. Gradually the eastern provinces of Canada became the new arms and ammunition center of North America, Canada rearming as the United States disarmed, much of this at the behest of England. Canada was also the only source for the

Resistance of replacement parts, magazines, and explosives. It was partly for this reason, Deacon had always understood, that the Soviets had begun the invasion of Canada across the Bering Strait, from Buffalo, and from Washington State fifteen years ago. But the invasion had stalled in the wild country of Canada just as it had stalled in the wild country of the United States. It was said that parts of Montana and Idaho held communities where no National Police, Spetznas, or regular Soviet Army had ever been seen.

They left the cave, Martin slinging his M-16 crossbody under his right arm, his pack slung on his back. Alice hand-carried her M-16, like a piece of luggage by the carrying handle. Rain was falling steadily and hailstones were on the ground, melting now, no hail falling since they had begun the trek. She looked ridiculously tiny, the rain poncho covering her like a tent, the lip of the hood extending well forward of her face.

"You know, this could be something else we're walking into," he told his daughter, breaking the silence that had endured for nearly a mile as he reckoned it. They were ascending to the height of the ridge, the ground loose, slippery, the going slow. He had decided upon six hours as maximum round-trip time before leaving the cave, leaving the rest of the Resistance team. "I said, this could be something else, kid—maybe a trap, maybe some Natpo setup."

"I don't think so," she answered offhandedly.

He had no idea whom she took after, in either his wife's family or his own. She had his wife's diminutive size, the appearance of delicacy, but skin coloring, hair color, eye color—none of these characteristics fit either of them. Her hair was red, her eyes a bright yet deep green. She was fair, freckled on her back, her shoulders, even a few freckles remaining on her face, though most of those had vanished with maturity. His first child had been more olive-complected, like his wife and himself. Young James Deacon had died at age sixteen in a fire fight with the Spetznas and the Natpos, hurtling his body over a grenade to save the lives of his friends and giving his life in the process.

Martin's wife, Linda, had died giving birth to Alice when James had been only five. And at eleven, when young James had died, Alice had stopped playing with dolls, stopped staying among the women of the camp and cried, screamed, and raged until Martin had shown her how to use a gun and pledged that as soon as she could use one well enough, she could fight. At age twenty-four, she was nearly halfway through the dog-eared set of *Britannica III* that had become their band's primary source of teaching. When she wasn't fighting, she worked with the young, teaching—both from books and from experience, the ways of warfare.

She had become as good as or better than any of his men. She had taken to martial-arts instruction, the use of a knife, and the use of firearms like second nature.

They were climbing almost vertically now, Alice moving rapidly. Finally he called up to her, "Hey, kid—remember how old I am?"

"Who could forget?" she called back, laughing.

"So slow up already."

"Bullshit." She laughed back, but she slowed.

Before going down into the valley that lay on the far side of the ridge, he planned to use his binoculars—the ones given him by James Hope that last night—and scan the ridgeline and the valley below. He had been halfway joking about a Natpo or Spetznas trap, but it was possible. The Natpos at least in recent years seemed to avoid combat under bad weather conditions—the laziness that came with too much success, he had often assumed. And the bad weather had become the best times to travel. The heavier the rain, the colder the air, the deeper the snow in the mountains, the safer it was—at least from the Natpos. Although the Spetznas were better fighters and were known to torture captives for information, the Spetznas usually would grant their captives an honorable death. But the Natpos would torture, just for the fun of it, it seemed. And the means of execution they would choose were oftentimes several levels beneath barbarism.

He had seen a man once who had fallen into the hands of the Natpos. His tongue had been stitched to his lower lip with wire and his nostrils split—blood would have run from the nose constantly, seeping into the mouth via the distended tongue. The man had been stripped naked and buried in snow up to his chin, left to die that way.

Martin had buried the body, Alice helping him. And the man wasn't even in the Resistance.

Alice was waiting for him, prone across the rocks as he reached the height of the ridge. He dragged his bones across the rocks and lay there beside her, catching his breath. "This war better get over real soon. I need a rest."

"You're stronger and tougher than any man you've got in the Resistance, even if you are older. And I should know, because I'm stronger and tougher than you are." She smiled.

She had a very cute little nose that wrinkled when she smiled. A raindrop fell from the hood of her poncho and settled on the very tip of her nose, and with the back of her left hand she brushed the raindrop away.

Martin Deacon shrugged. Women are crazy, he thought, and had thought for some time. His daughter just confirmed his suspicions. He reached under his poncho, finding the case for the binoculars. They were 8X30s, black rubber armored. The case and the binoculars had no common origin, had never had. James Hope had told him once that the binoculars had been imported only for a short period of time, and when they had first come into the country, no case had been offered, so James Hope had one built for it. The case—black ballistic nylon—was rock-scoured and muddy. The lens caps no longer read "Aimpoint." But the binoculars were as clear as they had been the first time James Hope had let him look through them. He settled them to his eyes. As the years had gone by, the focusing became harder, not because of a defect in the 8X30s, but because of his eyes. Fortunately, his arms were still long enough for reading.

He worked the individual focus knobs, first scanning the ridgeline.

"Daddy, I see something—those furrows. Follow them back."

"I'm checking the ridgeline. I'm more concerned about an ambush."

"It was a plane crash! Look!"

Martin Deacon gave up. In some ways Alice reminded him of Jennifer Hope—Jennifer was Alice's middle name. Just as gutsy, just as reckless, even a better fighter because she had grown up with it. And just as stubborn. He swung the glasses toward the valley floor. Long black and red clay furrows were plowed across the green of grass and late-summer wildflowers. Chunks of aircraft were littered about the valley like discarded toys of some giant child. He looked to the very base of the ridge—a blackened crater. The aircraft would have exploded there.

"Daddy, over there—to your right—hurry!"

He swung the glasses obediently in the direction indicated. He saw what looked like two men, one carrying the other on his back.

"That's a National Security Directorate plane. See the markings?"

"How can I see the markings? You've got the binoculars."

"Okay, okay. And there's two guys out there."

"All right. Let's check 'em out. If they're alive and well when we get to them and they're Natpos or somethin', fine—we kill 'em. If they're injured, we fix 'em up and kill 'em. But we can't just leave 'em."

"Why do I listen to you? Probably radioed in their position . . ."

Alice took the binoculars from him, fiddled with the focus knobs for a minute, and stared down into the valley. Deacon just shook his head. "If they radioed for help before they went down and gave a position, they'd stay with the aircraft, right?"

"Right." He nodded.

"So they didn't radio, because they're going away from the aircraft. And anyway, the one big one is carrying the smaller one on his back. The little guy must be hurt."

"Jees—all right!" Deacon took the binoculars back, continuing to scan the ridgeline—it still could be a trap. He had no idea who the hell these men were.

Michael had decided to leave the valley because they had been too exposed there. The mountains of Tennessee and North Carolina crawled with the self-styled Resistance fighters who killed anyone who wasn't one of them.

Milton Letjak had regained consciousness, and Michael had gotten their last position from the man. But after a time Letjak had fallen into the deep sleep of exhaustion. Michael had changed them both into warmer, dry clothing, though it hadn't stayed dry for long. Then he scrounged from his flight bag and Letjak's flight bag what might prove useful—extra socks, a sweater for each of them, the cockpit flashlight, an aerial map of the terrain. He had packed it all along with his medical bag into his own flight bag. And he wore the Russian paratrooper's jacket—which was insane, he knew, in the territory of the gun fanatics, but it would be equally as insane to suffer in the wet and be cold.

The gun lunatics—he thought of them now. And for a moment, he wished that he, too, had a gun, like one of the ones Marshal Blotsky had let him try. There was a Swiss Army knife in his medical bag. It was their only weapon, and hardly something designed for use as a weapon.

He could throw rocks, or he could find a stout piece of tree limb and use it as a club, he supposed. In one of the proscribed books he had read—all students read proscribed books simply because they were proscribed—the scientist Einstein, who had worked under President Franklin D. Roosevelt to perfect the atomic bomb for the United States to use against her ally Russia, had said he had no idea what the weapons of World War III would be, but World War IV would be fought with rocks and clubs.

Fine words for a man who had duped the American people and planned to vaporize their Soviet comrades.

He kept walking, turning his mind away from Letjak's weight on his back. Mercifully, Letjak still slept. He had over six inches on Letjak's five-foot-ten frame and outweighed him by fifty pounds; he had judged Letjak at about one-sixty.

From the map, it seemed they were not too many miles from Chattanooga and its environs. Chattanooga was civilized. Considerable Soviet or National Security Directorate traffic would be on the roads. And, of course, once the plane did not arrive at Brezhnev International in New York, a search would be started. The closer he could get himself and Letjak to Chattanooga, the speedier their rescue, he reasoned. As best he could fathom—and he had taken the astronaut survival courses, had always felt at home in the woods—he was heading almost due west.

If the rain would stop and the cloud cover clear before sunset, a more precise fix could be taken, perhaps saving them miles of useless travel.

Michael kept walking.

He began to talk to the sleeping Letjak. "Milt, everything's going to be fine—just fine." But he was talking more to himself, trying to convince himself more than Letjak.

They reached the far end of the valley now, and there were two ways up toward the ridgeline that blocked his path; one was rocky and steep, the other a gentler incline. Michael took the second path, starting up along it, careful of his footing—wet pine needles, leaves, and the grass itself made for slippery footing.

The tree cover was starting to close in, and he liked the idea of it. It would be too early for search planes, even if Chattanooga had them on radar when they went down. And the trees would provide some measure of cover from the armed lunatics he feared.

The path took a bend, almost a right angle, but to his left, and he followed it, the added pull of the incline making his burden seem all the greater. But there was no convenient place to put Letjak down, and the pilot still slept.

Michael kept walking.

Pine trees, magnificent in their diversity, reminded him of the trees that dotted the lower elevations near his home in Colorado.

"Move and you're dead meat, fella!"

It was a woman's voice. Michael turned to face the voice. But he saw no one.

"She means it!" A man's voice, older but strong-sounding, too.

"Hey—look, I got an injured man here. Broken leg, broken ribs, some broken fingers, maybe a slight concussion."

"Shut up," the woman's voice called out. The voice sounded too sweet to mean it really, but somehow Michael thought she did.

"Look—I'm unarmed." Michael extended his hands from his sides. He repeated, "Unarmed."

It was the man's voice again. "Hate to say this, but if you're unarmed, you're an asshole." Michael was inclined to agree at this point.

Then he heard the woman's voice again—all the threat was gone from it, a softness there that somehow he liked. "But God, he's pretty, though." She laughed.

Chapter Sixteen

Martin Deacon had been watching the young man intently, as if Michael were a ghost from the long-ago past.

They had erected a shelter beneath the trees and brought the injured man—a pilot, Michael had said—in out of the rain that still bled down from the darkening gray skies. The young man named Michael had said he was a doctor, then set to treating the pilot—examining his splint, examining the bandaged rib cage, checking the tape that held the bandages in place. She had volunteered to help change the pilot out of his wet clothes, and her father had surprised her by flat out telling her she couldn't. She had waited outside for several minutes. Shortly Michael and then her father had emerged into the rain.

"So what the hell was wrong with helping to change him? He's got two of 'em or something?"

Her father just looked at her and turned away for a second, then spoke but didn't turn back. "Alice, you know who this man says he is?"

"No."

"He's Michael Borden. Now, nobody'd be damn fool enough to say they was a Borden unless they were, not to me. And even if he is a damn fool, he's an honest one."

"Borden—"

"Three-time Olympic gold medalist in the decathlon, doctor of medicine, shining young star of the Kremlin—"

"Knock it off, huh?" It was the young man speaking. She looked at him, said nothing.

"Son of Arnold Borden—that's who he is."

She stabbed the M-16 toward him. "Mother-fucker—"

"Shut up, Alice—now!"

She looked at her father. She never remembered him

154

telling her to shut up—well, maybe just once or twice, she told herself. He was good-looking, this son of the murderous bastard any man or woman in the Resistance would have willingly endured torture or death to kill.

"What are you going to do, try to use me as a lever against my father?"

"No," Deacon told him.

"Kill us—or what? At least spare Milton Letjak—all he is is a pilot, a chauffeur. And he needs attention."

"You're a doctor," Martin Deacon said, staring at him. "You can attend him. And we don't kill wounded men. We wait till they're well." Her father's eyes smiled. "What have you heard about us?"

Her eyes moved to the young man's gray eyes. His eyes flickered once, then set hard. They were pretty eyes, she thought. He had a high forehead, his hair thick, dark brown, longer than the hair styles of the Natpos and the Spetznas but not as long as her father's. He was about thirty, she guessed, six-foot-four, from the set of his arms and his shoulders, muscular, and she found herself smiling at that. Men like this built muscles, her father had told her, but for no purpose, she thought. The purpose for strength was to fight the enemy. But she wondered—an athlete, an Olympian—who was he?

"Well, what have you heard about us?" Her father squared off, facing Michael Borden through the rain.

"That you kill anyone who isn't one of your own band of lunatics, that you sometimes resort to cannibalism, that—"

"Shut up!" she screamed. "You lying—"

"No, Alice." She glared at her father, and her father still looked at Michael Borden. "You heard wrong, son. I'm gonna prove that to you. You could never walk your pilot friend out without him dying on you, and if you left him here alone there's wild dogs, other things might easily kill an unarmed man. And if you left him with us, you'd be thinkin' we killed him. So you're both stayin' with us. And while his body heals, well, your mind can heal. You can learn the truth about the Americans who fight for freedom, not the Commie crap you've been fed."

"Truth—the truth of crazy men who value killing over everything else, who live like animals, who stalk other human beings? Is that your truth?"

She watched as her father closed his eyes. "No—and if you open your mind to it, you'll be able to tell easy enough who's telling the truth and who's telling the lies."

"Then I'm a prisoner." It was a statement, not a question.

"Prisoner or guest, your choice. Don't make no difference to me," Deacon answered.

"How does one answer an invitation from a man wearing two knives, two handguns, and carrying a rifle?"

Alice's eyes never left her father as Michael Borden had answered him, and now she started to laugh, her father telling him, "That's only the stuff you can see, son." And Michael Borden laughed, too.

They had walked well into the night. Michael took shifts with some of the Resistance people, litter-carrying Letjak, who was sedated to ease the strain of travel. Michael still rubbed his forearms—they ached from the strain of the dead weight of the litter—and he walked beside the one called Martin Deacon. The very pretty girl named Alice, who was Deacon's daughter, strode ahead of them, breaking the trail.

"Tell me something," Michael began.

"That's why we're keepin' you with us, Dr. Borden—so I can tell you something. So ask away."

"You have abdominal pain—"

"None of your business," Deacon snapped. "Ask me about something else."

Michael shook his head, looking down toward his feet— he had changed into the hiking boots he had packed for the Moscow winter. "That's a stupid attitude—let a problem like that go unchecked and—"

"Look, son, you either shut up or change the subject. Got me?"

Michael shrugged. "All right. Why are you here?"

"This little walk of ours should be ending in about an hour—at least for the night. There isn't enough time to give you a proper answer."

"So start. I've got nothing but time, it looks like."

He looked at Deacon hard when he said it, and Deacon's face remained unmoved. The rain had stopped, the cloud cover breaking, giving way to a full moon under which it was almost bright enough to read. Deacon began to speak. "I was like a lot of other folks—fewer of us these days, maybe, thanks to the brainwashing they done on young folks like you."

"Why not your daughter?"

"She was born out here, raised out here."

"So you brainwashed her instead," Michael told him.

"No—let her see the truth. How the Natpos kill sometimes just for the fun of it; how human rights are just a thing of the past far as the government's concerned. How the Commies control the United States through Lester Saile as their puppet; how the Commies caused the death of my son, her brother, and forced us into exile so when Alice was born there wasn't any doctor and my wife died. How they killed my best friend—James Hope—and killed his wife. It was Arnold Borden who did it, and Marshal Blotsky. They even killed Hope's boy Stephen—worthless shit that he was."

Michael shook his head. "You've got it wrong. Marshal Blotsky told me how it was. They cornered James Hope, and Stephen Hope was with them. Stephen picked up an assault rifle and killed his mother, his father, and their newborn child." Michael picked his way over a rise in the ground, the footing slippery with the mud from the day's rains. "Then some member of the Resistance killed Stephen Hope. The whole family was wiped out."

"There was a daughter. Did they ever tell you about Jennifer?"

"I don't remember mention of a daughter," Michael answered.

"She died trying to save her father and a bunch of Resistance fighters when they walked into a Spetznas trap. Caught 'em in the open at the base of the spillway there on the Ocoee River—"

"I don't know the area," Michael interjected.

"Well, the Spetznas under Blotsky started shootin' and then opened the spillway. Them that didn't get shot drowned or smashed on the rocks, and the few that tried climbing out on the banks of the river got shot as they left the water. Jennifer was covering them. This is the way her father told it to me. She saw what was happening and she lit out across this suspension bridge they had—knocked out the Spetznas machine gunner, turned the gun on the Spetznas themselves.

Another one of the Spetznas got up there. She fought him with a knife and she got shot. Emptied the drum for the machine gun, was goin' for more ammo or a rifle or somethin'. Anyway, the Spetznas got up there on the bridge, took a few of 'em, and they bayoneted her."

"Sounds like a brave girl," Michael said, knowing nothing else to say.

"She was. My Alice is like her."

Michael asked something that suddenly came to his mind, after the shooting session with Marshal Blotsky. "Answer me this: I understand this James Hope carried some special guns—"

"Two Detonics Scoremaster .45s—stainless steel, his last name engraved on the right-slide flat of each of 'em. Most accurate .45s they made, and the strongest, too. They disappeared after he was murdered. But I got Jennifer's knife—it's the knife my daughter Alice carries."

For some reason, the thought of Alice—loudmouthed and very pretty—going into combat with a knife that had belonged to a dead girl made him shiver. "You want your daughter to . . ." He couldn't finish the question.

"To die like Jennifer Hope? Tell you somethin', Doctor—"

"Michael—"

"Michael—I'll tell ya somethin'. My son died when he was just a kid, but he was more a man than most men ever get to be. Died fighting for freedom. He saved the lives of maybe a dozen others by throwin' his body on a grenade—"

"Aww, shit," Michael said with a hiss.

"Yeah—it wasn't pretty. He died instantly, they tell me—if he didn't, he died well. So you asked about Alice. Would I want her dyin' like Jennifer Hope died? Well, I don't want her dyin' at all, but I'd rather have her die fighting for freedom than have to live her life in fear of the KGB, of the Natpos or the Spetznas. Answer your question?"

"Aside from those abdominal pains you don't want to talk about, you might also have some trouble a few feet higher up." Michael smiled.

"Yeah, well, maybe I do." Deacon laughed softly. "But if I'm nuts and the Commies are sane, well, I'll take bein' nuts any day of the week, son."

Michael asked it—the question he had wanted to ask. "Why the hell didn't you kill Letjak and me?"

Deacon laughed again. "You mean like your Commie masters told you we would? Why aren't we runnin' around with human bones danglin' off our equipment belts?"

"Yeah." Michael nodded. "Why?"

"Just 'cause you're that scumbag Arnold Borden's—"

Michael reached out, grabbed at Deacon, and spun him around. "Now you've got guns, knives, probably know martial arts—just fine. One more word about my father and I'll break your goddamned neck or die trying."

The others had stopped—Michael could feel it. Martin Deacon spoke. "You need a thicker skin, son. And how can a boy raised by the Commies call me goddamned, huh? How can somebody damn me who doesn't exist? You answer me that one, young man."

Michael felt his balled fists trembling—with rage, he wondered or fear—or maybe both?

Smoked venison, stringy-tasting but a little sweet and moist once the mouth worked on it a little; string beans in the shell that were eaten without cooking and tasted good; something that was like cream sherry in its sweetness and its body and was called scuppernong wine. After consuming as much as he had wanted—which had been a lot—he had slept.

When he opened his eyes, there had been no conscious memory of dreaming to ease the night, only dampness and some stiffness in his back.

He threw back the borrowed blankets and stood, stretching, his breath steaming as he exhaled. He checked Letjak, sleeping under the lean-to beside him; the brow showed no sign of fever as he touched his hands to the skin.

Michael heard sounds, soft because of the distance. He grabbed up his paratrooper's jacket and threaded his way among the sleepers. His watch read a little after six. The sky was still gray and there were deep shadows to the west in the valley below them. He paused as he neared an armed guard, but the woman—an American Indian, she had said that night around the campfire—smiled warmly enough and let him pass.

The sounds were louder now, grunts, like yells though,

too. He wondered if perhaps during the night some innocent had wandered into the camp and been seized by these self-styled freedom fighters and was being beaten. Was that why the American Indian woman had smiled so—so that he could see the beating, know what lay in store for him?

He crossed around a bracken of scrub pine and cedar, into a clearing.

There was only one person in the clearing, Martin Deacon. His lean, muscular body was naked from the waist up, his arms and legs moving as though performing some mystical, stylized ballet. And suddenly his body would spin and he would leap up and hands and feet would flash toward some invisible target.

"What the hell are you doing?"

Deacon spun, smiled, his left hand touching at his abdomen. "You mentioned martial arts last night. Haven't you ever seen the martial arts practiced?"

"No. It's outlawed, you know that. Just another way of killing people. Let me examine your abdomen. If you've got cramps, you shouldn't be—"

"Hey—I live my life the way I have to. You've never seen a display of martial arts? Not even with the National Police or the Spetznas?"

Michael gave up on the man—at least for the moment. "No. Only certain select persons in the National Security Forces are allowed any training like that. And no one ever sees the Spetznas train. What was that you were doing? Judo?"

"Judo? My God, man—you are benighted. That was Gung fu."

"So—that's what you do—this Gung fu?"

"I do a lot of things. The wise martial artist knows to one degree or another all the major forms, then blends them into a style of his own. But he'll always be heavier on one style over another, one form over another. Take off your shirt for a minute."

Michael shrugged, dropped the paratrooper jacket, and tugged the black, long-sleeved knit shirt over his head and off, balling the shirt and dropping it on top of his coat.

"Now," Deacon began, looking at him, "from what I know about you, from your build and musculature, I'd say you'd be best off putting major emphasis on tae kwon doe—it would allow you to utilize your strength and your muscle mass to greatest advantage. It's a combination of boxing, like you have to have seen in the Olympics, and the use of the feet, as in savate or Thai kick boxing—which you probably haven't seen. But it allows best use of your body. Judo's something altogether different—but you should learn some of that, too. They cut that out of the Olympics, didn't they?"

"Yes—I remember reading that it used to be an event. There used to be some sort of skiing and shooting event in the Winter Olympics."

"Biathlon," Deacon supplied. "And there's no more shooting in the Summer Olympics, is there?"

"The Soviet Union and the United States jointly protested to the Olympic Committee that encouraging such practices—"

"Bullshit," Deacon declared. "I'll teach you some if you want."

"I don't like guns—what they can do."

"It's the men who use them."

"Someone else told me that."

"Smart person."

"You'd shit a brick if you knew who."

"Well, then don't tell me—I've got enough problems with that part of my anatomy."

"Look," Michael insisted. "If it's something bad, I won't even tell you. How's that?"

"Stupid. But I meant martial arts. But I'll teach you guns, too, Michael."

Michael looked at the man. "I'll make you a deal. No guns, but you can teach me some of this tae kwon doe."

"What kind of deal?"

"I get to try to find out what's causing that abdominal pain."

"After I teach you."

"That's a cop-out." Michael grinned.

"But it's the only deal I'll make."

Michael shrugged. "All right, but you don't wanna wait too long."

"Then you'd better learn well. We can start with something right now. Ever watch a boxer?"

Michael nodded. "Yeah."

"Ever do any boxing?"

"No."

"Good—don't have anything to unlearn. But boxers, they use a stance called a T-stance. A right-handed boxer would put his left foot forward, his toe pointing forward, his right foot behind him, toe pointed right."

Michael shrugged. He tried it. "Like that?"

"Yeah—more or less. Only spread your legs out a little more, get your balance real good, 'cause I'm gonna come up to you and try to push you over."

Michael laughed. "I'm six-four-and-a-half, weigh two-ten, and you're going to knock me over? With your hands?"

"Yeah. Go on, get set."

"I'm set," Michael told him.

Deacon moved into some sort of fighting stance, half wheeled right, then thrust his left hand forward. Michael instinctively tried to block it but missed, feeling the impact against his chest. He started to fall, his balance gone, catching himself on his hands as he hit the dirt. It was still wet from the previous day's rain.

"Shit," Michael said with a snarl.

Deacon laughed. "Now I'll show you the right way to do it."

Michael picked himself up, started to dust the mud from his pants, but his hands were full of it and all he did was streak the mud from his hands onto his pants. He looked at his hands, his pants, and then at tall, lanky Martin Deacon, in his middle fifties if a day. And Michael doubled over laughing.

Chapter Seventeen

The mountain peaks were ringed with wisps of cloud, the green of foliage above the clouds and below. It made him think of a John Wayne movie he had seen once in which

Wayne played an Indian-fighter. Michael walked beside an Indian woman now. Harriet Rainwater was chattering again. "So—I saw Marty teaching you some martial arts. You're lucky."

"Why am I lucky?" Michael asked her, reaching over and grabbing the green metal container she carried. "Here—it looks heavy."

"It is heavy." She laughed.

"What the hell is it?"

"Eight hundred rounds of .223."

"Ammunition?"

"Can't run to the store and pick up some more when you run out. Yeah, ammunition. So—you like it?"

"The ammunition?"

"No, silly." She laughed, her chubby face lighting with it. Her face looked like she had a deep suntan. "I meant the martial arts. You're lucky."

"That's twice you've said I'm lucky. Why am I lucky?"

"Well, Marty's about the best there is. He had a martial-arts school before the Civilian Disarmament Act. That big, shiny .45 of his? And those fancy knives—had 'em buried in a survival canister before it all went down. They took all the rest of his stuff—guns, knives, tried arresting him and his wife. He got away from them, came up into the mountains, and then he joined the Resistance. He was James Hope's lieutenant, they say—and James Hope's best friend. Marty taught all of us what we need to know to defend ourselves. He's a fine man."

"How come a fine man is running around armed and killing people?"

"What do you believe in, Dr. Borden? Last night you were gonna duke it out with Marty over him callin' Arnold Borden some name."

"Yeah. So?"

"You believe in your father enough to take on an armed man, a killer like you call him, right?"

Michael saw her line of reasoning. "Right—and he believes in whatever he believes in enough to fight the National Security Forces and the Soviet military aid."

She laughed. "You are dumb—no offense. Those Soviet troops aren't aiding us, they're keeping the lid on 'cause the

Natpos are too fuckin' dumb. You must live inside a plastic bag."

"Ever occur to you that Marty and the rest of you are the ones who are dumb?"

"Yeah—but nobody tells us what to think." She shrugged, smiling. "We're free people. We decide things for ourselves. Nobody keeps us here. We keep ourselves here, in the mountains, fighting. Because we're in the right."

"That's a narrow-minded attitude," Michael told her.

"No kidding? Well, guess it takes one to know one." She laughed, telling him, "But you're a real gentleman—not too many guys these days will offer to carry a lady's spare ammo for her." She gave him a big smile.

By midday they stopped, not in the open, as men and women normally would on such a day, the sun bright, the air crisp but not cold. They stopped beneath the trees—and he suspected why, to avoid aerial observation. A sausage was passed around, each man and woman cutting a chunk from it. When the sausage was passed to him, Alice looked at him and laughed. "You don't even have a knife."

"I do—there's a knife in my bag," and he started to open his medical bag to search for the Swiss Army knife.

Martin Deacon slipped down beside him and reached into his battle vest. "Here—good for cutting sausages and other things." From beneath the vest, Deacon drew a knife with a blade the length of a man's hand from fingertip to wrist. The point of the dull-looking steel was at exactly the center of the knife, one edge sharpened, the other side not. The handle was round, like a tube, but looked like a sword handle—like Michael had seen in museums. The handle was wrapped with some sort of twine, it seemed, and the base of it looked as though it were designed to unscrew. Two words were on the knife. Nearest the handle, the name "Crain," and beneath it a stick figure facsimile of a bird—a crane, he presumed. Against the unsharpened side of the blade the second word read "Commando."

Michael took it to cut a slab of the sausage. "Thank you."

"Hang on to it for a while. You'll need it for the bread—gets kinda hard."

"Gee, I'd watch it, Daddy—looks like he might be really vicious with a knife," said Alice.

Michael took a bite of his sausage. He couldn't tell what kind, but it tasted good. Through the mouthful, he said to Alice, "You know, I understand your father taught you how to fight. Too bad nobody taught you how to be a lady, Alice."

"Look—" She was to her feet.

But so was her father. "Alice—be decent, girl."

"Hell, Daddy, I can't look at him. He's—"

"He's him, and Arnold Borden's another matter. Now pipe down and sit down!"

She sat down, and so did Martin Deacon. The bread came around, Michael cutting a chunk of similar size to what the others had cut. The knife seemed sharp and sturdy. He glanced across to the far side of the circle. Harriet Rainwater was helping Milton Letjak to eat—and she seemed to enjoy it. Michael wiped the knife off against his trousers, then carefully inverted it to return it handle-first to Martin Deacon. "Thank you very much. It looks like a fine knife."

"It is a fine knife—you use it for a while. I'll tell ya when I want it back. Got a belt sheath somewhere in my pack for it—find it for you to use when I'm through eating."

"What'll I need a knife for?"

"Never know. You learn one thing real quick out here—bein' prepared's a virtue, Michael."

Michael studied the knife in his hand. "Thank you again." He continued to eat.

They moved along the slopes of the incredibly green, cloud-piercing mountains, and throughout the afternoon he marveled that there could be men and women who killed their fellow man yet seemed so at home here.

Martin Deacon walked at the head of the column and raised his voice, making what Michael interpreted as a general announcement. Two men named Showalter and Chen carried Letjak's stretcher. "We're well inside the stronghold's perimeter. Jake'll know we're here by now, so when somebody jumps out of the rocks at us, take a look-see before pullin' the trigger. Don't wanna go killin' no friendlies." And he fell silent again.

Michael looked to Alice, who walked in total silence beside him. "What's he mean? Who's Jake?"

She looked at him with disgust in her eyes. "Jake Brown, war chief of the Eastern Cherokee—"

"You gotta be kiddin' me."

"You don't know anything, do you? The Eastern Cherokee declared war on the Russians and Lester Saile's damn government. The Cherokee homeland here is one place where not only the Natpos get their asses kicked, but the Spetznas go runnin' home to their mommies with their tails between their legs."

"That's a good thing? For you, maybe."

"For America."

"Aw, come on—don't give me that crap. Fine—I respect the fact that you and your father and the rest of you all figure my father's some kind of bad guy and the Russians are our enemies. But you're wrong. If you'd sit down for five minutes with my father or with Marshal Blotsky—"

"They'd be rammin' hot pokers up my ass to get me to tell 'em everything I know about the Resistance."

"Shut up," he snapped.

She grabbed his shirt front in her tiny fist, and she had to be standing on her toes, but her eyes still were below his chin. "What my father can get away with and what you can get away with are two different things, buster."

"My name isn't buster—and what you need is a belt across the ass."

She let go of his shirt, her hands at her sides, her rifle dangling under her right arm. "Anytime you figure you're man enough, you just try it, comrade."

Michael walked past her. *Macho* women, he thought. "Shit."

He looked up, stopped in his tracks, then started to reach for Martin's knife at his side.

Deacon, at the head of the column, was shouting at a man. "Damn it, Jake!"

The other man—Jake, apparently—was laughing, doubled over with it. He had a bow in his left hand, an assault rifle like Deacon's under his right arm. He was tall, Michael guessed his own height or better, lean as the trunk of one of the pine trees. His hair was almost black, past shoulder-length and thick, but gray-streaked. An errant gust of wind caught it, and the man pushed it back from his face. He wore camouflage-patterned trousers, a white sweater of the kind sold as Irish Fisherman's knit, and what looked like high-heeled cowboy boots. The Indian stood on top of a large, flat rock, and Martin Deacon held an arrow in his hand.

"White man 'fraid of little-bitty arrow?" It didn't sound like a real voice, but a stage voice, and then the laughter again.

"How about white man rams little-bitty arrow up red man's—"

"Tsk, tsk—hell of a thing to say." The Indian gave a hand signal and jumped down from the rock, landing less than a yard in front of Deacon. Others—some with long hair, some not—came out from the rocks, joining him. Michael looked around. They were surrounded. He could see now what Alice had meant. This would be dangerous territory for anyone who was an enemy of these people.

The lodge house was red from the fire that burned at its center. Indian paraphernalia hung on the walls—war clubs, intricate beadwork, animal skins, as well as photos of former chiefs and dignitaries of the Cherokee Nation. A combination of lawn chairs and folding chairs were nestled close to the fire.

Martin Deacon smoked a cigar, genuine Havana, stolen from a shipment earmarked for one of the Cuban businessmen who seemed to be "miraculously" rising to the upper echelons of so many privately owned American businesses. Cuban Communists sucked, he had often said, but Cuban cigars smoked.

Jake Brown smoked a pipe—not a peace pipe, but a Meerschaum. "Now, Marty, how long I known you?"

"Ten, maybe twelve years."

"Right. So why didn't ya put the bag on Michael Borden and we could get anything we want out of his old man? Medical supplies, the stuff that's perishable and hard to get outta Canada and down here without spoiling, maybe. Maybe— who knows?" He raised his palms skyward and shrugged, then let his hands drop to his lap, chewing his pipe stem.

"That's bad for your teeth."

"I'm an orthodontist, remember—before I became a war chief. Boy, did I make the bucks wiring white kids' mouths. So I know what's bad for my teeth. So it's bad for my teeth. So what else is new? So why you treatin' the Borden guy like an honored guest?"

Marty let himself inhale on the cigar, massaging his abdomen as he spoke. "He's not Michael Borden. He's James Hope's boy." He cleared his throat. "And Michael's as good a name as any for him. James woulda probably named him Michael. James's father was named Michael, I think."

"You're crazy, Marty. No kiddin'—you been out in the boonies too long, man." Jake reached into the pocket of his cammie pants and produced a leather thong, raised his hair with both hands, and draped the throng around his neck. "James Hope's whole family died. You know that and I know that."

"Nuts."

Jake squinted his eyes. "Nuts to you." He bunched his hair together in the way women used to call a pony tail, and he used the leather thong to tie it that way in place. "What makes you think he's James Hope's kid?"

"Nothing. I know he is." Martin Deacon grinned. The abdominal pain was subsiding. Soon it would be gone—for a while.

"Okay, so I'll rephrase the question. What makes you know he's Senator Hope's son?"

"Better—much better." Martin Deacon laughed. The pain was really going. "Okay, dig up on this, Jake. The night James died, I sent Habersham and Bob McDowall on ahead, and I doubled back just in case the Spetznas and the Natpos needed some extra encouragement to follow us. By that time it was all over inside the cave. I saw Arnold Borden walking out of the cave holding this baby in his arms, the kid screamin' like hell. I wanted to open up on 'em right there, but I knew the kid had to be James's. So I waited. For two hours I waited. Longest damn time in my life. If I got ulcers," he patted his stomach, "that's the night I got 'em. Finally I couldn't wait any longer, and I didn't wait for them all to clear out of camp. I went down, sneaked into the cave. There were bodies all over—Spetznas, our own. James was gunshot, dead. Melissa, the same. Stephen Hope—the little asshole—he was dead, too, riddled with bullets. Looked like handguns at short range. I always figured Blotsky and Arnold Borden did it. And if what Michael tells me he's heard about that night is halfway true, it all makes sense. Borden and James used to be partners in the old days of the FBI, right?

So Borden sees Stephen trigger his mom and dad and nearly kill the newborn baby. Borden starts shooting. And Blotsky—he's a soldier—maybe that was even too much for him. Blotsky joins in. So Arnold Borden and Marshal Blotsky are brothers in blood now, and Blotsky's got Borden by the short hair. See, one time I asked James if this Borden guy who was chasin' us was married. James says yeah, married. No kids. So I said some pruneface SOB like that wouldn't want kids.

"Anyway, James never liked talkin' bad of Borden—guess because they were friends all those years. Borden and his wife had been tryin' to have kids for years, but Margaret Borden had something wrong with her plumbing. They couldn't have kids. So what would you do if there was this healthy, newborn baby, you knew the parents, and the parents had been your friends once and you felt like dogshit over them bein' dead and you had all this guilt over it—and your wife couldn't have kids? Would you kill the baby?"

Jake knocked out his pipe against the heel of his cowboy boot. "So how do you know it's the same baby? My brother was a lawyer—and I used to watch *Perry Mason* reruns when I was a kid. It's all circumstantial."

"No. Because Marsha Devoe was one of the people I left behind with James to defend the cave just in case things went down bad. Marsha was gutshot, bleedin' to death. But she delivered the baby—helped Melissa. The baby had a birthmark on his back, a little below the level of his waist. I got hold of everything I could about Michael Borden in the Olympics but never saw a picture of him when he wasn't wearing at least an athletic shirt, or if he had no shirt on, then he was faced toward the camera. Well, this morning I got him to take off his shirt—taught him a little about the martial arts, right? Decked him. And when he got up, there was the birthmark—red, kinda uneven-shaped."

"Holy shit—I mean, that's heavy, man."

"Yeah." Deacon snapped the cigar butt into the fire, and Jake began refilling his pipe. "He's just the kinda man I knew Hope's son would grow into. See the physique on him—hell. And smart—sharp, real sharp. He's got Jennifer's eyes, and his mother's eyes, even if the color's different. He's got his father's look about him, though. What a man—God, his dad'd be proud. If only we can straighten him out."

Jake looked at him, eyes squinted against a cloud of pipe smoke. "So when you gonna tell him who he is?"

"I'm not," Deacon answered, shaking his head. "He's gotta find that out for himself, Jake. For openers he'll never trust a word I say. He just flat out won't believe it. I gotta turn him—make him see reason, make him realize what freedom is, what we're fighting for. That's what I gotta do. It's the only way. If Alice don't try killin' him first."

"Fine. Tell Alice."

"You ever know a woman who could keep a secret? Anyway, she didn't know James Hope. It wouldn't matter to her like it does to me. But God, Michael could turn this whole thing around for us, be the leader we've been lookin' for since James got killed. Hey—no offense, Jake..."

"Yeah, I know. Cherokee orthodontists lack charisma—except to other Cherokees."

"You got charisma, Jake. But hell, Michael is James Hope's boy."

Chapter Eighteen

Dr. Jessica Cornbloom had marvelous hands. She was starting after the appendix of a twelve-year-old boy. A simple operation, but somehow she made it simpler with a clean, modified transverse incision across the skin. Cornbloom called for a hemostat, the nurse stepping to her side. Michael only watched, but had scrubbed just in case. "Why are you here?" he asked her.

"Where else should I be?"

"You're very good."

"Thank you. But I still don't understand you."

"These people need medical help, but with hands like you've got... I watched that bowel resection you did on that wounded boy—"

"Facts of life, Doctor," she began, looking at him over her mask, then looking back to the twelve-year-old. "I'm one quarter Cherokee, but that makes me a Cherokee. The Russians are ticked with the Cherokees for declaring war. So anybody who can't prove they aren't Cherokee is up the creek. My license was lifted, my job at the clinic was said to be unnecessary. My round rear end it was. We three doctors were understaffed as it was. When I got booted out, it made it worse. The Russians and the people under Lester Saile don't like Jews, either. So I would've gotten kicked out anyway when they found out I was one quarter Jewish, too. Here I don't need a license—I've just gotta be good. And it doesn't matter what I am, even Cherokee. They'd be happy to have me if I were a green-skinned Martian or something."

She began crushing the base of the diseased appendix with a Kelly clamp, then tying the stump. "Here I get to do lots of work, some of it difficult. The people appreciate me. They pay me in Free Money, which isn't worth the paper it's printed on, but the thought's what counts. They do take Free Money at the grocery store. I buy smuggled material. After I stitch up people I go home at night and stitch up a dress. I feel good about it. My mother used to tell me she couldn't see how I could ever be a doctor. How could I sew up people when I couldn't embroider initials on a blouse? So that's why I'm here. How about you?"

Michael closed his eyes for a second, opened them, answered her. "We were in a plane crash and—"

"I know that—doctors always hear all the gossip. I mean, you've got a knife. You look so healthy it's disgusting." Her blue eyes smiled over the mask at him. "Why didn't you hit the trail out of here?"

"Martin Letjak is still recovering. I'll leave with him or I won't leave at all."

"Such loyalty. What's this Letjak? Old school buddy?" She was investigating for additional pathology now, the peritoneum being closed.

Michael said, "I don't even know him too well—he's one of my father's pilots."

"So for one of your father's pilots you're hanging around with a bunch of people who would just as soon kill you as look at you? Makes a lot of sense to me."

"Well, it does when you think about it."

"I think Alice has the hots for you."

"You're crazy. Too many operations."

"Hell, no, I'm not crazy. Only man I've ever known Alice Deacon to bad-mouth as much as she does you is her father—and she loves Marty fiercely."

"How about you? You a Mrs. anybody?"

She looked away, the abdominal wall closed, telling the nurse, "Put him together, Trixie." She walked around toward the base of the table. Michael heard the clinking sound of the instruments as the nurse got started. Jessica Cornbloom stepped through the swinging doors, Michael after her. Her gloves were already off, her hands tugging down her mask, tugging off the bandanna that held her hair back. She shook it loose—it was short, straight, pretty.

"He came up into the mountains, told me he loved me and I should go back with him. I told him I loved him and he should stay with me in the mountains. He cursed me out. I told him I still loved him—even if I didn't like his mouth." She licked her lips, stared at the floor for a second, then looked into Michael's eyes. "I never saw him again. Anyway, the one time I ever sewed anything when I lived with Donald, he told me it looked tacky. All along, he was right: It took tacky to know tacky." She walked away.

The Natpos and Spetznas never had attacked the city of Cherokee itself, and to keep the balance, the Resistance never attacked the Natpos or Spetznas in the city, an occasional patrol passing through greeted with jeers and hisses but not with bullets or arrows, Michael was told. For the Resistance, Michael imagined it an island of sanity in a sea of madness and violence. Letjak's leg was healing, but not with astonishing rapidity, and the ribs, as Letjak put it, "hurt only when I laugh."

It had been nine days. Michael worked with Jessica Cornbloom during the mornings and learned more about surgery than he had learned in medical school or during his internship. In the afternoons he would do his own workouts and long-distance runs, swimming for twenty minutes in the icy waters of the nearby lake. Then after his regular work-outs, he would meet Martin Deacon and they would work together on tae kwon doe. In the evenings Michael usually would dine with Martin and with Alice, Alice always sitting as far from him as possible, letting Jake or one of the other Cherokee Resistance leaders sit between them.

When it was announced they were going down to Cherokee, Alice had jumped from her seat around the campfire and screamed, "All right!"

There was a vintage vehicle that looked like one of the big old station wagons so popular in the capitalist society prior to the advent of the Peace Party. Michael had seen pictures of the vehicles. But it was even bigger, and the initials "GM" appeared on it—dated prior to the nationalization of the auto industry, he was sure.

But the vehicle seemed to run well, at least standing on the edge of the camp.

It was a morning of surprises. First Jake Brown arrived, no camouflage pants and no cowboy boots, but rather a pair of blue jeans and track shoes. His long hair was up under a slouch brown hat. "What do you call that?" Michael asked.

"A hat."

"No—I mean, what kind of hat?"

"It's a fedora, Michael, made by Stetson."

The next surprise was Martin Deacon. Marty wore no visible weapons but rather an old leather vest, a black baseball style-cap that read "Jack Daniels," a name Michael was familiar with from parties in his medical school days, and a faded plaid shirt and blue jeans.

"You're unarmed," Michael commented.

"I'm never unarmed—my whole body's a weapon." Marty laughed, giving Michael a quick double shot into the right bicep and dancing away. "But no—I'm armed. Just can't see 'em. Speaking of which, if you want to carry that knife I loaned you, stuff it under your shirt or something."

Michael removed the Crain Commando and its sheath, then paused, trying to consider how you carried a knife hidden under your shirt. Deacon helped him, and soon Michael had the knife wedged between his underpants and his whipcord slacks, his belt tightened an extra notch to hold it in place. Carrying concealed weapons seemed very uncomfortable, he reflected, but shrugged. When in Rome, he thought.

As he rezipped his paratrooper jacket came the third surprise—Alice. She wore a dress, the skirt full, reaching just below her knees, the upper portion concealed under a blue ski jacket with a hood, the ski jacket zipped to her neck. She wore no stockings, and her shoes looked more like low-rise hiking boots. The dress was blue, almost the same color as the jacket. She looked pretty.

He told her, "You look very nice."

She just looked at him, then smiled for an instant. "Thank you," she said, and walked away from him, hugging both her arms around her father's left arm.

"All right," Jake announced. "There shouldn't be any trouble. Everybody in town knows us. But just in case we run into the Spetznas or the Natpos, play it cool, huh?"

Michael knew the expression. He intended to.

They boarded the GM vehicle, and Michael wound up in the rear seat. Alice sat there, too, but hardly beside him— she seemed to hug the right-side door. Jake Brown drove. "Tell me, Michael, do they still make Cadillacs?"

"Yes." Michael nodded, looking at Jake Brown in the mirror. "Not here in the United States, but some of the automobile plants outside the continental United States—say, in Canada—continue making some models. You see Cadillacs sometimes, but they're imported now. Like a Mercedes."

"I owned a Cadillac—loaded, let me tell ya." Brown grinned. "Everything you could put into a car I had in that one. My wife liked it so much, she drove it more than I did." His voice trailed off.

Michael had learned one thing quickly, and that was not to ask these people of the Resistance about family, about friends, because there always seemed to be some little horror story waiting as the answer.

Marty spoke. "When we get in town, Jake and I have some business to attend to. Alice, you keep Michael out of trouble."

"I wanna go with you, Daddy," she said—a little petulantly, Michael thought.

"Michael can be trusted, I think, but we really can't let him run around Cherokee on his own. If the two of you bump into any Natpos or Spetznas, all they're gonna figure is you're just a young couple out for a walk. You still see that these days, they tell me. And Michael with that beard he's been growin' since we picked him up isn't gonna be that instantly recognizable as Arnold Borden's son."

Jake cut in. "I've got identity papers for both of you. Your dad and I talked this over before, Alice. Now, chances are you won't need papers. The Natpos come in and go out quick in Cherokee, but sometimes you get a Spetznas commander who doesn't take the advice of people who've been through Cherokee and tries comin' off like a hard ass. So be cool and you'll be all right."

"Any Spetznas comes after us, he's dead," she announced.

Michael looked at the set of her face. He realized she meant it.

The town of Cherokee itself had changed drastically since the Declaration of War, Jake Brown explained. Prior to the Declaration, even after the Civilian Disarmament Act and the Subversion Acts, Cherokee had been a popular tourist attraction—a real Indian village that could be toured, a respected outdoor drama, and what Jake had called "the usual" tourist things. But after the Declaration of War, the Cherokee reservation lands were placed off-limits to everyone, and the thriving business in tourism had dried up instantly. The economy had become agrarian-based, and it was partially because of the Cherokee Nation's efficiency at growing food crops that, as Jake Brown put it, "the Commies leave us alone." There was still trade between the Cherokee Nation and the rest of the American people, but it was black-market trade. The Russians never tried to stop it because, after the Agricultural Modernization Acts, so many of the private farms had ceased to produce. Any source of agricultural products was treated with care.

Jake dropped them at the junction of U.S. Highway 441 and Highway 19. Michael and Alice walked from the edge of the town toward its center, side by side. There were various curiosities: something called a water slide, falling-down signs for souvenir and gift shops, boarded-up restaurant windows, a place that announced wild animals available for viewing—but it, too, was closed.

"Look what your Commie friends did," Alice said at last, breaking the silence she had held since announcing her intensions of killing any Spetznas who got in her way. So far they had seen none—a few pickup trucks, a private car, a slow-moving farm tractor, a semitrailer-truck.

"But nobody told the Cherokees to go against the government."

"They didn't have much choice, did they? Your Commie friends saw to that."

Michael looked away from her, then into her green eyes. "There was an expression I heard once—and lady, do you fit it. Got a block on your shoulder."

She laughed.

"What the hell are you laughing about?"

"It's not a block—Jeez—the way you say it, 'You got a chip on your shoulder.' You did live in a vacuum."

"Hold my hand," he told her.

"Why the hell would I hold your hand?" she snapped.

He smiled at her. "Two reasons: last car that went by, the people were staring at us. We should be holding hands. Makes it look more believable."

"What's the second reason?" she asked guardedly.

"I want to."

"What, been in the mountains so long you're horny for anything?"

"How the hell does anybody reach you, Alice? I mean— hell, never mind." He stabbed both hands into the pockets of his paratrooper jacket, looking straight ahead. But after a moment, he felt something, and he looked down to his left side: her right hand was burrowing into his left pocket. He closed his hand around hers, looked at her, told her, "Truce."

"Let's just say a cease-fire."

"Fine." He held her hand very tightly.

They walked past a shopping center. All that seemed to be open for business was an eighteen-wheel truck-trailer combination, a man standing on the ground near it holding a fistful of paper money. Children and women crawled about inside the truck. Michael aimed them toward it, wanting to see.

"Guys like him," Alice narrated, "get a truckload full of contraband, bring it up here, and sell the stuff to the people in exchange for Free Money. Then they take the Free Money and buy grain, fruit, like that, smuggle it out, pay off Natpos who guard the roads, and get into Georgia with it and sell it to the government-owned grocery stores. Then they do the whole thing all over again."

"Guns, I suppose, or something equally as deadly," Michael surmised.

Alice only laughed, hugging his arm now as they stopped a few yards from the truck. A woman and two children climbed down, the children taking armloads of books the mother took down for them. She approached the man with the cash and began to bargain with him. Michael looked at Alice. "Books?"

"Sure. The Cherokees have their own paper mills and presses and their own writers, but books that originate outside the reservation are impossible to get—legally. After the Subversion Acts, most writers who could afford to, Daddy told me, left the country. Most of them went to Canada, but some of them got as far as Europe. There are more books written by free authors here in Cherokee than you'd find anywhere else in the country, I bet."

"Books," Michael repeated, staring at the truck a moment longer. Alice started to guide him away.

"Jake has a good collection of banned books: the Bible, the Torah, the Koran, the novels of Ayn Rand, Camus, history books—some really neat stuff. You oughta check it out."

"You realize what would happen to your friend Jake if the National Security Forces found out he had stuff like that?" And he thought of his own mother with her Bible.

"Yeah, I realize. So does Jake," Alice whispered. "But do you?"

Chapter Nineteen

They had left the level of the road—it was potholed in spots, but maintained enough that it could be driven—and dropped to the level of the stream, walking against its flow along the rocky embankment.

Alice was telling him, "After my brother James died, Daddy cried. My God did he cry. That's when I decided I was going to help. I've been fighting the Russians and the Natpos ever since. But, as I'm sure you'd be happy to note, it's a losing battle. Jake's the closest thing we have to a unified Resistance Command, and he isn't really. But he's a heck of a fine guy. Sometimes Daddy'll talk—makes it sound as if James Hope hadn't been killed, we would have beaten the Commies and gotten freedom back years ago. But I don't think so."

The water rushed, the sound constant, pleasant. Michael finally spoke. "I thought this James Hope was some sort of God, the way Marty talks about him."

"Daddy loved James Hope like a brother, or maybe like a father. I don't know which sometimes, and maybe Daddy doesn't, either. But you love somebody, you're blind to their faults. Maybe that's the only way you can love somebody. Maybe—maybe it isn't. I hope it isn't. But James Hope, best I can tell, he was tough, committed, strong, smart—but he didn't have the ability to do what everybody wanted him to do. And when he died, they kind of promoted him to sainthood and told themselves that if he had lived, it would be a better world, this would have happened, that would have happened. You know."

"No. I don't know," Michael said honestly.

"Okay. He was cut down, he never had the chance to do all the things he had planned for us. Trouble is, I don't know what he had planned for us. I don't think anybody did, including him. I get the impression," she said, letting go of his hand, looking into his face, "that he was just holding on. That he didn't really know what to do. He was waiting for the people to rise up behind him and he would lead them and they would carry him forward. You know?"

"Maybe—maybe I know." Michael shrugged. He moved his hands up along her arms, stopping just beneath her shoulders. "Can I kiss you?"

"Why?"

"The fish in the stream there are staring at us."

She laughed. She looked very pretty when she laughed,

he thought. "It's the Tukasegee River. And how do you know they're staring at us?"

"A sixth sense."

"All right. So kiss me."

Michael drew her body closer against him, her eyes closing, her lips parting, his mouth touching lightly against hers. He felt her fingertips as they touched lightly against his face, then her hands as they knotted into his hair. The wind was strong and cold and her face against his skin felt more alive than anything he had ever touched before.

He felt her hands against his chest, and gently she pushed away, but her hands stayed against him. "The fish really are looking, I bet," she said with a smile.

"I don't blame them," he told her.

"Come on—there's a restaurant that still stays open. Let you buy me a cup of coffee. They get it through the black market—and it's the real stuff."

"The real stuff, huh?" He put his arm around her waist, keeping her close to him as they began again to walk. "I like the real stuff," he told her.

They climbed again to the level of the road, but not until they had to, a large, all but empty parking lot, boarded-up stores, and near the center of the shopping center, a restaurant. A neon sign was outside, but the tubes were broken, the sign not illuminated.

He held the door for her and they went inside. "I'll help you with your coat," he told her.

She smiled up at him. "Better not." She whispered so only he could hear, "I've got a shoulder holster under it."

He looked away from her, then back at her, then started to laugh. A solitary woman wearing a print apron over a blue dress came from behind the counter and smiled. "Want a table, or the counter? We've got plenty of room."

"A table," said Alice as she looked up at him.

"Just as the lady says."

"Any one you want." The woman smiled. She was an Indian, Michael decided. As they started to the table, the lady called after them, "Coffee, or something to eat?"

"Coffee is all, I think," Alice said.

Michael nodded. As he sat down opposite her in a large

dining room, a glass-paneled wall overlooking the stream just outside, he said with a laugh, "I hope you've got money."

"Free Money—yeah." She reached into her pocket and then extended her bunched fist to him. He took what was in her hand and looked at it. He didn't recognize the picture of the man on the dollar bills she had handed him. He looked across the table at her. She answered before he could ask. "That's James Hope. Looks just like regular money otherwise."

"Yeah, it does." He held one of the dollar bills up to the light. But instead of examining the bill, he found himself staring at the face. It was one of those official-looking heroic poses, the jaw firm, resolute, the brow high, the expression thoughtful. "Looked like quite a guy."

"Looked like you—at least a little." His eyes flickered from her face back to the face on the dollar bill. "But you're better-looking," she said. And he looked at her again. "I'm startin' to like you, Michael—and I really didn't want to."

"Why didn't you want to?"

"Lots of reasons—who you are, knowing that you're gonna be leaving soon."

"You don't have to stay here. I haven't seen your face in any post offices."

"What? I couldn't go back—I've never been. This is the only city I've ever been in except once when we knocked over a Natpo armory in Memphis. I got to see Elvis Presley's home. We drove past it."

"Elvis Presley?"

"Yeah, the singer. They used to call him 'the King of Rock 'n' Roll,' you know. No—you don't know. But anyway, Jake introduced me to his stuff—I mean, what a singer. And a neat-lookin' guy! But you probably wouldn't have liked him. Had this big, fancy house—had to be a capitalist."

Michael let himself smile. He opened his coat, leaving it on, remembering the knife hidden under his shirt. "Look, I'm not a Communist. I'm not a Peace Partyist, either. I always tried to stay apolitical. I just believe in certain things. And you believe in certain other things."

"I was reading some of Jake's foreign newspapers. He gets 'em smuggled in. I saw a picture of your fiancée and you at some thing or another. What's her name?"

"Svetlana." Michael nodded.

"Svetlana—she looks pretty. Svetlana..." It seemed as though she were tasting the name. "I bet she's worried about you."

"Yeah," Michael agreed. "She's worried about me. But everything'll be all right when I get back."

"So while you're here, you and I could have this casual fling, right? And when your pilot is well, you can go back to Svetlana."

Michael didn't answer her. The woman came with two cups of coffee. They smelled good. She set a small crockery pitcher on the table. Michael looked into the pitcher. The woman smiled. "It's cream."

"Real?"

"Uh-huh." The woman laughed, then walked away.

"I like real cream," Alice told him, taking the pitcher, pouring some into his coffee, then into her own. "You'll like it, too."

"I've tried it in Europe, but never—" He sipped at the coffee. It was hot, burning him as it went down, but the smell seemed all the better.

"You wanna make love to me, Michael?"

"Yeah."

"Are you gonna tell Svetlana?"

"Maybe."

"All right. But just once."

He held the coffee cup between his hands, feeling the warmth. "Why?"

"Why just once, or why am I letting you?"

"Both," he answered.

"Why just once—because I don't want to become addicted to something I won't have. And why am I letting you at all—hell, if I know."

"You're very beautiful."

"So are you."

Michael set the coffee cup down and looked at her. "Come on. I mean—"

"Well, to me you are." She picked up her coffee cup, extending it toward him like a wineglass. "A toast, hmm?"

Michael raised his cup. "All right. Unless it's to the Resistance."

"No—to lack of resistance, I guess." She clincked her cup against his.

The door opened and he recognized the uniforms: National Police. Her cup clattered against his, and some of the coffee spilled as she set it down. He wondered if she had seen their reflection in the glass that dominated the far wall, or just sensed they were there.

"Michael—please don't," she whispered.

He smiled at her, sipped at his coffee, noticed that his own hand was shaking.

The National Police approached the counter near the cash register. There were three of them, a fourth standing beside the glass door leading to the abandoned parking lot.

Michael hissed to Alice through his teeth, "Is there a back way out of here?"

"Probably, but we'd never make it," she said. "If they're after us, it'll be a fight. You stay out of it."

"Bullshit," he said, sipping at his coffee again. His hand wasn't shaking quite as much, but he could feel his heart racing, like it did before a sporting event.

One of the National Policemen at the counter was talking loudly. "I hear you Indian bitches are pretty good. Some coffee for me and for my men. Then how about we go in back and—"

"If you and your men want coffee," the woman behind the counter told him, "I'll serve you coffee. If you want food, I'll serve you food. But nothing else."

The one who had spoken removed his hat, revealing short blond hair. He looked back at the man by the door and then at the other two who flanked him. He reached across the counter and grabbed the woman by the front of her dress and started hauling her over the counter.

Michael stood up, his chair knocking over backward.

Alice said with a hiss, "Michael—"

"And what do you want?" the blond snapped toward him.

"I want you to treat her the same way you want someone to treat your wife or your sister or your girlfriend—like a lady."

The blond still held the woman half prone across the counter, her face staring up at him, his eyes boring toward Michael. "Well, see—if I had a wife, or a sister they wouldn't be livin' in Cherokee land, and they wouldn't look like this bitch here—they'd have white skin. So why don't you shut the fuck up."

Michael balled his fists. "Why don't you let go of her and come over here and make me," Michael almost whispered. He realized his voice was trembling, his body was shaking.

"You stupid mother-fucker." The blond laughed. And he let go of the woman. She sprawled across the counter.

He started walking toward them, his two friends at the counter flanking him. He was pulling on black leather gloves. Michael stepped away from the table, his body moving without thinking into the fighting stance Martin Deacon had shown him.

"Oh—martial arts. Realize that's punishable by death, asshole?" The blond laughed, started to reach to his hip for the pistol there in the flapped holster that all but obscured it.

Alice screamed, "Michael—hit the floor!"

She was moving, her chair falling to the floor behind her. Michael threw himself down right, the table crashing down as a pistol appeared almost magically in Alice's hands and she fired twice. The crack of the pistol made Michael's ears ring. The blond-haired man's face was suddenly splotched with red, his body rocking back into his two men. The one by the door was drawing his gun. Alice swung the pistol toward the door, firing twice. The man's body snapped back as though a car had hit it, smashing outward through the glass of the door, pinned against the metal horizontal door handle that ran full width of the door. His body sagged, hooked on the door handle.

Alice swung the pistol right. One of the two with the dead blond-haired leader had his gun out. A chunk blew out of the table, another out of the floor as Alice dodged, Michael rolling toward a stainless steel table. Alice's gun went off— Michael could tell the difference somehow, not knowing if it were the sound of the gun or the rhythm of the way she used it. The third National Policeman went down.

The fourth one was running through the doorway, pushing past his bleeding comrade there. Alice fired. The man's right arm went limp, his pistol clattering to the floor as he cleared the doorway, his body lurching into a dead run.

"Gotta get him!" She screamed the words, broke into a run.

Michael pushed up to his feet. The Indian woman was already across the counter, picking up a gun. She tried handing it to him as he passed her, but Michael pushed the weapon away.

Alice was through the doorway, Michael at her heels. She fired. The pavement near the running man's feet chipped, chunks of it spraying upward.

The man kept running.

Michael threw himself into a sprint, passing her, arms at his sides as he shrugged out of the paratrooper coat. "Get it!" He ran, the fleeing National Policeman looking back toward him. Running harder now, Michael closed the distance.

"Michael! Out of the way!"

But Michael didn't change position, because he knew she was going to kill the man, and there had been enough of that. He kept closing the distance instead, the National Policeman across the parking lot now, running down toward the stream.

Twenty yards—fifteen—ten—five. Michael shouted, "Halt!"

The National Policeman was starting down from the lot, toward the streambank. Michael hurtled himself after the man, reaching for the man's shoulders, bulldogging him like a steer in a rodeo. He dragged the man down, the National Policeman's legs flailing, fists hammering at Michael's face as they rolled.

They smashed against a tree trunk, a rush of hot air from the man's lungs washing Michael's face. The man slammed his knee up, Michael twisting left, feeling the impact of the knee against his pelvis rather than his groin.

Michael pushed himself up, hauling the man up to a standing position. Two shots: The center of the National Policeman's head cracked like the shell of an egg, red blood and gray flecks oozing out through the crack. Michael held the man's uniform as the body crumpled, sagged to its knees.

Michael looked up to the parking lot. "You just killed him—in cold blood."

"Cold, hot—doesn't make any difference. He heard me call you Michael. That's a radio on his belt. If he's carrying it, it means more Natpos are around because the radios don't work too well in these mountains. Now you gonna mourn him and get caught, or run?"

Michael still held the body by the uniform front, still stared up at Alice—at the handgun in her right fist.

"How could you—"

"Kill or get killed—makes for easy choices. Maybe sometimes too easy. You coming?"

"What about her?" He jerked his thumb back in the direction of the restaurant.

"She'll have some of Jake's people over there quick—and she'll be gone. Their guns will go to the Resistance. Their boots will go to people who don't have any shoes. Their uniforms will go to people who don't have any clothes. The radios will have the crystals pulled and new ones put in and we'll use 'em."

"Aren't you gonna melt his body down for soap? This is a human being."

"He stopped being human when he became a Natpo. You coming or not?"

Michael let go of the man's uniform. The head sagged against the chest, the body rocked back against the tree trunk. There was blood on his fist where he had held the uniform, a man's blood.

"I don't have much choice, do I?"

"Sure you do. Stay here, explain who you are, and get them to let you shave your beard off before they shoot you on sight—so they'll know you're Michael Borden and not some Resistance slob like me. Tell 'em everything Daddy trusted you with, about Jake Brown, about the camp up in the mountains, everything."

"Why don't you shoot me?"

"I love you, damnit."

Michael looked at the dead man, at the pistol Alice held, at her eyes. She started down the slope toward him.

Two men and a woman appeared at the top of the embankment, pistols in their hands. He started to shout to Alice, but she was already wheeling, her gun flashing toward them like some sort of magic wand in a fairy tale. "Calvin!"

"Alice—get the hell out of here. Take your friend there with you. Natpos—coming now!"

"Right." She turned, half skidded, half ran down the embankment. She was beside him now. "Come on!"

Michael nodded. His breathing was coming hard, but not from the run or the fight. She broke into a dead run along the stream bank, jumping out onto a flat rock, skipping to another, running through the shallow water. Michael started after her. If there was a God like these people in the Resistance spoke of, then why did He let things like this happen? No voice came from the clouds, and Michael just ran.

Chapter Twenty

Comrade Director Arnold Borden's orders had been specific enough.

Captain William Waterman stepped down from the helicopter, bending beneath the beating rotors, adjusting his gunbelt. His men fanned out into the parking lot to cover him. It was about time, he thought.

The local National Police commander was waiting beside a shattered glass door. A piece of cardboard was suspended in the doorway across the metal door handle.

Captain Slocum walked forward, extending his hand.

Waterman took it, released it, wanted no part of it. "One of them died like that?"

"That's right. We used a piece of cardboard to represent the body—it was impossible to do a chalk drawing. The fourth man was shot to death—execution-style, it seems—down by the water, over there. The other two are represented by chalk drawings on the floor inside the restaurant. Their weapons were gone, clothes were gone, radios gone—stripped down to their underwear."

"Resistance," Waterman said matter-of-factly.

"Yes. We were able to reconstruct the position of the body on the door from the cuts and abrasions. The other positions are only approximate. The woman who runs the restaurant is missing."

"How many of them were there?"

"It must have been a Resistance nest, or perhaps they had some advance notice these men were coming into the restaurant. We estimate at least a half dozen Resistance gunmen were involved. Footprints down by the water indicate that many at least."

Waterman pulled on his gloves slowly, not looking at the local man as he spoke. "Captain Slocum, I want the town burned. I want forty hostages taken, marched to some prominent place in town, and executed."

"But Captain Waterman, that's—"

"That's what?"

"I mean, that isn't legal, is it?"

Waterman finished with the gloves and looked at Slocum's face. From the weak set of the jaw, the hesitant expression in the muscles surrounding the eyes, it was evident why the Cherokee area was the Resistance hotbed it was. "Comrade Director Borden has granted extraordinary powers to me in order that my Special Operations Group may find those responsible for shooting down the aircraft on which his son was a passenger."

"Shooting it down—but how?"

"We have strong indications that a Canadian surface-to-air missile was used in an attempt to disable the aircraft and bring it down so Dr. Michael Borden could be taken hostage and used in some sort of extortion plot against his father. The plot succeeded only in that the aircraft was brought down. Examination of the wreckage indicates the missile proved too effective and the aircraft was vaporized. Unidentified bits of human remains vacuumed out of the wreckage that did remain suggest all three persons—pilot, copilot, and Comrade Dr. Borden—were killed. It would seem apparent from the efficiency of this most recent murder that Canadian or British commandos are actively working with the self-styled Resistance, possibly some of the Special Air Service assassins."

"What will—" But then Slocum fell silent.

"What will we do?" Waterman began walking toward the restaurant. There was no use in seeing the chalk drawings, seeing the bullet holes, but it was expected, and so he would

view them all. "We shall first demonstrate to the Cherokee
Indians that despite the fact that their agricultural products
are necessary to the state, they can no longer ignore the laws
that govern the rest of the United States. Two hundred
Spetznas under the command of a colonel personally selected
by Marshal Blotsky will be in the area by sunset. Elements of
my Special Operations Group shall work directly with you
and with the Spetznas and serve as liaison and leadership.
The mountains will be scoured to bring these butchers to
book. Prisoners will be transferred to the detention center in
Nashville, where I will make my headquarters and personally
supervise their interrogation." He moved the door aside a
little, glass tinkling down as he stepped through, more glass
crunching under his boots as he began walking toward the
overturned table and chairs, stopping beside one of the chalk
marks.

"This was Lieutenant Wheeler—one of my finest young
officers," Slocum volunteered, his voice low.

Waterman looked at Slocum, then placed his left hand
on Slocum's right shoulder. "He shall be avenged—I promise
you that. Now, order that the town be burned, the hostages
rounded up and executed."

Slocum nodded, walked away, began issuing orders that
Waterman only half listened to.

Arnold Borden had said to do whatever was necessary to
verify the death of his son and punish those who had now
murdered these four National Police personnel. Soon the
town would be in flames. Soon the hostages would be executed. Necessity, so the old aphorism went, is the mother of
invention.

They were dark and lonely days, Helen thought. Mr.
Halsey had said hardly a word to her, and it was necessary to
prevent Mrs. Borden from seeing any newspapers, hearing
any radio broadcasts, watching any television programs that
would discuss the tragedy of young Mr. Michael.

Dr. Borozoi had sat down with Helen and the other
servants and told them so. "If Mrs. Borden learns of her son's
death, it will only hasten her own death. And none of us
wishes that. Yes—I am telling you to lie to her, but lie only

by evasion. If you care for Mrs. Borden—as I know all of you do—then you will do this."

Helen had cried when she had heard of Mr. Michael's death. Such a handsome, fine young white man—and he genuinely cared for her, she knew.

As she ironed Mrs. Borden's slips, she would think about him. As she brought Mrs. Borden her tea, she would think about him. And it was worse when she read the Bible for Mrs. Borden—to read God's word and yet to lie. It churned her stomach, and when she would leave the company of Mrs. Borden after sitting with her in the library and reading the Bible, she would go and cry.

Helen cried for Miss Svetlana, too. Comrade Director Borden had read a letter, crumpled it, and thrown it to the floor of the library, and Helen had picked it up to throw it away properly. The letter had been from Miss Svetlana, and Helen had read it. Miss Svetlana had talked about wanting to kill herself, but not doing it—because she believed in her heart that somehow Michael was alive and if she killed herself and he returned, it would be the final cheat. And Miss Svetlana had said something in the letter that touched Helen in her soul—that if there were a God, she would have prayed to Him.

And so in her own prayers each night and on Sunday when she met with the others in the old Presbyterian church— so few—she prayed that Miss Svetlana would find God and take strength in Him. She began praying that Michael had lived, but still she prayed for the repose of Michael's soul if he had not.

Sometimes, although she knew better, she thought that maybe Mrs. Borden knew, or at least suspected. Once while Helen had been reading from Luke, Mrs. Borden had interrupted her, saying, "Michael was baptized. My husband didn't want us to do it, because if somebody found out, it would be considered wrong. But I had Michael baptized anyway." Mrs. Borden had convinced Helen to be baptized more than a year ago.

She carefully hung her black maid's uniform on the rack in the closet, carefully placed her apron across the back of a straight-back chair, her cap on the dresser they had given her. She drew up her nightgown a little as she dropped to her knees and folded her hands together like Mrs. Borden had taught her. "Please, God, bless Michael," Helen whispered. She had wondered once whether God were white, but Mrs. Borden—never saying it in words—had taught her that things like that didn't matter. . . .

Individual freedom was something Martin Deacon spoke of often. Michael sat well back from the cave mouth near the fire, and Martin Deacon sat near him. Alice stood alone by the cave mouth. The others were already asleep. Michael had not wanted to move Milton Letjak again but had realized the necessity of getting away from the Cherokee lands with the Spetznas coming into the area, with the National Police helicopter gunships filling the air.

Progress had been slow, between the litter for Milton Letjak and evading surveillance by air. A few miles, then hiding, then a few hurried miles again.

They were returning to what Martin called "Resistance Base Camp," and Michael understood it was in Tennessee. They had already entered the state, or would after first light—he wasn't sure.

"How can you talk about human rights and kill people? That's the ultimate abrogation of human rights."

"Why do you ask a question, then make a statement that denies the possibility of an answer?"

"Answer it then," Michael told him.

"All right. But what about you and Alice? You haven't said more than two words in the three days since it happened."

"You did the same thing—asked a question, then made a statement that precluded an answer."

"*Touché*. So what about it?"

"She's angry at me—says I'm stupid because I worried over killing those men. But they were men. It didn't matter that they were wearing National Police uniforms. They were still men."

"Agreed. All killing is wrong. I'll give you that. But sometimes there isn't a clear-cut choice between an absolute right and an absolute wrong, Michael. Sometimes you have to choose between two wrongs, determining which one is the greater wrong. Let me ask you a question. Alice said you stood up to defend that woman in the restaurant. Why?"

Michael licked his lips—the fire made the cool air of the

mountains at night dry. "They were going to—well, Alice told you."

"What would you have done to prevent them from taking their liberties with Claudia?"

"Was that her name?"

"Yeah. Jake knows her, she's got two kids. Her husband was killed fighting against the Natpos. What would you have done to defend Claudia?"

"I don't know—something."

"Killed?"

"I don't know."

"Well, think about it." Martin smiled. "Would you have killed to prevent Claudia from being gang-raped?"

"Yeah," Michael whispered.

"You've fired a gun—you told me that. With your friend Marshal Blotsky. You said you did pretty well. Try taking a pistol out from concealment, pointing it at a man who is armed when there are three others who are armed. Even if you're Alice, you're half scared shitless. Even if you're just shooting the gun out of somebody's hand, or wounding them in the arm or leg. I used to read about Wyatt Earp."

"Who was he? Somebody in the Resistance?"

"Frontier peace officer and gunfighter. He was one of the few men on the American frontier who could do something like that—draw, fire, and wound if he cared to. Alice did the only thing she could do: killed. Easier and faster and surer to go for the center of mass."

"What about the man down by the water?" Michael insisted. "He wasn't even armed."

"Another example of the lesser of two evils—let him live and blab about you, or kill him. Let him live and finger Claudia, or kill him. Let him live and take some other innocent life someday, or kill him."

"Maybe if she hadn't shot him he would have quit the National Police."

"Maybe—but then he would have been killed. You don't quit, Michael. Didn't Arnold Borden ever tell you that?"

"No, he never told me that. And leave him out of it."

"How come some of his men were going to rape a defenseless woman?"

"Rotten apples in every barrel," Michael parried.

"True. But the whole barrel is rotten when it comes to them. You would have killed to save the woman in the restaurant. Is that a fact or not?"

Michael stared into the fire, listened to the hissing of the wood. "Yes—if it had come to that."

"So there was a situation presenting two evil alternatives. A, you let Claudia get raped by at least one man, maybe as many as four. B, you take violent action to prevent the rape but that might result in serious injury or death to the four men. You chose B. We choose option B all the time. That's why we're here, fighting in these mountains. The United States Constitution was raped by Lester Saile and the Peace Party, and the Communists held her down while Saile and his people did it. But it wasn't a one-time rape. They keep at it, raping her until she can't even moan with pain anymore, and they murder anybody who tries to stop them. Those are facts. Now, you can choose to ignore them, but they're facts anyway, Michael. So we must make a choice. Kill the Natpos, as many as we can. Kill the Spetznas, as many as we can. Kill the KGB, as many as we can. And maybe someday if God's on our side and we fight the good fight long enough, the rape will stop and those of us who are left can help the Constitution to dress her wounds, clean herself up, and go on." Martin Deacon massaged his abdomen—Michael had given up asking.

Michael shook his head. "You're saying that communism is evil. I've been taught otherwise. I believe otherwise. You're saying Lester Saile has destroyed the Constitution and the country—but he saved us from nuclear annihilation."

"You've been taught, Michael. But what if what you believe in is all a pack of lies? What if we're right—Alice and me, the people like us—Jake, Claudia, all of us? What if?"

"But it isn't," Michael said, shaking his head.

"What if, though? Then in a way you were helping those four Natpo bastards to rape Claudia, you helped kill my son, you helped keep my wife from medical attention." And Martin Deacon drew his shiny pistol from its holster—Michael had been told it was a .45. He pointed it at Michael across the fire. "What if that's all true, and if I'm the butcher I'm painted to be? What if I kill you?" He held the gun for a moment longer, then shifted it into his left hand, as though weighing it in his palm.

"But I won't kill you. If you go on the way you are,

Michael, you'll be more guilty than those four Natpos. Because you're a leader, born to it. Some of the Army guys who drifted through the Resistance in the early days would say leaders are made, not born. You can teach the techniques, sure—but there's gotta be something there to begin with. And you've got that. So what's the greater evil—that I let you live and become one of their leaders and maybe someday cause the Resistance to die out, take the last hope of freedom away from America, or that I kill you? Save all that. If you figure it out and decide you want a gun, let me know."

Martin Deacon stood up from the fire, stared across it for a moment. Still holding his gun, he started toward the mouth of the cave where his daughter stood, then disappeared through and into the blackness that lay beyond the orange glow of the fire.

Michael stared after him for a long time. And then his eyes drifted to Alice. Her hands were in her pockets, and the harness for her shoulder holster hung on her shoulders, which seemed to sag under it.

He stood up, walking toward the mouth of the cave. He stood beside her. "Hi."

She turned around, looking up at him. "Michael?"

"Yes."

"Do you like my father?"

"Yes. Hell if I know why."

"Do you believe my father?"

"I believe that he believes what he says."

"But you don't understand yet, do you?"

He didn't answer her, just stood beside her and stared into the darkness.

Chapter Twenty-one

It had taken three more days of hard travel, three nights of sitting all but silently about the low campfire under a rocky overhang. There could be no campfires in the woods because even if they were held low, heat-sensing equipment used by the National Police could detect such a fire. But in a cave, or under the overhang of rocks, there was reduced likelihood of such aerial observation.

By midday of the fourth day, they had come into a rocky divide, and even before Alice had told him they were about to enter the Resistance camp, he had sensed it in the quickening pace of the others. Alice had walked ahead, joining her father, Michael taking his turn on Letjak's litter. It was then that Harriet Rainwater came alongside him and began to speak. "I wanted to thank you, Michael.'

"For what?" Michael smiled back.

"Well, you know—what you did in Cherokee for Claudia Dobbs. It must have been rough getting into it with the men who work for your father."

"When I go back I'm going to tell my father about it—"

"You shouldn't, Michael. You'll get in trouble."

"No, he's got to be told that he's got people like that in the National Police. There's got to be some way to use psychoscreening tests to weed out people like that before they ever get in," he told her.

"You live in a very simple world, don't you? I mean, it'd be real nice if the world was like that, Michael—but it just isn't. I feel sorry for you."

He looked at Harriet, not knowing what to say to her. She leaned up to him and kissed him on the cheek. "For being so nice," she explained, and she walked ahead.

The divide turned into a canyon of sorts, brush and scrub pines clinging to the sides, the sides of the canyon rising for what seemed two hundred feet or more. As they walked on, a stream seemed to appear out of nowhere, flowing at first like a tiny silvery ribbon of fast-moving water, growing beside them with each step they took, descending deeper into the canyon. It seemed to Michael a poor place for a camp, too much high ground on either side that would be too easy for an enemy to take. The place, despite its beauty, its idyllic setting, unnerved him. He remembered the old expression "It gives me the creeps"—and it did.

The weight of Milton Letjak seemed to grow as the incline grew, but Michael set his shoulders and walked on, his neck muscles aching with it. He kept going, the stream breaking suddenly left, wide now, perhaps twenty yards across, the water moving faster, rising, falling, breaking over wet-black rocks. To the right, there was a second stream, a waterfall high and white and roaring, dropping like a curtain from the right-side canyon wall. Martin and Alice were starting toward it, Harriet behind them. Michael angled toward them.

He judged the distance to the waterfall as perhaps a hundred yards now, the noise of it almost deafening as they neared it. Harriet slowed, waited, then fell in step beside him, unfolding a rain poncho. "We have to cross under the falls—no sense in Milton's cast getting wetter than it has to." She covered Letjak with the poncho.

She fell in step beside Michael again, starting to dig into the borrowed backpack he wore. She unfolded his poncho and was draping it over him. There was a moment of enforced blindness as she passed it over his head, letting it fall around him, then pulling up the hood for him, pulling it well forward over his forehead.

"Thank you," he told her, shaking his head to settle it under the poncho's hood.

Harriet only smiled, pulling her own poncho on, then saying, "I'll stick with you. Footing's a little tricky when we enter the pool."

"We have to walk through there?"

"Where the water is the whitest—it's the shallowest there—then cross under the falls by the big yellow rock. Sometimes it's really slippery, sometimes not so bad. Trouble is you never know until you're there, and if you don't watch your step you could take a nasty spill."

"Tell me something?" He realized he was shouting so she could hear him over the sound of the falling water. "What are you doing here—I mean, with the Resistance?"

"I'm a Cherokee, my tribe's at war. And I'm an American— but my country isn't my country anymore. That's why I'm here, Michael—to try to make things okay again." And she smiled, pulling her hood up, covering her sheening short black hair with it, pulling her rifle under the folds of the poncho.

Alice and Marty were near to the curtain of water now, Marty looking back, pulling up his hood, then passing from sight behind the falling white water. Alice pulled the hood of her poncho up and stood there, near the falls, spray forming a rainbow in the light around her. Her rifle and her hands with it vanished beneath the poncho.

Michael looked at her as he passed—and she smiled at him.

He glanced back. Harriet was at the center of the litter now, helping a little with the weight—he could feel that. Michael bowed his head as he entered beneath the waterfall, the pressure suddenly strong, then suddenly gone, the hammering sounds of the water against the hood of the poncho deafening for an instant. His trousers below the hem of the poncho were soaked, his boots soaked through. So much for Soviet footgear, he thought.

Shaking some of the water free, he looked up. Armed guards stood on both sides of a cave the size of a dining room in a large house, one of the guards nodding to him as though they had somehow met before. There was no rear of the cave, the rock ending abruptly. Michael was careful of his footing, the rock slippery beneath his hiking boots.

Beyond the cave, there was a green meadow. Smoke rose from fires here and there. Men, women, and children moved about the meadow, tents raised in orderly rows, a pickup truck parked at the far side, and beyond that, a horse corral. As he moved farther ahead, Michael could see the camp in greater detail. It was sectioned off. To his left and at the far side of the camp, children were seated on the ground in ranks of semicircles, a woman standing before them, a chalkboard erected against a rock—a classroom. To the far right and again to the far extreme of the camp, he could see men and women practicing what looked like the martial arts—a man threw a woman to the ground, she rolled, caught the man by the arm, and flattened him to the ground on his back.

There were smaller areas: two women and a man making arrows, bundles of arrows being carried off by older children. Down from the arrowmakers stood bales of hay with what appeared to be hand-drawn bull's-eye targets; men and women tested the bows. He smelled something foul in the air as they passed a smoldering fire, a pot bubbling over it. Some type of metal was inside the huge pot.

"What are they doing?" Michael asked Harriet as she

came along beside him. He was trying to shake the hood free of his head, and she reached up and pulled it down for him.

"They're making cast-lead bullets. We reload as much of our own ammunition as possible when we have the powder, and when we don't, we get powder from some friends up in Kentucky. Mammoth Caves. Ever been there?"

"No."

They have the raw materials for making black powder right there in the caves. During the War of 1812, I think it was, it was a primary source for black powder. We have a lot of black-powder firearms. We use them for hunting, in a pinch for added firepower in combat. One of our people—you don't know him—but he's in his seventies and he was a black-powder shooter ever since he was a boy. He can take a .54-caliber Hawken and without a scope or anything, he can pick off a Natpo at two hundred yards."

"Somehow that doesn't impress me."

"It should." She wasn't smiling anymore. "His wife and children were all murdered when the Natpos came to take his guns thirty years ago. He's been getting back at them for it ever since." She started gesturing about the camp. "We have a smokehouse over there for curing beef and venison. We put vegetables and some meat even under big plastic sheets and we dehydrate it—field rations, emergency food supply in case we have to move to another camp. We've been using this one for two years now. That's why there's so much permanent stuff here."

"Who runs this place?"

"We have an elected government that takes care of day-to-day affairs. Marty's the military commander, so he's sort of the overall leader when he has to be. Did you see those children over there?" She pointed toward the semicircles of children and the woman before the chalkboard against a rock.

"Yeah. School?"

"That's what Alice does when she isn't out on a patrol or a raid or something. The kids love her. She loves you, I think."

"She told me," Michael said.

"You gonna do anything about it?"

"I don't know."

"You should. These days, God—you never know if you're gonna be killed or not and never have another day."

"I oughta propose to you, Harriet," he told her.

She smiled, laughed. "My goodness—such a nice thing to say. But I'm even shorter than Alice. You'd get stoop-shouldered every time you kissed me."

"Hey, Michael!"

Michael looked behind him. Louie Chen, who held the other end of the heavy litter, was gesturing with his head. "We can set your pilot friend down."

"I'm for that." Michael bent, his shoulders burning as he released the litter to the ground. Chen—wiry, in his early twenties—started doing deep knee bends, flexing his arms as he did. Michael had mildly sedated Letjak to reduce the possibility of discomfort from the trip. Letjak was starting to come around. Michael dropped to his knees beside the man, pulling the poncho down that covered him, then removing his own poncho. "How you doin', Milt?"

"Feel half stiff—drunk, I mean, comrade Doctor."

"Call me Michael."

"Michael—all right."

"That's the sedative. It'll wear off, pal."

"I've been a pain in the ass to you," Letjak said with a smile.

"No, you haven't. Anyway, another week or so and that cast can come off. Then after a little while—"

"We can get outta here."

Michael nodded. Then, "You got a family, Milt?"

"A wife. We want kids soon as we can afford 'em. Don't make much as a pilot."

"Tell me something," Michael began, folding his poncho, then starting to shrug out of his pack.

"Sure—if I can."

"Even though you're a pilot, you're in the National Police—just like you would be if you carried a gun and hunted down the Resistance people. Right?"

"Yeah, I guess so."

"Could you quit? I mean, if you wanted to?"

The corners of Letjak's mouth turned down.

"Well," Michael insisted.

"They don't like people who've had firearms training

being let loose. Anyway, so much of the stuff you do you see top security stuff—get to know a lot of secrets even without trying."

Michael packed the poncho in the top of his pack, starting to close it. "Tell me—you owe me a favor. I'm collecting now."

"Tell you what?"

Michael looked at Letjak. "Are we the good guys? I mean, the National Security Forces, the Spetznas—"

"Look, Michael, you gotta understand—"

"I asked you an honest question. I saved your life. I set your leg. I carried you out. I've stuck by you. What you say won't go any farther. Are we the good guys?"

"I dunno. I used to think I did. Years ago—that's why I joined. And I wanted to fly. But, well—I've seen some things, done some things. So I don't know anymore, Michael. You find out—hey, tell me, huh?"

Michael bit his lower lip. He nodded, clapped Letjak on the shoulder, and rose stiffly to his feet. He saw Alice standing by the head of Letjak's stretcher, her dripping rain poncho still on, her red hair a tangle of waves, her assault rifle held as casually in her left hand as most women would hold a purse.

"We were gonna do something. Remember, we talked about it?"

"I remember."

"You still wanna?"

"Yeah."

"But just once. Remember?"

"I remember." Michael realized Chen was looking at them strangely. Michael shrugged.

"Louie, will Milton be all right with you?"

"Sure, Alice—sure thing," he nodded, smiling.

Alice extended her right hand. Michael took it in his left. She started walking toward the neatly spaced tents, a cool wind starting up, whipping the poncho around her legs, molding it against her. A horse whinnied from the corral. Children were shrieking—he looked toward the classroom area. The children were running in a dozen different directions. He guessed that school was out.

They kept walking, a child shouting, "Alice! Alice!"

Alice turned toward the voice, releasing Michael's hand. A little girl, blond, pigtailed, barefoot, and wearing pants that looked huge for her, was running across the grass.

Alice dropped to her knees, the poncho billowing around her in the wind. She gave her rifle to Michael. "Here—hold it for me?"

He hesitated.

She smiled up at him from her knees. "It hasn't bitten anybody in weeks—honest."

He took it. He knew what it was called by now: an M-16. He held it gingerly by the carrying handle as Alice swept the little blond girl up into her arms. "Oh, I missed you—you can hug tighter than that."

And the little girl squeezed her arms tightly around Alice's neck, then let go. She stood in front of Alice, smiling. "Who's he? He's cute."

Michael laughed.

"Yeah—he is kinda cute, I guess. He's Michael."

Michael shifted the rifle to his left hand, dropping to his knees beside Alice. He extended his right hand to the little girl. "Hi, sweetheart."

She took his hand, then stepped a pace back, very formally, curtsied, then turned and ran off.

"Harriet told me you work with the kids," Michael said.

"They're cute—and they're smart. I love 'em." She took her rifle from him.

Alice led Michael to a tent at the end of the row. "I like privacy—a little," she told him. She untied the rope closure for the tent flap, then passed through, Michael after her. The sunlight through the fabric of the tent diffused into a grayish half light.

She set the rifle down on a small table that looked made from split log sections cut small. There was a chair. A small mirror hung on one side of a tent pole, a lantern on the other. "Be it ever so humble." She laughed. There was no bed. "See, you wouldn't want a bed, because if you did, you might have things crawl into it. But if you carry your bed on your back..." And she shrugged out of the poncho, then out of her backpack.

He shrugged out of his pack. "If you spread your blankets and I spread mine, we'll be comfortable. Put the poncho down as a ground cloth."

He took the poncho, spreading it on the ground, looking up at her as she sat in the chair. She began to untie her boots. "Or would you rather I leave them on?" She laughed.

"No—that's okay," he told her.

He took her blankets from her pack, started to spread them. He heard one boot fall, then the other. He looked around as he got his own blankets, starting to put them down. She was unbuckling her pants, her utility belt already gone. She pushed her pants down, stepping out of them, her legs naked except for her socks. "Mind if I keep my socks on? My feet get cold."

"I'll keep them warm for you."

"Fair enough." She took off her socks. She stood up again, wearing just her panties, her shoulder holster, and the camouflage T-shirt that had been under her jacket. He took her in his arms. She kissed him lightly on the lips, drawing back before he could kiss her back. She slipped the shoulder holster off, ripping the gun from the holster, dropping to her knees on the blanket bed he had made, setting the pistol down at its edge. "Never know when you'll need it."

"No—I guess you don't," he told her, just to say something. He dropped to his knees beside her, his hands going to her T-shirt, starting to pull it up, off. She helped him. She wore no bra underneath. He started to reach for her breasts, but she leaned back, hooking her thumbs into the sides of her panties, pushing them down, off. She set them beside the gun. "I'll undress you. Okay?"

"Okay," he told her.

When she had done so, she confessed, "I never made love to anybody before—never once. So if you get me pregnant, I'll have your baby. I can name him Michael—keep me out of combat for a few weeks, but on the plus side, if Michael, Jr., grows up to be your size, it'll be worth it, make a fine fighter."

Alice slid up beside Michael, her hands exploring him, his arms closing her against him. His lips touched her forehead, her eyelids—her nose. He knotted his fingers in her hair, bringing his mouth down against hers. "You'll have to teach me," she whispered, his lips touching her throat.

"All right," he told her. His hands cupped against her breasts as he laid her back on the blankets.

Chapter Twenty-two

Thereafter, despite her original restriction, Michael had slept each night in the camp with Alice. She had asked him to teach her, but he had decided that very first time with her that she needed no teaching—some persons were naturally gifted. Her hands were like no hands he had ever been touched by. Making love to Alice was something so different from Svetlana. Svetlana was obsessed with sex, with the doing of it. With Alice it was something so totally different he could find no words even to express it in thought.

During the days, he had worked in the field clinic, doing what he could with the materials available. But he had been surprised at the general good health of most of the Resistance. The last day, before they would leave, Milt's cast off, the leg fully healed, the ribs healed, too, Harriet had come to him.

She had been embarrassed at first, smiling, talking—and then suddenly crying. She had given herself a breast examination, as was her habit—and found a lump. She had seemed more embarrassed still when he had asked to look at it. "You have a cyst. I'd bet that's all it is. If I could get you to a hospital, I could give you an examination that would tell for sure. Cancerous tissue shows up warm on certain tests. . . ."

"What can you do here? Will I lose my breast?"

"No, I don't think so," he told her.

Within an hour, he had removed the cyst and tissue surrounding it. In his best judgment it was not cancerous. When he told Harriet, she wept.

The 'experience with Harriet made him try one last time—with Martin Deacon. It had taken several minutes to track him down, at last finding Martin where he should have looked in the first place, he knew: in the martial arts training area.

Martin was demonstrating a fall. Michael called to him from the ring of bystanders.

"I'll be just a second—" The student came at him with a club, Martin blocking it, disarming the man. Hurtling the man to the ground, Martin poised his foot over the throat to crush the windpipe—which of course he didn't do.

He helped the man to his feet, then joined Michael, who asked, "Where can we talk?"

"Here's good."

"The stomach pains have to be taken care of, Marty. I'm leaving tomorrow."

"I don't need an examination. I need freedom. That'll make me cured of everything except swearing, 'cause I'll be so damn happy I'll be tellin' everybody."

"I'm serious," Michael told him. It was cool despite the bright sun.

"There's nothing you can examine here, anyway. Doctors always figure they've got to examine something. Let it be, Michael."

Michael shook his head. "No. You remember what you said? I let you teach me some martial arts, you'd let me examine you."

"Forget it."

"I won't forget it."

Martin started to walk away. Michael reached for him. Martin spun around, hands in a guard position. Michael licked his lips. "If that's the only way I can do it—to knock you on your ass—then I'll try it."

"You'll lose."

"If I do, you lose, too," Michael told him.

Martin laughed. "I taught you good—you've worked real hard at it these past few weeks. But you're not that good. Strength is okay, but skill is more necessary."

"Let's see," Michael told him.

"All right. You win, you get to examine anything you want. You lose, forget it. Right?"

"I can't forget it. But I'll stop mentioning it, at least until I figure I can beat you."

"After tomorrow you're gone, remember?"

"I remember."

"Alice remembers, too."

Michael looked down at his shoes, then back at Martin Deacon. "We gonna do it, or just talk about it?"

Deacon laughed. He stepped back into the circle where two men, one of them Chen, were doing Gung fu.

"Excuse me, gentlemen. My star pupil and I are gonna put on a little exhibition."

"It's a fight, Marty," Michael corrected, shrugging out of his paratrooper jacket.

"Okay, it's a fight." Deacon took off his shirt, tossing it to Chen. "Now, gentlemen, ladies, you're going to see something very valuable. My opponent is just about thirty. I'm pushing twice that. He weighs about two-ten. I think I'm still about one-seventy. At six-four-plus, he's got a three-inch height advantage and concurrent reach advantage. What's the chest, Michael?"

"Forty-eight."

"Bicep?"

"Nineteen and a half inches—last time I checked."

"So, a vastly superior opponent—physically. But as you will all see, skill is what counts."

Michael handed Chen his shirt, opened his belt, removed the Commando knife. He closed his belt, stepping into the circle.

"This'll be freestyle—just like it would be in real combat."

"This is real combat," Michael whispered.

"If you say so, Michael." Deacon seemed to spring into the air, twirling around like a ballet dancer, his feet snapping out, both feet hitting Michael's chest. Michael fell back, his lungs emptied, gasping for breath as he hit the ground and rolled. Martin came for him, missing as Michael sucked air, choked on it, but climbed to his feet.

He took up the guard stance Martin had taught him. Martin turned toward him now, going into a Gung fu position. Martin stood on one foot, hands moving, wrists limp, head slightly bowed—like a crane. Martin Deacon sprang, the foot that had been planted beneath him coming up, aimed for Michael's jaw. Michael sidestepped, sweeping the kick away with the left forearm, countering with a straight-arm jab to Martin's throat. Martin wheeled, the right foot kicking at him, then the left, then the right as Michael edged back. Throwing himself down, one leg sweeping, he caught Martin with one foot off the ground, bringing Martin down.

Martin's legs kicked out. He got up into a crouch, hands moving. Michael sprang to his feet.

Alice screamed, "Stop it, damn it! Both of you!"

As Michael started for Martin, Martin's hands wove up and down, like snakes ready to strike. Alice stepped between them. "Stop it!"

Michael slowed, edged back then. Martin Deacon dropped his hands.

"What the hell is the matter with the two of you? I know what you're fighting over. For Christ's sake, Daddy, let Michael see what's wrong! For my sake!" And Alice turned away and stomped off. Michael thought he heard her crying. He looked at Deacon, whose jaw set, then relaxed, his face seamed with a crooked grin. He shrugged his shoulders and walked away.

Alice had come into the tent. Martin was putting on his shirt. "You want me to talk in front of her?"

"Thanks a lot!"

"Yeah," Martin nodded.

"All right. You've got a tumor. I can feel it. Without opening you up or sending you through a CAT scan at a hospital, I can't tell what kind of tumor it is. It's not making you potbellied or anything—which makes me think all the more that it might be cancerous. Something like this should be expanding your abdomen, but it isn't. So it's drawing from your body. I've watched you eat. You're a healthy eater."

"I've always been skinny—funny metabolism."

"Fine, but you've got something in your gut there, and benign or malignant, it needs to come out."

"You can't do an operation like that in the field, though, can you?"

"I might be able to perform the operation, but you'd never recover from it. Anyway, I didn't train as a surgeon. I trained in space medicine, which helps you a hell of a lot on the ground sometimes."

Martin smiled.

"What should we do, Michael?" Alice asked him.

Michael looked at her, looked at her father. "I could give you a few more tests and get a better idea, but it still wouldn't solve the problem. If I got you into a major hospital in a major city, you'd stand a good chance, even if it is cancer."

"But we can't do that, can we?"

"Not unless you want to be executed—no."

"The boy's startin' to think," Martin observed, smiling at Alice.

Michael exhaled—it sounded like a sigh to him and should have been one, he decided. "Under the circumstances—"

"Forget it, right?"

He looked hard at Martin. "No. You talk about wanting to fight for freedom, as you call it. And you know I don't agree with you. But all that aside, in another few months you won't be able to fight for anything if you don't get yourself fixed up. What I'd recommend is that you smuggle yourself back into Cherokee territory, reach Jake's new base camp, then get Jessica Cornbloom to operate. She's very good. Better than I've seen in Moscow or New York or Chicago, better than anyone I've seen anywhere. She has fantastic hands—"

"You said I have fantastic hands," Alice interrupted. And she laughed—but the words and the laughter all sounded forced, and her eyes weren't laughing at all.

"You do." Michael grinned. "But she has fantastic hands for different reasons." And he looked at Martin Deacon. "Will you go?"

"How about another promise?"

"What?"

"You won't forget us here, what we said, what we believe in?"

"I don't have to promise that. You know it already, Marty. Some things happened to me that I'll never forget." It felt to him like a scene from one of the Communist Spirit films he had seen ever since boyhood, but he looked hard at Alice and knew she understood.

Chapter Twenty-three

They had been riding for several hours that morning—Martin Deacon, Alice, Harriet Rainwater, and Louie Chen accompanying Michael Borden and Milton Letjak. For Michael, being back on horseback was refreshing. But it was clear that for Milton Letjak it was a torture. Letjak seemed terrified of the animal he rode, the gentlest among the horses of the Resistance camp's remuda. By afternoon they would have neared U.S. 64, and there was always military traffic on 64 between Chattanooga and the mountains of North Carolina. Michael would shave off his beard and flag down a convoy vehicle and establish his identity, then return to his real world.

Alice had cried that morning, and they had made love for the last time, lingering over it like only lovers practiced with each other's bodies could. He had held her for a long time.

He had tried to avoid the questions inside him: Were these Resistance people on the side of good? Was he on the side of evil? Did he love Alice more than Svetlana?

He could not avoid the questions, but he attempted to avoid formulating answers for them, because the answers would only engender more irresolvable questions.

Harriet Rainwater had ridden ahead to scout and she was returning now, her usual smile somehow absent.

Alice reined in between Martin and Michael, Harriet slowing her mount, the horse drawing back for an instant, tossing his head. "It's clear up ahead," she said. "I checked down the defile and across the valley. If we stick to the far north, we can cross the valley and not bother following the ridge. Should save us a couple of hours of tricky riding."

"You look beat." Michael smiled.

"I am beat," Harriet admitted. "Indians are supposed to like riding horses. I know how, but I never liked it. Always afraid the damn things are gonna toss me off."

"Gonna miss you, Harriet," Michael said.

Martin spoke. "All right, we don't take the ridge. Down the defile and along the north edge of the valley." He was massaging his abdomen to relax it. Michael looked hard at him and Martin seemed to sense it, turned, and told him then, "And I won't forget about going to see Jessica Cornbloom and let her whittle on me. Soon as I can."

"I'll believe it when I hear it for a fact."

"He won't forget," Alice interrupted. "I promise you he won't."

Michael nodded, reached out, touched Alice's hand.

"Let's move out," Martin declared. Michael dug his heels into the roan mare a little, urging her ahead, riding now between Harriet and Alice, with Louie Chen and Milton Letjak behind them. Martin rode in the lead, alone.

The defile was tricky riding, the ground uneven, steep in spots. Michael stayed easy in the saddle, giving the animal her head but ready to take a heavier hand if needed. It was narrow in spots and so they had broken into a single file, Martin still at the lead, Alice behind him, then Michael, then Harriet, then Milt, and finally Louie Chen. It had been cool at night ever since the crash in the mountains weeks ago, but the days were cool now despite the sunshine and the clear skies. A breeze, cold when it touched you, rustled the trees that flanked the defile like solid walls. When it rained heavily, this would be a streambed, Michael realized, a torrent of water coursing along here. He was grateful it wasn't raining.

They were nearing the base of the defile when he heard Harriet crying. He edged around in his saddle, looking at her, smiled at her. "Hey—what's the matter?"

She looked as though she were trying to talk but couldn't, her chubby face appearing tortured. "You keep crying," he told her, "you're gonna get me doin' it. Gonna miss you people—especially you, Harriet. You've been a good friend."

She only nodded, sobbing more loudly now. Martin

called from the head of the file, "Hey, Harriet—if there're any Natpos around, they're gonna hear us comin' for a mile."

Alice made a hoarse stage whisper. "Daddy!"

It wasn't helping Harriet to stare at her, Michael decided, so he turned forward, keeping his eyes on the course of the defile, steeper as they neared the end. It was good that Harriet had scouted ahead, he told himself. Because if the Natpos—he was shocked, finding himself thinking with the term—were hidden in the valley, it would be impossible to take the defile up and out of the valley. It was a one-way street.

Michael decided to try talking to her again. "Harriet, what's the matter?" He tried to think what could be bothering her. "Look—I wasn't lying with that cyst. That's all it was. Honest. You'll be fine."

Martin's horse had reached the bottom, Alice following, Michael a little behind.

Harriet spoke, her voice choked. "They have my sister. They cut off her right hand and they said they'd cut her arms and legs off and leave her a basket case—if I didn't!"

Michael started, turning in the saddle. He heard the pistol discharge as he reached for Harriet's reins, but it was too late. Her body rocked back in the saddle, a gaping hole in the top of her skull, a spray of blood and bone chips filling the air. Blood gushed around the pistol that was still in her mouth as she fell to the ground. Alice screamed. Chen was trying to grab Milton Letjak's horse, which reared, Letjak crashing down, his head slamming against a large rock. Michael started to swing down from the saddle, but Milt's eyes were open unnaturally wide. It was death.

Gunfire—from beyond the base of the defile. Chen's horse reared, too, and Chen leaped from the saddle, clinging to a low-hanging tree limb, swinging down. The horse continued going, joining the pileup of falling horses and dead bodies. Michael spurred his mount ahead, staying low in the saddle, the animal vaulting the last few feet, skidding, almost going down, then rearing.

"Natpos—shit!" It was Martin. His assault rifle stabbed toward the north end of the valley, where Harriet had told them it was safe to ride.

Michael whispered, "Harriet—my God."

Alice shouted at him, "Michael, run for it!"

"What about Louie?"

"He'll make it—nobody'll catch him in these woods. Come on." She cracked the barrel of her rifle across the roan mare's rump.

Michael's horse lurched ahead, Michael looking back, Alice firing her assault rifle, Marty firing his, then both of them spurring their mounts ahead. Security vehicles came into view—the four-wheel-drive stake trucks used by the National Defense Forces troops, the black vans of the National Police.

A loudspeaker: "Throw down your weapons!"

Alice shouted, "Eat shit!"

Michael swung left in the saddle, keeping his profile low, looking back again. Alice and Marty were coming, quirting their animals with the barrels of their rifles.

Michael swung up in the saddle, reining back, Alice and Marty evening with him now, then Michael digging in his heels. "*Gyaagh*—come on, girl!"

The roan mare surged ahead, dead even with Deacon and Alice now, gunfire from behind them. He heard a whooshing sound, loud on the cool fall air. Then the ground rocked, a puff of white smoke, a black and orange fireball rising. Some kind of rocket, he guessed. Martin swung low in the saddle, hanging on by his right hand, only his right foot in the stirrup, his M-16 firing along his horse's flanks, toward their pursuers. Another whooshing sound.

"Rocket!" Michael shouted, reining his horse hard right instinctively. The animal reared, then vaulted ahead.

Michael could see Marty, but he couldn't see Alice.

He reined in, his animal rearing as it came out of the skid on its haunches, turning.

Alice's horse was down. Her father was starting back for her.

Alice lay behind her horse, her rifle propped across it, firing toward the Natpos, blowing out the windshield of one of the vans. The van careened across the valley floor, upending suddenly as it started climbing a rock, finally flipping over.

One of the stake trucks stopped, troops pouring from it. Alice's weapon either was out of ammunition, or something was wrong with it. The troops were charging toward her.

Michael dug in his heels, aiming the roan toward them.

Six men raised their assault rifles to fire. Michael drove the horse down on them, then threw himself from the saddle, hitting their bodies with his own. The horse fell into them. Michael kicked one of the men in the head, double-kicked another man in the abdomen, punched a third in the face. He grabbed up a rifle, holding it by the barrel, swinging the butt of the weapon against one man's chest, then on the backswing catching another in the shoulder. The horse was to her feet. Michael threw down the rifle, then reached for the saddle horn, the sixth man grabbing at him. Michael shook the man off, hurtling him to the ground. Swinging up into the saddle, not bothering to find the stirrups with his feet, Michael kicked hard at the roan, spurring her ahead. "Alice! Be ready!"

She started to run on an angle toward him, through gunfire, the burst of another rocket. Michael dropped low in the saddle, his left fist balled on the horn, his right arm scooping out—he had her, the muscles in his left forearm screaming at him as he drew their combined weight up, holding her against him. He felt it as she swung on. "I'm all right, Michael!"

"Hang on, Alice!"

Martin was riding a zigzag course, firing his assault rifle from behind his saddle, swinging up, changing magazines, starting back, firing again.

Michael shouted to him.

Alice screamed, "Daddy! I'm all right! Daddy!"

Martin's horse broke stride, wheeled left. Martin swung up into the saddle, firing the assault rifle behind him.

Michael urged the mare ahead, the far edge of the valley nearing. He looked back once at Alice. Deacon's horse was drawing near. "I love you!" Michael threw his left leg over the roan's neck, then pushed off, hitting the ground hard, rolling up, to his knees. Alice was in the saddle, starting to slow the roan. Martin Deacon looked back, Michael's eyes meeting his.

And then Deacon whacked the roan across the rump with the barrel of his rifle. Alice clung to the mare awkwardly, almost seeming to fight it as she stared back. Their horses disappeared as the ground dropped at the end of the valley.

Michael stood up. He raised his hands high over his head. The stake trucks were rolling toward him. Men on foot, their rifles at the ready, were running for him. He kept his hands high.

"I'm Michael Borden!" he shouted. "I'm Michael Borden!" Despite the beard, in the pocket of his paratrooper jacket he had the papers to prove it.

It was hot, mildly nauseating under the hood they had covered his head with. His wrists were cuffed, his hands behind him, and his feet were bound together at the ankles with thin, high-tensile-strength cord. They had taken his boots off, taken his paratrooper jacket, taken his papers. The feeling of warm nausea contrasted with the feeling of cold from the wind. The stake truck was moving, and he could hear the bizarre slang of the National Security troops—a combination of Russian and gutter English. They were talking about the woman who had gotten away, what they would have done with her. They were talking about the fat woman with the copper-colored skin who had blown the top of her fucking head off, as they put it. They were talking—endlessly, it seemed, and every once in a while, Michael would feel a kick against his rib cage or his rear end or his back as he sat there, at their feet, between the benches in the back of the truck.

The ride was interminable, the conversation of the men around him alternately disgusting and frightening. Eventually the truck stopped.

He sat there in the darkness of the hood, his muscles cramping from his bonds, listening, trying to determine his fate.

Helicopter rotor blades sliced the air—he heard them. Shouts. Loose talk about some "son-of-a-bitch" and more shouts. The screech of tires. Michael heard footsteps in the bed of the truck, coming nearer to him.

Something grabbed at his face, the hood wrenching away, some of the hair on his head with it. He squinted against the sunlight, not able to see.

The voice—he knew it and he opened his eyes a little, the face belonging to it just in front of him now. "Michael— good thing I was nearby. After what you did to some of these men, they would have been very upset with you. Very upset."

"Waterman," Michael whispered.

"See, hatchet men can come in handy, can't they?" Waterman laughed, rose from his crouched position, and shouted, "Some of you assholes get up here and set this man free! Comrade Director Borden is going to have your guts strung on his Christmas tree!"

Michael looked into the face of the man who had kicked him. He felt the handcuffs being unlocked, watching as one of the men cut free the plastic rope around his ankles.

The one who had kicked him bent to him, started to help him up. Michael swayed a bit, flexing, trying to restore circulation to arms and legs, his feet and hands. Waterman looked at him again and smiled again. "Obviously, Michael, the reason you attacked some of these men was because you realized they didn't recognize you and you were in fear of your life."

"Obviously," Michael nodded.

"I'll show it that way in my report."

"You're so kind."

"Like I told you that time, Michael—a guy like me could come in very handy."

"You're right," Michael told him.

They were at the end of the truckbed now.

"Can I help you down, Comrade Borden?"

It was the man who had kicked Michael who asked.

Michael turned to face the man and smiled. "I'll help you down." Michael's right fist snapped forward, catching the man at the base of the jaw, driving his body off the edge of the truck and to the ground. There was some laughter, the man shaking his head, his lips flared back, baring his teeth. Michael jumped from the truckbed to the ground, landing easily. "You wanna try to kick me again?" he asked the man.

"No—no, sir—no, Comrade Dr. Borden. It wasn't—"

Michael turned away from him.

Waterman was looking at him. "Michael, you're a surprising fellow." He placed a hand tentatively on Michael's shoulder as they started to walk toward the helicopter, its rotors spinning lazily in the midday sunlight. "We can contact your father by radio. As I understand it, your mother was never informed of your disappearance and presumed death. And, of course, I imagine you'll want to speak with Comrade Drusznina."

"Svetlana," Michael whispered. "Yes."

"I was sure you would," Waterman told him. "And, well, a good word to your father about my identifying you, saving you from a fate worse than death?"

"Yes." Michael nodded. He looked hard at Waterman. He knew about whom the anonymous voice had called "son-of-a-bitch." Waterman's parentage was unknown to him, but the description certainly fit.

Chapter Twenty-four

He had always thoroughly disliked Washington and quite enjoyed Alexandria, Virginia. He had called his mother on the phone after talking with Borozoi. The physician had advised against seeing her now—she was undergoing tests and would use Michael's presence as a means of avoiding the rest of the tests. The prognosis hadn't changed, but Borozoi still was trying. He had treated it as a casual call, apologizing to his mother for not writing, telling her that he had been so busy with his training in Moscow. His mother had lied about her health. He had expected that.

The overseas call to Moscow had come in later—Svetlana had traveled with her father on his Politburo business to Moscow. She would wait for Michael there. There had been genuine care, genuine love, as well as sensuality in her voice. Michael told her honestly he wanted very much to be with her.

The meeting with his father would come last—after a physical exam. A thorough physical—he had added a half inch to his chest and a half inch to his biceps. Other than that, his body seemed unaffected by his "ordeal," as the National Security Directorate physician had put it.

He had slept twelve hours, awakened at six, run six miles, and used the hotel gymnasium facilities He had showered, shaving his beard only, leaving the moustache.

Michael replaced his lost wardrobe with a fast, efficient shopping trip. He left the hotel, the temperature in Washington warmer than in the mountains, but the day still fine, crisp. He carried his trench coat over his shoulder. The Mercedes was waiting, Waterman's driver behind the wheel.

A short drive, across the Potomac to Alexandria, Michael telling the driver, "I'll see you at the hotel tonight with my things. Thanks."

The driver nodded, smiling—an unexpected day off, Michael surmised.

He walked. There was one item of clothing he had been looking for and hadn't found yet, but as he passed a storefront, he stopped. He shrugged—none of the coats in the window was what he wanted, but a half hour still remained before meeting his father a block away for lunch. He entered the store.

His photo had been all over the newspapers that morning. He hadn't read any of the articles, somehow assuming they would be lies anyway. But he wasn't surprised when the proprietor of the store, a youngish man, slightly overweight, addressed him by name. "Dr. Borden! I'm honored, sir."

"Thank you." Michael smiled.

"The whole nation—the whole world—was hoping the reports of your death would prove false. And thank—well, thank goodness—"

"You can say 'God' in front of me. I won't tell anybody."

The man's face froze, the man apparently not knowing how to take Michael's words.

Michael changed the subject. "I was looking for a coat. I have this Soviet paratrooper's jacket I've been wearing since college days. I lived in it all the time I was missing, and I'm looking to replace it. Are you familiar with those coats?"

"Yes—had one myself when I was in high school." The man's smile returned.

"Do you have anything warm like that, built to take a lot of use?"

"Would leather be all right?"

"Fine—I think. Show me."

The man nodded, still smiling, starting toward the back of the shop. "Would you follow me please, Dr. Borden?"

Michael followed him.

They stopped before a double row of racks, leather jackets on the bottom rack. Michael set down his trench coat.

"Now, sir—I would imagine you won't be wearing a leather coat over a sport coat—maybe only over a sweater."

Michael nodded, unbuttoning his blazer, slipping out of it, the man starting to help him.

"I'm a size—"

"Please—a little game I play. I like to eyeball customers. May I select?"

Michael shrugged. He watched, the proprietor moving his hands along the rack, stopping. He took a brown leather coat from the rack, holding it up in front of him—it seemed impossibly large against the man. "We have them with fur collars, and something like that might be to your liking, definitely warm, durable. Well, this is the only coat I'd stack against those paratrooper coats."

"How much?"

"Do you like it?"

"I do," Michael said. "Just what I was looking for."

"Then please—a gift, sir."

"No," Michael insisted. "Don't be ridiculous. I've got plenty of money."

"I'm sure you do, Dr. Borden. But I meant what I said. So many of us—we wanted them to be wrong, wanted you to be alive. I'd like to give it to you. Not just from me. Please, sir."

"Are you sure?"

"I really am. But a handshake, sir—I'd like that."

Michael extended his hand to the man. The man's grip was warm, sure.

"Thank you. If ever I can—"

"My son was always sickly. He watched you in your last Olympics—when you won the decathlon the third time. He told my wife and me he wanted to be like you. He started exercising. The state clinic said it would be all right. I mean, he'll never be like you. But he's been getting better, stronger, we think. You said it was all right to mention God—well, God bless you. Last night, when the news carried word of your being found, my son smiled for the first time since the reports of your death."

Michael didn't know what to say to the man. "What's your son's name?"

"Joey."

"Tell Joey to keep working at his body, tell him he's a lucky kid. Got a good father." Michael put his blazer back on, picked up his coat, the leather jacket, too. He started to walk toward the front of the store and then turned around to the man. "God bless you, too, and Joey." He walked out of the store.

Michael stood on the sidewalk a moment, not looking back inside the shop. He realized he was breathing hard, squinted his eyes tight shut a moment, then looked at his watch. Fifteen minutes remained before meeting his father. The security people would have been there for hours, checking rooftops, checking rear entrances to the restaurant, securing the buildings on both sides of the restaurant, the buildings directly opposite it, checking traffic patterns on the street outside. He was used to that, had been ever since they had moved to Colorado when his father had become director almost twenty years ago.

He started toward the restaurant, turning the corner onto the right block, seeing the black-uniformed Natpos everywhere, their black vans in "No Parking" areas, facing the opposite side of the street. More Natpos, rifles in their hands as they patrolled the rooftops.

A Natpo stopped him. "Papers!"

"I'm Michael Borden. Get out of my way!"

The man's eyes tightened, then there was a flash of recognition. He stepped back, saluted, shouting along the block, "Comrade Dr. Borden—let him pass!"

Michael nodded to the man and walked past more of the Natpos, to the door of the restaurant. He let himself in. The owner gushed, "Comrade Dr. Borden, it is a genuine pleasure, sir, to serve a man of your stature and to be honored by the presence of the comrade director."

"Thank you."

"Your table is prepared, sir—"

"Wonderful."

"We have an excellent wine to accompany the veal—"

"You got any beer?" Michael asked him.

"Beer—oh, yes. We have—"

"They still make Michelob, or did that get nationalized while I was gone?"

"No. No, it's still—"

"Bring me a Michelob, thank you." Michael slid into the booth.

He drummed his fingers on the table as he waited for the beer.

If Alice and Marty hadn't made it, would he have heard? he asked himself. The beer came—on draught. He tasted it—it was good. "Bring me a second one, huh?" he asked the waiter. The man bowed deferentially and left. Michael took a bigger swallow of the beer. He wondered if Louie Chen had made it. Chen was tough, resourceful, a good fighter.

He took another swallow of his beer. It tasted good. He put the glass down as the second glass arrived. The waiter started to remove the first glass, but Michael held his hand over it.

The sirens outside—his father was arriving. The sounds of the restaurant doors being opened too fast—a security team making a last-minute check. He caught a blur of black uniform and assault rifle in his peripheral vision. He finished the first beer, getting the eye of the waiter. "Bring me another, huh?" He started on the second beer.

He heard voices behind him: "a pleasure, comrade Director—an honor, comrade Director—a privilege, comrade Director—"

"Bullshit," Michael muttered, sipping at the fresh beer again.

Movement near the table. He looked up. His father stood there, extending his right hand. Michael took it.

"Mike."

"Dad."

"You look great."

"Thanks."

"See you started without me. The beer looks good." He gestured to a waiter. "Same he's having."

"Yes, comrade Director."

"Sit down," Michael told his father.

Arnold Borden slid into the booth, tenting his fingers on

the table. "See you got rid of your beard. I would, too, but it hides an ugly face," and his father laughed.

"I saw some stuff, Dad."

"I figured you did."

The beers arrived, Michael downing the second one, gripping the third schooner in his right fist.

"What kind of stuff?" Arnold Borden asked him.

"A woman—her name was Harriet Rainwater. She shot herself right in the mouth because the Natpos—"

"Natpos, huh?"

"Yeah—I got other names for 'em."

"Why did she shoot herself?"

"They had her sister. Cut her sister's hand off. Told her if she didn't betray us they'd cut off her sister's arms and legs and leave her alive—"

"Us?"

"Us—yeah."

"You made some friends, then?"

"There're some good people hiding up in the mountains and fighting your men and talking about freedom and stuff like that. They believe in God. They believe in themselves. They even believed in me."

"You're a likable young man."

"You gonna give me an answer?"

"You haven't given me a question." His father smiled.

"All right, here's a question: Are they telling the truth?"

Arnold Borden placed his hands under the table, out of view. Michael sipped at his beer. Borden hadn't touched his.

"What did they say, Mike?"

"That people are murdered because they disagree with the government. That the Constitution was raped by Lester Saile, and the Peace Party and the Communists helped him. That the Communists really run the United States these days. That guns aren't evil—just the men who use them sometimes. Even Marshal Blotsky told me that once."

"Marshal Blotsky had a sudden heart attack. But you wouldn't know about that."

Michael closed his eyes. "That you and Blotsky and the Spetznas and all of us—we're—"

"We're what?"

"Evil."

Borden laughed—it was forced. He picked up his beer, swallowed half the contents of the schooner. "What's evil?"

"Dismembering Harriet Rainwater's sister. Try that."

"Somebody got overzealous, took a gamble, and threatened the woman you're speaking of."

"What about the hand? Was that overzealous?"

"I can't address myself to something I have no knowledge of."

"Try this: Three Natpos threatened an American Indian woman with rape while a fourth stood guard at the door. The girl I was with—"

"Ah—a girl. That explains—"

"That doesn't explain shit, Dad," Michael said with a hiss, hammering the glass down on the table, the glass almost breaking in his hand. "The girl I was with saved the Indian woman—and I helped her."

"Michael, you were under a great deal of tension. I mean, I could recite chapter and verse to you. Some famous hostage situations. The hostage is so dependent for survival on his or her captors that this kind of cross-identification takes place, you know. And, well—you ally yourself with your tormenters. If you wound up helping this crazy girl in the mountains—"

"Don't say that again."

"All right." Borden nodded. "'This girl,' then—is that all right?"

"Yeah—"

"Damn it, Michael, you're pushing it—"

"What are you gonna do? Have somebody cut Mom's hand off to threaten me—"

His father's body moved. There was time to react, but Michael didn't react. His father's hand slapped hard across his left cheek. Michael's left eye began to tear, but he kept his eyes on his father. "Damnit, Michael—" A glass dropped somewhere in the restaurant. There were no other patrons.

"What have you done all these years, Dad?"

"I've done what I've had to do, Michael. Just like you'll do someday. And you had better watch your mouth. After Blotsky died, I heard about the thing with the Politburo. Now that you're still alive, I don't think any of that will have changed. But you could change it. You could fuck yourself over real good, son—real good."

"You mean instead of letting you do it for me?"

"Damn it, boy—those people in the mountains are crazy reactionaries. They want an America there never was and never could be, some kind of cockamamy total freedom where they can run around playing Batman—"

"Who's Batman?"

'"Never mind. My point is, they're a bunch of dangerous nuts. They kill people."

"If killing people makes you a dangerous nut, what about your guys—the Natpos?"

Arnold Borden drank more of his beer. "Look—for openers, you stop using that term—around me or around anybody else."

Michael took a swallow of his beer. "How come all these people seem to be doing is defending themselves against you?"

"As this nation's chief law-enforcement officer, I have a responsibility—"

"Sure—what kind of responsibility do people have who kill people for fun? What about guys like William Waterman? Where'd you dig him out of—the woodwork?"

"Waterman's a fine man, a good leader. He gets the job done, Michael—something you haven't been doing a damn bit of. If I'm so fuckin' terrible, then you oughta really worry, because the money I make and the influence I wield has gotten you everything you have. I suppose you screwed that girl you talked about. Told Svetlana about that? Next time you take a roll with Svetlana under the sheets, you might want to mention—"

"Shut up," Michael whispered.

"You don't tell me to shut up, boy. I heard you took care of six of my men, all by yourself. Finally put those muscles to some good besides gettin' gold medals and handshakes, huh?" His eyes were squinted tight, his eyes were hard. There was something in them Michael had never seen. "What? Learn how to use a gun, too? Or did you learn enough of that from Blotsky? I would have taught you—"

Michael kept his voice low—not out of fear of anyone

hearing, but out of fear of what he was thinking. "What happened to Blotsky?"

Arnold Borden sat back folding his hands across his stomach. "I told you—heart attack. Never regained consciousness."

"From what you told me, from what I heard, you and Marshal Blotsky were the last two to see James Hope alive."

"You stop mentioning that name, too, or you mark my words—"

"You were the last two. Did he know something?"

"What the hell are you talkin' about?"

"I don't know exactly. But it's a gut feeling I've got, and I don't like it."

"Well, at last we agree, son: I don't like it, either. And you mention it again and I'm gonna show you how much I don't like it."

Michael reached into his pocket. "I'm not too hungry— got a lot to do before I fly to Moscow. Be seein' ya." He stood up, grabbing the trench coat. He took the leather jacket as he tossed the bill on the table. It was Free Money Alice had given him back in the restaurant before hell had broken loose. He turned the bill around so it was right side up for Arnold Borden. "Recognize the picture?"

He didn't wait for an answer. One of the security people stepped in front of him, and he looked at the man for a split second. The security man stepped away.

Michael went out through the doors, trying to breathe.

Chapter Twenty-five

The flakes of snow were gentle against Michael's skin. His left hand was gloveless, and he held Svetlana's hand. She had met him at the airport, they had made love in her apartment near Red Square. Now they walked. Soon they would return to the apartment and make love again.

Michael looked at her. The snow clung to the fur of her coat, the same as it clung to the hair that peaked out from beneath the fur bonnet she wore.

She cleared her throat. Crowds were ranked in almost perfect order as they passed the Lenin Mausoleum. A few faces lightened as they passed, calling "hello." Michael waved back, making Svetlana walk faster to get away from them. The snow was falling more heavily now, but snow in Moscow was like sun in Florida, he reflected. You lived with it or moved if you could. "Was there a woman, Michael?"

"Yes."

"Did you make love to her?"

"Not at first—but later, yes."

"Do you love her?"

"Yes."

"Do you still love me?"

"Yes, I still love you. I'll never see her again."

"Do you still want to get married?"

He looked at her. "That circus they're planning up there..." He nodded skyward. "I don't know if I can go through with it." He shook his head. "I don't know what I know anymore, Svetlana."

"I can make you happy."

"I know you can," he told her.

"Let me make you happy—please?"

He started walking again, Svetlana beside him, the crunch of snow under her boots like the sound of something straining that was about to break. "All right. I'd like that," Michael told her.

They finished the circuit, entered through the security door, and took the elevator. Svetlana removed her fur hat, shaking it free of snow.

They stopped at the seventh floor and got out, Svetlana giving him the key from her purse. He opened the door, watched her as she passed through, closed the door, turned the bolt. Her purse was on the table in the hallway, and he opened it and dropped the key inside.

"Would you help me?"

She was sitting on the low-backed stool attached to the small sideways desk that served to hold the telephone. He dropped to his knees in front of her, reaching up along her calf, finding the top of the zipper, pulling it down, pulling off her right boot. She wore stockings of dark brown—probably nylon, but they felt like silk. He removed the second boot and she stood up, reaching her hand out to him. He stood.

"Get your boots off. I'll get a towel to dry your hair."

"All right." He sat on the stool she had just vacated and took his hiking boots off. He shrugged out of his leather jacket, hanging it beside her coat.

"I started the fire going—come into the living room," she called. Michael walked into the living room. "Here, sit down on the floor there." He leaned back against the couch. She toweled his hair dry of the snow. Her hands stopped moving, the towel draped half over his eyes. "Will you undress me?"

He did, and soon her hands were doing things to him, and after a time he entered her and she moved under him. He told himself it would be as it was before. . . .

The lights of the metro glowed warmly. Svetlana's father had offered Michael a chauffeured limousine, but he had refused it. He wondered who was the better Communist.

Each morning on the train, he would read. Each night on the train, he would read. There was much reading to do. He had come in halfway through a cycle, and there was no way to put off his training, even for a little while, or else the wedding that was to take place on the *Beacon of Peace* would have to be postponed. And now the wedding seemed more important than ever to Svetlana, who had told him she had the most beautiful feeling inside her. He wondered if she were pregnant. It was important to her father, who was to make a brief speech before the wedding actually began, a speech that would be seen in all the countries of the world where there was television, heard in all the countries of the world where there was radio. Official Soviet press estimates were that 90 percent of the people on the globe would watch the wedding. The thought had crossed Michael's mind that it was too bad his father or Svetlana's father didn't have to pay for it.

Day fell into day, all of it routine, the nights spent with Svetlana, making love to her, sitting by the fire with her in her apartment, which he shared, letting her cook for him. While he had been away she had taken up cooking and increased her exercise regimen so the cooking would not interfere with her body.

The classes at the Gagarin Institute for Advanced Space Flight focused on two subject areas that after years in Soviet-controlled educational systems he was used to—academics and politics. It bothered him greatly to spend time in the political education classes. He could have used the time studying, lovemaking, working out. But the classes were mandatory.

Professor Spleyetkin—his degree was in space and geopolitics—was doing as he usually did, talking. The others in the class—younger, less inured to it—sat either mesmerized or fidgeting. Michael had found that those who were mesmerized were usually those who were poorer in academics. Spleyetkin was speaking of the concept of individualism and the anachronistic implications it held. "The fallacy that the individual has some divine right over that right of the state is best exemplified, really, in the exploration of space."

Michael spoke—he didn't know why. "How is that, Comrade Professor Spleyetkin?"

Spleyetkin looked up from his notes, the sheen of his balding pate catching light for an instant, seeming to glow. He lowered his glasses to the bridge of his nose and looked over them. "Comrade Dr. Borden?"

"I asked, sir: how is that?"

"I was about to explain, sir." And he raised his glasses and looked back to the podium surface. He spoke from sketchy notes. "The individual—let us consider this concept for a moment. The individual—what does this mean?" It was a rhetorical question, clearly. "Someone who can morally justify selfishness. No more, no less. But selfishness, as we have all been taught from childhood, is immoral. Therefore, to justify selfishness is an immoral act." He thumped his right thumb down against the podium top for emphasis. "Therefore, the very basis of individuality is immorality.

"Those who cling to individualism may consider themselves, conversely, more moral than their less selfish fellows. But blindness of self is a problem as old as mankind itself. When this is translated into the arena of space exploration, the true nature of individualism becomes grossly apparent. Space has, from its very beginnings, been the effort of the group, not the individual. Even such daring pioneers as

Gagarin, after whom this institute is named, such men as the Mercury astronauts of the United States—all these men in their acts that were seemingly individual were in fact only the most visible edge of a group effort requiring the work of thousands, the support of millions."

Michael cleared his throat, raised his hand.

"Yes, Comrade Dr. Borden. A point?"

"Weren't these acts in and of themselves actually individual, comrade Professor? Certainly, team effort placed these men in space. But these were individuals performing the actual acts, individuals with their own personal reasons, goals, fears, strengths. Motivation, if you will. Why would a man—any man—risk his life in such a manner?"

He let the question hang. "These men were brave—risking their lives for the sake of—"

"But comrade Professor—your own words—they were 'risking their lives.' Each individual risked something he individually owned, not something collectively owned by the state. So at the edge of this collective effort, there was individual action. And in fact, each aspect, however apparently insignificant, of this collective act was an individual act. When the sum total of the individual acts are tallied, then the appearance is one of collective enterprise. But in fact the appearance is deceiving, sir."

"Your logic escapes me."

"I'm not a logician, sir. I merely suggest that this tremendous collective act to which you refer is nothing more than a wide range of individual acts viewed collectively. It is the eyes of the beholder that call this collective effort. Rather, collective efforts should be the term—that these were individual efforts and are considered collectively only."

"You champion the individual?"

"I'm not saying that. But I'm disagreeing with your premise, sir—with all respect."

"Yes—" Spleyetkin cleared his throat. "I am sure of your respect, but not so sure of your reasoning, sir. Are you using space, then, as a justification of individuality?"

"I'm not using it to justify anything, comrade Professor—which is just as I think it should be, with all due respect. It has always seemed to me that space is like athletics in the sense that it should remain free of politics, free of dogma. In that way will the greatest potential of space be realized, will the tremendous work of this institute reach its finest goal." He had learned the ways of argument that would keep the argument from being reported. But it had never concerned him before except as a means of avoiding bother. Somehow this issue concerned him in a more personal way.

The lecture went on, but at the conclusion, Professor Spleyetkin removed his glasses and looked across the lecture hall. "I would like to see Comrade Dr. Borden for a moment. You are dismissed, comrades."

Michael stayed in his seat, folding his notebook closed. There was nothing written there.

The men, the few women filtered from the lecture hall. Michael started to rise. "No—stay seated, Michael. May I call you Michael?"

"Certainly, comrade Professor. I am honored that you should want to."

Spleyetkin slowly climbed the low steps that were in reality platforms, on the platforms the students' desks ranked neatly side by side but now slightly disarrayed. "I realize you are very polite—and from an older student, this is most pleasant."

"Thank you, sir."

"I also realize you totally disagree with the subject of my lecture."

"I disagree only with your outlook, sir, and in this particular instance only."

"You should be entering the diplomatic service rather than the cosmonaut corps."

"I hardly think I'd be qualified for diplomacy, Comrade Professor Spleyetkin."

Spleyetkin gestured toward Michael with his glasses. "A bit of advice, then?"

"Yes, sir?"

"I greatly respect you—although it may not seem apparent." His eyes scanned his own body, rested a moment at his bay-windowed abdomen, then rose to Michael's eyes. "I, too, was once an athlete. I found the parties after the meets more alluring than the events themselves. So," he went on, settling his glasses on the bridge of his nose, "I feel a certain comradeship with you." He began feeling in the pockets of his brown suit for something. It turned out to be a pipe. He sucked at it, making a faint, whistling sound. "You should guard your tongue, Michael. I feel as you—that the ultimate purpose of space is for science, is for man. I view man collectively—perhaps it is superior logic, or only force of habit. You quite frankly view man individually. But regardless of this, regardless of your excellence in your studies here, your reputation, your skills as a doctor of medicine—if you continue to speak contrary to what our American friends formerly called the 'Party line,' you will fall into disfavor with those who can hurt you very badly, Michael. And I should hate to see this. All of us—myself included—at one time or another may harbor thoughts best left unspoken, or if they must be spoken, spoken to a loved one, whispered in a loved one's ear."

"Then there's no freedom of speech here."

"Here? You are naïve. There is freedom of speech if what your speech reflects is politically acceptable—and don't forget that, my young friend. I should hate for such a fine mind, such a fine body to . . ." He paused.

Michael supplied the words. "Cease to exist?"

Spleyetkin only shrugged his shoulders and smiled. He had found his tobacco and began filling his pipe.

Michael waited beside the bust of Lenin. Komsomolskaya Station seemed like a ballroom, but converted for the use of giant, winter-coated bees. There were people everywhere, moving to and from trains, to and from escalators, the chandeliers incredibly bright to compensate for the inefficiency of their lighting, the vaulted plaster ceiling as lit as a warm summer sky, the floor where the people walked beneath the lights in perpetual twilight, it seemed. If the place were empty, he told himself, the light would be dazzling, but as it was, those people who moved about the metro station named after the Young Communist League walked about in each other's shadow.

"Michael! Michael!"

He turned from the bust, looking for the single face.

"Michael!"

He lifted his knapsack and slipped between the knots of moving Muscovites, an occasional face upturned to stare in wonder. He started working the numbers in his head. The metro handled some five million passengers a day, he had read somewhere. He divided that by twenty-four: two hundred eight thousand, three hundred thirty-three passengers per hour.

Svetlana came into his arms, her face cold with the cold outside, her fur coat's shoulders wet, her hat wet as she pressed her face against his chest. He kissed her hard on the mouth and she grabbed his left hand with both of hers, her purse falling from her shoulder into the crook of her elbow. She tugged him with her. "Come on—we must hurry!"

He nodded, smiling, walking after her, broadening his stride as she ran on her high-heeled boots.

The escalators—gleaming, humming, packed with people—were ranked two up and two down on either side, and she led him to the interior escalator and he stepped on as she minced up a step to give him room. She turned around, almost his height now because of the boots, because of the raised height of the escalator step on which she stood, her arms wrapping around his neck. "I love you."

"I'm glad," he said.

She kissed his nose, and he could smell her lipstick.

"I got lipstick on your nose."

"Wonderful." He rubbed the back of his wrist against the tip of his nose. "Did I get it?"

"Uh-huh. Want to try again, Michael?"

"Later." He put his left arm around her back and drew her tightly against him. "I missed you, too," he told her.

"Wait until you see what I bought! In the car—and just for you."

They reached the top of the semicircular gray tunnel that was the shaft for the escalators, Svetlana taking his hand again.

They walked into the outside world, the snow falling in a white shower. The black Zil waited at the curbside, its exhaust melting snow beneath it and making great clouds of steam on the air.

Her father's chauffeur started out to get the passenger door, but Michael waved the man back, opening the door for Svetlana, letting her slide in, then going in after her, slamming the door shut.

"Good evening, Comrade Dr. Borden."

"Good evening, Fyodor. How's the traffic?"

Fyodor was practicing his English and didn't always get it right. "The traffic is homicide, comrade Doctor."

"Fyodor, that's *murder*."

"Yes—thank you very much," he said, and he was already starting the limousine into the homicidal traffic. There were not that many cars, nor were there ever, but the occasional slow-moving truck, the snow itself, the pedestrians— all made driving somewhat difficult.

"Michael, you want to see?"

"Okay." She was so pretty, little-girl pretty, and her eyes were lit with excitement. One glove was already off and she took off the other, tossing them both on his thighs as she started to unfold the top of the bag, taking out a white box. She smoothed the bag on her lap, her legs tight together, setting the box on top of it, opening the box lid. Michael took it before she gave it to him. She folded back white tissue paper. He didn't recognize the bag, but wherever she had bought it, it was expensive.

Her manicured fingertips raised a black negligee by its lacy straps, raising it high toward the roof of the limousine. She settled it against her chest, the black, see-through fabric against her fur coat like a voluptuous bear in drag somehow.

"What do you think?" She edged forward, turning around, perched on the very front of the seat. "It's complicated to take off—but I want you to try."

"I love you," he whispered, drawing her close to him, taking her across his lap. The box and the bag fell to the car floor, the black negligee still against her chest. He kissed her lips. They tasted faintly like candy. He looked up for an instant, telling Fyodor, "Part of my cosmonaut survival training— rest easy," and he kissed her again.

Chapter Twenty-six

The design of the space station had changed considerably from early conceptions to current reality. Michael had seen the drawings and sketches of the wheel-shaped stations, which were graceful but not very practical, at least not with existing technology. Someday, he thought, if the success of the *Beacon of Peace* were secured, there would be permanent space colonies. And someday—there were serious rumors that such a project was under way—there would be a colony on the moon, eventual settlement of Mars, exploration of the outer planets.

When he had first come aboard the *Beacon of Peace*, he had sat beside Svetlana in the special MkII shuttle craft, the cargo bay permanently sealed, converted to a cabin and limited-capacity cargo bay the size of a wide-bodied airliner.

He had since learned to fly the MkII, a perfect one-half scale of the original except for the cockpit accommodations, of course. It was used rarely these days for travel between Earth and low orbit, but used instead to transfer experiments into nongeosynchronous orbits, into lower or higher orbits, sometimes as a platform for experiments themselves. But he always remembered the first moment, seeing the *Beacon of Peace*, Svetlana's hand in his, her face lit with the same feelings he felt inside himself—expectation, awe, almost reverence.

Michael spoke into his headset. "This is MkII shuttle craft *Smolensk* requesting docking authorization. Over."

The voice came back through his headset—Andy Hall. "I copy that, *Smolensk*. Prepare for changeover to auto on my mark. Do you copy? Over."

"This is *Smolensk*. I copy, Andy. Over."

"Buy me some coffee, huh? Commencing countdown—now. Five. Four. Three. Activate auto control lock. Two. One. Mark. Release!"

Michael punched the button, then flipped the guard back over it, leaning back in his seat, staring ahead. Beside him, Andrea Wojnik laughed. "See—I told you being a pilot wasn't that much of a big deal. All you do is get her on the right trajectory and turn over the controls."

Michael removed his headset, just holding it beside his right ear in case something happened, his eyes focused on the docking bay, the movement of the MkII imperceptible except when the docking lock was focused on and its gradual increase in size detected.

"They've made space flight boring," Andrea said.

"Is that a subtle plug that I try to get Commander Umarov alone and pump him for more information on the Mars project?"

"Could you? I mean, maybe they've got the flight crew already picked—"

"I'll see what I can find out."

"Svetlana's a lucky lady, Michael."

Michael didn't say anything. He could hear the standard stuff he had heard on all his previous missions, but because he had the controls—even though the MkII was on automatic— he listened more intently. The docking was run entirely by computer, eliminating the possibility of human error. Andrea was speaking again. "Who do you think they'll get to captain the mission? Burnside or Balavadze?"

Michael thought for a moment, looked away from the docking lock, and told her, "I don't know, Andrea—I mean, they're both terrific pilots, both have command experience. The logical thing would be to put both of them on, flip a coin to see who had the command, and go. But when does anybody do the logical thing?" He smiled, looking away, back to the docking lock. It had grown since he had looked away. He could hear Andy Hall's voice, not speaking to him, but talking about a light showing on the computer that shouldn't be showing. This caused no alarm in Michael—there were two computer systems that could handle docking, one on line for other *Beacon*-related chores but ready for instant backup into the navigational system. "What's that stuff they brought up Tuesday?" he asked her suddenly.

"More computer junk, I guess."

"No—I mean the other stuff," he said.

"You mean the girders—"

"Yeah—looks like the stuff for a platform like this."

"Not enough of it though."

"Maybe not with living quarters. Any ideas?"

"I don't know—just some scuttlebut. Some of the crates have markings that don't seem to mean anything, in Russian or English. But Hattie Gould told me that she saw boxes like them once when she was a cargo pilot back on earth."

"So?"

"Looked military, but obviously camouflaged not to look military."

Michael then heard Andy Hall speaking to him: "Docking on my mark, *Smolensk*. Do you copy? Over."

"Copy you, control. Commence count. *Smolensk* over."

"Commencing now. Five. Four. Three. Entry. Two. One. Lock. You are docked, *Smolensk*. Over."

"I copy, Andy. Don't forget the coffee."

"Control out."

Michael set down the headset—there had been a slight clinking sound—and the starboard windshield now faced only the gray-white of the lower-level cylinder that was operations. *Smolensk* was safely docked to the space station. He released his seat restraint. He looked at Andrea. "I won't forget—about talking to Umarov."

She smiled and blew him a kiss on the air.

Svetlana wouldn't get off for an hour still, and Michael had checked the muscle-tissue cultures, rigged himself to the monitoring equipment, and done twenty minutes of strenuous exercise—curls, lifts, running in place, push-ups—and then showered while the computer evaluated the data from the monitoring equipment. As he pulled the sweater on—he wore no shirt—he studied the printout, water from his still-wet hair dripping onto it, beading oddly as water did always here in space. The gravity was only four fifths Earth gravity, and substances behaved oddly enough to be noticed. In this gravity, he could curl comfortably fifty pounds with each arm; on Earth, forty pounds was pushing it but manageable. He ran his left hand back through his hair, reading his data.

His mission on the *Beacon of Peace* could be summarized in a sentence: Develop a total fitness program for deep space and long-term space travelers that would as closely as possible compensate for changes in gravity and reduced physical activity, in order to minimize the aftereffects of such space activity on health and fitness.

He set down the printout, thrusting his hands into his blue jeans pockets as he started away from the machine. The data was inconclusive. He tested out as fit as ever, perhaps more fit because of the rigorous program of calisthenics and weight training, more rigorous than his Olympics days. But he had been an athlete to start with. Data with the other test subjects and data from the control subjects still were inconclusive. He shouldered through the swinging doors of his laboratory and into the yellow-and-blue-striped corridor. He imagined part of his disgruntlement was a function of age. Four days after marrying Svetlana he would be thirty, and with youth there was impatience. And what he had done these past weeks had sobered him greatly. He had begun his life's work, space medicine.

He reached Tube A, which was on the Earth side at the moment and pushed the elevator call button. He watched the indicator—the red light was on, meaning it was on Red Level.

He waited. The light shifted to yellow with a blue stripe. The door into the tube opened, and he stepped into the elevator.

He spoke into the sensor. "Orange, please."

He held to the handrail, the elevator moving downward—but it seemed lateral in relation to Earth as he watched. He could see the United States and Canada and Mexico. They looked blue and green and peaceful. The elevator stopped. The speaker announced: "You have now reached Orange Level. Please exit carefully. Thank you."

Michael walked along the main corridor toward the center where the dining hall was, checking his Rolex—he was two minutes late for Andy Hall, which could well be six hours early, since as communications officer Andy did double duty on navigation, and the *Beacon* had been very busy in the last week with shipments from Earth. Some of the pilots would stop in the lab. Some of them would talk. The Sino-Soviet situation seemed serious—deteriorating rapidly.

He pushed through the Plexiglas doors into the dining hall. He hated the see-through doors because it seemed to destroy any detachment from the rest of the station, something he felt psychologically necessary for persons with demanding jobs who were trying to relax and eat at the same time. He had memoed something about it to Commander Umarov but not heard anything in response yet.

But the shutters were open. And he could see a crescent of Earth and Coonrise—and those were worth seeing.

Andy Hall was waiting. Michael threaded his way through

the irregularly spaced tables toward the table Andy had grabbed nearest the open viewing panels.

Michael sat down.

"You just want coffee—I'm gonna eat. First chance I've had to relax all day."

Michael shook his head. "No—Svetlana'll be off in less than an hour. We'll eat together. You could always wait an hour and join us."

"Maybe tomorrow—got an MkI coming up in less than two hours. Don't know where they're gonna put the crap when it gets here—that spot a mile out with that steel net is starting to look like a garbage dump. And some of the stuff this trip they tell me can't be stored in space. Like some of the stuff at the beginning of the week. If they were gonna use this place as a warehouse they should have built it bigger."

Michael listened. He had wondered about some of the strange cargo aboard.

"Ever tell you the one about the student at the Polytechnic who was so dumb he spent fifty bucks to spend the night in a warehouse?" Andy cleared his throat. "Get it? Warehouse? He thought he was spending fifty bucks for—"

"A whorehouse—I know."

"So I'm not a comedian." Andy stood up, turned the triangular sign from "Vacant" to "Occupied," setting the lexan in the middle of the table.

Michael stood up, following him, Andy heading for the hot-foods line.

The men and women of the *Beacon* wore either their uniform dark coveralls or civilian casual clothes, all except for the ones in black—the men and women of the Security Group. They were both Soviet and American, both KGB and Natpo.

Andy was doing as he usually did, at least whenever Michael was around him—eating "internationally": *piroshki* (meat-filled deep-fried pastry) and French fries, a slice of apple pie with Swiss cheese on top. Michael took his coffee and a waxed cardboard container of milk, shaking the milk because it separated sometimes during the flight up.

He followed Andy back to the table, the dining hall filling up with some of the construction people who had been up now for the past two weeks—they worked their own shift schedules.

Andy sat down, Michael opposite him. "How can you eat all that fried crap? Aren't those nutrition lectures having any effect on you?"

"Look—they make it, I eat it."

"Yeah, I can see that you eat it. Why don't you volunteer to be a test subject for me? Wear a few electrodes and get yourself into shape again."

"What do you mean, 'again'? I was never in shape. I barely made it through NASA, and by the time I got to Gagarin, hell—I was surprised I didn't have a heart attack. No, I'm here because of my magic fingers. Got the touch the electronic stuff drops its pantyhose for. Tell me," he said, shoving fries into his mouth, "where you gonna find a guy who's a fuckin' genius with radios, knows computers inside out, and can repair anything that runs off electricity?"

"Sitting right opposite me at this table. Was that the right answer?"

"Yeah, that was the right answer," he said, adding *piroshki* to French fries as though he were adding insult to injury.

Michael looked up when he heard the voice. "May I join you?"

He had seen her before, a lieutenant with the Security Group, a Natpo originally because she was American.

She spoke again. "So many of the tables are filled, and I didn't want to have a table all to myself. And you have such a lovely view here."

"Please." Michael smiled, standing, getting her chair. She sat down, shifting her holster forward slightly on her belt. She drew her club from its ring and set it down on the floor beside her. "I must ask—well, I'm sure you've read my file."

"Yes—in my job I have to—"

"Well, certainly." Michael smiled. "So you know I've been around people who used weapons every day. That club—why the handle at a right angle to the shaft?"

"It's a Monadnock. It's a special type of nightstick—more versatile than an ordinary stick."

"Use it much here?" He smiled. He looked at her name tag. "Lieutenant Zimmer?"

"No—not here."

"And in the holster—I mean, wouldn't a conventional rearm punch a hole in the place and kill us all?"

"That's doubtful, but we use only low-velocity ammunition. Special springs—see?" She drew her pistol and set it on the table. "This is a Beretta 92-F, but we use weakened springs to function with the weakened ammunition. It's very safe. No need to worry."

"I'm so greatly relieved, Lieutenant."

She sipped at her coffee—black. Michael poured some milk into his.

"Maybe you can tell me something, comrade Doctor?"

"Michael—please." Her eyes were blue, strikingly blue with her short, mannishly cut black hair, her face pale. She wasn't spending enough time in the booths. He made a mental note to send out a health bulletin about it.

"I'm Phyllis." As she closed the flap on her holster, the gun gone from the table, she extended her right hand. Michael took the fingers in his.

"Phyllis, this is Andy Hall. Or have you met?"

"I've seen him. Hi, Andy."

"Hiya." He continued eating. "These are pretty good, ya know?"

Michael said to Phyllis, "So what were you interested in?"

She smiled at him, dropped her eyes for a moment, then looked frankly at him. "Well, what I meant was your experiments."

"Oh, my experiments. They progress. Was there anything specific?"

"You don't like Security Group people, do you?"

"What's not to like? I've never said that, Phyllis. In fact, I'd like to get one of your people over into the lab. Your unit seems to have very high physical standards, and any one of you would make admirable test subjects."

She smiled. "Even a woman?"

"Oh, certainly. I have a number of women involved in the program right now."

"It's not like those television shows they have with family fitness—I mean, just calisthenics and aerobics—"

"Well," Michael said with a grin, "that's certainly part of

it. But we do weight training, running in place, running on treadmills. In the gravity-free chamber, we even tried some simulated swimming. You'd love it."

"I'll think about it, Michael."

"Good. I imagine it must be pretty boring up here for you guys. I mean, who could you possibly have to arrest?"

Through a mouthful of food, Andy volunteered, "Arrest the asshole who did the circuit diagram for the inertial guidance box in the navigational computer, huh?"

She laughed—it seemed a genuine laugh. "No, we're just up here to make sure everything runs smoothly from a security standpoint, Andy. And you're right, Michael. It is sort of boring."

He sipped at his coffee. "Like I said, Phyllis—come over and get involved. You'll find it stimulating."

She pursed her lips over her coffee and smiled. It was the first time he'd ever seen a Natpo in lipstick.

He locked the doors. "Why are you doing that, Michael?" Svetlana asked.

"If I'm working out, I don't like people popping in on me."

Svetlana climbed aboard the bicycle—it was one of the fitness machines reset to compensate for the reduced gravity. She began to pedal, the rear wheels humming as it went speedily nowhere. Michael skinned out of his sweatpants, watching Svetlana. The leotard she wore was designed to be as little leotard as possible, but she wore it only when she trained with other women or trained with him, so he didn't mind it. In addition to her work in astrophysics, she led three groups of women in exercise programs both he and Svetlana had designed specifically for women, and since she had already been in peerless physical condition before reaching the *Beacon*, her body seemed to grow more magnificent almost hourly. He tossed the pants over a pommel horse, taking off his sweatshirt, putting it beside the pants.

"What are you gonna do, Michael?"

"Some exercises I learned a while back—but don't talk about 'em to anybody. They're kinda secret."

"Part of your new program?"

"No, not that. Just something I'm working on."

She giggled. "It sounds positively mysterious." She leaned into her machine, her thighs, her arms, her cleavage already glistening with sweat.

He tugged up his shorts, kicking out of his shoes, knocking them across the floor toward the pommel horse as he bent to drag another mat into place.

He placed both feet together, knees slightly flexed, right arm drawn back tight against his side, the fist bunched, his left hand raised, palm outward. He snapped his right foot forward, his right fist punching into an imaginary solar plexus, left arm rising slightly, then his left arm snapping back down, tight to his side, the fist bunched, his right forearm up at a diagonal from his right eye.

He relaxed, tried it again. The humming of the bicycle had stopped.

Svetlana had drawn her legs up onto the seat, perched there like a little bird in a cage. "What do you call that?"

"Well, it depends on what it's part of, really—but one of the names, if I remember it, is *jodan-age-uke*."

"It looks like dancing, Michael."

"It isn't dancing. But I understand if you get really good at it it's sort of like ballet."

He planted his left foot hard and twisted his upper body left and snapped his right leg out into a double kick, his foot flat, the ball of the foot leading. He spun onto his right foot, back-kicking the left foot into an imaginary opponent, then wheeling a double kick with the right foot, advancing, a double kick with the left.

"That's martial arts. I saw a movie once—"

"Now, you'd be the first person to tell me you aren't supposed to watch movies like that."

"All right." She shrugged, extending her upturned wrists to him. "Arrest me—please," and she laughed.

"Arrest you," he repeated slowly, stopping for breath.

He walked over to her on the exercise machine, lifting her up into his arms. She laughed, leaning her head against his chest. Her flesh, like his, was slick with sweat. He kissed her hard on the mouth.

Chapter Twenty-seven

Since there couldn't be a Christmas party, nor a New Year's Eve party, there was a December Thirty-first's Eve party. Christmas was officially frowned on. And although New Year's Eve wasn't, the wedding was to take place New Year's Eve at the stroke of midnight, and there was to be an official reception.

But several persons aboard the *Beacon of Peace* were of like mind to Andy Hall—drinking, dancing, eating, and general carousing were good for the soul. Svetlana had thrown herself into the party arrangements among work, the fitness classes, and last-minute preparations for the wedding. Michael had helped, too. And it was also a welcome party for the press shuttle that had arrived that morning. Newcomers were always an excuse to get together for a drink.

Michael had issued a medical alert: "Dancing in four fifths gravity may prove hazardous. You may do so at your own risk." People had laughed about it and it hadn't wasted that much paper and the paper was reprocessed anyway.

He glanced at his watch: The party would be starting in less than a half hour. He sat opposite Commander Alexii Umarov, who once again reassured him, "Right with you, Michael."

Umarov was the son of a Russian cultural attaché to Washington and spoke perfect idiomatic English, as did Svetlana. Most other Russians didn't—but, and he thought of the party, they were expert vodka smugglers. Alcholic beverages were officially taboo aboard the *Beacon*, but with Umarov's help, the taboo had been overcome.

"Okay." Umarov threw down his pen. "What can I do for you?"

"Wanted to confirm a rumor—or maybe get some inside dope."

"Unofficial, right?"

"Right, Commander. About the Mars flight—"

"Okay." Umarov tented his fingers, cleared his throat, and said, "I was asked to recommend any personnel I thought might be worthwhile for the Mars expedition—I mean, if there is going to be a Mars expedition." Umarov winked. "Which, of course, is all rumor. Right?"

"Oh, you bet." Michael grinned.

"So I recommended Andrea Wojnik for backup pilot. It's gonna be Burnside. Balavadze stepped aside in favor of him, which is really something."

"No shit," Michael agreed.

"The mission came first, and Balavadze reportedly told them that he figured Burnside was the better man."

"What?" He felt like an old woman gossiping over a white picket fence.

"I recommended you for medical officer and Svetlana for science officer. If it comes through, neither one of you has to take it. I told them you'd only go if she could go, and vice versa."

"I don't know what to say, Alexii—"

"Don't say anything. If it works and you decide to do it, tell me thanks and buy me a cup of coffee. Okay?"

"Okay." Michael nodded, standing, extending his hand to Umarov across the desk. "Okay."

"Don't mention it—please." Umarov ran his hands across his high forehead and back through his thinning black hair and looked down to his paperwork again. Michael let himself out, past the empty reception desk, then into the corridor of Red Level, the corridor filling, both elevators on either side opening and loading men and women. Michael packed aboard one elevator, taking it down to Orange Level. Phyllis Zimmer had turned out to be a wild and crazy girl when it came to party planning and had even volunteered for the exercise and fitness experiments in her spare time, then joined one of Svetlana's workout groups.

He remembered the old adage about judging a book by its cover. He supposed it also extended to judging a woman by her uniform.

He turned into the dining hall—it was filling up, the doors opening and more people flooding in. The hot-foods bar was now just a bar, and as his eyes scanned for Svetlana, he made his way toward it. Andrea Wojnik was tending bar, but he couldn't tell her the news. Umarov was right: If she got the appointment to the Mars expedition, she'd be ecstatic, but if she didn't, she'd be very disappointed.

"Whatcha want—vodka or vodka?" she asked Michael.

"Beer. But since we can't have any, I'll take vodka." Phyllis Zimmer and Andy Hall crowded next to him—they had been seen around a lot lately, together. It was like living in a dormitory, he thought—everybody knew everybody else's business. Phyllis wasn't in her regular uniform. She was wearing her dress uniform: black jacket, white blouse, black tie, and black skirt. She had pretty legs, he noticed. "Where's your gun?"

"In my purse. Wanna see?" And she laughed. He noticed the empty glass in her hand, guessing she had started early. He was just as happy he was getting married in a little over twenty-four hours and had tomorrow off—he didn't even want to think of blood-testing anyone in the room.

"Gimme lots of orange juice with that vodka, Andrea." He looked from Andrea back to Phyllis Zimmer. "Seen Svetlana around?"

"No. She isn't here yet."

Andy was eating a handful of popcorn—it shocked Michael. Popcorn was a healthy food.

"You guys have a good time," he said a little loudly so they could hear him, taking his drink from Andrea. "Thanks, kid." He sipped at it—too strong. "More orange juice."

"I can't stand healthy people," she said with a laugh, adding more orange juice to the glass.

"Tough—I can't stand sick people. So if I've gotta work with sick people, then you've gotta work with healthy people." He gave her a wink, starting away from the crowded bar.

There were some unfamiliar faces in the crowd—the newspeople from the press shuttle, he guessed. True to the spirit of the wedding, the news crew was comprised of Soviet and U.S. journalists.

He saw a face—and he almost dropped his drink. It was Louie Chen. "Holy shit," he whispered, drinking off half the contents of the glass. He looked around the room then started toward the man, edging close to him.

Chen was talking to two Security people, animatedly, laughing. Chen turned away—Chen's eyes caught his. Chen walked over to him. "Excuse me, aren't you Comrade Dr. Michael Borden? I've always wanted to meet you, sir!"

Michael took Chen's hand, smiling, saying low through his teeth, "I'm glad you're alive. But what the hell you doin' here?"

Chen kept smiling. "Terrible thing about a party in space—you can't even talk about the weather because there isn't any," Chen said loudly.

"Right," Michael agreed. "Do you have much of a crew with you, Mr.—?"

"Fong—Larry Fong, comrade Doctor."

"Mr. Fong—much of a crew with you?"

"Oh, yes, the best. If you follow broadcast journalism you'll recognize some faces, I'm sure."

Michael saw a very familiar person coming across the room and wearing a white cocktail dress, bright against the tan of her skin. It was Alice Deacon.

She stopped beside Chen and extended her right hand to him. He took it. She smiled. "You didn't get me pregnant," she whispered.

Michael almost dropped the glass again. "What are you doing here?" he whispered.

"You just do what you planned and you'll be fine and so will your bride."

"You're not—you're—you can't—"

"Blow the whistle on us, then—comrade."

"Michael!"

Svetlana's voice. Michael turned, looked into the crowd, saw her face. "Svetlana!" He called back.

She wore a black cocktail dress, her hair up, small earrings of gold, a thin gold chain around her neck. She was knifing her way through the gathering throng, toward him. "Hi!" She put her arms around his neck and he drew her close to him, kissing her neck, his eyes meeting Alice's eyes. "Umm—I missed you." Svetlana smiled.

"I want you to meet some people," he told her, turning her around.

"Hi—I'm Larry Fong with the U.S. pool."

"Hi, Larry. Glad you could make the party." She shot him her Number Two best smile. Number One was seen only in bed.

"And I'm Juliette Morris," Alice lied, shaking hands with Svetlana in the awkward way women sometimes have when shaking hands with members of their own sex.

"You're so pretty," Svetlana told her.

"Thank you," Alice replied.

"Are you with the press, too?"

"Yes. We're all hoping you and Comrade Dr. Borden have a wedding the world will never forget."

"You're sweet. Thank you," Svetlana told her.

Michael cleared his throat. "How about a drink?" He looked at Svetlana. He looked at Alice. "I know I could use another one."

"Wonderful," Alice agreed.

"Tell me, Miss Morris: How is it to be a reporter?"

"Miss Morris isn't necessary. Just Juliette."

"And I'm Svetlana."

They were nearing the bar, Michael not listening anymore. Alice and Louie Chen. He wondered if he would recognize anyone else. Or were the two of them alone? His mind raced. Louie Chen had been in broadcasting before joining the Resistance. And Alice—she picked up on anything, a mind like few he had ever experienced.

He set his glass down on the bar. Phyllis Zimmer and Andy were helping Andrea Wojnik with the overflow. Phyllis looked nearing drunkenness, but quite happy about something. Everyone ordered drinks, and Phyllis met Juliette and Larry.

Alice was saying to Svetlana, "I can't wait to see your dress. I understand it's just dripping with Polish lace—"

"I can't wait to wear it," Svetlana enthused.

"I want to get every detail from you," Alice told her.

Michael was still trying to figure what they were doing there—but then suddenly he knew. He started talking to Louie Chen. "Tell me, Mr. Fong—Larry—what do you do? Miss Morris is a reporter, I take it."

"I'm the second cameraman. I make sure our end of everything comes off just as planned. We've got a crew with us." His epicanthic-lidded eyes lit with a smile.

"All the best equipment, I bet—the newest."

"Well, not the newest. But what we've got is good and reliable and will get the job done for us."

Someone was playing records—he could hear "Midnight in Moscow." At least it was appropriate, he told himself. But he was more concerned about tomorrow midnight aboard the *Beacon of Peace*. "All set for the broadcast, then?" he volunteered.

Chen smiled again. "Got it all nailed down. All you and your lovely bride need do is relax, enjoy yourselves, and know that you're the focal point of an event of great historical significance. You know, it may sound silly for an old hand at this like I am, but I'm excited."

There would be no way to talk to either of them privately, and no way to stop them except to turn them in. He couldn't do that.

Svetlana and Michael had shared the same room since coming aboard the *Beacon*, her father having sent her two angry letters and making one angry radiotelephone call about it.

Alone, after the party, Michael stared at her and after a moment she asked, "Why are you staring?"

"I love you—that's reason enough to stare."

"Those people. I could see it in her eyes. She's the one, isn't she?"

"What are you talking about?"

"You never lied to me—at least I don't think you ever lied to me."

"No—I never lied," he told her.

She was taking off her stockings, wearing just her bra and her slip. He leaned back across the bed. She said, "There was something in the way she looked at you—I mean, I watch other women look at you quite a lot. You're good-looking. You're a celebrity. I think half the women in the world would climb into bed with you in a minute."

"Come on, Svetlana—"

"Let me finish. I saw it in her eyes. She's the one you made love to when you were with the Resistance—"

"How do you know this room isn't bugged by Phyllis Zimmer's people?"

Svetlana laughed. "For astrophysics, you need to know a little bit about electronics. I like privacy. It isn't bugged. Isn't she?"

"Yes."

"Why are they here?"

"I don't know for sure. But I think I know."

"To do something tomorrow night."

"Yeah, I think so." He nodded.

"Do you have anything to do with it?"

"Yeah—I'm marrying you. And that's their excuse."

She leaned down beside him. "You want to marry me?" Her eyes were tear-rimmed.

"Yes—I really do. God help us both."

She didn't kiss him—but she smiled, sniffed, sat up, picked up her stockings, and started putting them on. "What are you doing?"

"If this lady is going to try to mess up my wedding, I've got a right to know how. Put your pants on, Michael."

"Hey—look—"

"I know, you can't turn her in, and they wouldn't be up here with a bomb to blow us all up. Would they?"

"I don't think so. That wouldn't serve any purpose. I think they're planning to get control of the broadcast somehow and beam a message of their own to all those televisions and radios that'll be on."

"What's her real name?" Svetlana wanted to know.

"Alice," Michael said.

Svetlana nodded, smoothing down her slip, walking to the closet. She took down a white top that looked like an expensive, low-necked T-shirt and pulled it on over her head. She was digging again. "She wanted to know all about my dress—fine. I'll tell her now. In here—where I know nobody can hear."

"This is crazy," Michael told her.

"I've got to know, Michael—please?" She looked at him, her hands holding a black skirt.

Michael closed his eyes, opened them, nodded. "Just be careful."

"I will. You go and have a walk or something." She began stepping into the skirt. "Michael, can I ask you something?"

"What?" There were a thousand questions she could have asked, and she really hadn't asked him anything since that time in the street when she had asked him and he had told her about Alice, about being lovers with her.

"Who's right?"

He sat up. "I think they are." He stood up and started to put on his pants.

The dining hall looked as though a hurricane had swept through a bar. And when you looked through the open viewing ports toward Earth, it was always strange because there was no time unless you looked for the band of day and the band of night, where one began and one ended. Time aboard the *Beacon of Peace* was artificial, like the air, like the gravity—it was set to coincide with Greenwich Mean Time. The air tasted at times like that in an office building. The gravity, he had noticed, made people dance more wildly and drunk more quickly.

He sat on a chair, his feet propped on the ledge of the "window," looking into space, looking down at Earth. For a time, here, he had put some of it behind him, some of the experiences with the Resistance. But not the questions.

Michael wondered about Marty Deacon. Was it cancer, had it gotten worse, or was he dead?

This was a suicide mission—perhaps Marty was dead. He couldn't see Marty letting Alice go on something like this. But perhaps they had a shuttle—one of the MiG-Boeings.

And he wondered about Louie Chen—there was an air of professionalism about him tonight that Michael had never detected during those weeks with the Resistance. He wondered, sipped at his glass of water, and wondered.

"Hi, Michael!

Michael swung his legs down, stood. Svetlana's face beamed, but it always did. Her hands had disappeared into the pockets of her black skirt, and her hair was down. "Well—you satisfy that woman reporter's curiosity, or what?"

There were other people still in the room—a couple dancing, Phyllis Zimmer and Andy sitting and talking very earnestly in the far corner, some others standing around the bar. Andrea Wojnik, plain by the most objective of standards, had never enjoyed such popularity as tonight.

"She told me if she ever gets married, she wants a dress just like mine." Svetlana smiled. "Can I join you? It looks pretty tonight."

He grabbed another chair, pulled it up beside his,

waited until she sat, sat down himself as she crossed her legs, arranged her skirt. He propped his feet on the "windowsill" again. In less than ten hours, they would be married—he could tell time from the light and shadow on the Earth below. "Well?"

"You were right," she whispered softly, reaching over to him, taking his glass of water. He watched her as she touched her lips to the rim of the glass. "Water?"

"Yeah."

"Oh, yuch."

"What was I right about?" He put his hand in her lap and held her left hand, her right still holding the glass to her lips. Her teeth played against the rim, her eyes staring straight ahead.

"During the wedding. She told me that if we stay out of it, we'll be all right, no one will be hurt. That's what she said."

"You tell her it's suicide?"

"I told her. She said she had a way out."

"Bullshit. She can have all the ways out she wants."

"What are you going to do?"

"Play it by ear. I have to—I can't . . ."

"I will, too—whatever. Make love to me—in case something goes wrong. Please?"

"I'm sorry," Michael told Svetlana. "If there were some way I could—ah, shit." He sighed

"I know. You said it was a circus—this whole thing. Well, if they wanted a circus, they're going to get it, aren't they, Michael?"

"Yeah," Michael whispered.

"Hey, Michael?"

He looked around. It was Phyllis Zimmer, her high heels gone, looking a little silly in her stocking feet and her uniform, Andy beside her.

"Hey, Michael—look—got a question. I was talkin' to Phyllis here. We need a second opinion. You and Svetlana help us out?"

Svetlana moved to the edge of her chair and turned around, staring up at them. Michael stood, one foot on the windowsill, leaning down against his knee. "If we can, Andy. What's up?"

"I told Phyllis I wanna marry her. She said she wanted to marry me. But she told me that once you join the National Police they won't let you out. I told her that was a lot of bull. What do you say?"

Michael looked at Phyllis, then at Svetlana. "I'm afraid she's right."

"There gotta be some changes made, old buddy." Andy grinned.

"Yeah—you're right there," and Michael reminded himself to breathe.

Chapter Twenty-eight

Phyllis was helping Svetlana dress. "Now in the United States—I don't know how it is in Russia—we always say, 'something old, something new, something borrowed, and something blue.'"

"You were so silly last night."

"Thanks for reminding me. What's blue around here?"

"I don't know. Yes I do: my garter. I read a book on American wedding customs. Do you really want to marry Andy?"

"Uh-huh," Phyllis answered, dropping to her knees, unpinning the train. "But I can't. Female officers can't be married. I'd quit. Andy makes a good living. We could live on what he makes. But I can't quit."

Svetlana picked up the headpiece and the veil, Phyllis standing, shifting her holster back, starting to take the headpiece from her. "Can you sit down without messing up the train?"

"I don't think so."

She watched Phyllis's face in the mirror. Phyllis nodded. "What are we going to do? We're going to move in together as soon as there's a way of switching accommodations around."

"If they don't want you married, how are they going to look on you living with a man—I mean, permanently?"

"I don't think they'll like it."

"I'll ask Michael to talk to his father," Svetlana volunteered, bending so Phyllis could position the headpiece in her hair—they were almost exactly the same height. "Ouch—"

"Sorry." Phyllis removed the pin and began to try again. "I don't think that would do any good. I know Michael would talk to Director Borden. But Director Borden can't make an exception in our case."

"You love Andy. Right?"

"Yeah, I love Andy. Don't know why—I mean, he overeats, he's got the manners of a pig, he swears too much, and he works crazy hours. I thought *my* hours were bad."

The headpiece was set. Svetlana reached up to try the veil, Phyllis helping her. "Are you working tonight?"

"You mean security for the wedding. Yeah. Why?"

Svetlana smiled at her. "Just curious. Who's in charge?"

"Captain Metterling. Real gung ho."

"I want to help you when you get married."

"Don't hold your breath," Phyllis told her.

"How much influence do you think I've got?"

"A lot. Why?"

"You go change into your prettiest dress."

"It doesn't look good with a gun." Phyllis laughed. "What are you thinking about?"

"The one thing I did forget. I need a maid of honor. Will you be my maid of honor?"

"Me?"

"The ceremony isn't for an hour. Captain Metterling can replace you on guard duty. I'm all dressed. You can bring your things here, and I can help you."

She watched Phyllis in the mirror, then caught up her dress and turned to look at her. "Well, what do you say?"

Phyllis touched at her hair. "I'm not—"

Svetlana put her arms around Phyllis and hugged her. "Please, do this for me?"

Phyllis answered. "I guess—if Metterling says so—sure!" And Phyllis hugged her back. Svetlana closed her eyes....

*   *   *

Alice entered the storage room—they had given her a key. The sound equipment and cameras were already in place, and she had said she was going to get a backup unit for checking sound levels. Louie Chen was charming the Natpos and the *Beacon* officers.

She opened the metal box, lead-lined, in which they carried extra tape cassettes. She started removing them three at a time. The case was separated into compartments, each lead shielded. She thought about Michael and Svetlana. She didn't want to hurt them—especially him.

She removed a divider, reaching beneath it. These cassettes she removed one at a time, opening the plastic protective case, removing the cassette in each. These cassettes were heavier than the others. She opened her purse for her nail file—it had taken her six weeks in preparation for the mission to grow nails to an acceptable length.

She used the rounded portion of the nail file to pry open the cassette itself.

The trigger guard of the little stainless steel pistol was positioned around one of the sprocket holes. Alice lifted the gun free. She worked back the slide of the Detonics Combat Master, chambering a round from the top of the magazine, upping the safety, leaving it cocked and locked. From the cassette, she removed the spare magazine that had been held in place by metal spring clips. She glanced quickly at the top round in the magazine. It had taken Jake Brown months to find them. Then his best gunsmith had taken them apart, reconstructed the method of manufacture. The liquid Teflon solution had required breaking into a warehouse for chemicals. But at least according to what her father said, they were exact re-creations of Glaser Safety Slugs, the perfect thing to use here if it were necessary. No penetration, no ricochet, almost instant certain death or decapitation for anyone struck. Her father had told her they were the safest thing to use in a combat situation where there might be innocent bystanders. She hoped he was right.

Alice removed the second Detonics minigun, working the slide, upping the safety, removing the spare magazine from the second cassette. After the little Detonics pistols and their special ammunition supply were exhausted, she would rely on the special spring-kit-fitted Berettas and the special low-velocity, low-penetration ammunition of the Security Group.

She placed both pistols in her purse, the spare magazine for one of them in the right pocket of her dress, the spare magazine for the other rubber-banded already to the butt of the second pistol.

Taking the fake cassettes, Alice put the pieces back together, replaced them in the case, then replaced the real cassettes and the lead divider sections.

Louie already had the broadcast tape.

She closed the videocassette box, then began searching for the audio-level monitoring device. Louie had gotten the idea for the operation, and only then revealed to her father, Martin Deacon, that he worked for the Chinese. With their help, dossiers on newspeople had been gotten together, and those who could be relied upon for help were approached. Then the process had begun. There were a surprising number of young female broadcast reporters who matched her general description. Gradually, over the weeks since the inception of the plan, the appearances had been matched. There really was a Juliette Morris, but the real one was five-foot seven, had brown hair, and none of what Northerners called a southern accent. The real Juliette had begun tinting her hair, wearing lower-heeled shoes, while Alice had worked with the few Northerners in their Resistance group, smoothing away as much of her regional speech patterns as possible, tinting her hair from red to auburn, and practicing wearing high heels—something she had never done. For the first time in her life, Alice had also begun wearing a bra—unlike the purse and the lipstick, it was something she could well do without—the bra padded to match the figure of Juliette Morris. With the help of an Israeli who was what Louie Chen had called a "mole" in the National Security Directorate, Alice's fingerprints and identity photo had been substituted for that of the real Juliette. The real Juliette was now in Canada, in hiding. She had sacrificed her career, her friends, everything. Alice admired her for that.

It had been simpler for Louie Chen to take over the identity of Larry Fong, although their appearances matched less. A camera- and soundman was needed who would not be known to the rest of the members of the pool. Fong had been perfect in that regard. The same changes were made on

Fong's own identity card as was done with Juliette Morris's. Fong had gone to Canada as well, but after this was over, his wife and two children, already prepared to flee, would join him. At precisely midnight they would be spirited away by the Resistance, taken to safety before any Natpo reprisals could be undertaken.

Alice found the audio-level monitor, closing the case she had extracted it from, checking the small gold watch on her wrist. She had to hurry.

Her father had not wanted her to go. She had fought him to go. Chen had insisted that the chance for escape in the confusion they would generate was excellent. One of the MiG-Boeing SW9 shuttle craft would be ready for them. Someone aboard the *Beacon of Peace* would prepare it for them, a trusted agent, someone whose identity they were not given for the protection of that agent should they be caught.

They would take over the wedding ceremony, running their own tape through the master feed for the pool coverage, showing the misery and suffering of the concentration camps where once-free Americans were held like cattle. They would show the hideously mutilated faces and bodies of Natpo torture victims, the poison-gas attacks of the Soviet Union against the Chinese, Israeli, and Egyptian armies, show the remains of the napalmed Israeli border settlements. And before the signal could be jammed, they would give documentary evidence that the Russians, with the help of Lester Saile, were arming the *Beacon of Peace* as a nuclear weapons platform. The gas bombs would go off, throwing the station into total confusion, disorienting those aboard, while she and Chen made their way to the MiG-Boeing.

She considered her chances for survival exceedingly low, partly because she had argued so frequently with her father that her chances were excellent. Chen's revelation that he was a Chinese agent had opened a new world for them, a world of hope. There was an active Allied network made up of daring men and women throughout Canada, Western Europe, and Chinese Asia, working against the Soviet Union and the Soviet-dominated United States government. War between China and Russia was imminent, and likely nuclear war. But the other powers, beset with their own struggles against communism, were poised to side with China against

Russia. This action would so disrupt Soviet control of North America that the Soviets would be forced to commit troops throughout the United States, more troops into Canada. This would allow the Western Europeans, the British, the Chinese, the Egyptians, and the Israelis to launch a massive land and sea war against the Soviet Union, averting nuclear conflict, to crush communism and restore freedom in Soviet-occupied lands.

Considering what the broadcast was intended to achieve, the sacrifice of her own life was of little consequence. She found herself taking comfort in Michael's marriage to Svetlana. She had considered Svetlana Drusznina to be a spoiled Russian bitch. But she had been wrong. It was clear that Svetlana genuinely loved Michael. When Svetlana had called her to come and see the wedding dress, Alice had been wary.

Svetlana had been frank. "There are no listening devices in here, Alice. Do you intend to destroy the *Beacon*? I want Michael to live. If the only way he can live is for you to have him—"

Svetlana had then begun to cry.

Alice had held her hands. Alice had told her the truth, but only the details of the plan that directly concerned the wedding ceremony itself. Svetlana had been reassured.

She looked at her borrowed watch again as she exited the storage room. Svetlana would be dressed now. Soon it would all begin. Then it would all be over.

Chapter Twenty-nine

Svetlana's father stopped Michael as he walked toward the Command Level auditorium, along the corridor of Red Level. He looked more overstuffed in a tuxedo than Michael felt.

"Michael, I wanted to talk to you for a moment...." Mr. Drusznin shot his left cuff and looked at his watch. "I must join Svetlana soon—I am giving her away. Your American weddings—very complicated. Svetlana's mother and I went to the Commissariat and filled out the proper papers and we were married. It was very simple. But nowdays there is a return to these more formal customs, in my country, too." He draped his right arm across Michael's shoulders. "You are getting a fine girl."

"I know that, sir."

"Call me 'Papa'—please, Michael."

"Papa." Michael grinned.

Mr. Drusznin spoke. "There is much talk in the Politburo that you will one day be the American president, after Lester Saile can no longer serve."

"Yes, I've heard the talk."

"There is talk also that if the proposed Mars mission gets under way, Svetlana will be the science officer and you the medical officer."

"I've heard that as a rumor only."

"The two of you—after tonight particularly—will stand for something very fine together." Mr. Drusznin placed both hands on Michael's shoulders, looking up at him. "You are an astute young man, perhaps more so after your near misfortune with the American Resistance."

"I don't understand."

"The era of men such as Lester Saile is coming to an end, I think."

"And men like my father?"

"You take my dearest possession—you have a right to know what is in my heart. Do you know how long I have been Politburo representative to your government?" He didn't wait for an answer. "Twenty-three years, since Svetlana was so very tiny." He squeezed his hands together in front of him as though closing an invisible concertina, but very gently. "When her mother died, I was very sad. I was faced with raising Svetlana all alone. For a man who lives in large houses and has many servants, that may sound strange. But the responsibility was mine."

"I understand. She's a wonderful woman. You did a fine job of raising her."

"But I saw things, Michael. I wasn't like some fathers—who could leave, pretend that the child was raised somehow magically and one day was an adult. I began to think. What was I raising her to be? In what sort of world would she live? I was a good friend to Feyodor Mikhail Blotsky—"

"I was very sorry when he died," Michael interrupted. He thrust his hands into his pockets, staring out the viewing port toward the platform that was growing inexorably in the distance—a platform for what? He thought he knew.

"He told me things—he liked to drink a little. I all but stopped drinking myself." Mr. Drusznin laughed, Michael watching the dark reflection of Svetlana's father's face and his own in the viewing port. "He used to laugh and say that each drink I did not drink, he drank for me. He was a soldier—and he respected honor."

"I know that."

"He was a brutal man, but a good man. And he made me see things."

"What things?"

"There will be war—between our countries and China. We have based missiles in your country for the past eighteen years. They are aimed at Western Europe, Canada, and China. Our own missiles are aimed at the same places. The old weapons systems you destroyed, we have converted to our own use. The peace was a lie."

"I've been getting that impression."

"The platform you are watching out there"—Mr. Drusznin gestured dismissively toward it—"it is for nuclear weapons to launch against China and Western Europe."

"That's insanity. We'll all die."

"You cannot change this."

"Why can't I?"

"You cannot. Perhaps, someday, if anyone survives—"

Michael turned away from the platform that hovered near them, stared into Mr. Drusznin's eyes. "Are you telling me to take Svetlana somewhere? Or not to have children with her? What are you telling me?"

"I am telling you that when it comes, do not hate me because of it. I have fought against it as much as I dared. But there is nothing now that can stop it. Men like me must fight to hold back. There may be many good years yet, but—"

Michael embraced him.

*   *   *

The dress Svetlana wore was like a setting, her face the jewel that crowned it. She stood on the opposite side of the stage from Michael. The auditorium seats were filled with the crew of the *Beacon of Peace* who were not essential to its immediate function. At the center of the stage, Alexii Umarov stood as commander of the *Beacon*, there to perform the ceremony. Svetlana's father stood at the small podium at the side of the stage near her, addressing the four television cameras, two each from the United States and the Soviet Union.

Michael saw Louie Chen, his camera dollying back, the Soviet director murmuring into a headset. Alice sat on the edge of the dolly, her legs crossed, a notepad on her lap, a smile set on her face.

His eyes drifted back to Svetlana. Behind her stood Phyllis Zimmer, wearing an off-white dress with a straight skirt, holding her hands together in front of her. Phyllis seemed to glow, he thought.

He searched the crowd for Captain Metterling of Security. Metterling stood by the rear of the auditorium near the wide doors, which were closed. Security personnel were posted at strategic positions throughout the auditorium, but no rifles were in evidence. He didn't even know if they had any weapons beyond their clubs and their pistols.

He became conscious of Svetlana's father's words: "... millions who witness this ceremony. I have spoken as the official adviser for the Union of Soviet Socialist Republics to the United States for more than two decades. But now I speak as a father. These are two fine young people, and they symbolize more than a union between two nations of historic destiny. They symbolize mankind—the continuation, the celebration of life." Mr. Drusznin finished and stepped down.

Commander Umarov stepped forward. Michael caught his cue and started to walk from stage left. Mr. Drusznin and Svetlana reached center stage together. Mr. Drusznin put back Svetlana's veil, kissed her, and Svetlana hugged him tightly. Michael reached out with his left hand, her right hand resting atop his now as she turned and he heard the rustle of fabric as Phyllis straightened Svetlana's train.

Commander Umarov began to speak. "Comrades, as commander of the *Beacon of Peace*, I have overseen many firsts. And now tonight, the first wedding performed here at the edge of man's greatest frontier. Michael, do you take—"

"All right!"

Michael started to turn. There was a scream—a shot. Alice pushed between him and Svetlana, a gleaming pistol to Svetlana's head. "Nobody moves or she dies. We don't want to kill anybody. Louie!"

"It's running!"

With the lights, it was hard to see. Michael saw a blur of black, heard a shouted command to drop the gun, then heard the booming of gunshots. Louie Chen ran across the stage, firing, black-uniformed Security personnel going down. Chen's body doubled forward, stitches of red across his chest—blood and gunshot wounds.

Alice pushed Svetlana away, into Michael's arms. Michael held Svetlana tight against him, shielding her with his body. Umarov leaped for Alice, who cracked him against the side of the head with the pistol.

She started to run, the high heels clicking on the stage surface, then the sound lost in the boom of a gunshot. Alice fell forward, skidding across the stage surface, rolling to her back, firing into the face of one of the Security Group. The man's face was a wet red pulp as he fell back. She was up, the side of her dress stained red, her left leg dragging.

Then Phyllis Zimmer tackled her, the two women rolling across the stage, more Security personnel running toward them. Alice was up, her tiny right fist swinging out, Phyllis Zimmer's head snapping back.

Alice pushed Phyllis down. As Alice was starting into the wings, a figure jumped toward her. Alice reeled back, falling, firing her pistol, emptying it as the man swung a nightstick down toward her head. The man's body lurched away, falling.

Alice was to her knees, something falling out of the butt of her pistol—it was called a magazine, he remembered. Michael smelled something—gas, nausea welling up in him.

She was sticking a fresh magazine up the butt of the pistol.

A woman from the Security Group stabbed a pistol toward Alice and fired as Alice moved. The gun flew from her right fist to the stage floor, Alice's left sleeve drenched with blood.

Alice started to her feet. One of the Security Group personnel kicked her down. She fell.

Michael pushed Svetlana into her father's arms.

"Michael! No!" Svetlana screamed.

Security Group Captain Metterling was running up the center aisle.

One of the men from the Security Group—Michael knew him, disliked him—was placing a pistol to Alice's head.

Michael shoved forward, knocking one of the Security Group people down, another starting to swing his club. Michael blocked the arm with a crossed wrist block, knee rising into the man's crotch.

Alice was shouting at the man about to kill her. "The broadcast is running, fucker!"

Michael reached out, his hand closing over the pistol, the web of flesh between his thumb and first finger between the hammer and the slide. Martin had taught him that one. Someone at the edge of his peripheral vision threw up—the gas.

The Security man wheeled right. Michael's right knee smashed up against the forearm, his right hand grabbing the pistol just behind the muzzle. The grip was gone as Michael's knee contacted the security man's arm, Michael holding the pistol now, turning half right, his left elbow smashing into the Security man's chest.

Michael turned, the pistol still in his hand.

"Comrade Dr. Borden!"

The voice was Metterling's.

"Here—take it!" Michael shouted, holding the gun high above his head.

"What are you doing, comrade Doctor?"

Michael's mind raced. He looked at Alice, at Svetlana. She clung to her father's arms. "This idiot was gonna kill the woman here. Why do that? She must be Resistance. If she's alive, she can be made to talk."

Metterling stepped forward, taking the gun, working the safety down, the hammer falling, his eyes burning like hot pokers. "This—this martial arts—"

"The Resistance made me learn it. Kind of a joke, I guess—they thought it was. I couldn't see this girl being killed. She is too valuable—no matter what she has done."

Metterling looked at Alice. A voice shouted, "I have severed the cable—the broadcast is stopped!"

Alice lay there on the floor, bleeding. She started to laugh.

Michael dropped to his knees. "This woman needs medical attention, Metterling. Send somebody for my bag!" Alice just stared up at him, the laughter still in her eyes. Michael went to Svetlana, who stood over Louie Chen. Phyllis was with her, as was Umarov. "How is—"

"Dead, Michael," Umarov said flatly.

Svetlana looked at him sadly. The front of the wedding dress was stained red with blood.

Chapter Thirty

Svetlana wore only a white slip, her hair uncombed, her face tear-streaked. They were alone. It had been hours since the Resistance attack and the broadcast, the aftermath consuming the rest of the night. Before he had entered their room, he had looked at his watch: 7:00 A.M. GMT. He closed the door.

Svetlana stood in front of the closet door mirror. "What's going to happen?"

"She's alive."

"What are you going to do?"

"I got the bullets out. Nothing really tricky. She lost a lot of blood, but I sedated her so she can rest and they can't question her."

"If they use drugs, they'll know we knew."

"Yeah."

"What'll they do to her, Michael?" Svetlana's voice sounded strained.

"I don't know. Her father told me some things the Spetznas and the National Police do to people. The National Police are worse, he said. They're sending her down to Colorado later today, as soon as she comes out of it. There's the main detention center there. And my father's there."

"Can't you talk to him?" She had turned around now, facing him over her left shoulder.

"Nothing I can do will prevent him from doing his duty. I learned that."

"Michael?" she said with a moan.

Michael breathed out, hard, sitting on the edge of the bed. He couldn't remember where he'd left the jacket from the tuxedo—the tie was still around his neck, but open. He pulled it off. His sleeves were rolled up. His shoes had bloodstains on them. "When I do whatever I have to do, you make some official announcement, and talk about it privately a lot, to people who talk to other people."

"Michael?" She sounded like an injured child.

"I was never really sure I loved you."

"I know."

"And after Alice—I thought I loved her more. I don't—I loved her differently. But now I'm sure I won't be back. And I love you. You're gonna have to say you were shocked at what I did, that you never suspected I harbored counterrevolutionary tendencies. You should marry somebody else."

"I won't," she whispered.

"It's not just Alice. Some stuff your father said. Some stuff I've been feeling. They lied to us, Svetlana. Our books in school lied to us, our newspapers lied to us, the television, the radio, the people we trusted. My father—just a pile of lies and shit. They have missiles aimed at Western Europe and China siloed on U.S. soil. That platform they're building— it's to launch nuclear weapons against China. They're gonna blow up the whole world—and they're too stupid to care. They told us we had peace, and we never did. They taught us to love peace—and they never wanted peace."

"Are you going to join the Resistance?"

"I'll get Alice free somehow. And if we don't get killed— yeah. Maybe there's something to do to stop them."

"I want to go with you, Michael."

"You can't. You do as I say. Denounce me—call me ever filthy name you can think of. Marry somebody." Michael stood up, walked to his dresser, and started to pull out socks, underwear, a knit shirt, a pair of blue jeans. His track shoes were on the floor beside the dresser, and he bent over to pick them up. "Go and stay with your father, Svetlana."

"Michael?"

It sounded silly to say it, because she knew it. But she said it as he walked through the doorway. "I'll always love you."

He closed the door, walked the Orange Level hall, his eyes and his throat tight. Exhausted and confused, he stepped into the shower. He turned on the water. Now he could let himself cry, he told himself.

When he came back from the shower, Svetlana was gone.

BOOK THREE
THE FREEMAN

Chapter Thirty-one

Helen remembered every detail: Michael and Miss Svetlana coming to the center of the stage, Michael so handsome in his tuxedo, Miss Svetlana's dress so beautiful, the smile on her face so gorgeous when her father had lifted the veil and she had kissed him.

Then all of a sudden those awful people and their guns—the Chinese man and the woman who was supposed to be a reporter. And then those awful pictures. She closed her eyes against them even now. Men and women in concentration camps behind barbed wire, the announcer had said. Pictures of people who had been tortured by the National Police and the Russian soldiers: women with their breasts cut off, men with their testicles removed, people with lips sawn away, tongues cut out, eyes gouged. Children—their bodies mangled with what had been said were beatings in order to force information from their parents.

The planes with their red stars, flying over battlefields and spraying poison gas, killing the Chinese, the Jews, the Egyptians.

But what had frightened her most—the announcer had shown photographs that proved that the Russians and the United States were building a platform in space to fire nuclear missiles. Then suddenly the screen had gone fuzzy gray and the man who read the evening news had come on, explaining that armed terrorists had disrupted the wedding of Michael Borden and Svetlana Drusznina, that after killing dozens of innocent bystanders, the terrorists were subdued, and that Michael and Svetlana were uninjured. The news announcer attempted to explain away the Resistance broadcast as antigovernment propaganda. The so-called torture victims were really the subjects of bizarre medical experiments being carried out in Canada under the influence of the Chinese, experiments with drugs for possible use in germ warfare against the United States and the Soviet Union. The troops shown being gassed were really Spetznas disguised in the uniforms of enemy soldiers, being gassed by Chinese planes with counterfeit Soviet markings. The Chinese were using gas and germs against the heroic Soviet soldiers and their U.S. allies, as were the Canadians and their puppet masters, the English. There was a global anti-U.S. and anti-Soviet conspiracy among England, China, Israel, Egypt, Canada, Australia, and France, their stooges. Helen had asked Director Borden what stooges were—but he had sat there, white-lipped, not speaking.

As to the "missile-launching platform" in space near the *Beacon of Peace*—the official explanation was that this demonstrated the thorough evil and deceitfulness of the conspirators and the treachery of the armed terrorist lunatics who called themselves the Resistance. This was simply a platform that would be used to build the special space ship that would take people to Mars soon.

Helen looked at her little wristwatch—Michael would be here soon. Director Borden was away on business. Mrs. Borden was in bad shape—in shock after the terrorist attack aboard the space station. At least Michael was safe, Helen thought. . . .

The Mercedes stopped, and Michael bounded out of the car. He hunched his shoulders under the jacket, not quite used to the vagaries of terrestrial temperature—the thermometer had read just above the freezing point when they had passed the Financial Union building.

Helen greeted him at the door. Michael took the stairs three at a time, picking Helen up as he hugged her. "You look prettier than ever," he told her.

"Michael," she cooed. He kissed her on the cheek as he set her down. She tugged at her apron, at her dress, patted at her hair under the cap. "I was so worried. How's Miss Svetlana?"

Michael swallowed. "She's fine." He grinned. "Just fine. Mom awake?"

"No, Michael." The driver started to hand Helen one of

Michael's two bags. Michael grabbed it instead. But she took the other one from him.

Inside, he said, "You were telling me about Mom. My father said she was all right. That was—"

"She's fine now, sleeping. I just looked in on her. Can I fix you some breakfast?"

"Sure," Michael told her. "But only if you'll have something with me."

She smiled, started to laugh. "All right."

Michael set down his bag, took the suitbag, hung it on the hall tree—a habit his father hated. "My father home?"

"No. He left with that Captain Waterman."

"Sweet William—yes. Come on, you got me hungry with that talk about breakfast."

He followed her into the kitchen and sat at the servants' table while she cooked eggs sunny side up, a small steak, made fresh hashed brown potatoes, and brewed coffee. He sipped at a glass of orange juice as they talked. She explained what had happened to his mother, what she had thought of the broadcast, about the terrorists. He told her they weren't terrorists but freedom fighters. He admitted the difference could be subtle and confusing. He told her the broadcast was true: The television announcer had read lies to his viewers. He took out two plates and two settings of flatware. She insisted she wasn't hungry. He insisted she was, telling her he didn't like eating alone.

He cut the steak in half, helped Helen into her chair, told her he would get the coffee, and asked her if his father had said anything. "Just to keep you here, Michael."

"Helen, I'm gonna ask two favors."

"Sure, Michael. You know—"

"I know." He smiled. "Don't tell anybody we talked, that I told you the truth about last night."

"All right."

"And take care of my mother for me. When she's gone, watch yourself, and if things start to get bad, get out of here. I wouldn't want anything to happen to you. Mom left some things for you when she dies—"

"No, Michael—"

"You take 'em, use 'em. They're wrapped in brown paper on the floor in the corner of that big closet in her room."

"Yes, Michael."

"Eat—come on. Before it gets cold." And he began to eat, telling her through a mouthful of food, "This is good."

"What about Miss Svetlana? What'll—"

"She's gonna marry somebody else. I told her to. I can't take her with me where I'm going. Now—after we're through eating, I'm gonna wake up my mother, and you do me another favor. Go to my room and get out all my blue jeans, the three heaviest sweaters I've got, my ski gloves—both pairs. Those Natpo combat boots I've got packed away—see if you can find 'em. Sweat socks, underpants, that set of thermal underwear I always take with me when I go skiing— anything else that'll fit in the two flight bags in the closet and might be useful for a wide range of temperature extremes."

"Where are you going, Michael?"

"Can't tell you, Helen."

"But—"

"You can tell me something, though. Does Dad keep any guns here?"

"Michael! What could you do with a gun?"

"Not as much as I wish I could. Wish I'd taken Marshal Blotsky seriously."

Helen cleared her throat. "Just before he died he left a present for you. He told me I should hold on to it, put it away safely, and give it to you after he died. I didn't know where to send it. I—"

"Where is it?"

"In my room."

"Go get it? Please?"

"Yes, Michael." She ran from the room, Michael staring into his coffee. Blotsky had been murdered—he was more sure of it each time he considered it. Blotsky had known something about James Hope and the Resistance. But what?

He thought of Alice, wrists and ankles shackled against his medical counsel; she had been taken from the shuttle into one of the black Natpo vans. He knew where they were transporting her, what they would do to her. He looked at his watch; his father and William Waterman would be there now. But Michael had sedated her again. It wouldn't start to wear off for an hour. From her chart, the doctors at the detention center would know better than to give her anything until the sedative had worn off.

That gave him an hour, perhaps a little longer.

He could hear the clicking of Helen's shoes in the corridor, turned as she entered the room. She held a box, sealed with tamper-resistant tape wrapped completely around it.

He took the box from Helen. It felt heavy.

Sawing through the tape was like sawing through rope, something he had done in the survival course in the desert in Iran. He kept sawing.

"There's more tape underneath, Michael," Helen said.

"Keep cutting. Whatever it is, he didn't want anybody prying." Michael kept cutting, into the second layer now, tearing the first layer away in chunks and strips. He finally got it open and reached inside. His hands stopped when he felt something in plastic. He drew it out of the box. It was a pistol, oil-slicked though under the plastic; it was identical to the one Marshal Blotsky had said James Hope had used.

Michael tore open the bag.

As he drew the pistol out, he stopped, the right side of the pistol catching the overhead light. He smudged some of the oil away from the metal surface with a napkin.

A single word was deeply engraved upon it: "Hope."

Helen was exploring the box. "Michael—there's other stuff in here. And this."

She held a sealed envelope. Michael took it, setting the pistol down on the tablecloth, turning the envelope over in his hands. He tore it open. He recognized Blotsky's handwriting.

Michael—

Some things you might someday need. If you never need them, all the better. But something tells me you will. The pistol is one of the two James Hope carried. The other one is not in my possession. It is a Detonics Scoremaster. 45. You will see James Hope's last name engraved on the right-slide flat. The man who took the other pistol took it for different rea-

sons. I took this one because I have always enjoyed fine firearms. With it, I took all the accessories. You will find them in the box. Something called a Milt Sparks Six-Pack—spare magazines for the pistol. A plastic bag containing approximately two hundred rounds of ammunition taken from the cave where James Hope died. It is 185-grain jacketed hollow-point type. The case-head stamps read "Federal" —they made good ammunition. I have also included the necessary implements with which to clean the pistol and maintain it, two extra pairs of the rubber Pachmayr grips like those on the gun, and my best wishes. If you are reading this anytime within the present decade,. I will likely have opened my mouth once too often.

Bless you.

Blotsky

"What are you gonna do with this stuff?" Helen asked as he put down the letter.

"Use it," he told her.

With the cleaning materials was a typed set of instructions telling him how to disassemble the pistol for something called "field stripping" and cleaning. He followed the directions, cleaned the pistol, reassembled it in reverse order—surprisingly simple, he learned—then set about loading it.

The sight of the hammer raised unnerved him, so he followed Blotsky's instructions for lowering it, learned that the thumb safety didn't work with the hammer down, but the grip safety worked either way.

He took the pistol and carefully secured it under his shirt after first wiping off more of the excess oil. It felt cold against his skin. He took the single loose spare magazine, loaded it as well, and pocketed it. The hollow-point bullets each had an enormous cavity. He loaded the other six magazines in the compartmented black leather pouch called a Six-Pack, then replaced them in the pouch. He gave the box to Helen. "Put the cleaning kit, the Six-Pack, the bag of ammunition, and the letter into one of my flight bags. Pack some clothes around them. Get rid of the box. I'm going to see my mother."

He went to his mother's door, knocked. "Mom? It's Michael."

There was no answer. He knocked again.

"Michael?"

"Yes, Mom. Can I come in?"

"Yes—Yes."

He had not seen her in months, and in his frequent calls to her, she had always told him she was doing better. In his frequent calls to Borozoi, the physician had always told him she was sinking. Borozoi, Michael saw, had been the one telling the truth.

"Michael, come closer."

He sat on the edge of the bed beside her, smiling down on her. "How you doin'?"

"I'm fine—I really am. But I was up so late. Is Svetlana really all right?"

"Svetlana's really all right. She sends her love. Svetlana's dad said to tell you he wants another game of chess when he's back."

"I don't think he'll get it," she whispered, her cheeks sinking as she exhaled.

"Come on—you just told me you're fine."

"I lied," she said with a smile.

He leaned his head against her chest, and she held him, whispering, "What's this I hear about the wedding—it has been put off?"

"Yeah. There's something I have to do first."

"What, Michael?" She pushed him away a little, and he sat back. She tried to sit up. "I haven't been married to a policeman all these years for nothing. That's a gun."

"Yeah," he told her. "Don't worry about it."

"Just because I lie to you about my health doesn't mean you have to lie to me. Let me see the gun."

"All right." He nodded, sucking in a breath, reaching under his shirt, drawing the gun for her to see.

"That's James Hope's gun, isn't it? Where did you get it? No—don't tell me." She closed her eyes, the lids fluttering for an instant. He reached for her neck to feel for a pulse, but her eyes opened and she had a clear look in them he hadn't seen for a very long time. "Michael, go to the wall and take the painting of that ugly drunk Lester Saile off the wall and open the wall safe."

"What?"

"Just do it—hurry."

He stood up, stuffing the pistol into his pants under his belt, walking across the room, reaching to the frame, and taking the picture down. The wallpaper beneath it was unfaded, and there was a small wall safe set into it. "The combination is thirty-six right, left thirteen, and then right to zero."

He repeated it as he tried it—and he heard a click. "When did you put this in?"

"Your father put it in right after we moved here. He set the combination himself, but he was always bad at memorizing things like that, and he wrote it down. I memorized it. Turn the handle and open it."

He turned the handle, swinging the safe door open. There was a wooden box inside.

"Take the box out, Michael."

The box was heavy. It had a brass-hinged keeper, a hasp of sorts, but there was no lock in it. He lifted the hasp and lifted the lid of the box.

A pistol—a Scoremaster, identical to the one in his belt. "Hope" was engraved on the right side of the slide. "James Hope's second gun," Michael murmured.

"Now you have both of them. You're the one who should."

"Marshal Blotsky left the other one for me."

"It should still work—I can smell the oil each time your father opens the safe to clean it. I smelled the oil again last week."

"Mom, I can't—"

"Take it—it's yours."

"But—"

"I loved you from the first moment I saw you. Your father said someone had called you an angel—so we named you Michael. Neither one of us ever thought to give you a middle name. And your last name—you're James and Melissa Hope's son." She leaned back against the headboard. He crossed the room to her, dropped to his knees beside the bed, setting the second pistol on the nightstand beside her. "We couldn't—Arnold never killed your parents. Your brother, Stephen, did."

"Why?"

"Stephen was one of those people who couldn't drink. When he was sixteen, he decided he was going to try it. Your father—your real father—wasn't home. Neither was your sister, Jennifer. Stephen got very drunk. The servants were gone. He tried to—"

"He tried to what?" Michael whispered.

"He tried to rape your mother."

Michael closed his eyes, listened to his mother's voice—his mother, the woman who had loved him, cared for him. He could feel the tears as she spoke.

"He tried but did not succeed. She told me. We were always close—she said she had to tell somebody. I always knew why he killed his parents, why he hated his father. But she never told James."

Michael cleared his throat.

"Your other father—my husband—was a good man once. And we always loved you. I always loved you."

He leaned over her, cocooning her in his arms. "Mom," he whispered—and he felt, as the breath stopped, the rising and falling of her chest stop. He held her tightly and cried aloud.

Chapter Thirty-two

Michael drove the Mercedes, listening to the car radio.

"Tentative findings have been released today in the terrorist attack against the *Beacon of Peace*. Gas bombs had been placed aboard the *Beacon* by the terrorists prior to the attack, the canisters containing what a National Police spokesperson describes as lethal chemical agents long ago banned by civilized nations but currently produced by the Chinese and smuggled to the terrorists through Canada. Large caches of this gas may exist throughout the United States and Mexico, it was further reported, and the National Police have begun a massive search effort to locate the deadly poison gas before terrorists can strike again.

"In a further development, Director Arnold Borden of the National Security Directorate and commander of the National Security Forces announced that the terrorists who attacked the *Beacon of Peace* were using specially handmade bullets designed to kill victims slowly and in great pain, their special design the subject of specific legislation just prior to the Civilian Disarmament Act. When questioned following his statement to the press, Director Borden confirmed that these types of deadly killer bullets are used by special units of the Chinese infantry and by the British killer elite force known as the SAS, or Special Assassination Squads.

"In Washington, a spokesman for President Lester Saile decried the use of these mass-murder bullets and death-gas bombs and made a direct appeal to the Soviet Union for additional units of Spetznas to assist the National Security Forces in this crackdown.

"This just handed me: Using his special emergency powers, Director Arnold Borden has issued this statement: 'In the interest of public safety, I am instituting the following measures after consultation with President Saile and his advisers. First, a 9:00 P.M. to 6:00 A.M. curfew will be in effect until this terrorist crisis has passed. Those whose special work needs require them to travel during the restricted period will be issued special documentation at their place of work. Any other persons requiring special permits to travel between these hours must report to their nearest National Police post.

" 'Second, in order to curb further violence by these armed fanatics, the search and seizure policies previously used to enforce the Civilian Disarmament Act and the Subversion Acts will be temporarily extended. Innocent persons are advised to open their homes freely to the National Police and to cooperate fully in searches. Any contraband items seized may be appealed by appropriate methods through the

National Police, who will inform you of your rights under these emergency measures.

" 'Third, I am asking the Congress today to pass legislation immediately that would outlaw the possession, manufacture, or use of any cutting instrument with a blade thickness in excess of one-eighth inch. Further, that such special cutting instruments as may be required for work-related activities—such as axes—must be brought securely wrapped and tied along with appropriate documentation of need to the nearest National Police post immediately upon enactment. Further, that following enactment, there will be a ten-day grace period for the turning in of such potentially lethal devices at locations to be establised by the National Police. Following the grace period, any such devices held without proper authorization will be subject to confiscation, and those holding such devices, subject to criminal penalties to be spelled out in the legislation.

" 'Fourth, I am requesting the cooperation of all loyal Americans in defeating this terrorist threat. Any reported violation of law, when proven, will entitle the person originally reporting the violation to special financial compensation. This shall be considered an incentive toward good citizenship, and concurrent with the financial compensation, a certificate of award shall be presented by local National Police officials. If you know anyone who is in violation of the law, report that person at once—it might save your life.' "

Michael shut off the radio, no longer wanting to listen to the "news."

Possession of the two pistols he carried under his shirt, one behind each hipbone, butt forward, qualified him for life imprisonment. Use of the pistols qualified him for the death penalty.

He wondered what they could do to him beyond that—because he had other things planned.

In each trouser pocket, he now carried a spare magazine. He counted mentally as the guards approached, the gate still closed. Eight in each gun—that made sixteen. Seven in each of the two spare magazines on his body. All told, thirty rounds. He wondered if that would be enough.

Michael brought the Mercedes to a full stop in front of the security barricade, the closed chain-link gates beyond.

Apparently the guards recognized him, the shorter of the two men saluting with his rifle as Michael rolled down the window of the Mercedes. "Comrade Dr. Borden."

"Hi—listen. I understand my dad's here, or is coming here. I wanted to go inside. Gotta talk to him. Something I just thought of about the terrorist attack on the *Beacon* that might help him nail some of the bastards."

"Certainly, Comrade Dr. Borden. Comrade Drusznina is well?"

"Svetlana is fine, thank you." Michael rolled up the window to discourage further questions—he didn't have any further answers.

The shorter man opened the chain-link gates. Michael noted that the barricade was designed to block entrance, not exit. He gave a little wave. His palms sweated as he gripped the steering wheel. He started the Mercedes forward, noticing in the rearview mirror the taller guard running toward him, his rifle in his hands.

Michael licked his lips. Had he done something wrong? Was there some kind of special detection equipment that had told them he had brought firearms through the gates?

He stopped, his right hand moving from the steering wheel, resting across his thighs, ready to grasp the pistol behind his left hipbone. He had no idea if he could actually use it, actually kill. The thought scared him.

He rolled the window down with his left hand as the guard approached. "Comrade Dr. Borden—please?"

"What's wrong?"

"My daughter is a great fan of your athletic achievement. Would it be all right—" He extended a blank index card and a pen. Michael swallowed, took the pen and card. "She'll go crazy over this."

"What's her name?"

"Mary Ann."

"Pretty name." He signed the card, "All my best to Mary Ann—Michael Borden." He wondered what the guard would have said if he had signed it *Michael Hope*.

He handed back the card and the pen.

"Thank you, comrade Doctor—very much."

He raised the window. He had dripped perspiration from his hands onto the card. He hoped it wouldn't trigger suspicion in the guard's mind.

He stepped on the accelerator, the Mercedes rolling ahead.

The Administration Building was at the far side of the compound—his father probably would be there. If they were about to interrogate Alice, she would be fully out of the sedative now, ready for them.

He stopped the car in front of the Administration Building. He distrusted buildings—there might be electronic equipment that could detect guns. But the men and women he had seen moving about the compound carried guns. Wouldn't their guns set off the electronic alarms? He guessed that something could be installed in the Natpos' guns to avoid setting off the detectors.

Michael made a decision: He drew both pistols, slipped them far back under the seat, keeping them well below the level of any windows in the car. The spare magazines from his pocket went under the seat as well.

He got out, locking the car, looking around.

He saw a Natpo—whose black winter coat made his chest look broad and his arms look muscular. The Natpo was walking out of the main yard and along the side of the Administration Building, his pistol carried low along his side, just above the knee.

Michael glanced around, up toward the Administration Building, into the yard. He followed the Natpo along the side of the building, the trees that lined the walkway bare of leaves.

There was a garage behind the Administration Building. A stiff wind blew as Michael followed the Natpo. He could wait until the man reached the garage, but there might be other Natpos there, or service personnel.

He raised his voice after the man. "Excuse me—officer?"

The man turned around, his trooper cap cocked to an angle on his head, almost obscuring his right eyebrow. "What?"

"Excuse me. I'm Michael Borden. I was wondering—"

The man's face lit, his attitude changing. "Comrade Doctor, forgive me. I didn't recognize you."

Michael grinned, still walking toward the man, who was now walking back toward him.

They stopped, less than a yard apart. Michael glanced around, extended his right hand. "How are you?"

"Fine." The man grinned back, taking Michael's hand. Michael jerked him forward.

Michael's left fist crossed the man's jaw, his right knee smashing into the man's crotch. As the man doubled forward, Michael's right knee smashed up again as Michael murmured, "I hate to do this." He felt his knee contact bone, felt the right hand go limp in his. He caught the man up under the armpits as the man sagged.

Michael looked ahead and behind, then up to the building beside him—nothing, he determined. He hadn't thought of what to do with the Natpo. "Shit," he murmured, hauling the man closer to the building wall, dragging him through the hedgerow, and setting him down as gently as possible. The man's mouth was bleeding heavily. Michael searched his pockets, found a handkerchief, and wiped the blood away. In the instant before it reappeared, he saw that he had split the man's lower lip, but no teeth were broken. The man was unconscious.

Michael turned the man's head to the side so the blood would run out of the mouth and not into it and gag him. Michael took the pistol out of the holster. It was a Beretta like the one Phyllis Zimmer carried, but a metal band circled the grip just beneath the trigger guard, below the magazine release. Set into the band was a stud over the right-grip panel. He had guessed right. He held the pistol, removed the magazine, and gently drew the slide back—a round was chambered. He reinserted the magazine, trying to dope out the safety and the general operation of the pistol. Marshal Blotsky had let him fire one, he remembered. Push the safety up, the opposite of a .45.

He did it—somehow he could feel that the pistol worked. There was no need to cock it; just pull the trigger for the first shot, then work the safety, and the hammer would fall but the gun wouldn't go off.

He nodded to himself.

On the man's belt was a small pocket. Inside it were two

more loaded magazines. Michael pocketed them, then stuck the gun in his trouser band under his leather jacket.

He stood up, looked around, stepped over the hedgerow, and walked back toward the front of the Administration Building. He entered.

A cheerless-looking woman looked up from a desk at the far end of the entry hall. "Yes?"

"I'm Michael Borden—looking for my dad. Kind of urgent."

"Comrade Dr. Borden?" She was Russian.

"Is he here? It's real important."

"I can call the comrade director."

"What—he's not here?" Michael approached the desk. No sound, no alarm—he had made the right decision in stealing the Beretta rather than using his own guns.

"He is at the Intelligence Acquisition Building. I believe the comrade director interviews one of the terrorists from the *Beacon of Peace*."

"That's what I came to talk to him about. I'll go right over." Michael smiled at the woman. "Have a nice day." He turned and started back for the doors. It was possible she might call ahead—likely, perhaps. But short of shooting her or hitting her and raising a possible alarm, there was nothing he could do. In any event, he told himself, taking the steps down toward the Mercedes, zipping his coat against the cold, there would be nothing suspicious in his coming to see his father.

As he unlocked the Mercedes he noticed there was blood on his right knee, from the Natpo's mouth. He wondered if the woman had noticed it. He climbed in, locking the door, gunning the engine to life. He tried rubbing out the bloodstain, the palm of his hand bloody now. He wiped it on the maroon carpet on the drive-shaft hump. He put the Mercedes in reverse, backed out of the slot, put it in drive, and started for the parking area marked "Visitors" in front of the Intelligence Acquisition Building.

He was halfway up the steps, when the door opened.

"Michael! What a pleasant surprise."

It was William Waterman. "Captain—how's the hatchet man business?"

"Booming, actually. I believe the comrade director mentioned he had specifically requested you to stay at home."

Michael continued up the steps, reaching the top, standing an arm's length from Waterman. "You asked me to trust you once."

"Yes. Somehow I don't think you do."

"I'll start. That terrorist woman was one of the Resistance group I was with during that episode in the Smokies."

Waterman's black, deep-set eyes narrowed. Michael wondered if it were the sun, which had just broken from cover and now flooded the front of the Intelligence Acquisition Building, or just suspicion. "You know her? But why didn't you say this before, Michael?"

"I figured—well, hell—would you have told Captain Metterling up there on the *Beacon* if your father were the director, Metterling's boss?"

Waterman considered this. He clapped his hands to his forearms—he wore no coat. "Come inside. I'll take you to your father, Michael; he's with the woman now."

"I won't forget this," Michael told Waterman, trying not to lay it on too thick. Waterman held the door for him.

Waterman said, "I won't let *you* forget it, Michael. You may find I am a surprisingly useful fellow to have around."

"I'm starting to see that." Michael nodded, waiting in the lobby as Waterman entered. "I'll tell you one thing: We could have used you up there when it happened. I haven't seen so many guns in my life."

"Guns are only for those who know how to use them, Michael—a special elite. Those self-styled freedom-fighter crazies don't have the training, the experience."

"I was listening to the radio," Michael said, passing ahead of Waterman through the arch—again no sound, no alarm. "Were those really special bullets in their ammunition?"

Waterman laughed, beside Michael now, walking past two armed guards, entering a corridor that seemed to run the length of the building. "Just between the two of us, Michael—all they did was duplicate something called Glaser Safety Slugs—they were made years ago. The National Police have some stockpiled. My Special Operations Group uses them from time to time. Actually, they're rather the opposite of that official statement. Virtually no penetration problems, no ricochets, an instant put-down of your opponent without endangering innocent bystanders. This woman and her chink friend—"

"Chink?"

"Another word for Chinese. They selected the perfect ammunition for the job."

Michael grinned. "Gee—someday, do you think I could try some? I mean, I went shooting once with Marshal Blotsky, and I'll confess, it kind of got me interested."

"I'll arrange it sometime." Waterman nodded knowingly. The corridor was going down now, looping on itself, heading toward the front of the building again. The click of Waterman's boots and the click of his own were becoming more audible as the angle increased downward. "Are those combat boots?"

"Well—when in Rome," Michael said.

"You did very well up there. You took a big risk keeping the girl from being shot. But I understand you fought well."

"Just a couple of things I picked up out there in the Smokies. I don't even remember what I did."

"You know, Michael—if you don't mind my saying so—a man in your position should master some techniques of self-defense. I can teach you a few tricks. There might someday be a time when fellows like me aren't around to take care of you."

Michael smiled. "What a radical idea."

"It is always wise to anticipate the other fellow's moves—" He rapped a punch toward Michael. Michael dodged but let himself walk into the other fist—a tap. Waterman laughed. "So you see what I mean?"

"Yes, I do." Michael nodded. "Dad isn't alone in there with her, is he?"

"She's strapped down to a table, and her wrists are cuffed behind her—most uncomfortable. The doctor should be along any minute to administer the drugs we'll use."

Michael turned around quickly, calling to Waterman, "What the hell was that?"

Waterman spun around, reaching for his gun. Michael already had the Beretta in his fist, crashing the pistol sideways along the back of Waterman's head.

Waterman staggered, fell. Michael caught him before he split his head on the concrete floor.

Waterman's eyes were closed—but he was still breathing. Michael reached to Waterman's holster—the Beretta was there. He took the two spare magazines from the belt. He shoved the first pistol away under his jacket, quickly inspected Waterman's to make sure the chamber was loaded. It was.

He shoved the second pistol under his belt and left Waterman where he lay. Michael was running now. He had no idea which room—but he ran on, stopping before a double-doored room that could have been an operating theater. Was it for torture?

He tried the doors. They swung inward.

His father turned around, starting to say, "Doctor, I—"

Michael drew the two pistols, aiming them at his father's chest, his arms outstretched. "Wrong doctor."

"What the fuck—"

"Let her off the table."

"The hell I will. So she's your Smokey Mountains screw, huh?"

"Shut up. Get her off the table."

Alice's voice: "Michael! You're crazy!"

"She's right. Put the guns down. You wouldn't shoot your own father."

"You're right—I wouldn't. But I just might shoot you." He pushed both safeties up into the fire position.

"You know."

"Mom's dead—she died in my arms. She told me. I've got my real father's pistols."

"The safe—but where'd—"

"Blotsky wanted me to have the guns. But I told you Mom died—"

"She was sick for a long time, Michael. I know you're under a lot of strain—maybe you snapped a little. Where the hell'd you get those?"

"Some big guy I left behind a hedge next to the Administration Building. The second one's Waterman's. He's in the corridor with a headache. When he wakes up, tell him to take two aspirin and call me in the morning."

"You're crazy—they'll cut you down, Michael. I won't be able to stop them."

"Let her loose."

"No."

"You don't care that Mom died? All right, so help me, let her loose or you'll be the first person I kill."

He watched his father, but Arnold Borden wasn't his father, he realized. "Cut her loose!" Michael shouted, edging away from the door so he could cover the entrance.

"Michael—it's taking too long. Get out of here!" Alice told him. Her speech sounded thick, slurred a little, but her head seemed clear.

Arnold Borden was undoing the straps. "This won't do you any good—either of you. I don't even have the keys for the handcuffs she's wearing."

"He's lying. Every Natpo carries a handcuff key."

She sat up with difficulty, but Michael didn't want to shift the pistols.

"Empty your pockets—now."

Arnold Borden glared at him. He started emptying his pockets onto the table. "You just remember this: I took you in, gave you the best of everything. I treated you like my own flesh and blood."

"That's why I didn't kill you when I walked into the room."

"James never knew it—but he must have had bad blood. That flake son of his Stephen, that kill-crazy daughter of his with her goddamned hero complex—"

"Shut up!"

"Make me, damn you!" Arnold Borden started toward him. Michael edged back. Alice snapped her right bare foot up, into Arnold Borden's testicles. Borden fell to his knees, doubling over.

She slipped off the table, winced with pain, the faded blue shift bunched up, showing the bandages on her left thigh. She stood there, shuffling through the contents of Borden's pockets by poking at them with her chin.

"Key ring—Michael—use the key."

Michael set one of the pistols down on the table, picked up the key ring. "You do this now," Arnold Borden was saying, his breathing labored, "and so help me, you'll never know peace. You'll be the most wanted man in this country, Michael."

"Bury Mom. Be good to Helen and to Mr. Halsey, or you'll never know a night's sleep," Michael whispered. He turned the key in the handcuffs, and the cuffs popped open, Alice shaking them off.

She grabbed up the pistol from the table, Michael holding the other. She aimed it at Arnold Borden. "No," Michael said.

"Why the hell not?"

"No. Use the cuffs. Take his tie and his handkerchief and gag him."

She looked at Michael. "He's right—you are fuckin' crazy."

Michael edged toward the door, still holding Borden's key ring. The handcuff key read "Safariland" on it. "These fit all handcuffs?"

"Except the maximum-security kind," she told him, bending over Borden, pulling a pistol from beneath his coat.

Michael started taking the key off the ring. "Never know when I might need it," he thought aloud.

Arnold Borden was talking. "I'll kill you next time. You'd better kill me now, Mike."

"No, I won't do that. But next time—if I have to. Alice, gag him!"

Alice twisted Arnold Borden's tie free of his neck, pulled his handkerchief from his pocket, stuffed the balled handkerchief into Arnold Borden's mouth, then tied the handkerchief in place with the necktie. Twisting the tie around a second time, she knotted it in Arnold Borden's open mouth. She put the pistol to his head and he moved his hands behind him. She edged him back toward the table—it was bolted to the floor. Michael alternated watching as she cuffed Arnold Borden to a table leg, both hands behind it, and watching the doors.

"Ready."

"Leave his gun. You don't steal guns from people you know."

She shook her head, took the magazine from the pistol, snapped the slide back, and threw the pistol across the room. The pistol clanged into a cabinet.

Michael took one last look at Arnold Borden's eyes—they were filled with hate. Michael's throat was tight, like it was when he'd told Svetlana that she should marry someone else, like it was when his mother had died. "Good-bye, Dad," he whispered.

He stepped into the corridor, Alice behind him now. He looked at her. Bandages were visible at the neck of the prisoner uniform dress, below the short sleeve. Her arm should have been in a sling. She shouldn't have been walking, but was.

"You got a plan?"

"Yeah—we get outta here." He started up the corridor. Alice was beside him, limping badly. "Can you make it? Or should I carry you?"

"I'm sorry about messin' up your wedding to Svetlana. Seems like a nice girl."

"She is, and you did. Keep the gun out of sight until we need it—*if* we need it."

"We'll need it. You really got Waterman's gun—he's the guy who was with your father. What was all that stuff in there, anyway?"

"My mother told me something before she died. I figure your father knew it all along but wanted me to find out for myself."

She sounded out of breath. "What?"

"I'm James Hope's son, the baby born in the cave that night."

"Holy shit."

"You might say it that way." Waterman was still out.

"What did you do to him?"

"Hit him with my gun."

"That's called cold-cocking him."

"Is that a fact?"

She stood over Waterman. "He's still breathing." She lifted her gun to strike him across the head. Michael caught her wrist. "Look—we're not fighting the Girl Scouts," she said.

"You don't murder people."

"With him it wouldn't be murder. He's the head of the Special Operations Group."

"With him it'd still be murder. I owed him one."

"Shit—you can only kill certain people, huh? You gonna tell me who they are?" He started walking away from her, Alice shouting after him, "Or is it gonna be a big goddamn guessing game?"

"Shut up!" he called back to her. If anyone in the building didn't know they were in the corridor, she had taken care of it. He almost thought she wanted it that way.

They rounded the bend, starting up to the first floor. At the end of the corridor, blocking their exit, he could see the two guards from the lobby. They had assault rifles.

Michael continued walking toward them, Alice behind him as he glanced back once. "You are crazy."

He kept walking. "Arnold Borden is a traitor to all of us!" Michael shouted. "He sold out his best friend to the Communists thirty years ago! He sold out his country! Join us!"

One of the men raised his assault rifle. Michael judged the distance as twenty yards. He raised his pistol, stabbed it forward and fired, once, then again and again, the man going down, gunfire from behind him, the second man going down, his rifle firing into the floor, the noise reverberating.

Michael stopped walking. He looked at the gun in his right hand.

Alice was shouting at him, "You're good with that—not great, but good! Come on!"

She was limping ahead. He stood there still.

She was picking up pistols and assault rifles from the guards, spare magazines, stripping away one of the dead men's shirts, putting the pistols and magazines in the shirt like a sack, looking back to him. "Michael!"

"I just killed a man!" he shouted to her.

"Welcome to the club!"

Michael looked again at the pistol he held.

There was nothing suddenly vile or evil about it. He felt only shock.

He broke into a dead run. His thumb found the safety, used it. The hammer dropped. He worked the safety back off. He kept running.

Chapter Thirty-three

Sirens were sounding. "You want me to drive?"

"No," he told her, sliding behind the wheel of the

Mercedes, reaching across the seat to pop her door lock. She slid in, the bundle in the dead man's shirt between them, the rifles between her knees. He put the Beretta on the seat, the magazines from his pockets. He started the Mercedes.

"Well—come on."

"Wait a minute," he whispered.

He reached under the seat. His father's pistols—his real father.

"The Hope Scoremasters!" Alice exclaimed.

"You make 'em sound like the Hope Diamond."

"They're worth more—believe me."

He reached for the two spare magazines from under the seat, pocketed them, shoved the pistols into his belt.

"I've never done this before, but I imagine if we roll the windows down we'll avoid some of the broken glass that might come our way."

"Good idea—yeah."

She leaned into the back seat, Michael putting the Mercedes into reverse, black-uniformed Natpos pouring from the Administration Building. He threw it into drive. He stomped on the accelerator. He heard Alice operating one of their rifles. "M-16—an oldie but a goodie!" she shouted over the roar of the engine, the growing roar of the slipstream. He was heading straight for the gates, gunfire in the background. He heard gunfire beside him, felt hot cartridge cases pelt his left cheek and neck.

"Step on it!"

He floored it, the engine roar loud now, the wind tearing at his face, the gates mere yards away. "Duck!" He closed his eyes, heard the ripping and tearing of metal, a thudding sound. He opened his eyes. The Mercedes was rocking up, bouncing, settling—over the barricade. One of the guards clung to the hood of the car, a pistol in his right hand, his face bloodied, pieces of the wire meshing of the gates lashing at him, clinging to the body of the car. Alice shoved the assault rifle out the window and across the hood. There was a long burst. The man's mouth opened, his body rolling from the hood, gone, the Mercedes bouncing as it rolled over something—the man, Michael realized.

"Where the hell are we going?"

"The airport," Michael told her, hauling the wheel into a

hard left, away from the detention center, more gunfir
behind them. He glanced up into the rearview mirror. Blac
vans were pouring from the detention center grounds, followin
him. A hole seemed to be opening in the roof of one of th
vans. "What's that—in the roof of that lead van?"

"Some Natpos' vans—they've got retractable gun mounts—
machine gun. Hold this heap steady, Michael!"

She was leaning out of the window now, firing the M-16
Michael looked into the rearview mirror. The machine gu
she had spoken of was firing back, the rear windshiel
spiderwebbing, chunks of glass spraying into the car. "Hol
her steady, Michael!"

He floored the Mercedes again, the van with the ma
chine gun closing. Alice fired again. In the rearview mirro
he could see the windshield of the van shattering, the va
veering off right, bouncing onto the curb, over a fire hydrant
The water from the hydrant gushered skyward. The secon
van slowed, then picked up speed. There were more van
behind it.

"Get back inside!" He didn't have time to see if sh
complied, taking the right hard, sharp, accelerating again
He knew Denver as well as the Natpos did. He kept driv
ing.

"How far to the airport?"

"Not too far."

"Regular airport or Natpo?"

"Neither one—just a small field. The National Security
Directorate uses it, Party officials. A lot of people keep
private planes there."

"You realize, they'll shoot us down."

"No, they won't. By the time they get us on airport rada
from the Denver airport, we'll be out of range, and the rang
on the radar at this airport is short. We'll make it."

"I can see why your last name is Hope."

He didn't answer her. Another of the vans was close
now. The sliding side doors opened, men leaning out, firing
Michael swerved the Mercedes from side to side, trying t
make it a harder target to hit. "How's your father's stomach
Did he see Jessica Cornbloom yet?"

"Yeah—he saw her."

"And?"

"And?"

"Cancer—inoperable. He's dying. Tumor's gone into a period where it isn't growing, she said, but she can't remove it because if she does it could do something—"

"Metastasize," he told her. "It breaks up. Cancer cells get into the bloodstream. The cancer can start up anywhere then."

"Isn't there anything to do?"

"Yeah. One thing, maybe."

He slowed, taking the next left, away from the city, the airport just a few miles now, he told himself. Alice leaned out the window again. As the first van rounded the corner, she fired. The van went out of control; he had no idea what she hit. It climbed the curb on the left side of the street, spun one hundred eighty degrees, and skidded laterally into a storefront, the glass shattering around it. The van stopped dead.

Michael punched the accelerator down to the floor—there were no more turns until they reached the airport itself. A red light—he hit the horn and drove through, swerving to avoid a semi that was crossing with the light. It was in the center of the street as he cleared the intersection. "Shoot out its tires—fast!"

He heard the rattle of gunfire again, glancing into the rearview mirror. The truck skidded, swerved, jacknifed, the trailer twisting, overturning.

Alice was laughing. "They're gonna have to go around on the sidewalk to get past it. You know what? You show promise, Michael. How you gonna explain this to Svetlana?"

"She'll understand."

"But—"

"I told her I had to do this. That she had to marry somebody else."

Alice said nothing for a moment. Then, "You love her, don't you?"

"Yes." He could see the boundary fence for the airport in the distance. "I always will."

The Natpos were coming again, a quarter mile back, he judged. He glanced at Alice—she was changing magazines in the rifle. "You gonna stay with us?"

"I'm gonna fight."

"Why'd you get me outta there?"

"Seemed like a good idea at the time." He started to slow, to make the turn into the airport gates. They would be locked, he reasoned. But he saw it in time—one of the deflection barriers.

He shouted to Alice, "Hang on—tight!" He cut the wheel hard right, taking the Mercedes over the curb, across the parkway, punching the nose of the car through the chain link fence. The engine temperature shot up. He cut the wheel left, aiming toward the center of the field.

"We're on fire, Michael!"

He smelled antifreeze. "Just your imagination." He was looking for a plane to steal—something preflighted and ready. The airport was busy; planes of all descriptions flew in and out all day and almost all night. He had landed there in the MiG-Boeing craft.

It was still on the runway.

Michael felt his eye sockets tightening, the corners of his mouth raising in a smile. They were always refueled as soon as they landed—unless they were to be serviced. And there was no service center here. For use in space, they had been made to start cold, without any engine warm-up time; heat constantly recirculated through the engine from the moment of ignition.

He cut the wheel right, flames leaping up now from the front of the car.

"You grab the weapons—everything you can carry. I'm grabbing the stuff in the trunk."

"Michael!"

"Once we're clear of the car, fire a burst into the gas tank. Will it blow up?"

"I think so."

"Great." He started to slow. Another advantage of the MiG-Boeing craft—it required no key; the ignition toggle switch operated it.

He stomped the break. "Run for it!" He saw a blur of Alice in motion, the flames from the engine block higher now. He half threw himself out of the car, the engine cut. To his feet—he ran to the trunk, popped the lid. He grabbed his two flight bags, running, for the MiG-Boeing.

Alice was halfway to it already, dropping her burden in

the dead man's shirt, throwing her rifle to her shoulder, firing. Michael kept running, hearing it, feeling it, the impact hammering against him. He stumbled, caught his balance, kept running. He looked back. Natpo vans were streaming across the field, the car a ball of orange and black fire.

Michael ran past her to open the passenger door of the MiG-Boeing craft. Someone was in the doorway—a black uniform. Michael grabbed one of the Scoremasters, drew the hammer back, made to fire. A burst of assault rifle fire from Alice, and the figure in the doorway went down.

Michael upped the .45's safety, thrusting the pistol back into his belt. He removed the wheel chocks, out of the way.

He reached the open fuselage door, hurling the bags inside, turning. Alice was limping worse now. He swept her up into his arms and put her inside, then hauled himself in. The dead Natpo lay in the doorway. Michael shouted to Alice, "Take care of him!"

He moved forward to the controls. If the craft hadn't been refueled, they were dead. Through the windshield he could see the Natpo vans, men pouring from them, armed with assault rifles.

Michael settled into the pilot's seat, looking back toward Alice. She was rolling the dead Natpo guard out of the open doorway. "How do I close this?"

"You don't. I can do it from here. Get out of the way." Michael found the door button on the upper center control panel and pushed it, hearing the pneumatic hiss, the chunking sound as it secured. He hit the lock switch. He searched now for the ignition.

"They're shooting at us. This thing armed?"

"No, it's not armed, but if it can fly through the atmosphere and into near Earth orbit, it oughta be a little bullet proof." He could see the Natpos firing, but hear no sounds of bullets hitting metal. He found the ignition, hitting it, the power already on. His left hand moved to the fuel mix controls, his right hand moving from the ignition to the throttles.

"You don't look like you ever flew one of these."

"I haven't." He grinned.

She slumped into the copilot's seat, fastening her safety harness.

Michael increased the RPMs. "That Natpo—what's the bastard doing?"

One of the Natpos, no assault rifle, just a pistol in his right hand, was running toward them, not even shooting. "He's goin' for the wheel chocks. If he gets them in place and we haven't moved, we'll flip nose down into the runway."

"What are you gonna do?"

"Move." He throttled out, the Natpo running wildly away, the MiG-Boeing moving ahead—slowly, but gathering speed. Some of the black Natpo vans were moving, another one of them with a machine-gun port in the roof. The machine gun was firing, but there was no sound, no detection of impact.

He checked the instrument panel. "I don't think we're fast enough."

"What?"

"This is a short runway."

The Natpo vans were pulling ahead now, trying to cut the MiG-Boeing off. Michael gave the craft more throttle, turning it now. The turn was almost too tight, too much flap. "When I tell you to, see that thing and the one next to it—you push 'em forward all the way."

"What are we gonna be doing?"

"Keeping the nose up—get ready." He was outdistancing the vans now, gunfire still coming from them, chipping chunks of runway surface. If a tire were hit, it would all be over. Michael started pulling up on the yoke, the airfield fence closer, closer—five hundred yards, four hundred. "Now—all the way!"

"Forward?"

"Yes, yes—forward!"

He drew back as if lifting the nose through muscle power rather than hydraulics. It was coming up, but the fence was two hundred yards ahead now, then a hundred.

"You got it all the way forward?"

"Yes."

"You're religious—pray!"

The nose lifted. Michael reached up for the landing gear switch. He worked it, feeling the gears rise, the fence whizzing beneath them and out of sight.

Alice slipped her safety harness, reached across to him,

and put her arms around his neck so tightly he almost let go
of the yoke. She kissed him on the cheek and started to
laugh.

Chapter Thirty-four

Michael Hope sat on the rock ledge, staring out across the
mists that filled the valley, the snow swirling around him. It
was not unpleasant to sit there. The collar of his leather
jacket was turned up against the snow and, beneath the
jacket, he wore a woolen sweater and a flannel shirt. A navy
blue watch cap protected his head.

He heard the crunching of snow behind him and snatched
up his rifle. But it was Martin.

"Join you?"

"Sure," Michael answered, looking back into the valley.

"Talked to Jake," Martin said. "In a manner of speaking.
He sent a man up."

"What's the news?" Michael asked, not really caring.

"Lots. Let's see: They got it that you suffocated your
mother with a pillow, slaughtered dozens of innocent office
workers at the detention center, and caused the deaths of
sixteen prisoners being held for questioning. You're responsible for the destruction of eight vehicles, including a stolen
Mercedes, the hijacking of a MiG-Boeing, the kidnapping of
a terrorist prisoner, the assault of several officers of the
National Police, the murder of an airport National Police
guard, the theft of deadly weapons, the discharge of deadly
weapons—"

"And the sinking of the *Titanic*," Michael added. "The
part about killing my mother—he's gonna pay for that. She'll
always be my mother."

"I never heard James Hope speak ill of her, Michael."

"Were the Chinese ever able to get anything on that file
code I gave Jake?"

"They're still working on it. What is it? Some secret weapon?" Martin laughed. "That'd be all we needed."

"No—I may as well tell you. It concerns you. After we landed in the Cherokee lands, when we were hiding out, I talked with Jessica Cornbloom."

"She's a pretty lady, but she's got a big mouth. I thought you doctors were supposed to keep things between you and a patient confidential." And he laughed again.

"It's nothin' to laugh about, Marty."

"Look—I got a year or two, maybe longer. That's kinda comforting. I mean, ever since I got into this Resistance business, I figured I was lucky if I lived to the next day. Kinda nice to know I've got all that time."

"Bullshit," Michael whispered.

"Yeah, well—there's nothin' we can do."

"That's what that file code is. When I was interning I met a doctor from New York who was working in the same hospital. He told me about this thing one night when we were both off and we grabbed a beer. A cancer vaccine. If it tested out—that's what he said he'd heard they were doing— then Jessica Cornbloom could operate, remove the tumor, and we could shoot you up with the vaccine. If you didn't die from the operation, you'd live. When the cancer cells escaped into the bloodstream, the vaccine would kill 'em."

"If the Russians got a cure for cancer, you can be damn sure they won't give me any of it."

"Two of our people developed it. If we could get the stuff, or duplicate it, we could—"

"Hey, Michael, why don't you face the facts? I'm dying of cancer. I have lived a full life. Got a fine daughter. Got you back. If you and Alice keep sleepin' together—"

"She is expecting already. Her period should have started about ten or twelve days after I got her out of the detention center. It didn't."

"You work fast—I mean, a pregnancy test?"

"Jessica gave it to her just before we started up here." Michael looked at his watch. "She's about six weeks pregnant."

"Okay, more fuel for my argument. Looks like I'm even gonna be a grandfather. Hope it's a boy."

Michael said, "I thought that sleeping with Alice again would make it easier about leaving Svetlana. It hasn't."

"Oh, boy."

"You tell Alice that, you won't have to wait to die of cancer."

Marty laughed. "In these last couple of weeks you've gotten a lot better in martial-arts training—I'll give you that. And you've turned into a terrific pistol shot and rifleman. You're a natural—you got great hand-eye coordination and a steady hand and a sensitive trigger finger and a hell of a good teacher."

"Self-praise sucks, Marty," Michael said with a smile.

"Yeah, well—but it's true. Takin' good to edged weapons, too. But—and this is the important one right here—you couldn't take me if your life depended on it."

"Old man." Michael grinned.

"Old man who can whip your ass, boy." Marty patted him on the shoulder. "Slide over a little—I need more of this rock to sit on." Michael slid to the left a little, his seat getting wet with the snow on the uncovered portion of the rock. "What you gonna do, Michael?"

"About what?"

"Well—take your pick. You're sleepin' with my daughter, tell me you love another woman more, yet my daughter's carrying your child. The Russians and the Peace Party people are putting a nuclear weapons platform in space. The Russians and the Chinese are on the brink of war—but I admit, they been that way a long time. Jerusalem fell to the Soviet Union a week ago, and the Israelis and the Egyptians have their backs to the wall—or maybe the sea. The British are pumping everything they can into Canada to hold back the Russians near Yellowknife, the capital of the Northwest Territories on Great Slave Lake; and the Natpos still have that curfew, are arresting people by the truckloads, and even got that silly-assed knife law through Congress. Add to that that you are personally on the top of every Natpo, Spetznas, and KGB shit list, and I think it leaves you a lot of choices in terms of what you're gonna do."

"I could try suicide but I don't believe in it," Michael said with a laugh. "What I said about Alice and Svetlana— well, I love Alice. I started to back when I was with you guys before."

"Jake showed me a newspaper. Svetlana's saying some things about you."

"I told her to."

"I kinda figured that. You wanna know what she said?"

"No. If I want lies, I can listen to the radio newspeople." Marty laughed.

Michael said, "I'll take care of Alice and the child. I'll be a good husband to her, Marty."

"What about the rest of it?"

"What are you looking to me for?"

"You're James Hope's son—just the name will bring people to us. We've already started hearing about Resistance cells springing up in university towns, in some of the larger cities—even one in Denver. If you're in it as Michael Borden, when they find out you're not Borden's son at all, but Michael Hope—this country'll rise up. There's enough old guys like me around who remember him, are gonna see this as a new chance for freedom, are gonna follow you. But that means you gotta lead. Those pistols you carry—they mean a lot more than you think."

"I know what they mean."

Martin Deacon's voice sounded strange. Michael looked at him. "You know, Michael, there isn't much recoil in a .45. People used to talk about it like there was, but there really isn't much. But still—in a special way—it takes a real man to handle James Hope's guns. You showed you were man enough when you kept those Natpos off us in the valley that time after Harriet finked on us. God rest the poor girl's soul. You saved Alice—they woulda turned her into some kinda vegetable, let the Natpos fuck her over until she died. You know that. You proved what you are. Now maybe it's time to prove *who* you are. You can be like a messiah to us—"

"Aw, shit, Marty, don't talk like that."

"Let me finish, Michael. A messiah is a leader, a savior. You got it in you. Your real dad—for all the good things about him—I don't think had it, not like you do. You're the one. If you don't lead, well—maybe someday we'll win, maybe someday we'll lose it big. But we'll never get back what we had, boy. You're the only one who can do that." And he shook his head, looking away. "I feel it in my insides, Michael—you're the one. But you gotta take that extra step."

Michael stared out into the valley—the snow was coming more heavily now. The walk back to camp would be silent except for the crunching sounds his boots would make. Alice would have a hot meal for him. Most of the women cooked for their families, some of them pooling the cooking and eating communally. It wouldn't be many more weeks before her abdomen would visibly begin to swell. He wondered how long it would be before the Russians had their nuclear-weapons platform ready. He knew the Chinese would strike before it was finished. They would have no choice if they were to survive. And what Svetlana's father had told him—that missiles were siloed in the United States, aimed against China and Western Europe. The Chinese, despite their help, would be forced to target the United States for their own survival.

In the weeks since reaching Martin's stronghold in the Smokies, he had heard more about the British, the French, the Chinese, the Israelis, and the Egyptians—Canada and Australia, too. There were men in these governments who were ready to do something. But no one knew what.

He didn't look at Martin. "How well connected is Jake Brown?"

"Pretty well connected. Why?"

"See if he can arrange a face-to-face meeting for us with representatives of the European allies, the Chinese, the Israelis, and the Egyptians. Sort of what they used to call a summit conference. Do you think he could do that?"

"Won't know till we try, Michael."

Chapter Thirty-five

Six weeks passed. Michael and Martin made two trips to the stronghold near Cherokee by horseback. On the second trip they met with a British SAS man who had infiltrated from Canada with a message regarding a possibility of a summit, the content too important even to trust to a coded radio signal.

There was to be a summit meeting in two weeks. The ultimate location of the meeting was known only to the head of the British SIS (Secret Intelligence Service) and the head of the Mossad (the Israeli Intelligence Service), in exile in a London suburb for the past eight years. Chastain, the Special Air Service man, gaunt-featured, his black hair thinning prematurely, his eyes a peculiar shade of blue, began to draw on the chalkboard hung on the far wall of the counsel hut.

"Right—now. We've worked an exfiltration route for you blokes that I'm sure with your own knowledge of the area you'll make some minor changes with. Our Intelligence seems to indicate that the town of Commerce, Georgia, is relatively clean. It's equidistant from Atlanta, where the National Security Directorate and the Spetznas have put in a lot of manpower, and Greenville, South Carolina, which in the past several weeks has become a Spetznas staging area. But this little town of Commerce is clean. Some National Police—or Natpos, like you call 'em here—come through once in a while. That's about it. You'll rendezvous with me—lucky you." He smiled. "Then we work our way toward Charleston. I'll trust you gentlemen to warn me of any hot spots I don't know of and we can go around 'em. In Charleston, we have an agent—a good one, I'm told. The agent—don't know if it's a bleedin' man or woman—has the rest of the exfiltration details, or will have by the time we get there. You gentlemen meet me in Commerce two weeks from today. We have seventy-two hours to make it to Charleston, or the agent won't rendezvous with us. If we make it in time, you go to your summit meeting, and I get to go back home for a few weeks."

"Sergeant Chastain?" Michael Hope said.

"Yes, Doctor?"

"How long should it take to reach the point where the summit is taking place—that is, how long should we be gone?"

"His wife—my daughter," Marty said with a grin, "is pregnant. Baby isn't due for a long time yet. He's just nervous." He cracked his right palm down on Michael's knee.

"Don't rightly know, gentlemen," Chastain said. "But I

was told to say that you'll be gone no more than two weeks—if we don't all get ourselves killed gettin' there."

"Go ahead," Michael said with a smile, his voice low. "Build my confidence." Chastain, Michael decided, drew lousy maps.

Alice was whispering, "You know what I hate about winter?"

"What do you hate about winter?"

"You can never get a really hot shower. With wood, all we can do is get the water hot enough to be warm—yuch. You ever try washing hair as long as mine with water that isn't hot?"

"No—my hair's never been that long. I wish—"

"We lived in a city, with gas heat or something?"

"You'd be more comfortable."

"Junior's keepin' me warm."

Michael looked at her. The tents held reasonable warmth as long as you were dressed—which was a problem when you made love, changed clothes, or hadn't yet put on socks. He judged the temperature in the tent to be sixty degrees or less. The wood stove was the center of warmth, and when the temperature really dropped, he had shifted sides on the platform Martin had helped him build, so she slept on the warm side.

"You can handle things while we're gone?"

"I can handle things. But I want you to do me a favor."

"What—bring you back a present?"

She smiled. He could see her face, red-tinged, in the lamplight. "No. I've got a present for you." She reached under the bed, taking out her knife. "This was your sister's knife. She used it when she defended the bridge and saved your father's life. Jennifer died fighting with this, Daddy told me. It's a BuckMaster—a really fine production knife. Not as big as that Life Support System Daddy carries, but a fine knife. You take it. That Gerber boot knife's fine for some things, and your Swiss Army knife's fine for some other things. But this is what I want you to take with you."

"What are you gonna use?"

"I'm not planning on leading any raids. I don't think Junior would like it." She patted her abdomen beneath the blankets. "I'm just gonna keep everybody safe and the camp secure and wait for you to crawl back in bed with me."

He reached to her hand and took the knife. He set it on the table beside the rest of his gear, buttoning his shirt as he spoke. "When we get back we should have something we can do."

"Yeah. But you'll get to do it."

"You need a rest. Knit some booties or something."

"I never learned how to knit. I'll embroider something and show you when you come back."

Michael pulled on his sweater, running his fingers back through his hair, straightening the sweater then. He picked up the shoulder holster with the Beretta 92-F, slipping the harness onto his shoulders. It wasn't leather, but rather something Martin had told him was called ballistic nylon. The pistol hung diagonally, and he checked the thumb break. He settled the harness, the pouch for the two spare magazines edged with the base slightly forward, the way Martin had taught him.

"I wish I could tell you where we were going."

"What was it you told me about that SAS man—what's his name?"

"Demetrius Chastain—a sergeant."

She laughed. "Hell of a name. But didn't you tell me he had some kinda death pill to take in case he got caught?"

"Yeah."

"Just as well not to know. You and Daddy be careful. He's older than he acts like."

Michael grinned. "So are you, sweetheart." He picked up the double holster rig. The belt was a GI pistol belt, but black. The Sparks Six-Pack rode on the belt already, and Michael opened the belt hanger for the knife Alice had given him, slipped it under the belt behind his left holster, then closed the hanger. He picked up the little Gerber boot knife, sliding it inside his trouser waistband near the small of his back. The Swiss Army knife was always in the pocket of his jacket, as were his gloves.

He smiled at her.

"Turn around. Let me see how you look." She laughed. Michael grinned, turning around quickly.

She laughed again. "Very fashionable for a gunfight,

ella. Come and give Momma a kiss and a quick feel."
Michael went over to the bed. He could smell their lovemaking from the night before, his arms closing around her.

Snow was falling lightly, and Martin stood out front of Michael's tent. "Tough leavin' a warm girl alone in a bed, isn't it?"

"Yeah, it's tough."

"She'll be fine. Let's go. See she gave you Jennifer's knife. Figured she would." Martin shouldered into his pack. Michael already wore his, as well as his poncho, slinging his rifle as he started toward the falls. "Kinda excited—much as a guy my age can get excited, of course," said Martin Deacon.

"When I'm your age—well..." Michael let it hang, pulling up the hood and holding his M-16 under the poncho. He nodded to the two guards. The cascade felt the temperature of ice as it hit the exposed skin of his hands, the hood of the poncho drawn far forward, and his shoulders hunched to keep the icy water from his face and hair. The rocks just beyond the downward rush of water were slick as ice.

Through the waterfall, Michael shook the poncho, but left it in place against the falling snow, waiting as Martin caught up with him. Michael took his rifle from beneath the poncho and slung it muzzle down over his right shoulder. Neither of them spoke as they walked.

There was almost a warmth to the snow as they started along the defile, the snow heavy enough to crunch beneath their boots, the occasional sound of a bird—but only those sounds broke the silence.

Michael began considering again what he would say to these potential allies. It was clear that the crux of any agreement would have to be somehow neutralizing a portion of the joint Soviet-U.S. threat, so the Chinese could retarget missiles away from North America and into the heart of the Soviet Union. Only in that way might a global thermonuclear war be averted.

In the books given him by Alice and Martin, in the books and old newspapers Jake Brown had shown him in Cherokee, he had read of those who had truly worked for peace, only to become beguiled by Lester Saile and the hard core of his Peace Party. Michael had heard men and women

talking around the fires at night, saying that Saile had always
been working for the Communists. Michael remained silent
during these talks, listening instead. Over the past several
weeks, he had formulated his own opinion. And unlike the
others, Michael had the advantage, however dubious, of
having spoken to Lester Saile, shared table with him, seen
Saile at the peak of his glory, seen him drunk to the point of
near unconsciousness.

Saile had not been a Communist—not in the beginning,
Michael had decided. Perhaps the judgment of history would
prove him wrong, but he saw no calculating Soviet agent in
Lester Saile, selling out the United States as part of some
Communist plan for world domination—a common phrase
used around the campfires. He saw instead a man who had
once genuinely believed that total disarmament would be a
way to cure mankind's ills, and right or wrong, had pursued
these goals. But somewhere, Lester Saile had sold out—not
only his country, but also his soul. The personal power of his
position had corrupted him, and the more power he had
gained, the more he had become corrupted. Michael had
considered, too, the old aphorism about power tending to
corrupt—but he found it simplistic. Power was an individual
matter and affected individuals differently. Martin Deacon
wielded power—over the lives of his Resistance band of some
fifty souls, within the larger Resistance network, even among
the Cherokee through his association with War Chief Jake
Brown. But Deacon seemed unaffected by power in any way
except by its burdens and responsibilities. Svetlana's father—
in some ways the most powerful Russian in the United
States—was a decent, caring man who liked the wealth and
social position but never, to Michael's knowledge, had abused
personal power.

Saile had built an empire of lies, founded on lies, fueled
by lies, supported by institutionalized deprivation of rights
and constitutional guarantees, enforced by legalized murder
and false imprisonment.

Michael thought of Arnold Borden. Michael had forced
himself since that day to not think of the man as his father. It
was very hard to consider this demigod figure of James Hope
in any personal way, but James Hope was his father. He lay
awake at nights trying to personalize the photo on the Free

oney dollars—but the face remained a photo. And he had
oken with Marty about Melissa Hope, his natural mother.
.d about Jennifer Hope, who had died the day he was born.
.d about Stephen Hope. Perhaps Stephen's madness was
mewhere inside his own being.

But from Alice and her father, he had learned something
inestimable value. Alice had quoted the line to him once,
.t remembering the source. Michael had known the line but
.ver understood it: "Sufficient unto the day is the evil
.ereof."

In a way now, it was a personal motto, and without it he
.metimes thought that he would go mad. Svetlana had been
assigned to the *Beacon of Peace* after leaving it for several
.eeks, or so the smuggled New York papers said. And it was
.mored that Svetlana had been seeing Igor Balavadze, the
.an who had deferred command of the Mars mission to
.ylor Burnside. Balavadze had replaced Alexii Umarov as
.mmander of the *Beacon of Peace*. Michael had the consum-
.g fear that some night, one of the dreams of Svetlana would
.use him to call her name in his sleep—and then Alice
.ould know.

They had reached the top of the defile, starting along the
.dge now, but just below its height to avoid profiling them-
.lves against the sky when the sun would rise. Michael had
.scussed the matter with Marty. With Jake Brown meeting
.em three miles from camp with horses, there was no sense
. rousting a third man to ride with him and Marty to the
.ndezvous with Jake, only to ride back again leading the two
.her horses. Michael and Marty had elected to walk. Later
.ey would ride with Jake Brown throughout the morning
.d early afternoon to a spot along the Tennessee-Georgia
.order. Other transporation would await them to get them to
.e small town called Commerce in northeastern Georgia,
.here Sergeant Demetrius Chastain would be waiting to
.ccompany them on the next leg of the exfiltration route.

They were nearing the rendezvous with the orthodontist
.rned Cherokee war chief when Marty began to speak.
.Whatchya gonna tell 'em at his meeting, Michael?"

"That we have to eliminate the Soviet nuclear threat
.ithin the United States and from aboard the *Beacon*. It can't
.ke them much longer until that platform is ready to launch.

And once it is, the Chinese won't have any choice but to mass-launch against us. Nobody in his right mind could blame them."

Marty grinned, but then the smile faded. "Looks like push is finally comin' to shove, Michael."

Jake Brown interrupted Michael's thoughts of his unborn child. Michael reined in between Jake and Marty, three of Jake's men behind them. The sun was shining brightly now, making the snow impossibly white beneath it, the sounds of snow dripping from the pine boughs and rock ledges like the sound of rain. "I make it we've got about another two miles and we'll be at the rendezvous point. Sometimes I wish I still had my old Cadillac. This business of bein' war chief gets me into some weird shit, I'll tell ya."

"Who are we meeting? How are we getting through Georgia?" Deacon asked.

"There's a Resistance unit that works the mountains near Helen, Georgia—that place that looks like an Alpine village—"

"A what?" Michael asked.

"Big tourist attraction in the old days. Still gets some play, I understand. The town turned itself into an Alpine village, right in the Georgia mountains. Anyway, the people we're meeting work the mountains around there—got a camp somewhere on Mount Yonah, I hear. They're kinda close-mouthed about it. But anyway, they've got a truck waiting to haul us." Jake Brown pushed his long hair back past his shoulders, settling his cowboy hat again.

"Let's get on with it then," Michael said.

"Right." Jake Brown turned to the three mounted men behind them. "Floyd, you and Clay and Bob: Do like we planned."

The three men wheeled their horses around as Michael looked back, the horses kicking up clods of snow and mud as they started toward the higher ridgeline.

Michael turned back to Jake. Michael, resting his hand on the saddle horn, shifted his weight. He had long since removed the poncho, and he hunched his neck down into the collar of his leather jacket. "Just in case of a trap?"

"You catch on quick, Michael. I trust these Georgia boys

implicitly—but God knows if they were followed. And if they were, Floyd and the others'll be a little insurance."

"'Less it's something big," Marty murmured. "Then, they'll be able to get back and tell how heroically we died." Marty kneed his animal, a bay like the others rode, and stared down from the ridgeline, his horse kicking up a cloud of powdery snow.

Michael heeled his own mount, starting after him, Jake Brown beside and a little behind Michael.

It proved slow going as they worked away from the lower ridgeline, downward and laterally toward the intersection of U.S. 441 and what proved to be a rutted, snow-splotched ranch road. Four men were waiting beside a black Natpo van, dressed in camouflage fatigues with improvised white snow smocks over their jackets. Michael got a feeling of unease seeing the Natpo van but rode ahead, taking over the lead from Marty.

Marty said with a rasp, "Slow up, Michael." Michael reined back, Marty and Jake flanking him now. "There's somethin' wrong. That one fella—there isn't any magazine in his M-16."

"Let's get the hell out of here," Jake said with a hiss through his teeth. Michael looked at the Cherokee, a smile plastered across his face but his eyes tight-muscled and hard.

Michael returned the wave from one of the four men beside the van. All four were at the rear of the van, the van's doors open. A long, low ditch paralleled the highway, at a right angle to the ranch road.

"If we stay on our horses, got a better chance to get away if it goes sour," Marty advised.

"You taught me that if horses aren't used to gunfire they can go crazy with it. Jake stays with the horses. We'll walk the last fifty yards," Michael said.

"Agreed." Marty nodded. Michael reined in, drawing back tight, slipping down from the saddle. He left his rifle muzzle down diagonally across his back, but as his hands passed his holsters, he popped the releases for the flaps covering the Scoremasters. Marty swung down, their eyes meeting a moment. Marty unzipped his coat—both his pistols, the Randall .45 and the Beretta 92-F, were beneath it.

Michael handed the reins of his mount up to Jake, Marty

doing the same. Michael noticed Jake's right hand drifting to the revolver he carried crossdraw at his left side. "You guys be cool, huh?"

"Oh, yeah." Michael nodded, eyeing Marty, then plastering a grin on his face, starting slowly toward the van. "How you guys doin'?"

"Fine. And y'all?"

"A little cold. Nice vehicle you got," Michael shouted across the snow and mud. "Just steal it recently?"

The one of the four who had spoken paused for an instant. Then, "A couple of hours ago—it won't be reported yet."

"Wonderful," Marty called. Then under his breath, "They got guns on 'em from the van."

"Yeah." Michael nodded.

"Drift left, boy. I'll drift right."

"No—I'll cross in front of you, so don't start shooting until I'm clear."

"Four of you all there is?" Marty called out.

The man beside the van's open rear doors nodded—a little too quickly.

"Do it now," Michael whispered, drawing the Scoremasters, thumb cocking the hammers, dodging past Marty. He fired both pistols toward the rear of the van as he shouted, "Hit the snow!"

The first two shots hit inside the van somewhere. Black-clad Natpos jumped from the back of the van. The side door opened. A machine gun started to fire. The four Georgia Resistance fighters grappled with the three Natpos from the back of the van. Michael fired both pistols from the hip again, killing one of the three. Martin Deacon was rolling across the snow, the snow churning behind him in a ripple effect, the machine gun lacing into it. Marty then got up to his knees, the .45 in his balled fists bucking once, then again. The machine gun stopped.

Natpos rose from the ditch paralleling the paved road. Michael wheeled toward them, firing his pistols. One man down, another. A shriek—like something Michael had never heard before—and Michael threw himself toward the van for cover, rolling onto his back. It was Jake Brown, his mount tearing toward the Natpos coming out of the ditch, his M-16 in his right hand, his revolver in his left, both guns firing, the reins in Jake's teeth. The cowboy hat flew off or was shot off.

Jake's shoulder-length hair caught in the wind, his eyebrows cocked up, lips drawn back, teeth gritted on the reins.

Michael rolled onto his stomach, firing both pistols at the charging Natpos. Men were going down. The Scoremasters were empty, Michael stabbing them into their holsters, swinging the M-16 forward, working the trigger as he drew up into a crouch beside the rear tires of the van.

The two Georgia Resistance men who were still standing, Natpo assault rifles in their hands, attacked the ditch. Michael rose to his full height, running forward, dodging as Jake's horse nearly crashed into him.

Michael's M-16 was empty and he let it fall to his side on its sling. Reaching under his coat, he grabbed the Beretta, working the safety up, double-actioning the first shot into the abdomen of one of the Natpos, putting two more shots into the man's chest and neck.

The machine gun was firing again. Michael spun toward it, ready to empty the Baretta. Marty held it, a belt for the weapon slung from his shoulders, brass flying in a spray around him. "Hit the dirt!"

Michael threw himself down, the machine gun firing over him. The Natpos from the ditch were going down. Michael put the Beretta out, firing, catching one man with two shots into the head. He shifted the muzzle. Another man went down, hands flying out from his body as he bounced back into the snow.

Michael shifted the Beretta into his left hand, pushing himself up with his right, climbing to his feet.

He could hear Martin Deacon shouting, "Damn, I taught you good, Michael!"

Chapter Thirty-six

They had buried eleven dead Natpos under snow and mud after cleaning them of weapons, identification papers, and cigarettes.

They rode now in the Natpo van, the bodies of the two dead Georgia Resistance fighters covered under a tarp. The only one of the four who wasn't injured was driving the van. Michael rebandaged the arm of the fourth man—the blood had started seeping through.

By the time Floyd and the other two Cherokees had reached the battle scene, the shooting had been over, and Michael and Marty had been checking that none of the Natpos remained alive. None had.

"How'd they get you?" Marty asked finally.

The one whose arm Michael was bandaging answered. "It was my fault—if it was anybody's."

"Take it easy," Michael told him. "Doesn't matter whose fault it was." Michael said louder, so the others could hear, "We're still on our way."

"They left two Natpos with our truck—probably parked where we left it. The leader didn't want to radio in—figured he'd get himself credit for the arrest."

Michael called up to the driver. "How'd they get the location for the meeting out of you?"

"Y'all tell 'em," the injured man said, "or I will."

"Billy's brother—only fifteen—first time out with us. A good boy, but when the Natpos jumped us, one the Natpos put a gun to Dee Dee Bryce's head—"

"Who's Dee Dee Bryce?" Jake Brown asked.

The injured man spoke. "My girl—they put a gun to her head, said they'd kill her. Billy spilled his guts to save her."

"Billy and your girl—are they still alive, you think?" Marty Deacon asked with a rasp.

"I dunno," the injured man whispered, lowering his head.

Michael's and Marty's eyes met. Michael called to the driver, "Just where's this truck of yours located?"

"Broke down about three miles up the road, and we got it behind a billboard with an old faded Coca-Cola sign about two hundred yards off the road near some pines."

"You stop the van here about a half mile up, then pull off the road," Marty began. "Then give us ten minutes or so and start drivin'. With this tinted glass, they won't see who's drivin' until you get right up on 'em and open the door. When you do, we'll take care of these two Natpos."

"And we'll see if Dee Dee and Billy are still alive,"
Michael added. Michael had learned that killing got easier,
like anything else, with experience. He had learned that a
few minutes ago. But this time Marty was already touching
up the blade of his Life Support/System I knife with a stone.

Michael edged forward across the snow, on knees and
elbows, the BuckMaster that Alice had given him—the one
Jennifer had died with thirty years ago—in his right fist.
Marty had told him that to sneak up on a man successfully,
you needed to think about something else. So he tried to
remember all the things about knife fighting and sentry
removal that Marty had taught him.

In a few minutes Michael was nearly upon his target.
The black leather jacket of the Natpo was either new or
recently saddle-soaped, because it caught a little of the
sunlight, making hot spots.

Marty had told him to do it nice and simple—come up to
the man, knock him forward off the log on which he sat, and
stab him in the neck, ripping out the voice box, then finish
the job with a hard thrust into the right kidney.

But Michael stood now, walking slowly toward the man,
the knife raised point up in his right hand, his left hand palm
outward.

The Natpo's rifle was propped against the tree.

Michael was not ready to slash a human being's throat.
He focused his attention not on the man, but on the rifle and
what he would do about it, on the daggerlike fighting knife
slung from the man's belt over the left hip.

Michael was two feet behind the man. He glanced over
him, could see Marty approaching the truck. The second
Natpo was asleep at the wheel, the door open despite the
cold.

Marty disappeared behind the truck.

Michael kicked the Natpo's assault rifle to the ground.
The Natpo wheeled to his feet.

Michael stood, waiting. The man might go for his pistol
at his hip—but if he did, Michael was in easy distance for a
thrust into the chest.

The Natpo laughed instead. Slowly the Natpo reached

for his knife, drawing it from the sheath, the knife leaving the sheath making an audible clicking sound. "I've seen your picture—I'm gonna be famous," the Natpo whispered.

Michael did not move.

The Natpo lunged with the knife. It was double-edged. Michael's left hand dropped and snapped back. He turned ninety degrees to the left, slicing the BuckMaster forward and downward in an arc to his left, the blade's primary edge hacking across the top of the Natpo's forearm. Blood filled the Natpo's hand. Michael snapped the knife back, the butt cap hitting the Natpo's forehead. The head whiplashed back. Michael's balled fist swung left, the primary edge slicing across the man's chin, snapping his head back. Michael hacked down into the subclavian artery, stepping back as the blood sprayed. The Natpo's knees buckled, the body flopping into the snow.

Michael shifted the steel into his left fist, grabbing for one of the Scoremasters with his right hand, running for the Resistance truck. He heard a shot as Marty jumped down from the back of the truck.

Michael looked into Marty's eyes. The eyes had a dead look.

Marty started toward the man Michael had killed, saying, "Come on—you didn't follow my directions, Michael. I caught your act a little after I killed the guy in the cab. Looks like you did okay, though." Marty dropped into a crouch beside the dead Natpo, stabbing his big knife into the snow, rolling the body over in the snow, red smears where the body had been. He opened the man's holster and withdrew the Beretta 92-F, then opened his coat as he stood. Michael noticed the shoulder holster Marty wore was empty. Marty began methodically checking the Natpo's pistol. "Nice thing about these Berettas—they work like a Swiss watch, and they shoot right on the money." Marty holstered it.

"Where's your gun?"

Marty picked up his knife, fisting it into an ice-pick hold. "The mother-fuckers made Billy hump Dee Dee, then they cut his nuts off and let him bleed to death. Then they humped her. Beat the hell out of the poor girl. Carved her up. She wanted to die—well, so I let her. That's"—and he stabbed the knife in his hand into the Natpo's chest, twisted it—"that's where my damn gun is, Michael." He withdrew the knife, wiping the blade clean of blood on the Natpo's trousers.

The man with the bandaged arm, the Resistance cell leader, had not stopped crying. The other surviving Resistance man from Georgia stopped the truck once for the man with the bandaged arm to get out and vomit.

Michael, Marty, and Jake had buried the dead girl and the dead boy, then put the two dead Natpos into the van and torched the gas tank.

There were bloodstains on the Resistance truck's wooden bed. Though Michael and Marty had wiped the blood up, the stains remained.

They reached the outskirts of Commerce, Georgia, by 4:00 P.M., using the forged travel documents to cross the Natpo post at the junction of Interstate 85 and U.S. 441. Michael, Marty, Jake, and the man with the injured arm crossed the interstate a mile north on foot, hiding in the woods until the Resistance driver had cleared the checkpoint and picked them up.

The driver called through the open window hole in the back of the cab, "We're goin' a block west, then crossin' the railroad tracks. Got a long block of residential area—some of the houses are abandoned. Then we drive past a Presbyterian church and meet this contact of y'all's in a parking lot between a couple of school buildings. We gotta play it easy, 'cause the guy's gonna be drivin' a Natpo van."

"Here we go again," Jake Brown observed, braiding his hair as he talked.

"Damnit." Marty grinned. "If you don't look like old Willie Nelson used to look—but with a suntan!"

"Shut up," Jake shot back.

Small shopping centers were on both sides, most of the stores seeming to be abandoned, the homes on both sides now. Michael peered ahead through the window opening—once proud, he thought, but most of them in disuse or disrepair or both. They stopped, turned right, then made a quick left. The church was unmistakable and unlike the private residences they had passed, the grass neatly cut, the snow long behind them in the mountains. The building itself seemed well maintained.

It was as if the man with the bandaged arm read Michael's thoughts. "Folks in this part of the country will keep their church good even if they can't keep their homes up."

Michael nodded. He had never been in a church in his life, except when his mother had sneaked him off to be baptized when he was an infant, as she had told him.

"Me," the man with the injured arm, whose sweetheart and brother had died, whispered hoarsely, "All I got's God now." The man cleared his throat. "And my country. Gonna kill me every Natpo I can find. Gonna get this country back—gonna..." The man began again to cry.

Mary folded his arm about the man's shoulders, the man's head sagging into his hands.

More houses, modern-looking, but many of them abandoned. Then the truck began to slow, low buildings on the left at the end of a long, curving drive. The school. The truck took the drive slowly, Marty moving away from the injured man, his assault rifle poised. Jake Brown posted himself opposite Marty at the rear of the truck, his assault rifle ready as well.

Michael looked forward again as the building was nearer, the truck slowing, then stopping.

"Why we stoppin'?"

"Relax, Marty. It's a gate—chained, padlocked, but the lock's open," Michael advised.

The driver got out, looked from side to side, then opened the gates, climbed back in, and drove ahead, stopped again. Michael watched through the slats as the driver went back to close the gates, then returned. The truck started forward again, past a garage door, into a small parking lot. Through the windshield, Michael could see a black Natpo van, a uniformed man standing beside it. The build was right—and as the man removed his cap, so was the face. Demetrius Chastain waved his cap and started walking toward them.

"It's Chastain—I think everything's okay," Michael announced.

The tarp at the back of the truck flipped up, Marty jumping out, Jake after him.

Michael looked at the injured man. He said to him, "I've got a lot of reasons to hate, too—but the important thing is to get the job done. If we become obsessed with the killing, we'll lose sight of our goal. And that'll only help the Natpos and the Communists, not this country."

The man didn't answer, simply stared down toward the floor. Michael touched the man's shoulder, then jumped down from the truckbed to the parking lot.

"Sergeant Chastain," Michael said, nodding, taking Chastain's gloveless right hand.

"Dr. Borden—I mean Dr. Hope."

Michael started forward along the side of the truck, Marty beside him, Jake heading for the van. Marty called up to the driver, "Sorry about what happened. Good luck, huh?"

"Yeah." The man nodded, then cut the wheel and drove the truck slowly away.

Chastain's voice called from behind them, "Got Natpo uniforms for you gentlemen. But I have no idea what we'll be doing with Chief Brown's hair."

Marty smiled—but it was a sad smile. "If my wife were around, she'd have some ideas, God rest her soul."

Marty started for the van, Michael after him. Michael remembered something he had realized early in his first stay with the Resistance. More than hatred of the Communists and the Natpos, more than love of freedom, if there were a single bond that united them all—death.

Chapter Thirty-seven

The trip to Charleston, South Carolina, was uneventful—boring perhaps was a better description. Michael had never learned how to play cards with any degree of sufficiency, so he watched as Chastain, Marty, and Jake Brown played gin rummy, one driving, the other two playing, except for the turns Michael took at the wheel when all three of them played. He drove more often than their numbers required, to give himself something to do.

Eventually the card game wore out, Marty and Jake sleeping, but Michael, overslept already, sliding up front to sit beside Demetrius Chastain as the gaunt-featured SAS sergeant drove the last leg of the trip into Charleston. There would be no more checkpoints to worry about, and Chastain whistled a song as he drove.

"What are you whistling?"

"You gentlemen would call it 'My Country 'Tis of Thee.' We call it 'God Save The King.'"

"Got a family?"

"Yes. Two sons who want to be in the SAS like their old man, and a wife who makes them practice piano. And yourself, sir?"

"We aren't legally married—but yeah. A wife. Baby on the way."

"That's a good time. Now, I was fortunate. I was—was home with the wife for each delivery. Women like to make a fellow think that childbirth is bloody hell, and for some of them it is, but my wife—she had babies like fallin' off a log. That's another Americanism I picked up from you Yanks up there in Canada."

"Lot of Americans up there?"

"A whole bloody lot—good fighters, some of them so young they never even saw the United States. The big thing up there when you come in off assignment is American movies. Cowboys and detectives and soldiers of fortune and barbarians and karate fighters and all. Got a gang of you Yanks up there that fight with us in the SAS sometimes. Call themselves 'The John Wayne Brigade'—tough, good men to fight with."

Michael stared ahead, into the Charleston streets. "Why did England get involved with this in the first place?"

"Well, when they started invading Canada—the bloody Commies and the Security Directorate forces—of course there wasn't much choice. Before that, the government had been doing what it could. The Israelis and the Egyptians were having a tough go at it, of course, and the French got themselves so embroiled in the Middle East that they were in it up to their bloody eyeballs. All that Russian sea power hovering around Australia and New Zealand made us nervous, too. Well, the handwriting was on the bloody wall, as they say. The Commies would be comin' after us. So we beat 'em to the punch, like you Yanks say it. We came after them." He turned toward Michael and shot Michael a grin. "And Canada was a natural place to press the fight. When your own armed forces were dissolved thrity years ago, lots of blokes from the Delta Force, the SEALs, lots of Airborne Ranger types came to Canada to escape the death squads. When Saile's government took over and the Spetznas started doing some of his dirty work, a hit list was made. The National Police tracked down officers, senior noncommissioned officers, men like that—people with specialized counterterrorist training who could use that training against the Commies and Saile. If you Yanks ever do get your country back, there'll be a lot of wounds to heal, there will."

"I've had the same conversation a few times." Michael smiled.

"What are those fancy guns you're carrying under your uniform?" Chastain asked.

"Detonics Scoremaster .45s—they were my father's guns. How about you? What's the pistol under your jacket?"

"FN High Power. This side of the Atlantic you'd call it a Browning. The rest of my gear's stashed. I've been doing some thinking, Doctor."

"Yeah?"

"Well, I wish you a lot of luck with this conference. We've all been chippin' away at the Commies in the National Security Directorate for a long time, but sort of separately, if you get my drift—and well—"

"Organization? I'm not going to be able to bring organization to anything. Just maybe get something rolling."

"Word is," Chastain said, "that you being James Hope's son, well—just you bein' with us might turn things around."

They drove nowhere near the Charleston Harbor area. The security there was too tight. Chastain took them along side streets, sometimes with his headlights off. Michael asked if Chastain had driven in Charleston before, but Chastain had only smiled, saying he had memorized a street map and hoped the map was correct.

Marty and Jake had awakened, the two of them peering
ahead, wedged between Michael and Demetrius Chastain as
the Natpo van finally stopped. "Now, here's the bloody
dangerous part, gentlemen. I'm to flash my headlights three
times and wait. If our contact has been captured, then
chances are good the Natpo or the Spetznas or both'll be
waiting for us, and when we flash the headlights be all over
us like a two-bob tent."

"I got the back doors," Marty said with a hiss.

"I got the side," Jake added.

Michael drew the Scoremasters from under his jacket.

Chastain drew the High Power and set it over his right
thigh, his thumb resting over the hammer spur, his left hand
working the lights three times.

The lights went out, Michael squeezing his eyes shut for
an instant, then opening them, peering through the windshield into the darkness.

Chastain began to whisper. "Our contact's in the same fix
we are. If the Natpos got us, this could be a van loaded with
real Natpos. Might wait until tomorrow for the last rendezvous to meet us."

"Where do we hide until then?"

"Good question, Doctor. I don't really know. But I'm
sure we'll find a nice, cozy spot."

A figure emerged from the shadows.

"Should be a countersign. If there isn't, I drive, you
shoot, Doctor."

"Certainly, Sergeant." Michael nodded, his fingers over
the window button already.

A light flashed once, then three times, then once.

"The recognition signal—but the Natpos could've gotten
that if they picked up the contact."

"Is there more? A code phrase?"

"There is, but we still won't be certain until we're on the
way that it isn't some trap. Chief Brown?"

"Right!"

"Be ready, sir, with that side door, for our guest."

"Ready, Sergeant."

"Thank you, sir."

The figure came closer still, no more flashing lights.

Chastain laughed softly, saying, "I hate this bloody business."

The figure began taking shape—a coat down nearly to the ankles, a hat that closely fitted the head, the shoulders seeming broad beneath the head but somehow not broad enough for a man's.

The figure passed by Michael's side of the van, Michael still unable to see any face. There was a knock on the door—the same pattern used in the light response—and Michael looked over his left shoulder as he heard the sound of the door sliding open.

The figure was pulled into the van, onto the floor. Marty's Life Support knife went to the figure's throat. It was a woman, the knit hat framed at the neck and forehead with curls. "What is this?"

Chastain turned around. "Darling? What's the code phrase?"

"Oh, Jesus. Do I have to?"

"Either tell us the code phrase," Chastain said with a smile, Jake slamming the door, Chastain lighting a cigarette, "or this nice old gentleman will cut your bloody throat."

Her face—smallish with a turned-up nose—took a hard set and she said, unsmiling, "My body has ached for you since that last time, sweetheart."

Chastain emotionlessly answered, "And my body has ached for your touch." Then Chastain laughed. "Let the young lady up, please—and I'm certainly glad it's a young lady, because I had no desire to exchange pleasantries like that with another man."

Marty moved back, making the big knife disappear. "Sorry, honey," he told her, not sounding like he meant it.

"Drive, Sergeant," she ordered, sitting up.

"Where to, miss?"

"Out toward Edisto Beach. I'll tell you where to stop. I'm Mary. That's all you need to know."

"Right you are, miss. The lights in the van went off, Chastain starting the engine again, the vehicle rolling.

The drive took better than an hour and a half, Chastain taking side streets and part of the time driving with lights off. At last the woman spoke again. "Turn here." She had crouched between Michael and Chastain for the past two miles or so,

Jake and Marty already changing clothes in the back of the van.

Chastain turned left, Mary telling him, "Slow down—take it around back of that old house at the end of the driveway."

Michael unlimbered his pistols, ready. He glanced into the rearview mirror, twisting in his seat so he could. Marty was naked from the waist up but holding his assault rifle and crouched by the rear doors.

Chastain crossed from the driveway into the grass, rolling to a stop as he cut a left behind the smallish old house. "Anyone live here, miss?"

"No." She peered through the windshield. "Blink your lights like you did for me, only run the pattern twice."

"Very good, miss." Chastain began blinking the lights. Finally the blinking stopped, and from the darkness came the blinking of a flashlight, the same pattern Mary had used. It stopped, then repeated.

She breathed audibly. "Okay, come meet the people, then get changed. I won't say it was nice, but good luck." She started for the side door, Jake rolling it open, Michael stepping down into the darkness, slamming the door quickly to kill the dome light, Chastain doing the same on the other side.

"Sergeant Chastain?" a voice called from the darkness. "Sir?"

The voice sounded British or perhaps Canadian. The man matching the voice appeared from the corner of the house, Chastain saluting when he saw the British uniform. The officer returned it, saying, "Lieutenant Thornbridge. You did well, Sergeant."

"Thank you, sir!"

"At ease, Sergeant." Demetrius Chastain stepped back.

"Gentlemen," Thornbridge said—he sounded very British, the rank pronounced "leftenant," the speech slightly nasal—"we'll have time for proper introductions later. Please change to more suitable attire, then follow me—not a moment to lose." He shot out his cuff, apparently to look at a watch. "Not a moment to lose," he repeated.

Mary hadn't waited to say good-bye, simply left.

*   *   *

The rubber rafts—two of them—had carried Michael, Martin, Jake, Chastain, Thornbridge, and the two other men about a mile from shore. A power fishing boat had been waiting, the transfer to the vessel smooth, the boat very fast, heading farther out to sea.

"I thought these waters were patrolled," Jake had asked at one point.

Thornbridge had only nodded and said, "Yes, they were, actually."

The boat had continued on, by Michael's Rolex more than an hour longer out toward open sea, finally stopping. One of the two men in civilian clothes who had operated the rafts took a lantern and started signaling with it into the darkness. After several tries there was answering light, a voice from the flying bridge behind and above the foredeck on which they stood, saying, "I'm proceeding at one quarter— look for her running lights," one of the civilian-clad raftsmen calling back, "Aye, sir!"

Thornbridge announced after several minutes, "One of the best places for a clandestine meeting, gentlemen: H.M.S. *Stalwart*." Looming before them in the darkness was a submarine.

There had been hot showers, hot food, and now there was rum—it had been offered hot or cold, and Michael had taken his cold. They sat in what had been identified to him as the officers' wardroom, in the forward section of the submarine that Michael had been told was now submerged and running north.

Like Marty and Jake, Michael had kept his weapons with him, except for the assault rifle. He sat now, sipping at the dark rum—it was warm enough against his insides without being heated—as five men and a Chinese woman entered the room. Michael stood, Marty following his lead, Jake already standing, leaning against a bulkhead. Chastain was not present.

This was the conference.

The Chinese woman spoke. "I am Han Xiaomei, director of what is most simply explained as the Secret Intelligence Service of the People's Republic of China. I've been asked to make introductions." She was about forty, beautiful, with perfect teeth. Michael saw Jake noticing them. "I'll begin to my right. This is Sir Carleton Mitchell-Black, head of British Intelligence." Tall, he had the look of once being quite fit but no longer having the time for himself, his gray hair thinning on top, his glasses wire-framed and split for bifocal use. "This next gentleman is Marc Lumierre, our French counterpart." Lumierre was perhaps in his late fifties, tall, lean, very fit-looking, his hair almost totally white, his black eyes curiously watching Michael. "Next, Nathan Ibanez-Loeb, our Israeli counterpart." She turned to the man on her immediate left. "This is Omar Shalizar, our Egyptian counterpart, and this rather impressive-looking gentleman is Brigadier Llewelyn Hite, head of the British SAS and overall director of Allied Small-Unit Operations." Shalizar was as short as Brigadier Hite was tall, as fat as Hite was lean, as flabby as Hite was muscular. Hite wore wire-rimmed glasses, Shalizar wore none.

An exchange of handshakes proceeded as Han Xiaomei and the others took seats on the opposite side of the long mess table from Michael, Marty, and Jake. Jake sat between Michael and Marty, in a way the only one of the three of them representing a "government" as such.

Han Xiaomei spoke, her voice a lilting alto, her English, if accented at all, slightly British. "We can speak preliminarily for a time this evening, gentlemen, and then begin our discussions in depth tomorrow. Brigadier Hite might care to address our current situation."

Hite rose, setting his pipe down on the table. "Madame Han, gentlemen: H.M.S. *Stalwart* is well within international waters and moving north along the coastline of the United States. Two other undersea vessels accompany us, flanking us. Frogmen from the *Stalwart* were used to disable the sensing devices implanted along the coastline at the point of exfiltration, these same frogmen dispatching two patrol boat crews as well. Other than the obvious fact that something is about, the Russians and the National Security Directorate should have no idea what. When the conference is completed, *Stalwart* will come within helicopter reach of the Canadian coastline and our American friends will be picked up, taken to the nearest secure R.C.A.F. base, and flown home. Hopefully, none of you will find yourselves adverse to parachuting from aircraft."

Michael realized his palms were sweating—he rubbed them against his thighs before starting to speak. "We need some sort of unified action against the missile bases on U.S. soil and the missile-launching platform being completed near the *Beacon of Peace*. It seems obvious, Madame Han, that once the Soviets have the missiles ready to launch from low Earth orbit, the People's Republic of China won't have any choice but to undertake a mass preemptive launch against the missiles on U.S. soil, and likely France and Great Britain will join in. We're talking about ending the world, or certainly destroying a major portion of it."

Madame Han's lips grew thin and she did not smile as she answered, "Your observation would seem to be very well taken, Dr. Hope."

Nathan Ibanez-Loeb spoke—short, wiry, salt-and-pepper gray, an unlit cigarette hanging from the left corner of his mouth. "The Mossad has a long history of doing the impossible, even for a time against our good friends the Egyptians and the British. I think what you are suggesting falls within this category."

Michael looked at Hite. "I'm suggesting a preemptive strike of our own—against those missile sites, if we can do it."

Shalizar—his voice whiskey crackling, low—said, "If I am to understand correctly, Doctor, then you would propose a series of coordinated commando strikes against these missile silos."

"And the one in space, if I am understanding correctly?" Lumierre added.

"Yes." Michael nodded. "Otherwise, what have we got? Unavoidable nuclear destruction."

"Tricky business—must be hundreds of those sites, perhaps more," Sir Carleton said thoughtfully.

"It could be done, I think," Ibanez-Loeb added, finally lighting his cigarette.

"It would require considerable manpower," Hite said slowly. "We're not talking about sending average soldiers up against these sites, but experienced commandos. An international force would be the only way. SAS, of course, but all the Allies putting in their best people."

"The People's Republic would of course cooperate in

such a venture—if it were planned in such a manner that success were possible."

"It could be done—I agree," Lumierre said, smiling. "We have some fine people of our own, and those desert warriors of Mr. Ibanez-Loeb and Mr. Shalizar do this sort of thing all the time."

"The sites are known—we have them targeted already," Madame Han said quickly.

"As do we," Mitchell-Black added, lighting a cigarette. He offered the case, Marty taking one, Jake taking one, too. Michael did not.

"As do we," Lumierre said. "I would suggest Brigadier Hite to command the enterprise in conjunction with the appropriate field commanders."

Mitchell-Black looked at Madame Han, then at Lumierre. "We should compare our information on the locations—just to make sure."

"I agree." Madame Han nodded.

"My Resistance people," Jake said, "should cover most of the areas where sites will be located. They can help with getting up-to-date data on roads, escape routes, and flesh out the commando teams sent in."

"We'll need that—if the Communists get wind—" Brigadier Hite seemed to remember Madame Han. "A thousand apologies, madame—the Russians."

"All one thousand are graciously accepted," she said with a smile.

"Quite—but if the Russians get wind of the operation, they'll either increase security around the sites or order a mass launch."

"The key," Shalizar said quietly, "is to assault the missile platform near the *Beacon of Peace* prior to the Soviets' being able to launch."

"If the missiles are destroyed," Lumierre added somberly, "after they are armed and their destruction should result in detonation—then the game would be up for us all."

"Precisely so, Lumierre." Mitchell-Black nodded. He smacked his lips, stubbed out his cigarette. "The orbit is low. The amount of nuclear material would cause an electromagnetic pulse, almost certainly obliterate much of the ozone layer, perhaps irradiate the upper atmosphere."

"Poison ourselves and all die," Marty said. "I've been listening to all of it. The thing makes sense, but only if it can be done before the Russians arm their damn missiles. We can blow up the platform, the whole damn space station."

"A lot of innocent people aboard the *Beacon*," Michael said, shaking his head. "You're talking about mass murder. We do that, we're as bad as the Russians and the National Security Directorate. A lot of those people up there probably would help us if they could," Michael added. "The way to get rid of both at once would be to take over the *Beacon*, let those who want to join us, join us. Those who don't can take shuttles and get off. One man, maybe two could stay behind and get into the control center, work the vector adjustment engines—"

"What?"

"Orbits decay; to keep them from doing that, you mount small engines on the exterior of the station. They give the *Beacon* its spin for gravity. But if you devise the correct data for thrust and direction, you could use the engines to push the *Beacon* out of orbit and crash it into the missile platform. The two of them would destroy each other. They'd start to reenter the atmosphere—what was left of them, except for a few superhardened pieces of equipment. They'd burn up. Somebody might wind up with a piece of debris the size of a kitchen stove in his backyard. It wouldn't be without hazards, but it's the surest method to destroy both of them."

Hite looked at Mitchell-Black. "Sir Carleton, what sort of detailed data have we on the *Beacon of Peace*?"

"I could answer that better," Ibanez-Loeb said matter-of-factly. "We've had an agent aboard the *Beacon* since it was first put into operation. Clever fellow. Provided all the data we've ever asked for, one who first leaked the building of the platform. Also thoroughly able to get the technical data we would need to play footsie with those vectoring engines Dr. Hope spoke of."

"How soon will the missiles be armed?" Marty asked.

Madame Han answered, "Three weeks ago, information we received indicated sabotage had been discovered in the targeting computer—which was good news, because our agents were responsible for it. Reprogramming the targeting computer was begun ten days ago, and then testing. The missiles couldn't be ready for arming for another eight weeks."

Hite thumped his palm down on the table. "Excellent— then we give ourselves seven weeks and strike. Seven has always been a sort of lucky number for me, actually."

Michael looked at the man. The only time Michael had sustained a serious injury throughout his athletic career had been in a relay race in college, not even an important one. The number he'd worn pinned to his shirt had been seven.

Chapter Thirty-eight

There was a small gymnasium and Michael found it, his watch set to Eastern Standard Time reading just a few minutes after six. He ran more now than he had in the past, and his weight training was not as effective because he had no real equipment. His body conformation was changing, growing leaner. As he closed the door to the gym, his eyes surveyed the equipment—three long barbells, various collars, additional weight plates, twenty-pound dumbbells—a progressive-resistance machine. Michael set to work building the plates on each side of one of the barbells into something that would be decent to work with. A workout this morning would be especially important because it was impossible to go for a run on a submarine.

He began with simple curls, doing a set of fifteen, pausing for a few moments to work with a muscle stretcher, then another set of the curls, this time taking each curl into a lift. Another pause. Calisthenics—push-ups that made his arms burn, squats, stretching exercises. Another set of curls, again each curl into a lift.

On the progressive-resistance machine he began with sit-ups, then moved into chinning. The door opened from the companionway as he dismounted from the machine. It was the Frenchman, Lumierre.

"Monsieur Lumierre—you're up early for a spy." Michael smiled.

"I can come back when you're through—"

"No," Michael interrupted. "Just gonna wind down a little." He took up a twenty-pound dumbbell in his right hand—he wished for a thirty—and began curling it, each curl into a lift. Lumierre stripped off his sweater, his lean, older man's upper torso rippling with good definition, but little mass because of his weight. "You're a runner," Michael said between lifts.

"You are right. Have you never heard of me? Martin Deacon didn't recognize me last night. But it has been thirty years, and my friend was the more prominent of the two of us."

Michael shifted the dumbbell to his left fist, began the curls and raises with his left arm. "Thirty years—you're the—"

"The photographer friend of the ill-fated young journalist Jean-Pierre Petrovitch. He loved your sister very much. They died the same day, within minutes of each other, really."

Michael continued the curls and lifts, Lumierre setting himself up on the progressive-resistance machine. "You prefer weights?"

"I always have—seem more real than one of those. But I use them—used to have several good machines to vary my workout. How did you wind up head of French Intelligence?"

"The story is simple enough," he said, beginning his lifts, pausing between each raising and lowering, speaking only as he lowered. "I worked for French Intelligence even then. I was a journalist, a photographer—did a lot of military-related work. The government asked me to gather data for them. I was a patriotic man—then and now—so I did what I was asked." Michael shifted the dumbbell, Lumierre lowering, sitting up, mopping sweat from his neck with a towel. "After the death of my friend and the death of your sister, I was no longer content to report events. I wanted to change events."

"Have you done that?" Michael kept working his right arm.

"Perhaps—a man cannot ever say. You will feel as I when you become my age."

Michael shifted to the left arm.

"I wanted to meet you—when I heard you were alive. You remind me of your sister—which is a very strange thing to say to a man in a gymnasium." He laughed. "Something about you—a competence. I am impressed, my young friend. And I wanted to tell you this: Aside from the interests of my government, I have a personal commitment. That your nation should again be free."

Lumierre extended his right hand, and Michael took it.

Deacon was complaining. "Not too much room for my routine—but I limbered up, at least." Marty was eating less and less, Michael noticed, barely touching the bowl of cereal, the toast not touched at all.

Michael finished the second glass of orange juice, saying, "You notice anything special about Marc Lumierre?"

Marty grinned, leaning forward in his chair as Jake passed behind them, sitting down on Michael's right. The mess was filling up, a new duty shift ready to start in less than a quarter of an hour as Michael glanced at his watch. "He's the photographer—the one with the man Jennifer fell in love with. I kept waiting for Lumierre to say something last night during the meeting. I don't think he remembers me."

"He remembers you." Michael laughed. "We worked out together this morning. He thought you didn't remember him."

Marty just shook his head.

"My butt's gonna get tired. We have another meeting today," Jake commented.

"Then prepare for it to get tired, Chief—"

"Cut it out with the 'chief' stuff," Jake told Marty good-naturedly.

"I never ate with a head of state before," Marty continued. "That was inspiring the way the deck officer and that other fella saluted you and piped you aboard."

"Shut up, will ya?"

"Well, I mean it. Weren't you inspired, Michael?"

"Hell, yes—touched."

"You are both touched," Jake declared, plunging his spoon into his breakfast cereal.

Michael sipped at his coffee, saying, "I'm doing the raid on the *Beacon*."

"Figured you would." Marty nodded, sipping at his coffee. "You're the logical man. Just don't get killed. Alice'd never let me hear the end of it. But I guess there isn't much danger of that. I'm goin', too."

"Hey—now, that's—"

"Look, you're always the one remindin' me about this—" He patted his abdomen—the cancer. "One thing I always wanted to do when I was a kid was to be up into space and play Buck Rogers."

"Okay." Michael nodded. "Now all we've gotta do is convince them."

There was a tour of the bridge, but Michael, Marty, and Jake weren't allowed to see any of the more secret equipment, in the event they might be captured. But the captain had let Marty try the attack periscope and sit in one of the diving chairs and feel the controls.

The meeting with the Intelligence heads began at nine. Madame Han Xiaomei wore purple silk pants that looked like pajama bottoms and a knee-length blue brocade tunic that could have been a dress except it was slit along both side seams to her waist. She looked very pretty—and very mysterious. Hite said he had been up most of the night preparing preliminary materials for the raids on the missile installations—and his dark-circled eyes looked it. "I have come to a decision regarding the assault on the *Beacon of Peace*."

Madame Han asked him, "Its feasibility?"

"No—the nature of the commando team I want to send against it, madame."

Michael interrupted. "I've been thinking about that, too—"

"I rather thought you would have, Dr. Hope. And I'm afraid there's no other way to tackle the job, and I hope you'll agree. You must be there, Dr. Hope."

Marty, beside Michael, said under his breath, "Hope we can knock off the bad guys that easy."

Chapter Thirty-nine

The R.C.A.F. helicopter landed on the missile deck of *Stalwart* in a whirlwind of icy spray. Crewmen of *Stalwart*, secured mooring lines to the helicopter's pontoon framework.

Madame Han Xiaomei was swathed in a fur coat to her ankles and a matching fur hat, but they looked more practical than elegant, considering the temperature. Michael stood beside her in a corner of the sail, to starboard and well aft of the others. "You had something you wished to ask me," she said with a smile, her voice clear, subdued yet audible despite the noise of the helicopter's swishing rotor blades and the pounding of the whitecapped sea against *Stalwart*'s black hull.

"Yes."

"About the cancer vaccine the Soviets had kept suppressed."

"Why would they do that?"

"The Soviet Union has population concerns. That is assuredly part of it, both within the Soviet Union and in its conquered territories. But the real reason is that the president of France developed inoperable cancer eight years ago. If the Soviets were to release the anticancer drug, it might save his life. There still is a strong Communist Party movement in France, dominated by the Soviets as it always has been. If the drug is not released, the Soviets cannot be accused of being inhumane by withholding it from France. Therefore, the drug is restricted only to the privileged few within the Soviet hierarchy and within the hierarchy of their satellite nations. Lester Saile was treated with it three years ago, and lives."

"Nobody can get it? My friend Marty Deacon is—"

Madame Han said, "I anticipated this conversation—from your earlier inquiries made through Chief Brown. I consulted with Brigadier Hite. He agreed. Amid the confusion of the other commando raids when the missile installations are assaulted, a separate team will be assigned the task of penetrating the National Institutes of Health, where the two scientists who developed the drug have been forced to reside since their work bore fruit. The team will capture samples of the drug, any formula data available, and attempt to free the two scientists—a Dr. Shallert and a Dr. Rosenblatt, I believe. They and their discovery will be spirited to England. The first two persons to receive the drug will be the president of France, and your friend Martin Deacon." She smiled. "After that, others such as myself can test its efficacy."

"I didn't know—"

"You weren't supposed to." She smiled. "Such a mission was not practical before. Now it can be tried."

Michael looked at Madame Han. "May I kiss you, Madame Han?"

"Yes—you may." Michael touched his lips to her left cheek. "May your God go with you," she whispered.

"And with you, too," he told her, releasing her hand, starting toward the ladder, climbing it downward. Marty Deacon and Jake Brown were already on the deck. A seaman standing behind *Stalwart*'s captain handed Michael his assault rifle. Michael started toward the chopper but he felt a hand at his elbow and turned around. It was Lumierre, and coming down the ladder was Brigadier Hite. "Monsieur Lumierre."

"I came to wish you *bonne chance, mon ami*. We will see each other again."

"I'm sure of it," Michael told him, taking Lumierre's hand.

Hite stood beside them now and spoke. "You're sure that MiG-Boeing SW9 will be up to it?"

"I'm sure—I've gotta get back. Lots to do." He was already thinking of Alice.

"You'll be briefed on the rendezvous times and the time frame for the radar disruption. Good luck, Dr. Hope."

"Thank you, sir." Michael released Lumierre's hand, took Hite's, then told Hite, "You just make sure I have the data I'll need to get those vectoring engines going the way I want."

"Right." They broke the handclasp, Michael starting to run for the helicopter now, tossing his rifle up to a corpsman, clambering aboard the chopper.

Jake was there. Marty was there. And so was Sergeant Demetrius Chastain. Michael looked at Chastain as the chopper's tension lines were released and the rotor speed heightened.

The machine began lifting off the submarine's deck. "What the hell are you doing here?"

"Same question I asked him." Marty grinned.

"I started thinking, gentlemen, how marvelously impressed my two boys would be when I told them I'd been to outer space and back."

"Bullshit," Jake Brown announced.

Captain William Waterman sat in the dimly lit office. He heard the door to the library open, and stood up.

"That was my wife's chair—she'd never have it re-upholstered."

"It looks very nice this way, comrade Director."

The door slammed as Waterman turned around, watching Arnold Borden cross the room. Waterman stood at attention as Borden extended his hand. Waterman took it, released it. Director Borden sat down on the opposite side of the hearth, saying, "Sit down, Captain."

Waterman sat down, leaning back slightly. It was like sitting in a coffin. If he had known whose chair it had been, he never would have sat in it. But he had never been brought to the holy of holies before, the Borden household library. So he sat in the chair and tried to mask his distaste for it.

"Your men did good work."

"Thank you, comrade Director."

"We've been looking for that camp since long before Michael joined them."

"It was a matter of patience, sir—and perseverance. My men have the best training. I had no doubt they would succeed where the others had failed."

"You're not a modest man, Captain."

"I'm truthful, comrade Director—unless being otherwise seems necessary."

Director Borden let himself smile. But Waterman couldn't see Borden's eyes clearly.

"I want all of them dead. I don't want any prisoners."

Throwing away the possibility for gathering potentially

valuable intelligence seemed horribly stupid, Waterman thought. He told Borden, "My thoughts exactly, sir."

"We do think alike, I've noticed."

"I am flattered, comrade Director. Michael, too?"

"Especially Michael. Alive, with the rumors circulating that he's James Hope's son, he's a rallying point. But dead, it should destroy the backbone of the Resistance. If they have pinned their star to his name, well—then all the better."

"I promise to make it as quick as circumstances will allow."

"Whatever it takes, Captain."

"Yes, comrade Director. What should be done with the noncombatants—the children, the elderly?"

"You already have an order that covers that. That's why I picked you and your men, not the Spetznas."

"Yes, comrade Director."

Borden stood, Waterman starting to rise as well, but Borden waved him back into the chair. Borden paced toward the venetian blinds, his coat drawn back, hands on his hips. His white hair and beard gave him a ghostly look as he turned and looked back, the gray light surrounding him, not illuminating his face. "I've come to rely on you, Bill."

"Thank you, sir."

"You took care of the Blotsky matter in a very efficient manner."

"Thank you, comrade Director."

"If you succeed at this—I've never appointed a deputy director, but I think I should."

"Yes, sir."

"Good luck, Captain."

"Thank you, sir." Waterman rose, stood at attention for a moment, then turned and started across the room. It was always a rewarding experience meeting personally with the comrade director. There was always something to learn from him.

The weather had begun to turn warmer after Michael had gone—and even without him in bed beside her in their tent at night, it was almost too warm with the stove going. Each day except one, when she had been nauseous, she had faithfully done the exercises Michael had worked out for her own health and the baby's.

Mentally, she had been listing the questions she would

ask when Michael returned. And two questions were paramount: Was there any word on whether the cancer drug really existed? If so, could it be obtained to save her father?

Today Alice walked the perimeter of the camp as part of the exercise program Michael had worked out for her. Not only did her old jeans and shirts not fit her, but also the shoulder holster fitted awkwardly. The butt of her pistol kept bumping against her left breast, and her breasts had been getting sensitive. But being armed was more important.

What bothered her most—and pregnancy had nothing to do with it—was that there was nothing to do. Natpo activity in the surrounding area had been very light, and the Spetznas had pulled out. That was only temporary, she knew. They would be back. They always came back. But there was not even anything unusual about this with which she could have occupied her mind.

She squinted against the sunrise as she changed directions, continuing her walk. Sometimes Natpo activity would drop off. Sometimes the Spetznas would pull out. The few patrols she sent out brought back no information of interest. She would have led a patrol herself, except that she had promised Michael and her father that she wouldn't. And a pregnant lady leading a recon patrol was a little stupid, she admitted to herself. She scratched at Junior under her T-shirt— the T-shirt was getting tight for her, too.

She smiled to herself—Michael had better appreciate this. But she knew he did.

Alice no longer worried about Svetlana. Michael had mentioned Svetlana once or twice in his sleep, but in a way that only comforted Alice that Michael could love so deeply— because she knew he loved her that way, too. Those times he had mentioned Svetlana, she had taken Michael in her arms, held him until the dream passed, and when he opened his eyes, it was her name—Alice—that he spoke.

The mornings were all her own, with her thoughts. The guards by the waterfall, the guards in the higher reaches of the camp perimeter, all were lost in their own thoughts— waiting for the change of tour, planning to sleep or to eat or to make love or preparing mentally for their next patrol. But their thoughts were not on her, and she was alone.

She scratched Junior again, whispering to him, "You be

good—or I'll tell your daddy when he gets home. And your granddaddy, too. Now, shh." And she walked on.

Chapter Forty

William Waterman removed his pistol belt and set it flat on the floor of the van. He stood outside of the van, taking the left-handed holster into his hands and removing the Beretta from it. He set the holster over the web equipment belt and began working the clips to secure it in the right position.

Lieutenant Riddler approached, Waterman seeing Riddler at the farthest right extension of his peripheral vision. "Yes, Lieutenant?"

"Ground forces are in position, sir. The gunships are ready, and the rappelling team is in position at the lip of the canyon."

"Any signs we've been spotted?" The holster was secured now, and he replaced the pistol in it.

"None, sir."

The wind was blowing cold and strong, and Waterman hunched his neck against the collar of his leather jacket as he turned to look at Lieutenant Riddler. "What else, Riddler?"

"Sir, some of the men—they—well, about the orders to kill everybody. I mean, including the little children?"

"You will learn, Riddler, as I have learned, that orders are given for one reason: to be obeyed. Do you choose to question the authority of Director Borden? I wouldn't, but if you care to write a letter to him, I'll make certain it reaches the comrade director as quickly as possible."

"No, sir, I was just expressing the concerns of some of the men."

"I understand that, Lieutenant, I really do. I'll join you in leading the ground forces, by the way."

"Thank you, sir."

"I'll catch up to you, Riddler."

"Yes, sir." Riddler nodded, running off at a jog trot, his rifle at high port.

Waterman buckled on his pistol belt, positioning it to distribute the weight. He pondered Riddler's concerns, deciding on his course of action as he started away from the van. He broke into a run, a steady pace that wouldn't even work up a sweat. He glanced at his watch—the Rolex was so new the crystal wasn't scratched yet. Purchased with the money from the sale of Marshal Blotsky's pistol collection into the black market. Then, of course, he had ordered a raid on the black-market arms dealer's establishment, reconfiscated the pistols along with other arms, and kept the money. The arms dealer had died resisting arrest.

There was the sum of eighteen thousand dollars left after the purchase of the Rolex and a new motorcycle.

He could see Riddler and the ground assault force up ahead, Riddler holding them at parade rest, addressing them. As Waterman came closer, Riddler called them to attention. Waterman slowed his pace, walking in a brisk commando walk as he crossed in front of them. Riddler stood at attention, saluting.

Waterman called, "At ease" and began to address them. "We shall today eradicate the oldest existing terrorist band in the United States. And 'eradicate' is the word. Many of those we shall fight have been raised in these mountains, trained from childhood to kill every black uniform, trained to hate. Because of this, all of them are potential enemies. A child may conceal explosives beneath his or her clothing, just waiting to be detonated when within range of you or your comrades. The young girl—much better to keep her alive and get a fast lay, right?" There was some laughter—he had designed the remark to elicit it. "But what happens when she has a razor blade taped under her breast or up her ass, huh?" The laughter that hadn't already subsided did so now. "All of them die. Every one." He looked at his wristwatch. "We're moving out, Lieutenant. Let's go." Waterman started up into the rocks.

The climb was slow. They moved in silence. Waterman timed them as they moved over the rugged terrain. His snipers were already in position, using Steyr-Mannlicher Special Rifles, each rifle meticulously fired for accuracy at ranges of over a thousand meters, each with its own custom 7.62mm load, each wedded to the man who fired it. The rifles were at least four decades old, but brand new and taken from the cosmoline they had been packaged in when he had found them for his Special Operations Group marksmen.

He scrambled over an outcropping of lichen-covered gray granite, glancing at his watch again. In seven minutes, the snipers would take out the sentries on the south wall of canyon, and his men would storm along the ravine, up the slope to the wall, then open fire, assaulting the camp from its rear flank. Machine gunners and mortar teams were positioned on the east wall, and a special shock team would storm the waterfall from the outside. The steeper west wall would be the special task for the rappelling team, while the gunship would close from the north.

He had evaluated the tactical situation, the anticipated strength and firepower of the enemy. He had estimated the bulk of the fighting would end in six minutes, pockets of the Resistance holding out for another three at most.

Waterman glanced back and down. Riddler was becoming a problem. It was not that Waterman expected his men to be devoid of conscience, because conscience was part of the whole man. But battle was not a matter of conscience. And Riddler's weakness set a poor example, because Riddler had not expressed the concerns of the men, Watermen knew, but the concerns from within himself.

They had nearly reached the top, Waterman consulting his wristwatch again. Another minute remained. He watched the sweep second hand: another fifty seconds.

He raised his hand, signaling a halt. He watched the second hand. Thirty seconds. Twenty. Ten. Five. A shot, then another and another, the echo of the shots reverberating along the rocks.

"Forward!" He screamed the word from his soul as he hauled himself up, flipped the last rock obstacle, and threw himself into the run along the ravine. Sporadic gunfire erupted from beyond the incline, within the canyon itself. "Forward!" He started up the slope, drawing a pistol from each holster, running, the machine-gun teams and mortar teams breaking off to right and left as he glanced toward them.

The height of the slope—the canyon wall. His men

weren't straggling; they were running at top speed. One mortar position was already in place, the second one nearly set. A machine gunner at his back was already opening fire. The second team opened fire.

"Down the slope—follow me!" Waterman opened fire, his pistols useless at the range, his men opening fire, charging ahead, pausing to fire a burst at a target of opportunity, running again. The rappelling teams were starting down the west wall. On the east wall, four mortar emplacements and six machine-gun emplacements opened fire. In the distance, between the explosions of the mortar rounds, he could hear the roar of gunships coming from the north.

A woman in a printed skirt—a pistol in one hand, an assault rifle in the other—came running, rallying men and women and even children around her. She was either fat or pregnant.

The rappelling teams were coming under heavy ground fire. The woman positioned children with assault rifles beneath them. The woman seemed to vanish in the puff of white smoke and gray gravel of mortar impact—but she was to her feet, running, firing toward the shock team that had penetrated the waterfall.

Waterman shouted to Riddler, "Get ten men—follow me!"

"Yes, sir."

Waterman started laterally along the slope, toward the east wall, running, holstering his pistols, picking up a rifle from a fallen National Policeman. He looked back. Riddler was coming with ten men. Waterman slowed his run, the others catching him, Waterman leading them to cover behind low outcroppings of granite. "All of us are going after that woman. She's rallying them."

The gunships were coming in—it would be risky penetrating the canyon floor, but there was no choice. The casualties he was sustaining in the Special Operations Group were visibly mounting. "Let's go—move it!" He started down, fire from his own machine-gun positions coming dangerously close.

The woman was firing a pistol from each hand now.

"Close with her! Now!" Waterman let his men pass him, Riddler leading them, the woman whirling toward them, firing. One man went down, then another. The woman's body

twisted and fell. She was firing from her knees now. Another
man down, then another.

Riddler held back. Waterman pushed past him, one of
the woman's pistols empty, the second one firing out into two
of his men, the slide locking back.

She was pregnant, and Waterman recognized her: the
girl from the attack on the *Beacon of Peace*, the woman
Michael had come to rescue. Waterman shouted to the
woman, "For your crimes!" He burst-fired the assault rifle
into her chest and abdomen, firing again and again. Her body
twiched with each shot, lurching back. Had he severed the
spine? Her arms flopped twice, and she was still.

Riddler shouted, "Fuckin' murder—that's—"

Waterman turned around and shot Riddler in the face,
the left eye imploding. Waterman let the rifle fall from his
gloved hands to the ground.

He drew both pistols, stepping over the red-haired girl,
blood oozing everywhere from wounds, his eyes scanning the
camp. He wanted Michael Hope now.

There had been six days of instruction in the HALO
technique—High Altitude, Low Opening. Michael had jumped
before, Svetlana temporarily obsessed with sky-diving, Michael
obsessed with Svetlana. Martin Deacon had jumped, but
more than thirty years before. Jake never had jumped. After
the six days, they had boarded a Stealth-equipped British-
made private passenger jet used by the SAS and crossed the
border, across Lake Superior and over Upper Peninsula Michi-
gan. They had run a zigzag path, flying often at treetop
height, climbing for altitude only when they had encountered
the foothills of the Appalachians, following the contour of the
mountain range southwestward then, to the Tennessee-North
Carolina border.

In full combat geat, Chastain was the first to stand at the
door, Marty next, then Jake, lastly Michael. The green light
came on. Chastain jumped. There were no static lines. Marty
shouted, "Geronimo!" Michael smiled—Marty had explained
the origin of the old term the first time he had used it. Jake
stood at the door. "Push me, Michael!"

Michael pushed him, counted, then jumped. The wind
rushing around him suddenly was all he could hear. The night

was gray, the air temperature cold, the sound of his body's slipstream like a whisper in the otherwise total stillness. Michael's eyes scanned the grayness below, looking for a sign of any of the other three. He checked his altimeter: His descent rate was what it should be. Beneath him he saw the flower of a khaki-and-black camouflage chute—it would be Chastain's. Another chute a little south of Chastain's—it would be Marty's.

Michael's eyes focused on the altimeter, watching the needle spin, watching the red digital diode readout. His fist locked to the rip-cord handle for his primary chute. Almost directly below him, Jake's chute opened, seemed to catch, then billowed fully open. Michael was still falling, vectoring his body away from Jake's chute now, pulling the primary cord. His shoulders, his neck felt the lurch as the chute was suddenly open, dragging him slighly upward, it seemed, his hands already working the guidelines to control the descent.

Trees were everywhere; he tried working himself away from them. But it was no good. The treetops were punching up toward him. Michael tucked his body, his feet impacting, his arms flailing out now, grabbing at a limb. Something hammered at his left rib cage—a sudden jerk, his grip loosening. He swung free for a moment, shaking his head to clear it.

Michael tested his weight against the chute: It was tangled solidly. Beneath him, through the darkness, he thought he could see the ground. His left hand found the BuckMaster and drew it from the sheath, using the clip point to saw through the parachute line that supported his right side. One, then another; his body lurched and sagged, and he almost lost the knife. As he swung there, he switched it to his right hand, sheathing it then. He snapped his legs, starting his body into a pendulum motion, laterally, toward an overhanging limb. His left hand reached out, missing, then reached out again—he had it. He swung his left foot over the limb, testing it for his weight. It creaked but did not crack.

He hit the release for his harness, peeling out of it, rolling his body onto the limb. Coiled at the base of his pack was 150 feet of double-braided nylon black rappelling rope, seven-sixteenths inch in diameter. He unhitched it from his web gear, fingering the end, securing it in the notch where the limb joined the main trunk. His equipment vest was fitted with an integral harness and he worked the hardware now, using the eared figure-eight descender.

He started down, brushing away small branches, skirting the limbs, feeding out his rope slowly. Beneath him he could see the ground now, stopping his descent, listening to the night. He began again to descend, swinging down, freeing himself of the rope, his hardware tinkling loudly as he drew the Beretta, working off the safety.

No movement.

He waited for several minutes. Still nothing. Michael resafed the pistol, holstered it, and began working to retrieve his rope. The rope recoiled, he freed his assault rifle from the drop case, feeding a thirty-round magazine up the M-16's magazine well. He slung the rifle, remembering to remove his drop helmet, securing it to his pack by the chin strap, biting off his left glove, running his hand back through his hair. He stuffed the glove away, removing the right one, stuffing it away as well.

He found his lensatic compass, orienting himself, folding the compass closed, replacing it in its pouch, starting along the azimuth toward the rendezvous site.

Marty had cut his left hand as he sideswiped a tree. Michael had bandaged the hand, letting Chastain look at his banged-up ribs. The SAS man's diagnosis matched Michael's own: nothing of consequence beyond a potential bruise. Jake had been fine.

They had been walking for more than two hours when Chastain said with a hiss, "Hello!"

Marty wheeled toward him, Michael starting back, Marty dropping to his knees, feeling the ground. "Tire treads— same impression pattern the Natpos use."

"Are you sure?" Chastain asked.

"Hell, yes, I'm sure; they use Pirellis. No tread pattern like it."

"More tire marks over here," Jake called softly. "Five or six trucks, I'd say."

"Natpos," Marty whispered. "Okay, let's fan out. Be ready."

"These seem fresh," Chastain volunteered.

"Too damn fresh," Marty murmured, then started ahead.

Michael swung his M-16 forward, his right fist closed on the pistol grip.

There was more sign of vehicular traffic that shouldn't have been there—the signs of helicopter skids. On a high point of the ridgeline, Marty found what he identified as a .308 shell casing, and when Chastain scanned in the direction of the camp with his starlight glasses, he saw no signs of fire. Marty used a cigarette lighter to inspect the shell casing. "This isn't commercial ammo. And the marks on the case show it wasn't fired from a semi-auto. Looks like a bolt-action or maybe a single-shot. A sniper—shit." He threw down the case in disgust.

Michael looked at Jake and at Chastain. "We'll split up here. You guys circle around and come up along the canyon wall from the south. You know the ravine there, Jake?"

"I can fake it."

Michael nodded, not knowing if they could see his face, hoping they couldn't. "Marty and I'll go in under the waterfall. Let's go. Any trouble, the two of you get the hell out. And Jake, you get some of your people."

Michael broke into an easy jog trot, Marty running beside him, along the east wall and well below its rim, angling down along the slope, between the rock walls that led to the waterfall.

It took twenty minutes of running, Marty never once slowing, saying nothing.

They stopped a hundred yards from the entrance to the waterfall and the pool just beyond the cascade.

Michael reached to Marty's pack, removing the poncho from it, turning around, Marty doing the same for him.

Michael pulled the poncho over his head, settling it over his equipment but leaving the rifle out. The hell with the gun getting wet, he thought.

He looked at Marty. "So help me," Marty whispered, "if they—holy Jesus, I hope our people are okay."

Michael walked ahead, holding the M-16 at his hip in an assault position, stepping into the pool along the shallow rocks. He stopped before the curtain of water.

He glanced toward Marty, could not see his face in the darkness. Michael reached up, pulling in place the poncho's hood, then started through the water, his boots soaked with it, the gun wet-slicked with it—and he was through.

Michael stood there looking with unbelief. They were all dead, piled where they fell, it looked.

He broke into a run, pushing back the hood of the poncho, screaming, "Alice! Alice! Alice!"

Two children, eyes opened to the night, a woman beside them. Five men as though huddled together, backs to each other, fighting some now unseen enemy. The clouds broke—moonlight—a flash of something—Michael wheeled toward it. "Alice!" It was the pink-print skirt Jessica Cornbloom had made for her. "Alice!"

Michael slowed the run, swinging the muzzle of the M-16 right and left toward the flanking canyon rims. He ran ahead, skidding to his knees beside her. Blood, dark wetness, everywhere. "Alice! Answer me!" He bent over her, tears spilling from his eyes.

There was a pulse in her neck—and slowly he raised her head to inspect the air passage. "Michael."

Her eyelids fluttered, opened. "Waterman—I waited for you—the fucker got Junior, Michael—he got—I love you—" The eyes stayed open, but the pulse was gone. Michael hugged her bloodied body to him. Her abdomen—bullet-riddled—was pressed against him. The tears flooded from him. "Alice—dear God, why? Alice—"

He could hear, but he didn't make sense of the words. Marty was shouting at heaven: "Goddamn you! Goddamn you!"

Chapter Forty-one

The enemy had not found the cache of supplies, arms, ammunition, and gasoline. So Michael and the others had strapped the two-gallon gas canisters to their equipment vests, carried more in their hands and arms. Even the horses had been slaughtered, but there would be time to burn the bodies of the animals later. They worked, the four of them, in almost total silence. It would have been impossible to bury the dead, there were too many. So they had piled the bodies as gently as the could, one upon the other, making a vast, gently angled mound of dead.

Chastain had said when Michael had taken his dead wife and child into his arms, "I can dig a grave for her, Michael."

Michael, still crying, had forced out, "No—no." And he had carried her in his arms toward the mound, the smell of gasoline heavy on the predawn air, a slight breeze blowing, only serving to spread the smell of the gasoline around them like a cloud.

Still holding Alice and the still child inside her, he dropped to his knees before the pyramid of the dead. Marty knelt beside him, kissing his daughter's closed eyes.

Jake stood, hands trembling.

Michael touched his mouth to hers, then placed her on the ground before the mound. He rested his head against her abdomen and the dead life there. "I don't know your name, but it would have been..." He began to choke, cleared his throat, whispered, "Hope." He forced his eyes to remain opened, the tears clouding his vision. "Waterman will never kill another child—I swear it." His right hand touched Alice's face; her flesh was cold to his touch. Marty's hands were on his shoulders.

He took her body in his arms, hugging her tight against him, his lips touching her hair. After a long time he let her go and he stood, stumbling a little, not turning his back to her, but stepping back. Jake's body was racked with tremors. He poured the gasoline, Chastain helping him.

Michael found the handle of his knife—Alice's knife, Jennifer's knife.

He unscrewed the butt cap, pouring the contents into his hands. It was the first time he had opened it since Alice had given it to him. Fishhooks. Fishing line. Two sinkers. A small cork bobber. Water purification tablets. Matches—he wanted the matches. He didn't want them ever. A piece of paper, the size of something one would take from a fortune cookie. He unfolded it, squinting his eyes tight against the tears. "I love you. Alice."

Michael dropped to his knees, the knife falling to the ground beside him, the survival gear falling. Through his tears, he saw a hand—Chastain's.

Marty stood beside Michael. Chastain struck the match.

The fire wasn't there—and then it was, flames licking skyward. Michael started to run toward Alice's body. Marty grabbed him. Jake grabbed him. He shook them off, took a step forward, then stood there.

Demetrius Chastain, his voice sounding very old was saying, "The Lord's my Shepherd, I'll not want; He makes me down to lie in pastures green; He leadeth me the silent waters by..."

Chapter Forty-two

Demetrius Chastain had the qualities of patience, insight, and in-depth understanding of technical knowledge that would have enabled him to teach neurosurgery had it been his field of expertise. But his field instead was counterterrorism and a highly personalized man-on-man combat.

For six weeks Michael arose each morning at six, utilizing improvised weight-training equipment—pieces of pipe with crudely forged cast iron plates. He ran six miles, whether the predawn was bitter cold or mild, dry or damp with ice or sleet. Shower, breakfast, and then target practice. His marksmanship improved. No longer was he just capable of center hits on man-size targets at ranges out to seventy-five yards. At ranges of twenty-five yards, rapid fire, he could dump seven .45 ACP slugs into a hole that could be covered by a teacup. But the Cherokee stronghold, on full alert since the discovery and destruction of the Resistance base camp in the Smokies, had no teacups.

A three-inch-diameter piece of pine wood was his measuring stick instead. With either hand, at one hundred yards, he could hit the head of a man-size silhouette using his Scoremasters or the Beretta military pistols. Deacon and Chastain taught him how to run and fire with center-of-mass accuracy at targets out to twenty-five yards, how to reload on the run—whether the relatively simple procedure of changing magazines in an autoloader or charging a revolver's cylinder two rounds at a time. His understanding of weapons increased; no longer did he possess just a comfortable familiarity with the guns he carried. Revolvers and semi-automatics, calibers he had never heard of. By the end of the first three weeks he could comfortably handle any 9mm Parabellum or .45 ACP semi-automatic available among the Cherokee Resistance fighters, a revolver in .38 Special, .357 Magnum, or .44 Magnum. An hour each morning of shooting handguns, a second hour each afternoon.

Not only handguns, but rifles and shotguns as well. At various yardages, he learned to fire guns with names he memorized: the SPAS-12, Remington 870, Ithaca 37, Remington 1100, even a shotgun he was told had been used in World War I, a Winchester 97 pump with bayonet lug. Assault rifles—the M-16, with which he was already modestly proficient, guns from Heckler & Hoch, from FN. Bolt-actions—Winchester Model 70's, Remington 700's, the superaccurate Steyr-Mannlicher SSG. There were the guns of the Natpo Special Operations Group snipers. The one Michael learned to fire had been taken from the body of a dead one. With each firearm, handgun, or long gun, he learned to field-strip, to reassemble, to clear stoppages. When a semi-automatic pistol jammed, you cleared it and continued, he learned. When a revolver jammed, you inverted the weapon in your hand and used it as a short club. Submachine guns—the SAS utilized Uzis and H&K MP5's, SDA3's, some of the Cherokees possessing MAC-10's and MAC-11's; Michael learned to use them all.

Between weapons sessions, more running, then hand-to-hand combat training with Martin Deacon and Demetrius Chastain. Marty taught Michael more of the martial arts, refining his techniques. Chastain taught him how to kill or cripple with the hands.

Knife fighting came next, and Michael quickly became

proficient. Once he was able to disarm Chastain and get a knife to Chastain's throat, but Michael told himself it was late in the day and Chastain was nearly a decade older than he. He learned the use of the shuriken throwing stars and spikes; the construction and use of garrotes from piano wire and wooden pegs; how to use a flexible, ring-ended saw to garrote a man or sever his head.

Michael learned something every minute of the day. More running. More fighting. More shooting. He learned. An inch to his biceps, an inch to his thighs, twelve pounds gone. Each day he thought of William Waterman; each night he saw Alice, and he saw Svetlana. No matter how tired he made himself, he saw Alice, he saw Svetlana. And when he would run, his thoughts focused on the child he would never know.

He always pictured the Resistance fighters—whom he had been taught to think of as armed lunatics—sitting around roaring campfires, plotting their evil deeds. They plotted no evil deeds, and their campfires didn't roar when they used campfires at all. Campfires were too easily spotted from the air, picked up by high-altitude observation craft on sensitized heat-visualization equipment.

When they had not worked on his skills, they had worked on the MiG-Boeing craft, arming it with machine guns for use against fighter aircraft if they got picked up on their way toward the *Beacon of Peace*. They checked and rechecked each system, each part. If the machine were somehow to fail, all would be lost. Jake Brown, though totally lacking in mechanical background, found a new talent when he worked with them. His fingers, used to detail work, adapted well to aircraft wiring.

In the beginning of the fifth week, Martin Deacon had doubled over and fallen, his teeth gritted, lips drawn back. Michael had rushed over to him. Chastain put down his knife and came, too. Marty had lain there, refusing to be carried off to the field hospital, refusing to be helped to his feet. The pain had passed, and Marty had walked off unaided.

The evening of the last day prior to the mass commando raids, Michael, Marty, Chastain, and Jake sat on benches in the counsel hut. Jake poured from what he called the drink of the gods—a bottle of Jack Daniels. The fire in the center of the lodge burned, not like a bonfire, but reassuringly warm. Jake Brown raised his glass, holding the Jack Daniels by the bottle's neck in his left hand. "A toast—to the three of you—"

"Hold it a minute, Jake," Marty said.

Michael looked at him. Marty lit a cigarette, setting down his glass. He stared into the fire. "It's gonna be the two of them, not the three of us. Sometimes I can barely stand up or sit down. My legs are going—shit. Don't even do that too well this past week or so."

"Jessica can—"

"Jessica can't bring back the dead. Neither can you, my doctor friend. I'd go. My ego tells me to go. With them beefin' up security on the *Beacon of Peace*, my guts tell me to go. Because if the Special Operations Group is up there, maybe that son-of-a-bitch Waterman is gonna be there, and I can beat you to killin' him, Michael. But me—both my children are dead. You're like my son—so even more of a reason for me to wanna go. But I'd get you guys killed with this." He gestured lamely toward his stomach. "So I'll wait here." Marty drew the two Crain knives, one from the sheath at his belt, the other from beneath his leather vest. "Michael, I was saving these for the grandchild. They're yours."

"No—"

"Look, boy, where I'm goin', whether its hospital, hell, or heaven, I won't be needin' 'em. But you promise me somethin'. If you get Waterman, don't use these knives. If you don't have to shoot him but can kill him with a blade, well . . ." He touched the handle of the knife on Michael's belt, the one Jennifer Hope had carried. "You use that one. Okay?"

"Okay," Michael whispered.

Marty raised his glass. "To the two of them: my son and his friend. Long life, and death to their enemies." Marty Deacon downed the glass of Jack.

Chapter Forty-three

William Waterman leaned back in his chair. "Sit down, Lieutenant Zimmer."

Phyllis Zimmer sat down.

"Tell me: How long have you been—what's the expression? —'keeping company' with this Andrew Hall, the communications whiz?"

"Since the first of January, Captain Waterman."

"But you knew him before?"

"Yes, sir; for several months. We were good friends for a long time before we—"

"Began sleeping together. That's very nice for you. I mean, everyone should have someone, Lieutenant Zimmer. I have a mistress. When I told her the SOG was taking over security here on the *Beacon*, she was displeased. I was glad she was." Waterman allowed himself to smile. "I imagine in another week or so she'll find a way to cheat on me, and when I eventually return to Earth, she'll lie and tell me she was faithful. Tell me: Do you think this Andrew Hall would cheat on you?"

"No, sir."

"Ah, but you're wrong." He leaned forward, tenting his fingers, his elbows on the desktop, his chin coming to rest over his fingers. "He has cheated on you from the very moment you met him. Shall I tell you about him?"

"I—you've got to be—"

He watched her eyes—she was fighting back tears. "But perhaps he hasn't cheated on you. You may both have been cheating—"

"I don't understand, sir."

"Lieutenant Zimmer, Andrew Hall is an Allied agent. We discovered it two days ago. There is apparently something big about to happen. It required more message-sending,

347

and he was observed—his volume of information needed to flow more greatly, so to speak. And as the flow increased, it was detected. That shuttle that was found waiting for the terrorists who attacked the *Beacon* on December thirty-first— they hadn't preflighted it. Someone else had. *He* had. The information our enemies use to work against us comes through him. But the question is"—and he leaned back, tapping the fingers of his right hand over his thigh—"did you aid him?"

"I never—Andy wouldn't—there has to be—"

"There is no mistake, Miss Zimmer. Those antiquated titles are what you in the Allied sphere or the Resistance prefer yourselves to be called by, aren't they?"

"I'm not—"

"At this moment, Mr. Hall is being arrested. I will soon discuss the matter with him. Leave your gun and your stick and think about it, Miss Zimmer. And remove your badge. Place it on the desk with the gun and the stick."

Phyllis stood up. She lifted the flap of the holster, drew the pistol slowly, and brought it forward now to lay it on the desktop. Waterman took out his own gun. His left first finger moved, then moved again. The noise, even of the reduced load, made his ears ring with each shot in the confined space of the office. Her eyes opened very wide—they were pretty enough eyes.

Her body slumped back, hitting the arm of the chair opposite the desk where a second earlier she had sat, the body flopping to the floor, the pistol falling from her grasp.

The door flew open. "Captain Waterman—are you all right?"

"Yes, Corporal. You'd best summon medical assistance immediately. When I confronted Lieutenant Zimmer, she admitted her complicity with the American Andrew Hall in this plot against us. She drew her weapon—but fortunately I was able to distract her and get off the first shot. Apparently she had been working with Hall and even with Michael Borden since well before the attack on the *Beacon*. Unfortunately, she didn't reveal any further information before the attempt on my life." He sat on the edge of the desk, weighing the pistol in his hand, then added to the corporal, "Hurry, man—maybe we can still save her life, get her to talk!"

"Yes, sir." The man ran out.

Waterman stared down at Phyllis Zimmer, the eyes wide open in death, blood covering the two wounds in her chest. "But," he smiled, "unfortunately, Miss Zimmer died." Waterman shrugged his shoulders and smiled again.

Just out of the shower, Svetlana entered her bedroom. She was taken aback by the presence of a man. He sat on her bed.

"We haven't met—but I've seen your picture often. And photos do you no justice at all." The man in black uniform, a pistol at each hip, rose and extended his right hand toward her, his lips smiling but his eyes not smiling. "I'm William Waterman—"

"I know who you are." She tightened the belt of her robe, then stabbed her hands into her pockets so he wouldn't see that her hands were shaking. "What are you doing in my room?"

"I'm sorry. The door was open, Comrade Drusznina, and I simply let myself in."

"It wasn't open—it was unlocked. There's a difference, Captain."

"A thousand apologies. I mustn't have been thinking." He still smiled. "I—I'm afraid I'm the bearer of unfortunate news. Concerning two friends of yours. Phyllis Zimmer and Andrew Hall."

"What's wrong with Phyllis?"

"She's dead. When I confronted her, well—"

"Confronted Phyllis with what?"

Waterman began to pace the room, his hands resting on the holsters at his hips. "First we caught Andrew Hall sending encrypted ultralow-frequency messages to the Allies. He was a spy for the Chinese, perhaps the British or Israelis—a traitor."

"That's ridiculous!"

"And then when Andrew Hall's misdeeds were brought to the attention of Lieutenant Zimmer, she confessed her involvement."

Svetlana realized she had sat down without even being aware of it, that her hands were out of her pockets, locked tight in her lap. When she looked away from Waterman's face—something she wanted to look away from very much—she saw that her knuckles were going white.

"She attempted to kill me. I was forced—reluctantly, I assure you—to shoot her before she was able to kill me. A very near thing."

"Let me get this straight. You shot Phyllis for being disloyal? You're crazy. Who the hell do you think was wrestling with that woman you people call a terrorist when the *Beacon* was attacked? Phyllis wasn't even armed! She risked her life—"

"Just an attempt to mask her own involvement in the sordid affair, I'm afraid."

"You just murdered an innocent woman. Where's—where's Andy Hall?"

"Where he will come to no harm—unless, of course, he doesn't tell us what we want to know."

Svetlana licked her lips. "Let me see him right now. Damn it—right now!"

"Sorry." Waterman grinned. "Really, that would be the worst thing you could do—for either of you."

"Either of us?" She stood up, walking to stand on the opposite side of the room from Waterman, her hands in the pockets of her robe again. "What are you saying?"

"I'll be frank, Comrade Drusznina. You're on shaky ground. Looks and a strong party connection won't save you in the face of the weight of evidence."

"Get out of here—leave me—"

"Not before I've finished."

"Fine. Then I'll leave."

She started for the door. She had other friends, people she could go to. Waterman's hand was on the door, slamming it shut. She turned around, her hands behind her on the knob, her back pressed against the jamb. "Let me out of here."

"No." This time he didn't even try to smile. "Look at things objectively for a moment. Here you are, beautiful and unsatisfied."

"Balavadze will—"

"I don't think so. I know quite a bit about Commander Balavadze. A brave man, to be sure. And a loyal one. But I'm sure he would be willing to admit to suspicions about you, Svetlana. He's—well, of course you know. But no one else does, except a few close friends, and the men he associates with. I always thought Balavadze backed off from that Mars mission because he was afraid he couldn't—"

"Shut up, damn you."

"No. I'm the one who tells you to shut up. I'm the one who'll tell you to jump and you'll ask how high. Or to screw me—or whatever—"

She started to slap him and he caught her hand and felt her face flushing and wanted to scream at him. Instead, she told him, "My father'll have your job."

"I don't think so." He let got of her hand, brushing her lips against it first. "Balavadze will agree to anything I tell him to. I do my homework—pictures, tapes. Ever hear two men make love?" And he started to laugh. "Real silly, I mean—but anyway," and he walked back toward the chair. She wanted to run into the corridor, but she couldn't move. "If Balavadze is implicated as a homosexual, and you're his lover, too, well—you'd be suspect as a lesbian or something. That would account for the unnatural involvement you had with Phyllis Zimmer, I suppose."

"Shut up!" She screamed the words so hard she felt her throat almost tear.

"So—what do we have? An Allied agent and saboteur, his coconspirator a dishonored National Policewoman, the coconspirator's lesbian lover in league with the Resistance terrorists. A heroic commander who happens to be homosexual and may well have been part of the entire conspiracy. Yes—and a dishonored father who will be removed from his post under a cloud of suspicion, exiled in his declining years with the memory of his executed daughter haunting him. What a sad picture. But it needn't be."

Svetlana didn't recognize her own voice. "What do you want from me?"

"Your love." Waterman smiled. "You see, when this tour is over, I'll be named deputy director under Comrade Director Borden. I think the Peace Party's on the way out, myself. Costly, inefficent, unnecessary. When Arnold Borden dies, to be certain that I assume his position, a strong Communist Party connection would be to my advantage. How much stronger could it be than marrying you?"

Her whole body was shaking.

"I'll hold off on interrogating Andrew Hall for a few

hours. Other administrative duties. Come to my office. You know where it is. Wear something pretty. Tell me you'll love me forever. And I'll protect you—the least I can do."

He started toward the door. She sank to her knees, no longer able to stand. He stopped as he rested his right hand on the knob. "You look very pretty that way." He closed the door behind him. Svetlana closed her eyes.

Chapter Forty-four

There would be no pretense once they approached the *Beacon of Peace*. There would be security personnel waiting at the docking bays. It would be a battle from the moment he opened the hatch of the shuttle craft.

Michael prepared for it as he would have prepared for any competition. Sleep—but not too much. Carbohydrates. A quiet, lonely walk.

He picked up the shoulder holster with the Beretta and slung it across his shoulders, adjusting the angle of the holster itself and of the double magazine carriers beneath his left arm. The Gerber MkI boot knife hung behind the magazines, inverted.

Michael took the Crain Commando, lashing it to his left calf above his boot on the inside, securing his leg lashings, checking the safety strap. He opened the belt on his blue jeans, partially unthreading it, then positioning the heavy black leather sheath of the Life Support/System I there, well forward of his left hip. He rethreaded the belt, closed it, checked the safety strap of the Life Support's sheath. It was secure.

Michael took his gunbelt from the bed—the twin stainless Detonics Scoremasters that had been his real father's, the knife that had been both his sister's and his wife's, the knife positioned behind the right-side holster now. A pouch on the belt held the SAS commando saw that he could use as a garrote. The Sparks Six-Pack was behind the left holster.

He picked up the two loose spare magazines for the Scoremasters, securing them in the snap-flapped patch pocket of his leather coat.

He pulled on his coat—it was no longer so new-looking, but just as serviceable. He took up the canvas bag Marty called a musette bag and Chastain called a kit bag; it was loaded with spare thirty-round magazines for the M-16. He slung the bag crossbody to his left side. He picked up his rifle.

Michael walked out of the borrowed room, not caring if he ever saw it again. There was no picture of Alice—none had ever been taken. No picture of their unborn child—none could ever be taken.

He closed the door and walked into the hallway, seeing Jessica Cornbloom standing there at the doorway to her surgery. "Hi."

He nodded.

"Look, he'll be fine. If that cancer serum comes through."

"Yeah." Michael nodded to her and walked past, into the night. He had reset his watch to Greenwich Mean Time, the time being used for the raids, the time used aboard the *Beacon*. Marty. Jake. Chastain. They all stood beside the jeep that he and Chastain would use to reach the MiG-Boeing.

Michael stopped. Marty spoke. "You come back, son."

"I will." He thought he was lying. But he reached out, closed his arms around Martin Deacon, and held the man. "I love you," he whispered, then walked away toward the jeep.

Svetlana fastened her bra, not bothering to look at herself in the mirror—she knew her body. She walked to the closet, taking down the long-sleeved, full-skirted, high-necked black dress. She put it on.

Jewelry. She had a very elegant string of pearls and put them on, knotting them between her breasts. Matching earrings. She left her watch on—he would get the point. . . .

She stepped into her high-heeled shoes, the skirt seeming at its proper midcalf length now as she studied herself in the mirror. After attending to her hair, she made her way to Waterman's office.

She opened the door here. No secretary.

William Waterman sat behind his desk, his feet up.

She approached the desk.

"Svetlana." He smiled.

She heard the sound—an alarm signal. She ignored it. She heard the computer voice. "The *Beacon* is under attack." She didn't care.

Waterman started to rise.

"Fuck you—but it won't be me doing it."

He came around the desk and his hand was a blur as it moved and she felt the stinging hardness of it against her left cheek and she started to lose her balance. She knew how to fall—any athlete did—but there wasn't time to do it right.

Chapter Forty-five

They had crossed through the upper atmosphere without encountering fighter resistance. The radar disruption Madame Han and the others had spoke of had worked. The docking bay was nearing, Michael doing it manually, something he had never done. Chastain was stationed beside the air-lock door, ready with his explosives. To Michael's left and right the MiG-Boeings painted over with Allied markings were coming in, starting to dock.

Michael's eyes flickered to the control panel, the docking bay closer now. Warnings were coming over the *Beacon* control band, "You are violating the territory of the Soviet Union and the United States! Turn back! Turn back!"

He punched the selector, flicking channels—chatter now from the other MiG-Boeings as they closed on the *Beacon*. "If they get the air locks open to space, there isn't enough air in one of these MiG-Boeings to handle the pressure; everything'll just get sucked out into the air lock."

"Hope they didn't have time." Chastain grinned. "How much longer, Michael?"

"A minute, maybe seventy seconds. Be ready!"

The symbolism of it wasn't lost on him—the docking bay being penetrated by the shuttle craft. This was rape rather than simple penetration, forcible. "Docking in ten seconds, eight, seven, six, five seconds, three, two, ONE—locked!"

Michael heard the pneumatic hiss of the air-lock door as he slipped his safety harness, grabbing up his rifle and Chastain's from the rack they had improvised on the bulk-head. He started back toward the air-lock door, Chastain already into the bridge between the MiG-Boeing's air lock and the *Beacon* lock, a circular shape of the grayish, claylike substance Michael had been taught to use—plastique.

"Look out—right—" Chastain dodged back, Michael taking cover behind the barricade they had built at the rear of the MiG-Boeing's passenger compartment. Michael covered his ears to the roar. The smell of the smoke from the explosion was sweet and faintly nauseating. Michael was up—to the air-lock handing off Chastain's rifle, Chastain running behind him. Air lock seven.

Black-uniformed security personnel advanced, some of them KGB, from the collar tabs. Michael swung the M-16 forward, the selector flipping under his thumb into the auto mode. He fired and dodged through the air lock. The outer air-lock door vanished except for shards of metal sprinkled about the floor of the air-lock compartment, imbedded into the bulkheads and the overhead. Gunfire ripped toward him as he dove for cover beside the interior air-lock controls, the panel ripping and the gauges shattering as pistol fire stitched into it.

The rattle of Chastain's H-K submachine gun was near-by. Michael sprang up, spraying the M-16 into the mass of guards.

An explosion—another MiG-Boeing blowing the air-lock opening.

Michael started forward, stepping over bodies, instinct developed over his time with the Resistance telling him to strip the dead guards of their weapons and ammunition. He didn't have time to bother.

Through the interior air-lock door—the gray-white corridor of the lower level—Chastain ran beside him. Another explosion. At the far ends of the corridor, black-uniformed security personnel were coming from the elevators, but more of the Allied commandos were emerging from the air-lock compartments. Chinese. Keffiyeh-clad Muslims. SAS personnel. Uniformed men with French-flag shoulder brassards.

Israeli commandos. Egyptian commandos fighting beside them, closing with the security forces at both ends of the fourth level. The fighting was hand-to-hand. Rifle butts smashing the security forces back. Pistol shots. The screams of men as knives flashed.

Chastain had his M-16 in his left hand, his submachine gun in the right and was running beside Michael toward the nearer of the two elevator tubes. Michael shouted to him, "We want Red Level—they'll have security men waiting. We'll get off on the second level—that's research—then take the access shaft."

"Like we planned—right!"

They neared the elevator shaft now, the fighting intensifying as the elevator door opened again, more of the security forces streaming out, clubs flailing, pistols firing. Michael and Chastain waded into the fray. The butt of his rifle tipped one man on the jaw, the man falling back, Michael ramming the flash deflector into another man's face, blood spurting as the nose broke, the eyes wide open in death. The ethmoid bone, Michael realized, had broken, the brain penetrated.

A club crashed down toward him, Michael blocking the club with his rifle, pushing the Natpo back. Michael's right foot smashed upward and forward, the toe of his combat boot catching the man in the groin. The club fell and the man started to go down, Michael smashing the rifle butt down against the side of the man's head.

He reached the door. Three Natpos and a KGB man were inside. Michael swung the M-16 on line, firing over the roar of Chastain's submachine gun. The KGB man and one of the Natpos went down. The other two Natpos followed, blood stitched across chests and necks and faces, splattered on the walls of the elevator.

"Hit the button!" Michael shouted, dragging the feet of one of the Natpos through the doorway. The door slapped closed with a smack, the computer voice droning on about elevator safety. Chastain stepped back from the elevator panel. Michael rammed the butt of his M-16 into the speaker. The voice went silent.

They were to Orange Level. He thought of Svetlana. "On the way down—I've got business here."

"I'll cover it for you."

Michael glanced at Chastain, nodded.

Orange Level where the living quarters were, was passed; then the blue-striped Yellow Level: research. "Hit the stop button—now!"

The elevator lurched, the doors opening, Michael and Chastain framing themselves on either side. Pistol fire greeted them.

"Count of three?"

"Count of three!" Michael shouted across.

"One—two—THREE!" Chastain thrust his assault rifle into the opening, Michael doing the same, a fresh magazine loaded. He emptied the weapon into the corridor. If a stray bullet punched a hole in the shell of the *Beacon*, the level would explode with the outrush of air into the vacuum surrounding them. If they didn't die instantly, their own bodies would explode with the depressurization.

Michael's assault rifle was empty. No time to reload. He pushed it back on its sling, drawing both of the Hope Scoremasters. Stepping into the corridor, he fired both pistols as he advanced. Two men down, a woman with a pistol in each hand down. Inside himself, he prayed he wouldn't meet Phyllis Zimmer this way.

Another security man went down—KGB collar tabs. Michael tucked in against the bulkhead beside double doors of the astrophysics lab. He kicked in the doors, stepping back as they swung inward. Gunfire erupted from inside, Chastain running past him, going into a roll, through the doors as they swung again, the H-K submachine gun firing.

Michael threw himself after Chastain, emptying both pistols toward three pushed-together lab tables, chunks of the lab-table surfaces powdering, chipping away, beakers smashing, an electrical fire starting in a spectrometer. Michael dropped to cover behind a lab table, dumping the magazines from both pistols, reloading with fresh ones from his belt, pocketing the empty ones.

Chastain was opposite him. A grenade, ready to be thrown, was in Chastain's left hand. Chastain pushed up, pitched the grenade, and tucked down, Michael ramming a fresh magazine into the M-16, snapping it out from cover as the Natpos ran from behind the three tables. Michael opened fire and Chastain fired his submachine gun. The four Natpos went down, dead.

Michael was up, running back for the corridor, Chastain shouting, "Just a minute—need my dummy grenade back!"

Michael reached the corridor, dumping the partially spent magazine for the assault rifle, loading a fresh one. He had one fully loaded magazine left, plus the partial.

He started up the corridor, hearing something behind him, wheeling toward the sound—Chastain. "Sure you want to go through with it this way, Michael?"

"Only way—you gotta make 'em think we're coming through the elevator."

Chastain thrust out his right hand. "Dark of the moon—like we blokes always say to each other in books."

"Right."

"When the lights flicker twice, I'll come running."

Michael nodded, turning into the service block, past the closet marked in English and Russian, "Emergency Only." He rammed the butt of the M-16 against the lock. Chastain pulled the door open—fire extinguishers, a fire hose, a pump valve. "Start flooding the corridor—might be interesting."

Chastain laughed. "You're really getting the hang of this, lad." Chastain started working the hose valve. Water started to drip, then gush, Michael stepping back. He gave Chastain a nod and ran for the rear of the block.

There was a door there marked in both languages, "Authorized Personnel Only."

Michael fired a burst of the M-16 at the lock, cutting out a chunk of the door, then smashed the flat of his right foot against it. The door split open.

The access shaft. Michael started for the ladder. He stopped, looked at the M-16. There was nothing personal about it. Waterman would be there, he hoped.

He unslung the rifle, unslung the musette bag with the spare magazines for it, throwing them both into the far corner. Water was already starting to flood across the floor. He looked back. Chastain had disappeared from the service block. Michael reached for the first rung of the ladder, starting to climb.

Sirens were sounding now, muted voices shouting over the PA system, the sounds of gunfire below him audible through the shaft. He kept climbing, the light here gray. Beneath him he heard the sounds of feet moving up the rungs. A shot ripped along the shaft, the noise in the perhaps three-foot-diameter tube deafening as Michael compressed his body against the ladder.

Another shot, one of the tubular rungs dimpling, Michael's ears ringing.

Michael fired the Scoremaster down the length of the shaft. Beneath him he saw the outline of a figure falling away from the ladder, down the shaft.

Michael took the partially spent magazine from the pistol, picking another full one from the Six-Pack on his belt. He upped the safety, holstered the pistol, then swung toward the ladder again.

The contact aboard the *Beacon*—who had given them the data for utilizing the vectoring engine to propel the *Beacon* toward the missile platform, who had given them the information on the access shaft, whose identity Michael still did not know—had said the shaft had one hundred eighteen rungs between the second level and the first. Michael had been counting; eighty rungs remained. He kept moving, the light becoming more dim, darkness above him.

Seventy rungs remained.

Sixty. His palms sweated. His mouth was dry.

Fifty rungs.

No sound from the darkness above.

Twenty.

He squinted his eyes and swung away from the ladder. Light suddenly showed above him. There was a muted shout, a blast of gunfire but not a pistol this time, more like a submachine gun. Bullets tore along the sides of the tube, Michael swaying helplessly, clawing for the gun on his right hip. He had the gun, pointing it upward, firing, emptying the Scoremaster toward the top of the shaft.

The gunfire above him ceased.

No time to reload. Michael stabbed the empty pistol into his waistband.

Ten rungs. He drew the little Crain Commando from his left calf, putting the knife in his teeth. The top rung. There was no choice: He dove through, out of the shaft, snatching the knife from his teeth. Pistol shots hit the floor near his

head as he rolled. A man—bleeding heavily, dying, but not
soon enough—reached for the submachine gun on the floor
near him. Michael drew the right-hand Scoremaster, wiping
down the ambidextrous safety, firing, the man's body thudding back against the bulkhead. Movement to Michael's
right. The knife in Michael's hand flashed. He twisted his
body left on his knees and thrust the knife upward. The blade
gouged into the abdomen of a Natpo, the man's body doubling forward. Michael crashed the butt of the pistol against
the base of the man's skull.

To his feet. Michael wrenched out the knife, wiping the
blade clean on the clothes of the dead man.

He sheathed the knife, picking up the submachine gun.
He saw no spare magazines for it. It was a Soviet PPSh like
the Spetznas used. He started out of the service block,
reloading his pistols, holstering them. He checked the magazine for the submachine gun—it was one of the ones like he
had fired, converted to 9mm Parabellum. The magazine
seemed about half empty.

Michael edged along the wall, toward the electrical
panel.

The door to the service block opened. Michael returned
fire as pistol shots rang against the bulkhead. A woman's body
slammed back against the doorframe, her black uniform
red-splotched, smears of red blood along the doorframe where
her body had been.

He threw the submachine gun down, running now toward the electrical panel. There would be security men
waiting at the elevators on both sides. He would flicker the
lights in the *Beacon*, signaling Chastain and other of the
Allied forces who might have linked with him on the second
level. Then Michael would create the diversion needed to get
them out of the elevator shaft alive.

The panel was locked. He ran back from it, reaching
under his jacket for the Beretta. The high-speed 9mm was a
better choice for shattering the lock with a single shot—all he
could risk lest he destroy the electrical panel.

He worked the safety off, the pistol settling in both
hands. At twenty feet he fired, turning his face away as he
triggered the shot. He looked back. The lock was broken.

He ran forward, working the safety on the Beretta, lowering the hammer, working the safety back off.

The lock was shattered, the door jammed shut. "Shit." He reached for the PPSh. He used the submachine gun like a hammer, beating at the electrical-panel door, the door bending, buckling.

Using the Life Support knife, he inserted the blade as far in as he could where the panel door had buckled away from its frame. He pried, the panel door springing open.

A maze of circuit breakers. He sheathed the knife, remembering the data the agent aboard the *Beacon* had provided. He hit the third breaker from the left in the second row—overhead lights, he hoped. The lights flickered off. He worked the breaker. On. He worked the breaker to flicker the lights twice more, then left the breaker in the on position.

He started for the end of the service block. The door was closed. The Beretta into his waistband, he worked the door handle. The service blocks were soundproofed, as were some of the labs—it was possible nothing had been heard. Slowly he opened the door inward, grabbing for the Beretta again.

He looked through the crack, able to see only to his right. The elevator Chastain would be coming up in was guarded by eight men, at least four of them with submachine guns.

He stepped through slowly, watching the level indicator on the elevator.

He looked behind him toward the opposite end of the level—six security personnel there, submachine guns as well. He took the second Scoremaster, putting it into his belt.

Michael stepped fully into the hallway now, turning toward the eight by Chastain's elevator. The Baretta in his left, the Detonics in his right, Michael opened fire. Three men went down, the Beretta still firing as he stuffed the first Scoremaster into his belt and reached for the second. Two more down by the elevator Chastain would use, one down by the other elevator shaft.

Submachine gun fire ripped into the bulkhead beyond the service-block door. Michael, reloading, was almost out of ammo for the Scoremaster.

He edged back, waiting.

Submachine gun fire in the corridor. Someone shouted,

"SAS!" If it were a battle cry or a cry of danger from the Natpos or the KGB, he couldn't be sure. Michael waited. A Natpo stepped through the doorway, firing, a pistol in each hand. Michael threw himself down to the floor, firing both Scoremasters. Then he jumped back to his feet, shoving the Scoremasters into his holsters, running. To the doorway. He grabbed up the Beretta from the Natpo, then stepped into the corridor, firing both pistols until the slides locked back empty.

Chastain and three other men in SAS combat gear were running along the corridor, charging the remaining security personnel.

Michael threw down the two emptied Berettas, drawing his own, advancing on the second elevator shaft.

Chastain was beside him. "Let 'em clean up, Michael. Where the hell are the control sections?"

Michael reloaded the Beretta as he ran, shouting back, "Come on!" Opposite the service-block corridor was another, longer corridor, leading to the forward section of Red Level. He ran, Chastain even with him, the SAS sergeant's submachine gun at high port. Double doors loomed ahead of them. There would be security men behind the doors.

Michael shoved the Beretta back into his waistband, grabbing the Scoremaster. Waterman would be behind those doors.

Michael looked up to the overhead—a television security camera. He used the Scoremaster in his right fist to destroy it.

The doors opened, Chastain stepping out ahead of Michael. "Watch it!" Chastain warned. The H-K submachine gun began spraying toward the double doors. Two men and a woman armed with PPSh's went down, one of them still firing. Michael put a bullet into the woman's head. He pushed past Chastain, slowing as he neared the double doors. Chastain rammed a fresh magazine into his submachine gun.

Chastain called to Michael, "Worked once?" He grinned crazily, the dummy fragmentation grenade in his right fist. He let the grenade fly. Michael threw himself into a run, to the doors, jumping over one of the bodies. He grabbed up one of the Soviet submachine guns. He was through, Chastain behind him. Into the corridor beyond the doors, Michael firing to the right, Chastain firing to the left, they sprayed the security personnel barricaded behind overturned desks and tables. Some of them returned fire. Chastain shouted, "In there!"

Chastain ran forward, Michael after him, both of them diving into a corridor perhaps three feet deep. Chastain reloaded, Michael checking the magazine in the PPSh.

Michael fired the Soviet submachine gun beyond the wall of the niche, hosing it side to side and up and down to cover the greatest target spread. Chastain's gun roared behind him. The PPSh was empty. Michael drew the Scoremasters, emptying them as he shouted, "Let's get 'em!" He stepped into the open.

Chastain shouted, "Down!"

Michael dropped, the submachine gun in Chastain's hands roaring over him. Two more security personnel armed with submachine guns went down.

Michael scrambled to his feet, putting the last spare magazine into the Beretta. He picked up the Scoremasters. Ducking back into the niche, he used the partially spent magazine from earlier to reload one of them, the last full magazine for the other. Michael licked his lips. "When we step out of here, the control center's to the right, command center's to the left. Communications and operations are all on the lower level, but up here's where the master controls are. You can override everything. You learned as much about fucking with these vectoring engines as I did. I want Waterman."

"Thought you would, Michael—be seeing you!" Chastain stepped out, feet planted square, his beret low over his eyes, the H-K firing.

Michael broke cover, diving into the corridor, rolling, grabbing up one of the submachine guns. He fired as a chunk of the desk he was behind blew away. He shouted back to Chastain, "Don't forget your toy grenade, Demetrius!"

"Thank you very much, Michael!"

Michael was up, running, firing. Two men were beside the door at the far end. Bullets laced into the bulkhead near him. Michael threw himself beneath a desk, ramming the submachine gun forward, firing at floor level toward the feet of the two security men. There was a curse, a scream of pain.

Michael was up, firing out the submachine gun, the second man going down.

The first man was dragging his legs, crawling toward the submachine gun as Michael passed him. Michael pumped two rounds from the Scoremaster into the man's neck. Michael flattened himself against the bulkhead beside the door into the security offices. "Waterman!"

"Come and get me, Michael!"

Michael rammed one of the Scoremasters into his belt, his left hand reaching for the knob. Bullets screamed through the closed door, chunks of the door exploding outward. Michael tucked back.

He reached to the floor, grabbing up a PPSh, checking the magazine. It was almost full. He stepped away from the wall, locking both fists tight on the submachine gun, moving his body, not the gun, sawing his way through the door, burning the weapon empty, then throwing it to the floor. Then he hurtled his left shoulder against the door, which collapsed under his weight as he came up in a roll, both Scoremaster pistols in his fists.

Waterman stood by his viewport. Svetlana screamed, "Michael!" Waterman held Svetlana in front of him, one of two pistols at Svetlana's head.

"You win, Michael. No, gold medal, I'm afraid, this time. But I wanted you to see her die. I killed the other one, and the baby. This one, too."

Svetlana threw herself to the floor, Michael not daring to fire lest he penetrate the viewport and they be sucked into the vacuum. But he ran, vaulting the desktop, Waterman's pistols discharging. Michael felt something tear into his left thigh, a chunk of ceiling tile falling under the impact of the second round. Michael's right fist hammered the Scoremaster against Waterman's left shoulder. Waterman screamed with pain. Michael rammed the second Scoremaster into Waterman's abdomen. Waterman's left fist—a blur of motion—hit Michael's jaw and sent him sprawling back.

He rolled across the desk, fell to the floor. Waterman was to the far wall now, his guns gone. But Waterman held a black club high, charging for the desk. Michael saw Svetlana—she was between them. Michael threw himself toward her; no time to pick his guns from the floor. The club came crashing down across Michael's shoulders as he protected Svetlana. His right foot snapped up, back kicking Waterman in the crotch. Waterman's body crumpled and fell back.

Michael shoved Svetlana back, reached for the Beretta in his belt.

Waterman was to his knees, starting to his feet. "I didn't think you had the guts, Michael."

Michael handed Svetlana the pistol. He reached to his left side, drawing Marty's Life Support knife. "Nothing to do with guts," Michael said quietly. "Shooting you would be too fast."

"Michael!" Svetlana screamed.

"Stay by the door. Anybody comes in, just pull the trigger at any black uniform. With me?"

"Yes—always."

Michael edged away from her, the knife in his right fist, blade pointed up. Waterman edged back. Michael stopped, his eyes never leaving Waterman. He picked up Waterman's guns, one at a time, setting them on the desk. "Svetlana— those two pistols of mine—get them. Be careful not to touch the triggers."

"Yes, Michael."

Using only his left hand, Michael set the Berettas inside a desk drawer, closing it. "Just to keep it fair. Your club—my knife."

Waterman smiled. "You'll be dead. I know how to use this thing." Waterman twirled the club, shifting it from right hand to left. He feigned an advance. Michael backstepped, his left palm outward, the knife still raised.

Waterman twirled the club in his right hand, left palm outward, then stabbed at Michael, who turned a full three hundred sixty degrees. The blade was pointed downward now, primary edge to the left, the handle in both his fists.

"Very stylized, Michael—I like it."

"Bite it," Michael said with a hiss. Waterman twirled the club, thrusting with it, backing off, hacking downward with it. Michael twisted full around, blocking the downswing with the Life Support knife, twisting the club away as he forced it up. Then he hacked the knife laterally, across the base of Waterman's forearms. Waterman, shrieking with pain, fell back, no longer spinning the club but holding it straight out, protecting his body with it.

Michael raised the knife, edging toward Waterman.

Waterman pushed himself off the wall. His eyes flickered right and left. He threw the club. Michael batted it away with the knife.

Waterman lunged—but for Svetlana, grappling with her, grabbing for the Scoremasters. The Beretta clattered to the floor.

Waterman raised the Scoremasters.

Michael threw his right leg forward, lunging for Waterman, the blade of the Life Support cutting between Waterman's upraised hands into Waterman's chest. Waterman fell back, the pistols in his hands but his arms visibly unable to raise them.

Michael let go of the knife. Waterman staggered away from the wall, dropping to his knees now, the pistols falling from his hands.

Michael reached to his belt for Jennifer's knife. He unsheathed it, both fists balling around it. "For my sister—for my wife, Alice—for our baby!" Michael swung the blade, feeling the drag as it penetrated Waterman's neck beneath the left ear. Michael's full body weight was behind the thrust.

Svetlana screamed.

The stump of Waterman's neck sprayed blood. Waterman's head fell to the floor. The headless torso flopped forward. The fingers twitched, the legs seemed to vibrate. Michael looked for an instant at the head—it was almost as if the eyes were still alive. Michael looked away, his hands, his clothes, the knife dripping blood.

"Michael?"

He didn't say anything.

"You married—the girl—Alice?"

"Yes."

"A baby?"

"Waterman attacked the base camp. He murdered Alice, murdered the baby while it was still in her womb."

Svetlana ran to him, her arms going around his neck. He leaned his head against her shoulder. "I love you. Come with me."

"Yes," she whispered.

Chapter Forty-six

The *Beacon of Peace* began to shift beneath their feet. Michael wiped his hands clean of the blood, against the clothes that covered Waterman's headless body. He wiped the knife clean, sheathing it. He rolled the headless torso over, grasping the handle of the Life Support, wrenching it from Waterman's chest. He wiped the Life Support clean as well.

There was no gunfire now. He took his pistols, popped the magazines, and checked the number of remaining rounds, holstering them, cocked and locked. He found his Beretta on the floor, holding it in his right fist, his left hand closing over Svetlana's right. The very fabric of the *Beacon of Peace* was groaning now, the floor beneath their feet starting to buckle. "He's got it in motion," Michael whispered.

"Who?"

"An SAS sergeant named Chastain. Come on!" Michael broke into a run, dragging Svetlana after him.

"Wait a minute—can't run in these." He stopped. She kicked off one high heel, stood on one foot, and pulled off the other one.

They started to run again, along the corridor, quiet now except for a new alarm, a new recorded message. "The *Beacon of Peace* is experiencing severe orbital difficulties. Please move calmly to the elevator tubes and proceed in an orderly fashion to lower Gray Level, then move at once to the air-lock bays and board the shuttle craft that will be waiting for you. There is no cause for—aaaaaa—larrrrr—" The message groaned and died.

From the far end of the corridor, he could see Chastain. "We're heading right for it. Hey, she's pretty."

From beside him, Svetlana said breathlessly, "Whoever he is, he's got a good eye."

They met where the corridor began the T-shape into the main portion of Red Level. Chastain scanned behind them once, then looked at Michael. "Waterman?"

"Dead."

"Plugged into communications with the lower level. Chap named Andy Hall was your contact. The bad boys clipped him sending a transmission. He's been beaten badly but should live. Found him locked in a cell with a dead woman—she was a Natpo, but Hall fell to his knees and kissed her when they got him out of his shackles."

"Phyllis. My God, Waterman did it," Svetlana whispered.

"Some friend of yours?"

But before Michael could answer Chastain, the *Beacon* shuddered again, Michael grabbing Svetlana and running along the T of the corridor toward the main cylinder. Michael looked back; Chastain was running after them. The corridor floor beneath them was rippling now, twisting, buckling, the groans of the bulkheads and the overhead louder.

They reached the main cylinder, Chastain shouting, "If the lifts are out, we're done for!"

Michael didn't answer, running to the left, toward the elevator Chastain had used, Svetlana beside him. Her black dress was torn at the left shoulder, the sleeve hanging to her elbow. Her hair was tousled. One earring was missing. Yet her face glowed with the radiance he'd never forgotten.

To the elevator now, the interior and the corridor door held open by a dead body. Michael grabbed Svetlana, lifting her over the body, into the elevator. "Anybody else—"

"Gone—already gone."

Michael stepped inside, Chastain after him. Michael shoved the body free of the door and hit the floor button. The elevator moved down.

Chastain kept balling his fists on his submachine gun. "Everybody's gone from the three top levels. Our lads herded the civilian personnel down toward the larger shuttles. Some of them are already out there. . . ." Chastain pointed through the viewport. A shuttle moved in the distance, another just clearing the fourth level, starting away.

"What about the Natpos and the KGB—"

"Odd thing—not a one of them survived." Chastain grinned.

They were nearing the third level, the color of the framework for the elevator tube changing to orange. The tube started to tremble, the groaning sounds of metal bending, twisting.

"We won't make it," Svetlana said quietly.

Michael folded his left arm around her. "We'll make it."

At the fourth level the elevator lurched, then stopped dead.

"Blast!" Chastain exclaimed.

"What?" Michael snapped, punching the elevator buttons. Nothing responded.

"The bloody lift. Stand back. I'll fire one burst as a warning." Chastain leveled his submachine gun and fired a quick three-round burst through the bottom of the elevator door. "Halfway between levels, I hope—let's have a go." He fired through the bottom section of the elevator doors, about two feet from the floor, working the submachine gun laterally left to right, then right to left. "Try it, Michael."

Michael walked to the door, kicking at it. It gave partially.

"I'll do it again. Watch out!"

Michael held Svetlana to him, covering her ears this time.

The submachine gun sprayed—there was light coming through the larger groups of holes.

The submachine gun stopped, Chastain shrugging his shoulders.

Michael went to the door, then dropped to his knees, supporting himself on his hands and left knee, facing away from the door. He smashed his right foot back, the flat of the sole hitting the door. "It's coming!" He kicked again—again. "Got it!"

Michael peered through. The base of the elevator was four feet from the floor of the gray-white level—he could see the door.

"Corridor doors aren't as strong—kick with me," Michael ordered, pushing his feet through the opening. Chastain dropped down beside him. "On three. One—two—THREE!" With both feet, Michael hit the corridor elevator door, Chastain doing it simultaneously. The shaft around them trembled. The door burst outward, Michael rolling onto his stomach, slipping through. "Gimme Svetlana—"

But she was already sliding through. He reminded himself that when he'd met her she was an Olympic gymnast.

Chastain dropped down and through. Michael grabbed Svetlana by the hand, running now for air-lock opening seven.

The *Beacon* was lurching, Michael losing his balance, hitting the bulkhead to his right, catching Svetlana in his arms. Chastain had fallen to his knees but gotten up, swaying again. The *Beacon* shifted radically.

"She's gonna break up, Michael!" Chastain called.

Michael didn't say anything, dragging his way along the bulkhead, the cylinder's configuration to the mass of the station having changed now, he reasoned. If the cylinder ripped loose, it would spin inexorably, lose its atmospheric integrity.

The air lock—seven. Michael threw himself toward it, half dragging Svetlana. Chastain was coming. The cylinder lurched again. Michael caught himself, almost tripping over a dead Natpo, clambering toward the open door of the MiG-Boeing. The cylinder lurched maddeningly again. Michael fell forward, through the hatch. A pistol shot rang from the forward compartment. Michael rolled, snatching the Beretta from his belt, and fired.

It was a Natpo. Michael fired again, the Natpo's body doubling forward, then falling back, jackknifed against the control panel. Michael was to his feet, Svetlana beside him now.

Chastain was coming as Michael moved forward, the MiG-Boeing trembling. Through the craft's windshield the space station *Beacon of Peace* was visibly breaking up. The cylinder was twisting apart, the missile platform looming ahead, nearer. He heard the bulkhead door heaving to.

"Get us out of here, Michael. The *Beacon*'s loaded with impact-sensitive charges. One of these twisting motions could set them off and she'll blow!"

Michael pushed the dead Natpo away from the controls, then handed Svetlana the Beretta 9mm he had used to kill the Natpo. "Buckle in. Take the copilot's seat." Michael activated the controls. His eyes stopped on the docking release indicator. One of his bullets had smashed it.

"How's it going, Michael?"

"Chastain—buckle up back there."

He powered up, still eyeing the docking release indicator. If he worked the docking release control and hit the

throttle and somehow hadn't released, he'd rip out the MiG-
Boeing's air lock and they'd die instantly.

He looked at Svetlana.

"Michael," Chastain called to him, "don't you think,
lad—"

"Hang on!" Michael hit the docking release. The indicator be damned, he told himself. He felt Svetlana's hand on
his right forearm. His leg pained him. He hit the throttle,
praying. The MiG-Boeing lurched, then he had separation.
The shuttle was arcing away from the *Beacon*. The crippled
space station vanished from the right side of the windshield.
The missile platform came perilously near, then was gone as
he accelerated, vectoring hard to port.

Michael landed the MiG-Boeing in an abandoned corn-
field somewhere that he thought might be Georgia. There
had been only time enough to make sure he was over
someplace friendly, he hoped. Not only had the docking
release indicator been destroyed, but so had the oil pressure
gauge for the starboard engine. And the oil temperature
gauge had red-lined. There was no time to be picky about
landing areas. As they had reentered the atmosphere, there
had been brighter lights than usually came off the heat
shield—but from behind them. The *Beacon of Peace* had
collided with the missile-launching platform.

He left Chastain starting to break out the tool kit to
remove the starboard engine cowling—as soon as it cooled
enough to be touched with heavy gloves. As they had taken
the MiG-Boeing into the reentry loop, bright flashes of
light—explosions—had been visible dotting the United States.
The missile silos, each explosion a successful strike.

He held Svetlana's hand in his, walking quickly with her
beneath some high white pines, then up a gradual slope.

He wanted to see. And as he stopped along the height of
the ridgeline, Michael looked up, in the direction he thought
he should find the *Beacon of Peace* and the missile-launching
platform.

He wanted to see.

If the commando raid on the National Institutes of
Health had worked, Marty at least stood a chance to live. The
Russians and the Peace Party of Lester Saile would not give

up their hold on the United States—but with their missiles gone, at least there was a chance now. A good chance, he told himself.

Svetlana huddled against him, Michael holding her close, his arms around her.

He saw a flash of light in the darkness—it would be debris burning up. The *Beacon of Peace*, a lie, was now at least one less lie to fight.

Michael Hope watched the darkness, Svetlana's breath against his cheek, suddenly knowing inside himself what it had all been for. There was another flash in the darkness, for an instant brighter than any star—another bit of the lie that burned to ashes and was gone.

Relive the American Experience in Vietnam

BANTAM VIETNAM WAR BOOKS

☐ 25894 THE NEW FACE OF WAR: $3.95
          VIETNAM (Rev. Ed.)

☐ 05160 JOHNNY'S SONG $9.95
          Steve Mason (A Bantam Hardcover)

☐ 25041 THE 13TH VALLEY $4.50
          Del Vecchio

☐ 22956 FIELDS OF FIRE $3.95
          Webb

☐ 24104 A SENSE OF HONOR $3.50
          Webb

☐ 26029 12, 20 & 5 A DOCTOR'S YEAR $3.50
          IN VIETNAM John A. Parrish M.D.

Prices and availability subject to change without notice.

Buy them at your local bookstore or use this handy coupon for ordering:

The Fighting Elite ™

AMERICA'S GREAT MILITARY UNITS

by Ian Padden

Here is the magnificent new series that brings you into the world of America's most courageous and spectacular combat forces—the Fighting Elite. Each book is an exciting account of a particular military unit—its origins and training programs, its weaponry and deployment—and lets you re-live its most famous battles in tales of war and valor that will live forever. All the books include a special 8-page photo insert.